DATE DUE

THE LAUGHING WEST

▼▲▼▲▼▲▼▲▼▲▼▲▼▲▼▲▼▲▼▲▼▲▼▲▼▲▼▲▼▲▼▲▼▲▼▲▼▲

THE LAUGHING WEST:

Humorous Western Fiction
Past and Present
An Anthology

Compiled and Edited by
C. L. Sonnichsen

Swallow Press/
Ohio University Press
Athens

Library of Congress Cataloging-in-Publication Data

The Laughing West: humorous Western fiction past and present: an antholog.
compiled and edited by C. L. Sonnichsen.

p.   cm.

ISBN 0-8040-0901-5.   ISBN 0-8040-0902-3 (pbk.)

1. Western stories.   2. Humorous stories, American—West (U.S.)
I. Sonnichsèn, C. L. (Charles Leland), 1901–
PS648.W4L38   1988   813'.0874'08-dc19   87-26737

Introduction and Notes
© Copyright 1988 by C. L. Sonnichsen

Second printing 1988
Third printing 1989

*For Nancy
a delightful daughter*

Table of Contents

▼▲▼▲▼▲▼▲▼▲▼▲▼▲▼▲▼▲▼▲▼▲▼▲▼▲▼▲▼▲▼▲▼

Acknowledgments

▼▲▼▲▼▲▼▲▼▲▼▲▼▲▼▲▼▲▼▲▼▲▼▲▼▲▼▲▼▲▼▲▼▲▼

"Ancestral Eagles," excerpt from *Indian Stories from the Pueblos*, by Frank G. Applegate. © Copyright, 1929. Published by J. B. Lippincott, reprinted in 1977 by the Rio Grande Press. Reprinted by permission of the Rio Grande Press.

"The Marriage of Moon Wind," by Bill Gulick, from *Branded West: a Western Writers of America Anthology.* © Copyright, 1956. Published by Random House. Reprinted by permission of Western Writers of America and the author.

"Louis Champlain's Party," excerpt from *Stay Away Joe*, by Dan Cushman. © Copyright, 1953. Published by Viking Press. Reprinted by permission of the author.

"Little Piñon Fires," from *No High Adobe*, by Dorothy Pillsbury. © Copyright, 1930. Published by the University of New Mexico Press. Reprinted by permisison of the University of New Mexico Press.

"Life at Sagrado," excerpt from *Red Sky at Morning*, by Richard Bradford. © Copyright, 1968. Published by J. B. Lippincott. Reprinted by permission of Harper & Row, Publishers.

"Joe Mondragón Defies the Establishment," excerpt from *The Milagro Beanfield War*, by John Nichols. © Copyright, 1974, by John Nichols. Published by Holt, Rinehart, & Wilson. Reprinted by permission of Henry Holt, Inc.

"A Night in Town," from *Men and Horses*, by Ross Santee. © Copyright, 1928. Published by The Century Company. Reprinted by permission of The Ross Santee Corral: Mrs. W. S. Andrus, Mrs. James Whitsell and James Whitsell.

"Old Fooler in Action," extract from *The Rounders*, by Max Evans.

ACKNOWLEDGMENTS

© Copyright, 1950. Published by Random House, Inc. Reprinted by permission of Russell & Volkening, Inc., as agents for the author.

"Partners," extract from *The Cadillac Cowboys*, by Glendon Swarthout. © Copyright, 1964. Published by Simon & Schuster. Reprinted by permission of the author.

"The Real Wild Bill Hickok," excerpt from *Little Big Man*, by Thomas Berger. © Copyright, 1964. Published by Dial Press. Reprinted by permission of the Sterling Lord Agency, Inc.

"Tom Horn Meets Al Sieber," extract from *I, Tom Horn*, by Will Henry. © Copyright, 1974. Published by J. B. Lippincott. Reprinted by permission of the author.

"Jaimie Meets Jim Bridger," excerpt from *The Travels of Jaimie McPheeters*, by Robert Lewis Taylor. © Copyright, 1958, by Robert Lewis Taylor. Reprinted by permission of Doubleday & Co., Inc.

"Ike Bender's Indian Scare," excerpt from *The Road to Many a Wonder*, by David Wagoner. © Copyright, 1974, in hard cover. Published by Farrar, Straus & Giroux. Reprinted by permission of Farrar, Straus & Giroux, Inc.

"Flashy and Sonsee-array," excerpt from *Flashman and the Redskins*, by George MacDonald Fraser. © Copyright, 1982. Published by Alfred A. Knopf. Reprinted by permission of Alfred A. Knopf, Inc.

"Reel 11," excerpt from *God's Other Son*, by Don Imus. © Copyright, 1981, by John Donald Imus. Published by Simon & Schuster. Reprinted by permission of Simon & Schuster, Inc.

"Spotlight on Cullie Blanton," excerpt from *The One Eyed Man*, by Larry L. King. © Copyright, 1960. Published by New American Library. Reprinted by arrangement with NAL/Penguin, Inc.

"Seldom Seen Smith," extract from *The Monkey Wrench Gang*, by Edward Abbey. © Copyright, 1975. Published by J. B. Lippincott. Reprinted by permission of the author.

"The Founding of Caliche," excerpt from *The Return of the Virginian*, by H. Allen Smith. © Copyright, 1974, by H. Allen Smith. Published by Doubleday & Co. Reprinted by permission of Doubleday and Co., Inc.

"Janet and Her Songs," excerpt from *Baja Oklahoma*, by Dan Jenkins. © Copyright, 1981. Published by Atheneum. Reprinted by permission of Macmillan Publications Company.

"Freight Train," excerpt from *Peeper: a Comedy*, by William Brinkley. © Copyright, 1981. Published by Viking Press. Reprinted by permission of the Sterling Lord Agency, Inc.

"The History of Sheriff C. L. Hoke Birdsill," excerpt from *The Ballad of Dingus Magee*, by David Markson. © Copyright, 1965. Published by Dell Publishing. Reprinted by permission of the Sterling Lord Agency, Inc.

Introduction

▼▲▼▲▼▲▼▲▼▲▼▲▼▲▼▲▼▲▼▲▼▲▼▲▼▲▼▲▼▲▼

The Humorous West

THE TIME IS OCTOBER, 1905. THE PLACE IS MADAM MATTIE FOU-
quet's Mahogany Parlor of Recreation (the best little whorehouse in
Nacogdoches, Texas). A huge, red-headed oil-field worker named
Gideon Karnes has persuaded Madam Mattie to provide entertain-
ment for him and his lumberjack partner, Euphémon Boudreaux,
although the house has been reserved for a crew of trail-weary cowboys. When the cowboys arrive early, a confrontation ensues; Karnes
subdues all the punchers except their leader, an ancient range-
country Ulysses named L. R. Foyt.

> His tanned face was a craggy relief map of miles and years of expe-
> rience and endurance; his pale eyes were cool and framed in skeptical,
> humorous crowsfeet. Of middling height, he wore faded blue Sears Roe-
> buck bib overalls, and under them the colorless, faded red shirt of a set of
> long-handled flannel underwear. His huge hands and bony wrists were
> protruding from the frayed, flared too-short cuffs. Except for his boots
> and his bowed legs, he might have been taken for a particularly poor-off
> dirt farmer.

When Karnes comes at him, Foyt pulls a pistol from the bib of his
overalls and the war is over. In no time at all the men are partners in a
scheme to rob a train at Teague, Texas, 150 miles away, driving a herd
of scrub cows as cover.

The critical mass in this mixture may well be those bib overalls.
When one of Foyt's followers asks him why he wears this uncowboy-
like garment, he explains:

> Nobody but the actors in Wild West shows ever did that face-off-and-
> *reach*-pardner performance. If you had reason to shoot a man, it was far
> more sensible to dog him unawares and shoot him in the back . . . but
> if it ever did come to a face-to-face encounter, it was blamed foolishness to
> have your gun hanging out where your opponent could see you grab for
> it.

1

The better way was to use the bib. It provided a notable advantage when the chips were down.

> First you looked away from the other fellow, maybe over his head, and looked thoughtful, as if you had discovered a flea in your chest hair, then you stuck your hand inside the bib to scratch yourself, and then you brought your hand out full of pistol.

One of Foyt's victims, he declares, thanked him as he was carried out for "demonstrating the technique of itch-scratch-shoot."[1]

Foyt is the central character in Gary Jennings's 1978 novel *The Terrible Teague Bunch*, an outrageously humorous book that pokes fun at the stereotypes of the traditional western novel and shows how far we have come since *Wolfville* and Hopalong Cassidy in portraying comical cowboys and how happily we have upset the assumptions of *Riders of the Purple Sage* and *Destry Rides Again*. We have changed our minds about the West and its characters over the decades, as our literature clearly shows, and humorous fiction is a good place to study the changes. Comedy is our most civilized and civilizing form of writing. It cuts closer to the bone of truth than any other. It shames us and hurts us when we need shaming or hurting, and it tells us who we are.

If, as I believe, "As a man laugheth, so is he," then our humorous fiction, as James Thurber once remarked, is "one of our greatest natural resources,"[2] for in it we write our own autobiography and, at least in some cases, correct our mistakes. *The Terrible Teague Bunch*, in which the cowboy hero is shot full of holes, shows how we do it.

Specialists in American humor have written dozens of good analyses of the comic element in American literature, but none of them has much to say about humor in the West. Leslie Fiedler, the literary critic who once shed his radiance over Montana, is one of the few to discuss it. He thinks we need a good deal more of it. The romantic West, he insists, in *The Return of the Vanishing American*, has missed the whole point of western history. It was not the heroes and statesmen who built the country. It was "the gunslingers and pimps, habitual failures and refugees from law and order, as well as certain dogged pursuers of a dream who . . . actually made the West." We have not faced that fact in western writing, he thinks. "Those more sophisticated recent pop novels which play off, for laughs, the seamier side of Western history, against its sentimental expurgations, are not quite satisfactory, either. Yet to understand the West as somehow a joke comes a little closer to getting it straight."

As usual Fiedler overstates his case, but he has a sound idea. It is dangerous to idealize the West and its people as popular historians, romantic novelists, and standard Hollywood movies have always done. Westerners, like other human beings, were at times ridiculous, and Galahads were as scarce in Utah as they were in Chicago, a fact that was not obvious to Zane Grey when he created the solemn Lassiter in *Riders of the Purple Sage*, or to Jack Schaefer when he conceived that messiah with a six-gun, Shane. "Certainly," Fiedler goes on, "the decrabbed, castrated, Westerner, that clean, toe-twisting, hattipping white knight embodied finally in Gary Cooper, betrays the truth of American history."[3] In short, the application of a strong sense of humor would have saved us from the mythical or Hollywood West if we wanted or needed to be saved, giving us a truer picture of what went on in the "winning of the West."

Similar calls for a saving sense of humor have come down to us through the centuries. More often than not the theorists were talking about comedy in the theater, but always the basic questions were, Why do we laugh? and What do we laugh at? Nobody has yet found a satisfactory answer to the first, but everybody has had a try at the second, beginning with Plato, Aristotle, and Socrates. No two of them ever agree completely, but all concur in viewing comedy as a tool used by civilized man to get at the truth about life, change if for the better, or rebel against its failures and lunacies. Every important thinker has had his say: Cicero, Ben Jonson, Schopenhauer, Freud, Bergson, Koestler, and H. L. Mencken, to name a few.

In the second half of the twentieth century a great many scholars have become involved, and books and articles have proliferated in a steady stream—the intellectual offspring of psychologists, sociologists, philosophers, cultural historians, and buffs—all of whom conduct experiments and analyses and draw solemn conclusions. There are national and international societies for the study of humor and the comic, dominated by academic people who hold conventions, read papers, publish scholarly books and articles, and tend to squeeze the fun out of the study of laughter. They are capable of writing such paragraphs as this:

> The comic quality is a characteristic mode of aesthetic consciousness. Cocreative acts of author and reader attribute to the content of a literary work of art an objectivity of such a kind that we sense or interpret it as having the comic properties of continuance as itself and freedom in relation to a continued threat of alteration.[4]

Intensive attempts to describe and analyze, in the name of science, the aspects and uses of the comic can leave a nonspecialist shaken and dismayed.[5] It is a startling thing to listen to a suave and serious female professor analyzing scatalogical humor (known to most of us as dirty stories) before a roomful of specialists expanding their knowledge of human behavior.[6]

Much of their thought has been spent on how humor works—the tricks and devices, the machinery that leads to laughter. Wylie Sypher's list is simple: repetition, inversion, and reciprocal interference. Jesse Bier adds "comic catalog, anticlimax, reversalism, circular disqualification, and comic contrasts of formal and informal style."[7] These refinements need not detain a nonspecialist. The important thing is function—what is humorous writing trying to accomplish.

Building on Plato and Aristotle, commentators in the eighteenth and nineteenth centuries considered comedy a social corrective. Henry Fielding in 1742 declared himself a specialist in the "true ridiculous," which was made up of equal parts of vanity and hypocrisy, both demanding to be laughed at. "A dirty fellow riding through the streets in a cart" is not funny, but "seeing the same figure descending from his coach and six or bolting from a chair with his hat under his arm"[8] would provoke derisive laughter and perhaps convince the dirty fellow that he was making a fool of himself.

Progressing a little farther down this road, George Meredith in his novel *The Egoist* (1879) visualizes a Comic Spirit ranging the world in search of what Meredith calls egoism—meaning self-serving pride, impenetrable vanity, all the way up to the overweening assumptions of *hybris* in Greek tragedy. When the Egoist launches into his de-

4

scending spiral, the Comic Spirit is there, waiting for him to crash and make himself ridiculous. Meredith's parable, simply stated, says that the fear of being laughed at is the salt that keeps society from spoiling; laughter is the great purifier. Henri Bergson, whose *Essay on Comedy* is a foundation stone of modern thinking on the subject, agrees that comedy "corrects men's manners,"[9] and there is a general consensus that correction is one of the functions of the comic.

In the American West, however, this hardly holds true. Meredith and Bergson were talking about cultivated, educated men and women, at home in the drawing room, witty and in command of the language. Since drawing rooms on the frontier were nonexistent and civilized Frenchmen and Englishmen were scarce, drawing-room comedy could hardly develop. *Ruggles of Red Gap* (1910) is about as close as the Western United States could come. Ruggles, the English butler, does stand corrected at the end.

Besides, the country in general was headed in another direction. Satirical exposure seemed to suit us better than the urge to reform, and after the Civil War our humorists found more and more in American life to object to. They felt, with Sigmund Freud, that the primary purpose of humor was resistance to authority, and later writers saw in it "hostility," "deflationism," and the venting of our aggressions.[10] The slide toward black humor and sick humor, hastened by two world wars and the Depression, has brought us to the point where laughter has almost vanished from our fiction and only bitter satire and merciless exposure remain. We find words for it like "denigration" and "comic despair."[11]

In view of these radical changes in the constitution and direction of the humorous novel, finding a way through the jungle of concept and counterconcept is no easy task, but several ways in which the Comic Spirit serves us can be made out: It can aim at

1. *Correction.* Fear of ridicule, as noted, keeps the tissues of society healthy and the egoists (antisocial people) in line. Corrective comedy is more at home in Boston than in Boise.
2. *Self-preservation.* Our sense of humor helps us bear the unbearable. Uncle Remus's black people, represented by Br'er Rabbit, laugh slyly at their oppressors. Dust Bowl victims make up comical songs and tell funny stories about their predicament. One thinks of Stewart Edward

White's unfortunate settler in *Arizona Nights* who endured a spectacular run of bad luck, blow after blow, without impatience or resentment. When the last and worst happened, however, he laughed immoderately. Asked for an explanation, he replied: "Because it's so darn complete!" The West often makes the best of the worst by laughing at it.[12]

3. *Escape.* Humor offers escape from boredom on the one hand and from pressure and stress on the other. People laugh to keep from crying and from dying of ennui. In the West tall tales and cowboy "windies" helped people keep their sanity. They find a place in western novels, for example, Andy Adams's *The Log of a Cowboy* and Robert Lewis Taylor's *The Travels of Jaimie McPheeters*.

4. *Purgation.* Stephen Leacock and Konrad Lorenz define laughter as the expression of our savage, violent instincts.[13] Violence is certainly an integral part of the standard "Western," but Alfred Henry Lewis is one of the few in early times to laugh at it (Jack Moore "does the rope work for the stranglers"—the Wolfville vigilance committee).[14] The superviolent popular novels of such men as George C. Gilman and J. T. Edson (both Englishmen) are not intentionally humorous but violence is so exaggerated as to become comic.

5. *Ego support.* Our sense of the comic can provide us with a sometimes much-needed feeling of superiority. Aristotle had the idea but Thomas Hobbes in the seventeenth century gets credit for the theory that we laugh when others come to grief or make themselves ridiculous because it is not happening to us and we find ourselves in a superior position. Even this cynical view contributes to the idea that laughter helps us to cope, to survive, to make the best of things.

6. *Exposure.* We live in a sick society, the historians of culture tell us. "The triumph of indiscriminate black humor and sick jokes and literature is unmistakable," says Jesse Bier. "Such excess is a symptom of defeatist morale." Black humor and sick humor tell us and show us that our society is rotten to the core.[15] Western fiction, as will be argued later, has refused to go down this ghastly and forbidding road.

The functions of humor, however they are analyzed, have not changed over the centuries, but the words we use to describe them have. The old distinctions and definitions no longer hold. In the eighteenth century, for example, there was much debate about the difference between wit and humor. In our day the terms are practically synonymous, and *witty* and *humorous* are used interchangeably with *amusing, funny, ridiculous,* and even *side-splitting,* though careful speakers make proper distinctions. Something special needs to be said, however, about the words *humor* and *humorous.*

Humor was once a medical term referring to the four body fluids recognized by medieval doctors. Human differences, and sometimes human illnesses, were caused by an excess of black bile, yellow bile, blood, or phlegm. People were thus melancholy, choleric, sanguine, or phlegmatic. The connection with character was obvious. A man's special humorous constitution set him apart from others and gave him his individuality. A little of his special peculiarity made him amusing. A lot of it could make him a social liability. The term for a person who was pretty far out but still tolerable was *original genius*—"original" for short. Dramatists, beginning with Ben Jonson,[16] took up the idea and the eighteenth-century English novelists followed suit.

Storytellers had been fond of these oddballs ever since Aristotle's disciple Theophrastus described the ones he encountered in ancient Greece, and storytellers still are. Often they embody contradictions. Take Miss Piggy as an example (though she has not yet appeared in a novel). On the surface sticky-sweet, underneath she is a ruthless self-promoter. We laugh when her true tough self breaks through to the surface. She is a "character," an "original," a truly humorous figure in both the ancient and the modern sense.

The English two centuries ago rejoiced in the idea that their countrymen were more humorous—more crochety and cross-grained, more determinedly eccentric—than people of other nations. They were proud of their foibles and compared themselves favorably with the volatile French, the devious Italian, and the stolid German. Their enjoyment of humorous differences was passed on to their American cousins, the Yankees, the Southerners, and eventually the Westerners—the last inhabiting a region where individualists flourished more rugged than anything an eighteenth-century Englishman ever dreamed of—Davy Crockett (he was a westerner in his time), Mike Fink, Jim Bridger, Lottie Deno, Big-nosed Kate, and that famous female camp follower the Great Western. The fiction of the American West has availed itself fully of this storehouse of humor. Even the faultless hero whom Leslie Fiedler objects to is likely to have his "comic sidekick," almost a fixture in popular western fiction.[17]

These characters are intriguing because they do not conform or fit the conventional pattern. They fail to measure up. It could be said, indeed, that all humor, including western humor, is based on human failure, at least on human deviation from the norm. Sometimes it smiles at harmless eccentricity; sometimes it growls at overweening egotism; always it begins, as Schopenhauer was the first to point out, with a perception of incongruity. There are many names for it. Kierkegaard and Kafka call it "contradiction." Bergson talks about "a sudden dissolution of continuity."[18] Another way to say it is that running through our minds like the San Andreas Fault in California is a line dividing what should be from what is and shouldn't be. On one side is the normal, the accepted, the approved; on the other is deviation. The perception, usually sudden, that a person or an act is on the wrong side of the line—the little shock of recognition—is somehow funny and tickles us, causes us to smile or laugh.

It can also cause us, we must admit, to sigh or cry. A familiar illustration is the man who slips on the ice, gyrates wildly, and comes crashing down. His normal position is vertical. Suddenly he is horizontal. Very comical indeed! But if he breaks his neck and leaves a wife and eight children without means of support, the humor vanishes. Thus the same event can be both comic and tragic.

Over and over again the historians of culture make the point that "misery is the basis of comedy" and that laughter is a way of transcending the misery.[19]

Jerry Lewis, the comedian, says, "I need only call upon my sorrow to create laughter. Sorrow and laughter are so close. Hand in glove. Things that are funny are also often so sad, funny and terrifying at the same time. The fact that so many comedians are from Jewish families goes as far back as Pharaoh. The Jews saved their asses by their sense of humor."[20]

At least one theorist contends that pain and pleasure are found together and meet "to produce a third element, which partakes of both, like being pinched by a pretty girl." Hence, says Samuel S. Cox, "some humor makes us cry and some makes us laugh. Less prettiness and more pinching brings tears. More prettiness and less pinching, smiles."[21] Cox could not have foreseen the advent of black humor when he wrote those lines in 1876. Black humor is all pinch and no prettiness.

The material of tragedy and comedy, then, can be the same. Both involve human beings who do not conform, who are, as we say now, "out of sync." The tragedian takes one stance; the comedian another. The comedian's stance is not easy to define but it is easy to recognize, or was in former times. The comedian has his tongue in his cheek, is no respecter of persons or conventions, and has no illusions. He goes in for verbal humor, including dialect. He appears to be poking fun and creates laughter.

The humorist-comedian knows, however, that his business is to get at the truth. He destroys delusions and attacks prejudice and cant. He makes unpleasant things bearable. One remembers that in earlier centuries when the king had to face distressing facts, it was the court jester who found a way to tell him what he did not want to hear. In our time storytellers, rather than statisticians, are often the ones who convince us that pollution is about to choke us, that the big brothers of totalitarianism are reaching for us, that stockpiling more and more atomic bombs is the ultimate madness.

In our own country humor has always been a part of our culture, and it developed in its own way, departing somewhat from its European models. "We laugh harder, and need to in the United States," says Jesse Bier, "where pretense and rhetoric and sentimental shibboleth have been more solidified than elsewhere." Our humor is "caustic, wild, savage." It has strong roots in oral storytelling. It is "the voice of hard, fresh truth," springing from the grassroots.[22] The eastern states had their Jack Downings and Yankee Doodles but the Old Southwest (the South as we now know it) was particularly productive, its first triumphs coming in the 1840s. Hennig Cohen and William B. Dillingham's *Humor of the Old Southwest* (1964) is a standard work, featuring such characters as Sut Lovingood, Simon Suggs, and Mike Hooter. An eighteenth-century Englishman would have been delighted with these "originals" as they swaggered, bragged, courted, wagered, fought, and lied through life.

The *new* Southwest and the West in general owe much to this humorous tradition. It reappeared in the work of such men as Captain Randolph B. Marcy, Captain John G. Bourke, George H. Derby, and Dick Wick Hall.[23] Bret Harte and Mark Twain carried the banner in California and Nevada where miners, mule-skinners, scouts, and saloon hangers-on talked in "Western" dialect, told enormous lies, and exhibited peculiar standards of conduct. The

9

frontier eccentric reappeared in many forms in the new century, but he has undergone remarkable changes, especially in fiction. The crochety old cattleman of Alfred Henry Lewis's *Wolfville* (1897) is taken a good deal farther down the road by Larry McMurtry, for example, as he describes his Uncle L in *All My Friends Are Going to be Strangers* (1972).

> Ninety-two years had not mellowed him at all. . . . When I walked up he was down on his knees, stabbing at a hole in the ground with a big crowbar. . . . His little blue eyes were as clear and mean as ever. . . .
> "I still got ever goddamn one of my teeth," he said, opening his mouth to show me. . . . He spat in his gloves and went back to stabbing at the earth with the crowbar. Holes were one of his obsessions. Over the years he had scattered some three hundred corner postholes about the ranch to the peril of every creature that walked, including him. The theory behind them was that if he ever got around to building the fences he meant to build it would be nice to have the corner postholes already dug. But he had lived on the ranch fifty years and it had only two fences, both falling down. My own theory was that he dug the holes because he hated the earth and wanted to get in as many licks at it as he could, before he died. The earth might get him in the end, but it would have three hundred scars to show for it. Uncle L was not the kind of man who liked to be bested in a fight.[24]

Uncle L is a byproduct of the comic cowboy. Outside the confines of the cattle kingdom the evolutionary process has produced results just as startling as we encounter such weirdos as Sheriff C. L. Hoke Birdsill of David Markson's *Ballad of Dingus Magee* (1965) and the Reverend Billy Sol Hargus of Don Imus's *God's Other Son* (1981). Billy Sol does not know who his father is and comes to believe that he is the product of an immaculate conception. He refers to Jesus as "Brother" and he calls God "Dad."

Obviously western fiction has made some progress down the road to disillusion and the mirthless laughter of the leading Eastern novelists of our time, but it has not gone all the way. We may or may not continue down that road. The only certainty is that everything about us, including what we laugh at, is subject to change and illustrations are easy to find. Novels about cowboys, for example, show how our assumptions concerning the man on horseback have undergone radical revision in the course of a century. L. R. Foyt, with his bib overalls, has replaced the cowboy hero.

These things do not happen all at once. It took a long time to put Lassiter and Shane out of business, but almost from the beginning the nonheroic cowboy existed beside his heroic counterpart. Hopalong Cassidy in the early Bar-20 novels was sometimes drunk and disorderly. W. C. Tuttle, Henry Herbert Knibbs, Charles P. Snow (Charles Ballew), S. Omar Barker, John and David Shelley, Nelson Nye—all made fun of their cowboys. The antihero had not been born in western fiction, but characters with names like Rimfire Boggs and Wild Horse Shorty were nonheroic and sometimes ridiculous.[25]

Eugene Manlove Rhodes admitted in verse, with unconcealed resentment, that people in his day were defining the cowboy as a "hired man on horseback."[26] In later years we hear William W. Savage of the University of Oklahoma referring to cowboys as "an unfortunate breed of men," rangeland dropouts who remained dependent and insecure because they did not have the drive or the intelligence to become cattlemen. They were individuals of "no significance"; they were, in fact, "dull."[27]

Recent writers carry the downgrading process still further. Jane Kramer, after living for a year on a Texas Panhandle ranch, concluded in *The Last Cowboy* (1977) that her rangeland friends were trying hopelessly to live up to the cowboy myth in the age of agribusiness and the pickup.[28] John Erickson in *The Modern Cowboy* (1980) presents a firsthand account of the contemporary puncher's unglamorous life.[29] Western fiction, drawing on its greater resources of imagination and invention, adds an extra dimension to these revelations. "In those days," says L. R. Foyt, speaking of his youth, "a man could take satisfaction in a rough job well done—because what he was bucking was nature. But now he was bucking civilization." There is no place for the old-time cowboy in the modern world, he adds. "No place to call their own, not a woman nor a fambly nor a single dollar put away in their sock. All the happy prospects of a peckerwood in the petrified forest."[30] The humorous comparison reinforces the point.

The best and most thoughtful Western novelists of the last half of our century reach the same conclusion. They look on the modern

11

cowboy as an anachronism (Edward Abbey, *The Brave Cowboy*, 1956), as a survivor in a strange world (William Decker, *To Be a Man*, 1967), as a loser (J. P. S. Brown, *Jim Kane*, 1970), or as an ignorant brute (Marguerite Noble, *Filaree*, 1978). Add to this list Richard Gardner's *Scandalous John* (1963) and Robert Flynn's *North to Yesterday* (1967), both full of wry humor, which deal with mixed-up old cowboys trying to relive trail-driving days in the era of portable corrals and paved roads.

A truly funny example of this negative trend is Max Evans's *The Rounders*, which makes comic capital of the fortunes and misfortunes of two cowboys in virtual peonage to a rangeland capitalist named Jim Ed Love. They spend a hard and lonely winter gathering wild cattle for Jim Ed, with the aid and discomfort of a satanic horse named Old Fooler. On a typical cattle-gathering day Dusty and Wrangler come upon a big wild steer in the brush. Dusty and Old Fooler go after him.

> We had started around this piñon tree, and I had leaned over just enough so Old Fooler would know which side to go on. He acted like he was doing just what I wanted, but when he got to the tree, he whirled back the other way at full speed. So there I was trying to go around one side, and him going the other. My chest whopped into hard bark and off I went.
>
> I was laying there on my back trying to find the sky. My breath was gone and every move I made I could feel them busted ribs scraping against one another.[31]

Dusty gets even, when he is able to ride again, by putting Old Fooler back into the brush and running *him* into that same piñon tree.

In the spring the partners ride out with their catch, blow in their money, and are back in slavery next fall. They are dead-end kids in the cow country, but they don't know it, and most readers have been too busy laughing at them to know it either. Is there an element of cruelty in that laughter? The Greeks would have said yes.

The point to emphasize is that such laugh-provoking portrayals of the puncher and his life are more than good stories. They show what has happened to the image of the cowboy over the years. They contribute to history.

Changes in fictional humor are by no means limited to the cow people. Every corner of western fiction has gone through its own transformations. The lowly "greasers" of Alfred Henry Lewis's *Wolfville* (1897), for example, are not the simple souls, sympathetically portrayed, of Frank Applegate's *Native Tales of New Mexico* (1932), or the Mexican dreamer who retakes the Alamo for Mexico in James Lehrer's comic masterpiece *Viva Max* (1966). Similar developments take place in stories about Indians and blacks, peace officers and outlaws, country people and town people, picaros and prostitutes, as this book attempts to show.

Two truths stand out, however, as one examines humorous fiction in any or all of these categories. One is the shift from the country to the city. The other is the fact that our humor has grown grimmer and darker. These developments are to be expected since the nation is now more urban than rural, and the literature of the Western world has been darkening for more than a century. In our own country it would seem that there is no faith or hope left. We no longer believe in God and country. We no longer believe in ourselves. We no longer believe in life itself. Some humorists have been able to get some amusement out of the sorry spectacle. H. L. Mencken, writing soon after the end of World War I, sneered, "Well, here is the land of mirth. . . . Here the buffoonery never stops. . . . I am naturally sinful and such spectacles caress me. . . . I never get tired of the show, and it is worth every cent it costs."[32]

Forty years later not many were amused as the theater of the absurd, sick jokes, and black humor came upon us. Richard Boyd Hauck attributes this development to a prevailing conviction that life has no meaning. "A novelist's decision to create laughter out of the absurdity of everything appears to me to be an astonishing phenomenon. . . . What is startling in absurd American fiction is that straight reality is presented as being absurdly humorous." The novelists thus succeed in being "both nihilistic and cheerful."[33]

To most readers the cheerfulness is not apparent. Black humor, to ordinary people, is more black than humorous. Half a dozen excellent scholars try to explain it. A few are horrified by it. Sarah Blacher Cohen quotes Lenny Bruce: "Everything is rotten—mother is rotten, God is rotten, the flag is rotten," and adds, "Their favorite kind of comedy was scatological to convey their excremental vision of things. . . . They slaughtered every sacred cow they could corral and flaunted the carcasses before the pained owners.[34]

It would be too much to expect that Western fiction would escape the infection and the new freedoms have produced some startling results. The old-fashioned strait-laced formula western has taken the most conspicuous advantage of the new freedom to say and show everything. "Adult westerns," also known as "porno westerns," caught on in the 1970s and publishers, sometimes using a "house name" and employing half a dozen writers, flooded the market with "series" paperbacks featuring ⸱ hard-case sexual athlete—Slocum, Lashtrow, Klaw, Gunn, Ruff Justice, Easy Company, Longarm. The most successful and revolting of these is Longarm, who is as good in the bushes chasing criminals as he is in bed with a wide variety of willing women.

It is comforting to know, however, that hardcover western novels have resisted the infection rather well. Larry McMurtry and a number of friends and followers, mostly living in Texas, do indeed feel free to use any word and describe any act. Their characters are apt to be feckless and rootless and given to the pleasures of the flesh. They satirize the sinfulness and duplicity of ordinary folks, but they never reach the point of utter nihilism or decide that "absurd creation" is the only answer to an absurd universe. The West (in fiction) is not *that* wild.

And a whole host of what this anthologist must believe are saner writers are producing fiction that takes the true humorist's view of life, kindly or critical, and they make good literature out of it. This book shows what a few of them have done and can do. If some have never been heard of on the eastern seaboard, so much the worse for the Weary East. In the West we still know how to laugh, and in our era, this is no small distinction.

There will be objections to the plan and content of this collection, beginning with the absence of material from the West Coast—California, Washington, and Oregon. Where are Mark Twain and Bret Harte, Alan Moody and William Saroyan, H. L. Davis and Bernard Malamud? The answer is, they are not here because they belong in another world. The essential West, with which this book is concerned, is the West of cowboys and Indians, Mexicans and miners, mountain men and cavalrymen, stretching from Montana to Mexico with the Rocky Mountains as its backbone. When most people, including Europeans, say "West," this is what they are thinking of. It is the western heartland. Covering even this fraction of the United States in one volume is nearly impossible. There is no room for separate areas like the Great Plains and the West Coast. Let the Great Plains and the West Coast turn out their own anthologies. They are big enough and important enough to deserve them.

A reminder is in order that the humor here presented is fictional, with short stories and excerpts from novels as examples. Yarns, tall tales, reminiscent narratives, folklore, and anecdotes are not included by themselves. No Charley Russell, no Will Rogers, no Bill Nye, no Petroleum V. Nasby! Only bona fide fiction writers are displayed, and there are too many good ones to get even a fractional part of them in.

Any readers who feel hurt and betrayed by the omission of their favorite fictional humorist should know that this collection, when it first came off the typewriter, was 900 pages long and had to be cut. That favorite humorist was undoubtedly included and had to be, as they say in the world of football, waived. It was hard to see him go, but there was no more room at the inn.

The principle of selection is simple. The story has to have a western setting and characters; it has to take a humorous view of its subject; it has to have something to say, a point to make. Many chapters and stories were amusing enough but they lacked significance. Some recent ones were so fantastic and far out—*Blazing Saddles*, for example—that they would make little sense to an ordinary reader. Some were so frank in language and explicit in situation that a modest anthologist could not include them. And Texas writers had so much to satirize and have appeared in such numbers that they tried to dominate the book and had to be hustled firmly out.

A short essay precedes each subdivision, commenting on the quantity and character of the works included, and a brief note introduces each writer. When an excerpt from a novel is presented, the characters are identified and preceding events are outlined.

The book can be read for amusement and nothing else, but it can also provide some new ideas to people who are interested in humor and its uses in these United States, and it will introduce some good writers with something to offer who deserve a larger readership than they have had.

Anyone, even an anthologist, who puts together a book accumulates many debts. Friends who lent a hand in making this one include Dale Walker of El Paso, Ben Capps of Grand Prairie, David Grossblatt of Dallas, Jon Tuska of Portland, Oregon, S. Omar Barker of Las Vegas, New Mexico, Richard Etulain of Albuquerque, Jeanne Williams of Portal, Arizona, Nelson Nye, David Laird, Tom Sheridan , Leland Case, Bunny Fontana, and Don Bufkin of Tucson.

The staffs of the University of Arizona Library, the Tucson Public Library, and the University of Texas at El Paso Library responded to many a challenge. And my wife Carol was patient, as always, when her desk-bound husband found it difficult to leave bookmaking and smell the flowers. My thanks to all are hearty and sincere.

Notes

1. Gary Jennings, *The Terrible Teague Bunch* (New York: Norton, 1975), 26–50, 61, 136–37.

2. Quoted in Jesse Bier, *The Rise and Fall of American Humor* (New York: Holt, Rinehart & Winston, 1968), 2.

3. Leslie A. Fiedler, *The Return of the Vanishing American* (New York: Stein & Day, 1968), 136–37, 141.

4. George McFadden, *Discovering the Comic* (Princeton, N.J.: Princeton University Press, 1982), 4.

5. Discussions of all aspects of humor may be expected at such reunions as the annual conference on WHIM (Western Humor and Irony Membership) held in April at Arizona State University in Tempe.

6. For an introduction to the subject see Paul E. McGhee and Jeffrey H. Goldstein, *Handbook of Humor Research*, vol. 1: *Basic Issues* (New York, Berlin: Springer Verlag, 1982). Bibliographies are included. The literature is enormous and growing; the discipline has developed its own vocabulary. Dolf Zillman, for example, in discussing Hobbes's superiority theory, talks about "disparagement of the unaffiliated" (p. 87), and Howard R. Pollio discusses "smiling as an embodied social event" (p. 219).

7. See Wylie Sypher, *Comedy: An Essay on Comedy, George Meredith, Laughter, Henri Bergson* (Baltimore: Johns Hopkins University Press, 1956), 124. For Bier's view, see *Rise and Fall*, 352.

8. Henry Fielding, *Joseph Andrews and Shamela*, ed. Martin C. Battestin (London: Methuen, 1965), 10–11. *Joseph Andrews* was published in 1742.

9. Sypher, *Comedy*, 71, 187.

10. Bier, *Rise and Fall*, 16–20; Konrad Lorenz, *On Aggression*, trans. Marjorie Keir Wilson (New York: Harcourt Brace Jovanovich, 1974).

11. Bier, *Rise and Fall*, 295.

12. Stewart Edward White, *Arizona Nights* (New York: Hillman Books, n. d., original copyright 1907), 35.

13. Stephen Leacock, *Humor: Its Theory and Technique* (New York: Dodd, Mead, 1935); Lorenz, *On Aggression*.

14. Alfred Henry Lewis, *Wolfville* (New York: A. L. Burt, 1897), 18.

15. Bier, *Rise and Fall*, 468.

16. Louis Cazamian, *The Development of English Humor* (Durham: Duke University Press, 1952), 391.

17. Norris W. Yates, *The American Humorist: Conscience of the Twentieth Century* (Ames: Iowa State University Press, 1964), 12. Yates notes the persistent relationship between character and humor: "The closest thing to a 'key' that can be found in the printed humor of the period is the humorists' use of character types."

18. Sypher, *Comedy*, 264, 196, 76.

19. Eric Bentley, *The Life of Drama* (New York: Atheneum, 1967), p. 301.

20. Dotson Raider, "And Sometimes He Cries," interview with Jerry Lewis, *Parade Magazine*, April 22, 1984, p. 6. Compare Ralph Waldo Emerson, "The Comic," in *Works of Ralph Waldo Emerson* (Boston: Houghton Mifflin, 1880) 127–40.

21. Samuel S. Cox, *Why We Laugh* (New York: Harper & Row, 1876, repr. Benjamin Blom, 1969), 14.

22. Bier, *Rise and Fall*, 1, 2.

23. Captain Randolph P. Marcy, *Border Reminiscences* (1872); John G. Bourke, *On the Border with Crook* (1892); George H. Derby (John Phoenix), *The Squibob Papers* (1865); Dick Wick Hall, *Stories from the Salome Sun* (1968).

24. Larry McMurtry, *All My Friends Are Going to Be Strangers* (New York: Simon & Schuster, 1972), 180.

25. Rimfire Boggs is a character in *The Bandit of the Paloduro* (1934), by Charles Ballew (Charles H. Snow). Wild Horse Shorty is the central figure in Nelson Nye's novel of the same name (1934).

26. Eugene Manlove Rhodes, "The Hired Man on Horseback," in *Best Novels Short Stories*, ed. Frank V. Dearing (Boston: Houghton Mifflin, 1949), 551.

27. William W. Savage, Jr., *Cowboy Life* (Norman: University of Oklahoma Press, 1975), 3, 6.

28. Jane Kramer, *The Last Cowboy* (New York: Harper & Row, 1977), 3, 4.

29. John Erickson, *The Modern Cowboy* (Lincoln: University of Nebraska Press, 1981).

30. Jennings, *The Terrible Teague Bunch*, 49.

31. Max Evans, *The Rounders* (New York: Macmillan, 1960, repr. Bantam, 1965), 40–41.

32. H. L. Mencken, "On Being an American," *Prejudices*, 3rd series, New York: Alfred A. Knopf, 1922, p. 61.

33. Richard Boyd Hauck, *A Cheerful Nihilism: Confidence and the Absurd in American Humorous Fiction*. Bloomington: Indiana University Press. 1981, p. xii.

34. Sarah Blacher Cohen, *Comic Relief*. Urbana: University of Illinois Press, 1878, p. 23.

PART ONE

▼▲▼

Humor in the West—
A Changing Picture

*What we call the West was so full of humor in
reality that I do not believe that the Great
American Western can ever be written by an
author essentially lacking in humor.*

—Will Henry *

*. . . to understand the West as somehow a joke
comes a little closer to getting it straight*

—Leslie A. Fiedler **

---

* Dale L. Walker (ed.), *Will Henry's West* (El Paso: Texas Western Press, 1984).

** Leslie A. Fiedler, *The Return of the Vanishing American* (New York: Stein & Day, 1968).

Red Man's West: The Transformation of the Indian

▼▲▼▲▼▲▼▲▼▲▼▲▼▲▼▲▼▲▼▲▼▲▼▲▼▲▼▲▼▲▼▲▼▲▼

Frank G. Applegate—"Ancestral Eagles"
(from *Indian Stories from the Pueblos*)

Bill Gulick—"The Marriage of Moon Wind"
(from *Branded West*)

Dan Cushman—"Louis Champlain's Party,"
(from *Stay Away Joe*)

From Villain to Victim

▼▲▼

IT HAS NEVER BEEN EASY TO LAUGH ABOUT INDIANS. WHILE THE tribesmen, especially the Apaches, were a menace and a barrier to settlement, white attitudes alternated between outrage and contempt. When the Indian wars were over, however, it was possible for white observers to view the red survivors with new interest. Anthropologists, folklorists, and curious ladies from the East moved in on them, studied them, poked and pried at them, and even began to idealize them. Marah Ellis Ryan in *Indian Love Letters* (1907) dissolved the Hopis in sentiment, taking the same stance in fiction that popular composers did a little later in such tender ballads as "Red Wing," "Hiawatha's Melody," and "Indian Love Call." Harold Bell Wright's Apache character Natachee in *The Mine with the Iron Door* (1923) aimed vigorous swings at the encroaching white man. In 1925 Zane Grey in *The Vanishing American* allowed a Navajo boy and a white girl to fall in love, but he could not let them be happy together. In the 1930s several good novels took the side of the Indian (for example, Will Levington Comfort's *Apache*, 1931), and in 1947 Elliot Arnold in *Blood Brother* went all the way, making the white man the bad guy and the Indian the good guy. His views are still popular in the 1980s.

In his progress from villain to victim the red man did not, and could not, provoke much laughter, though he was sometimes treated with humorous contempt, as in Alfred Henry Lewis's *Wolfville*, published in 1897. One has to wait until the 1930s for Frank Applegate's charming little comedies, the sharp-edged humor of Mary Austin. An infusion of gall came along later with Dan Cushman's *Stay Away Joe* (1961) and Clair Huffaker's *Nobody Loves a Drunken Indian*, called *Flap* in the moving-picture version (1967). Serious trouble is just around the corner in such novels. Flap and Charlie Eagletooth in *Charlie Eagletooth's War* (1969) rebel openly against the government. The publishers describe Flap as "hilarious," but he has tragic overtones and could easily have dropped the comic mask as other Indian novels have done (such as Nasnaga's *Indians' Summer*, 1975).

The question is, do these humorous novelists and storytellers use their tools effectively? Some readers, including this anthologist, feel that their books do a better job of presenting the Indian and his situation than Dee Brown's best-selling *Bury My Heart at Wounded Knee* (1971) or Vine DeLoria's acerbic *Custer Died for Your Sins* (1970), both immune to laughter.

Ancestral Eagles

▼▲▼▲▼▲▼▲▼▲▼▲▼▲▼▲▼▲▼▲▼▲▼▲▼▲▼▲▼▲▼▲▼

Frank G. Applegate

Frank Applegate was a product of the University of Illinois, the Pennsylvania Academy of Fine Arts, and the Julian Academy of Art in Paris. In the 1920s he joined other fugitives from the East in the artists' colony at Santa Fe. A fine artist in his own right and a respected member of the Taos–Santa Fe complex, he spent much of his time in the field collecting folk art for the Museum of New Mexico. His travels brought him into daily contact with the Indians and Mexican-Americans of his adopted state, and he developed a special rapport with them. In *Indian Stories from the Pueblos* (1929) and *Native Tales of New Mexico* (1932) he looked at both groups with gentle humor, the kind that comes from love and respect. His little stories are a special gift to the humorous literature of the West.

TABO SALUKAMA, HOPI INDIAN, HAD, WHEN A SMALL LAD, BEEN snatched away from his parents by the Indian Police and sent by the Indian Agent, along with other Hopi boys and girls, hundreds of miles away to an Indian boarding school. At this school he had been kept for eight years without returning once to the pueblo and, during all this time, he had had it impressed upon him that Indians were savages and that their religious practices and ceremonies were the result of low and base superstitions. He was also taught that the middle-class American culture was the flower of highest civilization and that all Americans were one hundred per cent pure in their ideals, religious beliefs and practices. Likewise he was taught that the Indian Bureau and its agents were always solicitous for the welfare of the Indians and always stood ready to help them in any emergency. Tabo came gradually to believe all this, so that when he returned to his sky-high home, his head was full to overflowing with white man's nonsense and he disdained and disapproved all things Indian and was the despair of his parents. Nothing Indian was good enough for him. Hopi religious ceremonies and their worship of "false gods" dis-

From *Indian Stories from the Pueblos* (Philadelphia: Lippincott, 1929; Glorieta, N. M.: Rio Grande Press, 1977), 17–26.

gusted him and the eternal odors of stewing mutton and goat's meat sickened him. Corn meal porridge and dried peaches were, to him, no fit sort of substitute for boarding-school rolled oats and stewed prunes. Fortunately the keen air of the high altitude gave Tabo such an over-powering appetite that he soon overcame his repugnance for the hearty Indian food, and a few months later his mother gave him as husband to a nice Hopi girl who had shown herself proficient in the difficult art of grinding corn with the metate or mealing stone.

Tabo was now confronted with the emergency of making a living for himself and wife and he soon found out how profitless was all he had learned while at school. But his father-in-law took him in hand and taught him how to plant his corn and squashes and tend his peach trees, so that they would yield, even in the desert's sandy and thirsty soil. Tabo tried for a while to live according to the missionary's teach-ings and prayed fervently every day for his corn and squashes, but when his corn began to turn yellow, in spite of his prayers for rain, he suddenly lost faith in what the Indians call "the Sunday Jesus" and reverted to his ancient and primitive tribal gods and joined the other Hopis in their great rain-making ceremony. Soon afterwards the overdue summer rains arrived and confirmed his reborn faith in the old gods, so that thenceforward he was one with the Hopis in their belief that their own gods are best for them, although Jesus may be able to help the white man.

After this demonstration of the efficacy of the old tribal Katchinas, or Spirits, Tabo took part in all the religious rites and ceremonies of his people, and the death of a maternal uncle a few years later leaving him as chief of his clan, he became a very important figure in Hopi affairs.

Now one of the grandest ceremonies in all the Hopi calendar is the Niman Katchina, or farewell to the gods. These gods, or Katchinas, after dwelling with the Hopis during the spring and early summer, leave for their homes in the far distant San Francisco Mountains, which sparkle like a gem on the distant Hopi horizon and seem a fitting setting for the homes of gods. At dawn on the next day after the Katchinas have gone there is a ceremony by the chiefs of the clans at which each chief dispatches the spirit of a golden eagle that it may hurry to the returned gods with messages to remind them not to neglect sending the proper amount of rain to mature the Hopi corn for the year.

It is very essential that each clan chief have an eagle for this ceremony, so all the country round about Hopiland for fifty miles is carefully mapped out by the Hopis and a section set aside for each clan chief as his eagle hunting ground, on which no one else is to trespass in search of eagles. In the spring each clan chief seeks out the eagle nest in his territory and selects one of its eaglets and brings it to the pueblo, so that it may mature in time for the Niman ceremony.

Now one year when Tabo climbed up the crag where his eagle nest was located he found that someone had been ahead of him and stolen an eaglet. He was very much incensed at this but was too conservative to jeopardize the supply of eagles of future years by taking another one, so he descended the crag and started searching for the thief. He had not far to go for he soon met up with a Navajo Indian sheep herder who frequented that part of the country, and in whose possession he found the eagle.

When he accused the Navajo of the theft and demanded his eagle, the Navajo only laughed at him and told him, in what was the equivalent in Indian sign language, to go chase himself, that he had found the eagle on his own herding ground, and that it now belonged to him.

The Hopis are a peace-loving people and are reluctant to employ violence to further their ends, so Tabo left the Navajo and went trustingly straight to the Indian Agent, feeling sure that in this case where the right was so obviously on his side he would be able to procure swift and complete justice. The agent, who was new to the country and its problems, could make neither head nor tail of Tabo's story, but finally to get rid of him he gave Tabo a written order on the Navajo to give over the eagle. Tabo took the order with profuse thanks and trotted confidently back the forty miles to the sheep camp and trustingly handed the paper to the herder. Now this Navajo had not had the advantage of the schooling given Tabo, since, being a nomad in this great desert country, it had been easy for him to evade the Indian Police at the time when he should have gone to school, so he knew nothing of the "paper that talks." But he took the paper from Tabo and looked at it, then reached in his pouch and took out a familiar-looking bag and poured some tobacco from it into the creased paper, then carefully rolled up the paper and tobacco into a small cylinder, and placed one end of it in his mouth, lighted the other end of it with a match and proceeded to smoke it. Tabo looked on this desecration amazed and outraged and expected every moment to see the Navajo struck dead in some mysterious manner, but on nothing of the sort happening, he took courage and again demanded the eagle, whereupon the Navajo drove him from the camp.

Tabo again took his tale of woe to the agent, but the agent was by now bored by the affair, the ins and outs of which he could not comprehend, and had Tabo put out of his office.

Tabo now retired to his home to brood over the wrongs and the injustices of the agent. He finally reasoned that the agent was only a very small and rather ineffectual factor and that his intelligence was hardly adequate to understand the seriousness of the present crisis, in which the future crops and welfare of the Hopis were jeopardized by his incompetency, so Tabo came to the conclusion that the only thing to do was to apprise the chief at Washington of the emergency that was imminent.

The next day Tabo spent in composing and writing the following letter:

> Dear Chief of Indian Bureau:
> This same has come to pass here. Bad Navajo Indian have get my eagle wich i require for Niman Kachina, So no rain coming maybe for Hopis. Make corn die. Me i tell it to Hopi Indian agent. He say it to me, No require no eagle. Sunday Jesus Katchina send rain when need. i tell to him like hell no, i pray like hell one time with Jesus Katchina. He no send rain and corn get sick. Then i get rain from Hopi Katchina. I don get eagle pretty dam Quick now Hopis maybe got no corn. Navajo got too plenty sheeps no got use for eagles. Please big white chief for Indian, make police get eagle to me from naughty Navajo. i submit myself to your loving care,
>
> Tabo Salukama, Hopi Indian.

This letter a week later landed in the Indian Bureau at Washington and was duly laid on the desk of a young, newly appointed under clerk, who a few weeks before had been a salesman in a cigar store in Philadelphia and whose nearest acquaintance with an Indian, heretofore, had been with the wooden one in front of the building. After studying the letter the clerk read up on various subjects and sent back the following reply:

Mr. Taby Salukama, Dear Sir:

Your communication of recent date has been received and your problems have been given the greatest consideration by the bureau. The bureau is having sent to you under separate cover the following list of bulletins of the Department of Agriculture. #754 Raptores and their control. #1263 Proper Picking of Yellow Dent Seed Corn for Increased Germination. #968 Sheep Dips for Exterminating Ticks. #987 Methods of Dry Farming in Western Kansas. #547 Earth Worms and Their Contributions to Soil Upbuilding.

The Bureau feels assured that these bulletins will solve your difficulties for you. The bureau further suggests that you consult the nearest farm bureau relative to your problems. If, as you suggest, the eagles are carrying off your sheep you should take it up with the agent there and perhaps he can supply you with poisoned grain so that you may rid your pastures of these undesirable birds, or he may be able to procure a government hunter for a short period to shoot them.

Department of the Interior,
Indian Bureau

Tabo was overjoyed when he received a bulky package and a letter from Washington. He was sure that his troubles would soon be over and he would quickly have his precious eagle in his possession. It was about time too, for the Niman Katchina ceremony was only two weeks distant now. Tabo examined his mail, but not having time to figure out what it was all about, he hastened off to the agent to consult him further about it. The agent looked at the letter and the bulletins and then told Tabo he could go and try them on the Navajo if he liked, but not to bother the Indian Bureau with any more letters or to annoy him further. The truth of the matter was that the agent was reluctant to interfere with the Navajo, for Navajos are only too ready to take their own part when they think their rights are being invaded, while the Hopi is so peace loving that he will allow himself to be imposed upon.

This time when Tabo approached, the Navajo picked up a stone and threw it at him. Tabo was beginning to lose faith in the white man's help now, but he was willing to take one more chance on Washington, so he went home and this time he wrote a letter to the President. As he wrote he felt a resurgence of faith in the white man, for surely the great white father would not permit such rank injustice as had fallen to his lot. The President could even send soldiers to recover his eagle for him. Tabo's letter to the President ran:

Dear sir Precident of U. S.
Please send soldiers to get my eagle from Navajo, talk paper no damn good for Navajo. Niman Katchina coming too soon now. I don get eagle pretty dam quick now Hopis maybe starve for no rain to wet corn. Tell soldiers, look out, Navajo no good, throw stone to me for one time soon. Please dont wait to hesitate for the present and delay.

Loving,
Tabo Salukama.

The last ten days before the going of the gods, Tabo was in a fever of expectation. He scanned the horizon continually every day watching for the soldiers that were to come to restore his eagle before it should be too late, but on the morning before the Niman Katchina, instead of soldiers, came a letter marked "Office of the President." Tabo hastily tore it open and read:

Mr. Tabo Salukama
Dear Sir:
Your recent letter has been referred to the Indian Bureau and we trust that your claim will be speedily adjusted to your complete satisfaction.

Per_____, Secy.

The Niman ceremonies were over and the greatest of all the Hopi gods had gone back to their ancestral homes in the far away San Francisco Mountains. The next morning at dawn the spirits of the eagles must be released to carry messages to the great Katchina gods of the Hopis to remind them that they must not forget to arrange for plenty of rain for the Hopi cornfields. Tabo had, as a peaceful Indian, done his utmost in every peaceful way to recover his clan eagle, without success, so now his mind began to move in an old and almost obliterated groove. He returned to his home early that day and had his wife prepare a succulent and sustaining stew of mutton and dried peaches. At dusk he dispensed with all his clothing, with the exception of a gee string and moccasins, and covered his body with red ochre paint, with the exception of a few green stripes. Then he took a very old and much worn ancestral club from a niche over a roof beam and faded silently away in the night, as only an Indian can fade, in the direction of a distant and lonely sheep camp far out in the desert.

The next morning at dawn the full quota of eagle spirits was released by the Hopi clan chiefs to carry their messages to the all-powerful Katchinas in the distant San Francisco Mountains, although it might have been observed that one feather was missing from the tail of Tabo's eagle. Just at this moment a distant Navajo sheep herder discovered that the same missing feather was gripped tightly in his hand. The Navajo was recovering from a long spell of unconsciousness, in which he had imagined that he was flying through the air on the back of an eagle at a great height, when suddenly he had fallen on the ground, alighting on his head. Now with one hand he was feeling a great lump above his eyebrow, while with his eyes he was looking intently at the eagle feather, which he was already beginning, superstitiously, to blame for his great fall through the sky.

The Marriage of Moon Wind

▼▲▼▲▼▲▼▲▼▲▼▲▼▲▼▲▼▲▼▲▼▲▼▲▼▲▼▲▼▲▼▲▼▲▼▲▼

Bill Gulick

Old pro Bill Gulick, Missouri-born but long a resident of Walla Walla, Washington, is a successful writer of superior western fiction and has done excellent nonfiction studies of the western country. Always a humorist who enjoys the idiosyncracies of his Westerners, red or white, he never fails to see the funny side of the human predicament. He is a two-time winner of the Spur Award of the Western Writers of America, once for "The Marriage of Moon Wind," and has received the Wrangler Award from the National Cowboy Hall of Fame.

IT WAS THEIR LAST NIGHT ON THE TRAIL. OFF TO THE NORTHEAST the jagged, snowcapped peaks of the Wind River Mountains loomed tall against the darkening sky and the chill, thin air of the uplands was spiced with the pungent smell of sage and pine. But Tad Marshall was not interested in sights or smells at the moment. A rangy, well-put-together young man of twenty with curly golden hair and sharp blue eyes, he leaned forward and spoke to the grizzled ex-trapper sitting on the far side of the fire.

"You'll fix it for me?"

"I'll try," Buck Owens said grudgingly. "But don't hold me to blame for nothin' that happens. Like I told you before, Slewfoot Samuels eats greenhorns raw."

"He takes a bite out of me, he'll come down with the worst case of colic he ever had."

"You're cocky enough, I will say that."

"Don't mean to be. It's just that I come west to be a beaver trapper, not a mule tender."

"With the knack you got fer handlin' mules, Captain Sublette

From *Branded West: A Western Writers of America Anthology* (Boston: Houghton Mifflin, 1956). It was originally published in Gulick's collection, *White Men, Red Men and Mountain Men*, 1956, and appeared also in *The Saturday Evening Post Reader of Western Stories*, ed. E. N. Brandt, 1962.

won't want to lose you. He hears about this scheme you got to partner up with Slewfoot, he'll have a foamin' fit."

Tad shook his head. He liked Sublette and was real grateful for this chance to come west, but he wanted to see a chunk of the world with no dust-raising pack train clouding his view.

"Sublette can just have his fit. Me, I don't intend to go back to Missouri for a long spell."

"What're you runnin' away from—a mean pa?"

"Why, no. Pa treated me good."

"The law, maybe? You killed somebody back home?"

"Nothin' like that."

"Jest leaves one thing, then. Did you have woman trouble?"

Tad ran embarrassed fingers through his hair. "Guess you could call it that. There was three gals got the notion I was engaged to marry 'em. They all had brothers with itchy trigger fingers."

"Three gals wanted to marry you all at oncet?" Buck said in open admiration. "How'd that happen?"

"Darned if I know. Women have always pestered me, seems like. Now tell me some more about Slewfoot. You trapped with him for five years, you say?"

"Yeah. That's all I could stand him. Got a right queer sense of humor, Slewfoot has."

"A bit of joshin' never hurt nobody. I'll take the worst he can dish out, grin and come back for more."

"An' if you can't take it," Buck said, a gleam coming into his faded old eyes, "you'll stay with the mules like me 'n' the captain wants you to do?"

"Sure."

"Fine! I'll introduce you to Slewfoot tomorrow."

The word got around. During the half day it took the fur brigade to reach rendezvous grounds in the lush, grass-rich valley of the Green River, the men gossiped and grinned amongst themselves, and their attitude riled Tad.

Greenhorn though he was, Tad had learned considerable during the trip out from St. Louis. There were several kinds of trappers, he'd discovered. Some worked for wages and some for commissions, but the elite of the trade were the free trappers—men who roamed where they pleased, sold their furs to the highest bidder and were beholden to nobody.

Usually such men worked in pairs, but Slewfoot, who'd been queer to begin with, and was getting queerer every year, did his trapping with no other company than a Shoshone squaw he'd bought some years back. Campfire talk had it that Indian war parties rode miles out of their way to avoid him; she grizzly bears scared their cubs into behaving by mentioning his name; and beavers, when they heard he was in the neighborhood, simply crawled up on the creek banks and died.

None of which scared Tad. But it did make him look forward with considerable interest to meeting the man whose partner he hoped to be.

Shortly before noon they hit Green River and made camp. Already the valley was full of company men, free trappers and Indians from many tribes, come in from every corner of the West for a two-week carnival of trading, gambling, drinking, horse racing and fighting. Tad took it all in with keen, uncritical eyes. But other eyes in the party looked on with far less tolerance.

Traveling with the brigade that year was a minister named Thomas Rumford, a tall, hollow-cheeked, solemn-visaged man who was returning to a mission he had established some years earlier among the Nez Perce Indians, out Oregon way. Parson Rumford had made no bones of the fact that he disapproved of the language and personal habits of the mule tenders, and he liked even less the behavior of the celebrating trappers. While Tad was helping unload the mules, Parson Rumford came up, a reproachful look on his face.

"My boy, what's this I hear about your becoming a trapper?"

"Well, I was sort of figuring on it."

"Do you know what kind of man Slewfoot Samuels is?"

"Tell me he's some ornery. But I reckon I can put up with him."

Parson Rumford shook his head and stalked away. Feeling a shade uncomfortable, Tad finished unloading the mules. Then he saw Captain Sublette approaching, and the amused twinkle in Sublette's dark eyes made him forget the minister.

"Met your trapping partner yet?"

"No. Buck's takin' me over soon as we get through here."

"Well, the least I can do is wish you luck."

"Thank you kindly, Captain."

"And remind you that your mule-tending job will be waiting, in case things don't work out."

Feeling more and more edgy, Tad joined Buck and they threaded their way toward the Shoshone section of camp.

"Lived with that squaw so long he's more Injun than white, Buck explained. "Even thinks like an Injun."

"I'd as soon you hadn't told everybody in camp what I was figuring to do. They're layin' bets, just like it was a dog fight."

"Well, you got my sympathy. Slewfoot's got a knack fer figgerin' out the one thing best calculated to rile a man. Goes fer a fella's weak spot, you might say. What's yourn?"

"Don't know that I got one."

"Mine's rattlesnakes. Slewfoot shore made my life miserable, once he found that out." Buck shivered. "Kind of gives a man a turn wakin' up from a peaceable nap to find a five-foot rattler lyin' on his chest—even if it is dead."

"Slewfoot done that to you?"

"Yeah, an' then near laughed himself to death."

They stopped in front of a tepee where a squat, red-headed trapper in greasy buckskins sat dozing in the shade, and Buck nodded his head. "Thar he is. Ain't he a specimen?"

Before Tad could make much of a visual appraisal, Slewfoot Samuels opened his eyes. Tad got something of a shock. One eye was green, the other black, and they were as badly crossed as a pair of eyes could be. Slewfoot glared up in Buck's general direction, took a swig out of the jug of whisky sheltered between his crossed legs and spat.

"Howdy, Buck. This is the greenhorn you're figgerin' on palmin' off on me?"

"This is him. Name's Tad Marshall."

"Sit," Slewfoot grunted.

They sat and Buck reached for the jug. Slewfoot extended his right hand to Tad. "Shake."

Tad gave Slewfoot his hand, which Slewfoot promptly tried to crush into jelly. Half expecting such a stunt and having a muscle or two of his own, Tad gave just about as good as he got, and they let go with the first engagement pretty much a draw. Slewfoot took the jug away from Buck.

"Drink, Tad? Or have you been weaned from milk yet?"

Tad raised the jug to his lips, held it there while his Adam's apple bobbed six times, then passed it back. "Been watered some, ain't it?"

"Have to cut it a mite, else it eats the bottom out'n the jug."

Slewfoot's squaw, a clean, sturdy-looking woman, came out and got an armload of firewood from the pile beside the tepee, and Slewfoot grunted something to her in the Shoshone tongue. She stared curiously at Tad for a moment, grunted a reply and disappeared inside.

Several dogs lay dozing in the shade. A half-grown, smooth-haired white pup wandered into the tepee, let out a pained yip and came scooting out with its tail tucked between its legs, followed by the squaw's angry scolding. The pup came over to Slewfoot for sympathy, got it in the form of a friendly pat or two, then trotted to Tad, climbed up into his lap and went to sleep.

Slewfoot grinned. "Seems to like you."

"Yeah. Dogs usually take to me."

"Mighty fine pup. I got plans fer him."

A dark-eyed, attractive Indian girl appeared, started to go into the tepee; then, at a word from Slewfoot, stopped and stared in openmouthed amazement at Tad. He colored in spite of all he could do. Suddenly she giggled, murmured something in Shoshone, then quickly ducked into the tepee.

"Who's that?" Buck asked.

"My squaw's sister. Name's Moon Wind."

"Tad is quite a man with the ladies," Buck said, gazing innocently off into space. "They was three gals at oncet after him, back home. Caused him some trouble."

"A woman can pester a man," Slewfoot said, "less'n he knows how to handle her. Have to lodgepole mine ever' once in a while."

"Lodgepole?" Tad said.

"Beat her."

"Can't say I hold with beating women."

Slewfoot grinned. "Well, you may have to beat Moon Wind to make her leave you alone. She sure admired that yaller hair of yourn."

Slewfoot yawned. "I'm hungry. I'll git the women to stir up some vittles."

The squaw came to the tepee entrance. They talked for a spell, then Slewfoot looked ruefully at Tad. "She says we're plumb out of meat. Kind of hate to do this, but when a man's hungry he's got to eat. I'd be obliged, Tad, if you'd pass me that pup."

"This pup?"

"Shore. It's the fattest one we got."

"I ain't really hungry yet. Ate a big breakfast."

Slewfoot grabbed the pup by the scruff of the neck, handed it to his squaw and waved her inside, then turned to Buck and began a long-winded tale. Tad's mind wasn't on the story, but with Buck sliding a look his way every now and then, there was nothing for him to do but sit there and pretend to be enjoying the company. Would the squaw skin the thing, he wondered, or just toss it into the pot with the hair on? For the first time in his life, he felt a little sick to his stomach.

After a while the squaw brought out three wooden bowls of greasy, rank-smelling stew, and Tad, hoping his face didn't look as green as it felt, accepted his with a weak smile.

"Hungry now?" Slewfoot asked.

Glassy-eyed, Tad stared down at the mess in the bowl. If he didn't eat dog he'd have to eat crow, and, of the two, he reckoned tame meat was the easier to swallow. Grimly he dug in with his spoon.

"Why, yeah. I am. Hungry enough to eat a horse. Shame you didn't have a fat one to spare."

When they headed back to their own part of camp a while later, Buck asked, "How'd you like that stew?"

"Fine,'cept for its being a shade greasy."

"Bear meat usually is."

"Bear? I thought it was dog."

"Shoshones ain't dog eaters. Slewfoot could of lodgepoled his woman till Doomsday an' she still wouldn't of cooked that pup for us. That was just his idea of a joke."

"Didn't think it was very funny myself."

"You said you could take his worst, grin and come back for more."

"I can."

"Well, I'll hang around and watch the fun."

There were times during the next week or so when it wasn't easy for Tad to grin. The day Slewfoot near drowned him while pretending to teach him how to build a trout trap was one. The night Slewfoot put the physic in the whisky was another. But he came closest to losing his good nature the evening he got scalped by Moon Wind in sight of the whole camp.

Slewfoot arranged the thing, no doubt about that, even though it was rigged to look plumb accidental. The boys had got to finger wrestling around the campfire. Two trappers would pair off, face each other and interlace the fingers of both hands. At the word "go," they'd have at it, each one trying to force the other to his knees or break his back, according to how stubborn the fellow wanted to be.

Slewfoot threw all corners. Looking around for fresh meat, he allowed as how a certain young fellow from Missouri would chew good, so there was nothing for Tad to do but climb to his feet and give it a try.

Captain Sublette was watching. So were Buck Owens, Parson Rumford, the packtrain mule tenders and a whole mess of Indians. The bets flew thick and fast as Tad and Slewfoot squared off. Staring over Slewfoot's shoulder, Tad found himself looking right at Moon Wind, who was sitting on the ground with her deep black eyes glittering in the firelight and her soft red lips parted in excited anticipation. Kind of a purty little thing, Tad was thinking. A sight purtier than the girls back home. If only she wouldn't keep staring at him that way.

"Go!" Captain Sublette said.

Slewfoot grunted, heaved, and the next thing Tad knew, he was lying flat on his back on the ground. Dimly he heard the yelling of the crowd as he got to his feet.

Slewfoot gave him a cockeyed grin. "Want to try it again, partner?"

"Sure."

This time Tad kept his mind on the chore at hand. For some minutes they rocked this way and that, then Tad made his move. Slewfoot's knees buckled and he went down with a thud. The crowd roared even louder than before.

"Hurt you?" Tad asked solicitously.

"Once more," Slewfoot grunted, getting up.

They locked hands. Judging from the look on his face, Slewfoot really meant business this time. So did Tad. But the kind of business Slewfoot had in mind was a shade different from what Tad expected. Because they'd no more than got started good when Slewfoot dropped to his knees, heaved and threw Tad clean over his shoulders.

Tad did a complete somersault in the air, landing with his feet in the crowd and his head on the ground right close to Moon Wind's lap. Foolishly he grinned up at her. She gave him a shy smile. Then she whipped out a scalping knife, grabbed a handful of hair and lopped it off.

The crowd went crazy. So did Tad. He jumped up and made for Moon Wind, but she fled into the crowd. He whirled and went for Slewfoot, who was laughing fit to kill. Sublette, Buck Owens and half a dozen other men grabbed him and held him back.

"Easy, son; easy!" Sublette said between chuckles. "There aren't many men get scalped and live to brag about it!"

After a moment Tad quit struggling and they let him go. His face burning, he stalked off into the darkness.

Morosely Tad finished his breakfast and accepted the cup of coffee Buck poured for him. *Yellow-Hair-Scalped-by-a-Woman.* That was the name the Indians had given him. Buck eyed him sympathetically.

"I told you he was ornery. But you were so cocky—"

"He caught me off guard. It won't happen again."

"He's too cunning for you, boy. Why, I'll bet you right now he's windin' himself up to prank you agin."

"He gets wound up tight enough," Tad said grimly, "I'll give him one more twist and bust his mainspring."

"Better git ready to twist, then. Yonder he comes."

Uneasy despite his brag, Tad ran absent fingers over his cropped head as Slewfoot came shuffling up, looking as pleased with the world as a fresh-fed bear.

"Mornin', gents. Any coffee left in that pot?"

Buck poured him a cup. Slewfoot hunkered on his heels, his black eye studying Tad while his green one gazed at the mountains off in the distance. "That was a dirty trick we played on you last night, Tad. It's sort of laid heavy on my conscience. So I've decided to make it up to you."

"I can hear him tickin'," Buck muttered.

"Just how are you going to make it up to me?"

"I know you don't like yore new Injun name. So I had a talk with a Shoshone chief that happens to be a friend of mine. He says he'll fix it."

"How?"

"Why, he'll just adopt you into his tribe an' give you a new name. That'll cancel out the old one. It'll cost me a mite, but I figger I owe you somethin'."

"Adopt me?"

"Yeah. Injuns do that now an' then."

Buck eyed Slewfoot suspiciously. "Who is this chief?"

"Seven Bears."

"Why, ain't he the—"

"Yes, sir, he's the top man of the whole tribe. No Injun'll dare laugh at an adopted son of hisn."

Tad thought it over. If there was a catch to it, he sure couldn't see it. He looked at Buck. "What do you think?"

"I ain't sayin' a word."

"Well," Tad said, "in that case—"

The ceremony in Chief Seven Bears' tepee took a couple of hours. A dozen or so of the most important men in the tribe were there, and one look at their solemn faces told Tad this was serious business with them. Slewfoot must have been dead serious, too, because before the palaver began he gave Seven Bears a couple of horses, half a dozen red blankets, a used musket, several pounds of powder and lead, and a lot of other trinkets in exchange for his services.

When the ceremony was finally over, they left the tepee and Slewfoot walked to the edge of the Shoshone section of camp with him. His grin seemed genuine.

"How does it feel to be an Injun?"

"Fine. What was that new name he gave me?"

"White Mule. It's a good name."

"Reckon I'm obliged to you."

"Don't mention it. Well, I'll see you later."

Buck was taking a nap when Tad got back to his tent, but at the sound of his step the old trapper's eyes jerked open. "What'd they do to you?"

"It was all real friendly. Name's White Mule now."

"So he did do it! What'd it cost him?"

"Well, he gave Seven Bears some blankets, a couple of horses—"

"Hosses? Fer two hosses he could of bought you a—"

Buck suddenly broke off and stared at something behind Tad. He shook his head. "He did too. Look around, boy."

Tad turned around. Moon Wind was standing there, smiling shyly. Behind her were four horses, two of which he recognized as the ones Slewfoot had given Seven Bears a while ago, and all four were laden down with Indian housekeeping gear. As Tad stared at her with stricken eyes, Moon Wind gestured at him and at herself, then made a circling motion with both hands.

"She wants to know where she'd ought to pitch your tepee."

"My tepee?"

"Yourn and hern."

"She's—she's mine now?"

"Reckon she is. Slewfoot bought her for you."

"But Seven Bears—"

"Is her pa. Also happens to be Slewfoot's squaw's pa."

"Tell her I don't want her! Tell her to go home!"

Buck laid a restraining hand on Tad's forearm. "This may be just a prank where you an' Slewfoot're concerned, but I don't reckon it's one Moon Wind and her pa would laugh at much. She must of liked you. An' Seven Bears must have thought a lot of her, else he wouldn't of outfitted her so fancy an' given you back them two hosses of Slewfoot's as a special weddin' present."

"Well, I sure can't keep her!"

"Easy. They's a way out of this, maybe, but it'll take some tall thinkin'. Let her set up her tepee. You an' me are goin' to have a talk with Captain Sublette."

Captain Sublette was not in the habit of losing his temper, but when they told him what had happened he was fit to be tied. So was Parson

Rumford. When Tad declared that what he had a mind to do was grab a club and beat Slewfoot half to death, then make him take Moon Wind back to her father and explain the whole thing, the parson gave the idea his hearty approval. But Sublette shook his head.

"You can't send her back. No matter how much explaining Slewfoot did—assuming we could make him do any—the whole Shoshone tribe would be so angry they'd be down on our necks in a minute. You've got to accept her and pretend to live with her until rendezvous breaks up."

"I won't hear to such a thing!" Parson Rumford exclaimed.

"I said 'pretend,' sir . . . When the bridgade goes back to St. Louis, you'll go with it, Tad. I'll tell Moon Wind that you're coming back next summer to stay. That will save her pride and our necks."

"But I won't come back? Is that the idea?"

"Yes."

Tad gazed off at the mountain peaks rimming the valley. "Seems kind of a dirty trick to play on her. Lettin' her wait for a man that won't never be comin' back to her. It's downright deceitful."

"Better a little deceit than a full-scale Indian war. She won't wait for you long, I'll wager. Next year I'll cook up some story about your having died of smallpox or something, and she'll be free to pick herself another man."

Reluctantly Tad nodded, but the deceit of it still weighed on his mind. "She's an innocent little thing and not to blame for this. I'd kind of like to give her something to remember me by—for a while, anyhow. Could I draw some of my wages and buy her a trinket or two?"

Sublette smiled understandingly. "Of course."

Pausing with the clerk in charge of the trade goods to pick out a few items he thought might appeal to her, Tad walked back to the spot where his tent had been pitched. But the tent was gone. In its place stood a roomy, comfortable skin tepee around which a dozen or two Shoshone women bustled, chattering happily as they helped Moon Wind set her household in order.

Seeing Tad, the women smiled, exchanged knowing looks amongst themselves, then quickly wound up their tasks and drifted away.

When the last one had gone, he went to Moon Wind, who was on her knees building a fire.

"Moon Wind, I got something for you."

Her eyes lifted. Black eyes, they were, black and soft and deep. He got the sudden notion that she didn't know whether he was going to beat her for what she had done to him last night or caress her because she was now his woman. He took her hand and pulled her to her feet.

"These here trinkets are for you."

He dumped them into her hands. One by one, she examined them. First the glittering silver-backed mirror. Then the long double strand of imitation pearls. Then the small gold ring, which by some accident just managed to fit the third finger of her left hand. For a long moment she stared down at them. Then without a word she whirled away from him and ran toward the Shoshone section of camp.

She was gone so long that Tad, weary of trying to figure out what had got into her, went into the tepee and took himself a nap. Except for an unpleasant dream or two about Slewfoot, he slept fine. Presently he was awakened by angry voices arguing violently in the Shoshone tongue outside the tepee. He got up and went out to see what the ruckus was all about.

There, toe to toe, stood Slewfoot Samuels and his woman, jawing at each other like a pair of magpies. Off to one side and admiring her new trinkets stood Moon Wind.

Suddenly Slewfoot saw Tad and spun around. "What in the name of all unholy tarnation do you think you're doin'?"

"Me?" Tad said, "Why, I was just takin' a nap."

"That ain't what I'm talkin' about!"

"What are you talking about?"

"Them things!" Slewfoot roared, pointing a trembling hand at the ornaments Moon Wind was admiring. "That foofaraw she's wearin'! You got any idea how much that stuff costs?"

"Sure. I bought it. What business is that of yours?"

"My squaw wants the same fool trinkets!"

"Well, buy 'em for her."

"Waste a big chunk of my year's wages for junk like that?"

"Then don't buy 'em."

"If I don't, she'll pester the life out of me."

"Lodgepole her. That'll make her quit."

Slewfoot shot his woman a sidelong glance and shook his head. "Don't hardly dare to right now. She'd raise such a racket I'd have all her relatives on my neck." Slewfoot sidled closer, a pleading look in his eyes. "Look, boy, the joke's gone far enough. Now you take that foofaraw away from Moon Wind an' cuff her a time or two. Then my woman won't be jealous of her no more."

Tad looked at Slewfoot's squaw, who had gone over to Moon Wind and was gabbling with her over the beads, mirror and ring. Sure was queer how some men would spend any amount for their own pleasure, but wouldn't put out a dime for their women. He grinned and shook his head.

"Why, I don't have to cuff 'em to make 'em behave. Treat 'em kind, I say, if you want the best of 'em. Buy 'em presents, help 'em with the chores, give 'em the respect they're due and crave—that's the way I treat my women."

Slewfoot stared at him. "You're goin' to keep her?"

"Sure am. Going to marry her, in fact, soon as I can get Parson Rumford to tie the knot. Come to think about it, I'll make a real shindig of it. Invite her pa and ma and all her relatives. Invite the whole camp. After the wedding I'll throw a big feed with food and drinks for all."

"That'll cost you a year's wages!"

"What if it does? Man like me only gets married once."

"But when my woman sees it," Slewfoot said hoarsely, "she'll squawl to high heaven fer the same treatment. First thing you know, I won't dare lay a hand on her. She'll keep me broke buyin' her fofaraw. She'll have me totin' wood an' takin' care of the hosses an' wipin' my feet 'fore I come into the tepee—why, she'll have me actin' jest like a regular husband!"

"I wouldn't be at all surprised," Tad said, and strolled off in search of Parson Rumford.

It was quite an affair, that double wedding, and the party afterward was real good fun for all concerned. Except Slewfoot Samuels, who didn't seem to enjoy it much. He'd lost his sense of humor, somehow.

Maybe he'd get it back after they'd spent a few months in the mountains trapping beaver. Tad sure hoped so, anyhow. Worst thing you could have as a partner was a man that couldn't take a joke, grin and come back for more.

Louis Champlain's Party

▼▲▼▲▼▲▼▲▼▲▼▲▼▲▼▲▼▲▼▲▼▲▼▲▼▲▼▲▼▲▼▲▼▲▼▲▼▲▼

Dan Cushman

Born in Michigan, Dan Cushman graduated from the University of Montana and made Montana his home. Of his twenty-five novels, the best known is *Stay Away Joe*, a funny-sad look at a group of Métis (French-speaking Indians) living on a Montana reservation. Joe Champlain, at the center of the action, is an amoral opportunist just back from the service. Louis, his father, has been given a herd of pure-bred Herefords by the U. S. government Experiment Station in the hope of making him self-sufficient. Naturally this calls for a party. All Louis's Indian neighbors come, and he has to buy drinks and feed them. The herd begins to disappear as a result. Meanwhile Joe is up to all his old bad tricks and things go from bad to worse for the family.

The book created something of a sensation in 1953. It was made into a Broadway play and was the basis for *Brothers in Kickapoo*, an Elvis Presley movie. It won prizes and created much comment, not all of it favorable. Reviewers called it "wildy comic" and "delightful." Vine DeLoria in *Custer Died for Your Sins* recommended it as one of only three novels that give "a good idea of what Indians are all about." Dorothy M. Johnson (*A Man Called Horse*), says, however, "I never finished *Stay Away Joe* although the author was a friend of mine. The book was too true to Indian life on a reservation and it made me want to cry rather than laugh" (Letter to C. L. S., March 24, 1984).

I T WAS SUNUP, AND LOUIS LAY IN BED LISTENING, BUT THERE WAS no music or shouting, only the sounds of sleeping men and women rolled up in their blankets on the floor. He got up, quietly pulled on his clothes, and, taking long steps over the sleeping forms, went outside. There he warmed himself in the sunshine and looked around. Cars and rigs filled the yard; there were tents by the creek, and tarps stretched from cars and wagons to make lean-to shelters. There was no movement anywhere. Only he was awake. Spread across the little flat on the other side of the creek were his cattle, nineteen heifers and the young bull, grazing the buffalo grass.

"Goddam!" he said.

From *Stay Away Joe* (New York: Viking Press, 1953; Popular Library edition, 1961). Louis Champlain's Party is Chapter 4 of the novel, pp. 34–46.

The sun climbed in the cloudless sky. It promised to be a hot day, but the morning was fine. After an hour there was movement, and by eight o'clock most of the people were up, rusty and yawning, looking for breakfast.

Yesterday they had eaten everything in the house; today they took up a collection and sent Bix Red Eagle, Peter Old Squaw, and the fellows from Fort Belknap to Big Springs for grub and beer. They got back with it before noon, and from somewhere appeared a side of venison. Several cars had left, but more arrived, and then most of those that had left returned again. Indians came from the settlement on Hill Fifty-Seven in Great Falls, and old John and Agnes North Lodge from the Assiniboin reservation at Fort Peck, just under the Canadian border in eastern Montana.

Louis had spent the last of his winnings on beer, there was no grub in the house, and he had to eat at the cook-fire, where now another side of vension, together with spuds, carrots, onions, and turnips, was bubbling in a huge brass washboiler.

Seeing Louis dishing into the stew, old Matthew Horse Chaser struck his walking stick on the ground and crackled, "Look! Already the meat of the kettle becomes all bone, like the wolf of the cold moon! Soon Louis, our rich friend, will have to butcher one cow and feed his friends, or else they will starve."

Everyone laughed when old Horse Chaser said out loud what they had been saying on the quiet before Louis came down from the house with his plate in his hand. Louis laughed with a good show of teeth, but when he tried to eat, the food seemed to lodge in his throat.

Louis scraped up four dollars, borrowed six from Stephenpierre, and sent to Callahan's for beer. The cans were empty and strewn on the ground before he was back at the house. Cars shuttled steadily from the ranch to Callahan's, to Big Springs, and even to Havre, hauling beer. Car radios and the Philco in the house blared the Melody Wrangler's hit parade. By nightfall the dance was going again, and at ten o'clock there was a fight.

It was only a small fight at first. Ron Tilcup, a former jockey, fifty years old and weighing little more than one hundred pounds, struggled with big, sixteen-year-old Humphrey Hindshot, who kept laughing at the little man's bantam fury and holding him at long arm's reach, staying safe from Ron's wholly ineffectual haymakers. Finally, when Humphrey started pushing Ron around, Boob Dugan tried to stop him, and Frank Knife, misinterpreting Boob's actions, pulled him away, doing it too violently, and was clipped on the chin for his trouble. Frank got up from the floor, and the battle was on. They fought brutally, a toe-to-toe slugging match that lasted without particular advantage for at least ten minutes. Knife was then so tired he could not lift his arms. He tried to keep fighting, absorbing rights and lefts until his legs collapsed and he fell on hands and knees. Boob was on him with his riding boots, trying to stamp him against the floor. Knife, his nose and mouth running blood, got to a kneeling position, and Boob kicked him on the side of the head. Big Max Beaupre then pulled Boob off. They fought briefly, Boob retreating to a corner where he covered up while Beaupre pummeled him. Peter Buffalo thereupon swung at Beaupre, and Jiggs Rock Medicine hit Buffalo. The battle spread like flame through dry straw. In a matter of seconds the entire room surged with the struggle. Men were down, and men tramped over them. A bench crashed, and a stool sailed through the air. The battle petered out and then flared again in private fights. Outside, Bix Red Eagle lay like a dead man after being knocked down by Morrie Roque. One of Bix's companions from Fort Belknap, a very tall, skinny youth called Red Rider, ran to the jeep, started it, threw it in second, and raced after the fleeing Roque in a wild S turn with the rear tires showering dirt. Failing to get him by a hair when Roque dived headlong to safety, Red Rider, coming around for another try, forgot about the blacksmith shop and crashed into it, shattering the siding and two-by-fours and killing the engine. Within ten minutes the dance was going again. The jeep was unmoved, its front thrust through the wall, and two old squaws in blankets and moccasins were seated on its bumper, drinking Budweiser from cans, watching the dancers.

By the house Louis watched the near destruction of his blacksmith shop. He was preoccupied with his own problems. His supper had not agreed with him. Even now, everybody full and having a fine time, he was troubled by that fact that his money had purchased only a fraction of the food and liquor—yet he was rich, with his cattle in full sight whenever anybody looked. It seemed to him that every time he walked up to where people were talking they would stop or change the subject, and it made him feel like an outcast on his own ranch. Then he heard someone behind him, and turned to see Grandpere standing with his hands crossed over the knob of his diamond willow stick, hunched in the identical posture of old Matthew Horse Chaser at the stewpot that afternoon. Louis experienced a guilty start, for Horse Chaser's words had hurt him the worst of anything. He said, "Gran'pere, you should be in your bed."

"In the old days—" Grandpere started, and Louis cut him off. "Oh, lon la! Always the old days. You were young in the old days, Gran'pere."

"It was better!" Grandpere lifted his shoulders up and down, beating the stick on the ground. "I have years like the chokecherries in September, and I say it was better." He became crafty. "Tell me, my son, have you eaten tonight?"

Louis knew he had been talking to Horse Chaser or some of the other old men. "I ate. It is late, Gran'pere. Better you go to your tepee, get some sleep."

"My father was great hunter. With his knife he kill buffalo, with his hands he kill deer, with arrow the grizzly bear. This was in old days. Sometimes my father traveled far, many sleeps, to the river of yellow water and beyond, hunting the buffalo. When my father went out to hunt, the squaws followed him with skinning knives and fleshing stones, with poles and lines to jerk the meat. Ai-ai! He was a chief with many cayuse, *metatut* cayuse, *two-metatut* cayuse. Sometime, after a great hunt, would come to my father's tepee many friends, from three-four sleeps—many friends, dance, sing; and they were big days, strong days, those old days, you savvy? Did they come carrying their own meat? No. Did they bring their own tobac? No. My father, that strong chief, he would have lifted the scalp of that man who came carrying his own meat like the meat of my father's tepee was not good enough for him."

"You have been listening to that damn old Matt Horse Chaser."

"They were great times when I was young, before railroad, before Ford skunkwagon, before Philco devilbox. Buffalo I have seen on Box Elder flats, many buffalo, as far as I could look, like black spots on prairie, like the ducks that came in autumn in the old days," He lifted the stick in both hands and beat himself on his bony chest, crying, "*Watche!* Grandpere for hundred years has lived, like my people, not in shacks, but in tepee, always except in forty-below cold sleeping on the ground. Do I cough blood so the agent sends me away to hospital dying house? No. Grandpere live plenty long. See all white men, devilbox, skunkwagon come. See all white men go too. Pretty soon all white men die. Boom! like devilbox say. Boom! Boom! All white men blown up by bomb." He hopped around, driving his stick to the ground, saying, "Boom! Boom! Blow all white men up like devilbox say. Big bomb kill all white man off, blow 'em up. No house, out in tepee, out in cave, white men die. Boom! Injun live yet, you savvy? Maybe some day great herd buffalo come back."

"No, Gran'pere. You should stay away from the house and not listen to Edward R. Murrow on the damn radio. By gare, those bomb she's cost ten-twenty million dollaire, you think they will drop one on Big Springs, hey?"

He walked with Grandpere to his tepee, actually a wall tent, a very dilapidated, blackened from the fires that the old man liked to build inside, standing beyond a clump of thorn-apple bushes so Grandpere could sit in the doorway when he chose and be out of sight of the house.

Inside, Grandpere still talked, his voice coming from the tent darkness. "When they came to my father's house he always had the fattest of all buffaloes for them to eat. Tallow, like that, on the ribs of the young buffalo. Over coals of the red willow the squaws would roast the buffalo, and everyone ate until his belly was full, and no one brought food to the tepees of my people. That was in the old days."

Louis had started away but came back and stood, troubled and thoughtful. "Gran'pere!"

"Uh!"

"They talked about me, Louis Champlain? They are saying that I am a cheapskate?"

"They say that one night some Scotchman must have crept into your mother's tepee, that now you are rich and do not share food with your friends."

"Who said this thing? Matthew Horse Chaser? By gare, I wish that Horse Chaser was thirty years younger, I would beat him with my fists. Gran'pere, I do not think you should be friends with this Horse Chaser—"

"Did I say it was Horse Chaser?"

"Who, then?"

"Ai, it was good in old days, in my father's time, when the choke-cherries hung black and the fat on the antelope was white and thick. Ai, my father was a chief, many cayuse, many guns. From three-four sleeps came riders to the tepee of my father . . . ."

Louis left the old man still talking, shuffling around, finding his way into the heap of quilts, deer robes, and blankets that served as a bed. He walked to the house, soundless in his moccasins, and stood in the dark near the back door, looking inside to where Annie and the squaws were seated around the kitchen.

He spoke. "Ol' woman!"

She came outside. "What is the trouble?" she asked, having a hard time seeing him.

"I am going to sell one of the cows to Littlehorse."

Annie whispered, "Are you crazy?" and came down from the step to peer into his face. "Only two days you have had the cows, and already you want to sell and spend the money!"

He answered with unexpected fury, waving his arms out at the ranch yard. "My friends, they are here. From hundred mile they have come to celebrate with Louis Champlain his good fortune. Do I feed them, do I give them beer? Only maybe old bean soup. My own stomach I can feel my backbone through. How do I eat—me, the host? Do I say, 'Come, have big feast?' No. I, Louis Champlain, go to their fire, carrying my dish, lak bum, lak old Gros Ventre squaw, saying, 'Please, may I have food, I am so hun-gree.' In the old days it was not so in my family."

"You have been listening to Grandpere again."

"I say myself, in the old days it was not so. In the old days a man did not come and ask his squaw to sell one cow. In the old days, in a man's tepee was he a chief. By gare, yes. And now I say, ol' woman, I will sell those cow to Littlehorse." When she did not answer, but stood in sullen opposition, he grinned and said, "We still have plenty cow. Ol' Congréss come around and ask, we tell him this one cow she's lost in the brush."

51

"And how long will the money last that you get from one cow? They will drink it up in one night. Then you will sell another cow, and another, until pretty soon there will be nothing left. You know they will stay as long as there is anything left to drink. They will stay until sun-dance time."

"I will sell one cow," Louis said doggedly.

After Annie had gone back inside, Louis stood by himself in the dark, still not quite resigned to selling the cow to Littlehorse. The beat of the dance came plainly to him—the trumpet blasting rhythmically, Sylvester Bird Looking, a little more husky and nasal than before, singing "I Wouldn't Treat a Yellow Dog the Way You Treated Me." The blacksmith shop was brighter than before. They had torn some of the loose siding away and turned on the lights of the jeep, which augmented the lanterns. Among the cars were couples having private parties, drinking, and making love. Two of the younger bloods warwhooped and wrestled. A truck turned in from the county road and wallowed in the creek, its dual wheels giving it a hard time as it got past the mired Hudson. Finally it ground on in compound low, swung around undecided between the house and the blacksmith shop, decided on the latter, and rolled to a stop. It was an orange-yellow Montana state highway maintenance truck, so Louis supposed the driver must be Clyde Walschmidt, who had married one of the Bird Tracker twins. There proved to be four persons jammed in the cab of the truck—Clyde. a heavy, bald man of fifty; his wife, large with child; a second woman; and a tall, broad man in a gigantic white sombrero.

Sight of the tall young man brought Louis up rigid and popeyed. He shouted, "Ol' woman, come quick! See who has come home from Korea and Madison Square Garden! It is my boy Big Joe!"

Joe heard his father's voice and waited while Louis crossed the yard with long, downhill strides. They embraced, and Louis wept. He pulled Joe down and kissed him on the cheeks, talking French, Cree, and English all at the same time. The word of Joe's arrival spread, and the crowd swarmed from inside. They tore Big Joe away from his father and wrestled with him and called him strong names, and pounded on his back. Someone thrust a can of beer into his hand.

Louis kept pushing them away, trying to keep charge of Joe, saying, "This is my boy. Goddam, you let me talk to my boy. Two-three year I have not seen my boy. Joe, here's your papa, wait long tam."

"Grandpere still alive?"

"Sure." Louis turned to the crowd. "That's my Joe—always think of the old folks!"

Joe drank his beer, the entire can at one draft, without lowering it from his lips. "Ha!" he said and blew foam, and wiped his lips on the back of his hand. He kept glimpsing old acquaintances and shouting to them. Everyone tried to hand him beer, telling him he was far behind and had to catch up. He tilted a second can of beer and drank it without lowering it.

"Look at those Joe!" Stephenpierre shouted. "He's same old Joe all right."

"I want to see Grandpere," Joe said, tossing the can away over the heads of the crowd. "Brought something along for Grandpere."

One of the Laney kids went running to the tent for him. Big Joe was then on his third can of beer. He towered above everyone. He was six three or four; an extra two inches were added by the heels of his riding boots, and his huge white hat made him seem taller yet. He was broad and thick through, weighing about two hundred and ten pounds. with not an ounce of fat on him anywhere. He was slightly bowlegged—not in the hipsprung manner of a cowboy. but bowlegged as so many Indians are, starting with his toed-in feet and ending in his spread-apart hips. His legs were rather short in comparison with his trunk, which was very long. He was more Indian than anyone else in the family—his mother, Louis' first wife. having been a full-blood Assiniboin—and his face showed it being built in the classic lines of the warlike chiefs, with a low, slanting forehead, very high cheekbones, a huge nose, and a jaw that was square and big under the ears. He had a fresh haircut, and his sideburns were held stiff and comb-marked by pomade. In addition to the boots and big white hat, he wore Pendleton stockman's pants, a scarlet shirt with decorative pearl buttons, and a fawn-colored silk crepe neckerchief knotted like a four-in-hand and held to his shirt-front by means of a large Navajo silver concha.

Little Joe and Pete, who had been in bed, were now up and dressed and wriggling through the legs of the crowd to get to their big half-brother.

"It's Joe, it's Joe!" Little Joe shrilled, getting there first, pulling himself up by means of Big Joe's free arm. "Let's have a look at the Cadillac, Joe."

Pete cried, "Can I drive her, Joe? I know how to drive. I drove the old Chevvy."

"That damn Cadillac," said Big Joe.

Bronc Hoverty said, "Say, how about that Cadillac you wrote that you'd bought? What you doing hitching a ride in the highway truck?"

"I bought it all right. Drove from Umatilla to Great Falls in seven and a half hours. Stopped in Missoula for grub. You should have seen me hit that stretch this side of Helena. Hundred and eight miles an hour. Burned out the main bearings. Couple of connecting rods too. She was hammering like hell when I got into Great Falls. I left her there for repairs."

"Did you leave the saddle in it?" Little Joe screamed.

"Huh?"

"The silver-mounted saddle you won riding broncs in Fort Worth."

"Oh, that. I sold that."

"How about the diamond belt-buckle you won bull-dogging the steer in nine and a fifth?"

"Hah, I got that around someplace."

Bronc Hoverty, grinning, said, "Here, have another can of beer and tell us all about the Cadillac."

Joe still had half a can of beer, but he took the one Bronc handed him anyhow. He was not in the least bothered when everyone began to rib him about the Cadillac.

"I'll show all you bastards I got a Cadillac one of these days," Joe said.

"Does it say Chevvy on the front of it?"

"I'll drive up here about next week and take all your squaws away from you."

They all jeered and hooted at him, and Joe went on, drinking beer and shouting back, "One of these days I'll come back here and drive my Cadillac right through your tepees. By jeez, you need a hundred and sixty acres to turn that Cadillac around."

Soon Grandpere came, hobbling with his diamond willow stick, and everyone made way for him.

"You are a chief!" Grandpere said, stopping at a distance and peering up with his sunken eyes. He struck the stick up and down. "A chief come home from battle. *Watche!* All my people chiefs, kill plenty Sioux, steal plenty cayuse. When I was young I stood tall, like so. *Watche!* He is a chief like old days."

Joe said, "I brought something for you, Grandpere," and, limping slightly, as though his right boot were too small for him, he walked to the truck and got out a leather-bound canvas bag. He unstrapped the bag, dug down through clothes, spurs, and odd pieces of saddle gear, and came up with a worn manila envelope, which he opened. He took out something wrapped in an old red silk kerchief.

"Smell, Grandpere," he said, sticking it beneath the old man's nose.

Louis said, "Poor ol' Gran'pere, he's smell nothing in twenty-thirty year."

Grandpere steadied himself with the stick leaning against his waist, and, using both hands, unfolded the kerchief, revealing a tuft of black hair attached to a dried wrinkled piece of skin.

"A scalp!" he said.

"Didn't I promise I would bring a scalp home from Korea?"

The women all pretended to be repelled; they shrieked and crowded to escape, without moving away or making room for the men at the fringe who tried to get in for a look. Grandpere held the scalp overhead and did a jiggly war dance, first on one moccasin and then on the other. "Hoy-ya-ya-hoy-ya!" chanted Grandpere, waving the scalp overhead.

"It is not a scalp!" said Louis.

"Sure it's a scalp!" Joe said, finishing one can of beer and starting the other. "What the hell, nobody's going to tell me it's not a scalp. I took it myself."

"You should not bring it here."

"Why not? I promised Grandpere I'd bring him a scalp, and I brought him a scalp."

"You are a chief!" said Grandpere. "You have taken coup from the Communists."

Everyone wanted to examine the scalp, but Grandpere would not let it out of his fingers. In a few minutes the dance was again in progress, but with new fervor, for Joe was home from the war, and he gave it a patriotic purpose. The beer was low, and Louis searched for Chief Littlehorse so that he could sell the one cow; but Littlehorse and his wife had gone home, and no one else had the cash to buy. So Louis got Big Joe aside and asked, "You maybe have ten dollaire for beer?"

"Here's fifty dollars" Joe said, handing him a bill.

Louis had never before seen a fifty-dollar bill. He carried it in his hands to the house, where he held it out for the squaws and Annie to see.

"Look here at the money that my son Big Joe has brought home with him from Madison Square Garden. Some men have ten-dollaire bills, some twenty-dollaire—but Big Joe, oho! My Joe has *fifty*-dollaire bills. Look at those picture on bill. He's ol' U. S. Grant, le general; he presidenté long tam before your Louis was even born."

"Joe gave that to us?" Annie asked incredulously.

"To buy beer, drink up, have big tam. Oho, when those boy treat, he treats by gare! And in Great Falls, with burned-out bearings one Cadillac car! A hundred and eight mile an hour he drive those car."

With Stephenpierre he rode to Callahan's for beer. All evening, up until now, Louis had not touched a drop, but he decided now to celebrate the return of his boy with just one can. He drank the one, and then a couple, and then one more. He got to feeling very good on beer. He stopped the orchestra and made a speech. In French, English, and Cree, with tears hunting crooked courses down his cheeks. he told them how dear it was to his heart to have Joe, his firstborn, back with him—a hero, with the Purple Heart, and with two toes gone, shot off by the Communists in Korea. And he went on to speak highly of Mary, and of his cows, and of Gran'pere. who was the oldest man in the whole damn country, and yet, though perhaps 105 years old, would sleep in the house only eight or ten nights in the whole year, but sometimes at twenty below zero would sleep on the ground in his tent, showing what kind of men they were in the old days, and the kind of men the Champlains still were, by gare; The Champlains, Louis said, were always strong, big fighters, with many fast race-horses, and he himself when young had one tam danced the whole night through, from sundown to dawn without stopping once, ending with no soles at all on his moccasins, only the tops; but that was in the old days, in Canadá, vive la Canadá!—except for those damn Protes-tant red-coats police.

Everyone started shouting at Louis about dancing the soles from his moccasins, and he answered back, saying yes, by gare, he could do it yet if only someone would play the old-time tunes like "French Min-uet" or "A La Claire Fontaine." So old Jamie Croix borrowed the fiddle and sawed it dissonantly, while Louis, choosing for his partner Minnie Hindshot, did his best on minuet. But soon the crowd lost interest, Jamie was divested of the fiddle, and the blacksmith shop was filled with the push and shove of a fox trot to the tune of "Sneaking the Alley; Looking for You."

Louis still danced with Minnie Hindshot; then somehow he was dancing with Mary Whitecalf; and next he was outside, drinking with Connie Shortgun, Nellie Beaverbow, and Walt Stephenpierre.

Grandpere was still around, a can of beer in one hand, waving the scalp aloft on the diamond willow stick with the other. It occurred to Louis that Grandpere should be in his tent, and he went over to say so; but instead he found himself listening while Grandpere said. "In old time, long time ago, when war chief return to his village, from far off come tall smoke. Smoke tell 'em, pretty soon all squaw get ready, make big time. know from smoke war chief come back. plenty horse. plenty scalp you savvy? Pretty soon big feast. Whole damn fat buffalo. Young buffalo bull, you savvy? Fat young bull, roast on fire all day all night. All this for young war chief come home safe to tepee. you savvy?"

Grandpere was joined by old Matthew Horse Chaser, who said in Cree, "If I had a son like that Big Joe I would butcher a beef for him. I would show all tribe and white men too what I think of my son."

"By gare, yes!" Louis cried, throwing his empty beer can as hard as he could throw it. "*Watche*, everybody, you will see what kind of party Louis Champlain throw. You will see big whoop-up this tam, by gare. We will have a fine beef roast on fire just lak in old days."

On The Range:
The Unromantic Cowboy

▼▲▼▲▼▲▼▲▼▲▼▲▼▲▼▲▼▲▼▲▼▲▼▲▼▲▼▲▼▲▼▲▼▲▼

Ross Santee—"A Night in Town"
 (from *Men and Horses*)

Max Evans—"Old Fooler in Action"
 (from *The Rounders*)

Glendon Swarthout—"Partners"
 (from *The Cadillac Cowboys*)

The Cowboy: Hero No More

▼▲▼▲▼▲▼▲▼▲▼▲▼▲▼▲▼▲▼▲▼▲▼▲▼▲▼▲▼▲▼▲▼▲▼▲▼▲

THE INTRODUCTION TO THIS ANTHOLOGY DISCUSSED FICTION about the cowboy, attempting to show that the unheroic cowpuncher has been with us for many decades, sometimes in solo performance, sometimes accompanying the cowboy hero. Over the years negative feelings about the hired man on horseback have intensified until, in everything but the commercial western, he has emerged as a dull drudge, a misfit, a failure, a dead-end kid, or a man existing in the shadow of a legend he cannot live up to. The stories and excerpts that follow in this section, taking the humorous approach, paint a brighter picture of cowboy life than some of the novels mentioned in the Introduction, but the descent from hearty laughter to a sad smile cannot be mistaken or ignored.

Emerson Hough (*Heart's Desire*, 1905), Stewart Edward White (*Arizona Nights*, 1907), B. M. Bower (*The Happy Family*, 1910), and Eugene Manlove Rhodes (*Good Men and True*, 1910) enjoy their cowboys and savor their special predicaments, but Ross Santee (*Men and Horses*, 1926) makes it clear that cowboys come to grief like other people and sometimes find themselves in painfully funny situations. Max Evans (*The Rounders*, 1960) plays Dusty and Wrangler for laughs, but he shows that they are victims of the system and their own natures and that an appropriate sign over the door of their line-camp shack would be No Exit. Glendon Swarthout's commission man becomes a windbag and a fake when he leaves the ranch, and Larry McMurtry's Hud (*Horseman, Pass By*, 1961), an immortal opportunist, hits a new low when he commits rape and murder without being called to account. McMurtry has a gruesome sense of humor to go with his disillusion, and at the other end of the cattle country Thomas McGuane (*Nobody's Angel*, 1983) chronicles the decline of a Montana ranching family with some sardonic humor.

A Night in Town

▼▲▼▲▼▲▼▲▼▲▼▲▼▲▼▲▼▲▼▲▼▲▼▲▼▲▼▲▼▲▼▲▼▲▼

Ross Santee

Like Eugene Manlove Rhodes and Charley Russell, Ross Santee led from strength in portraying the cowboy, especially the Arizona cowboy operating in the country near Globe, where Ross was most at home.

Born in Iowa, he studied cartooning at the Chicago Art Institute, didn't make it in New York, and finally, in 1915, joined his sister in Arizona. He got a job as horse wrangler on the Bar-F-Bar Ranch and spent his best years on the range soaking up the color, the lingo, and the customs of the country. If anyone knew cowboys, it was Ross Santee.

As a consequence, his punchers are as real as they are funny, and Santee reveals the way they think as well as how they look and act. In "A Night in Town," for example, Slim never asks Shorty a direct question about his misfortunes. He makes remarks that open the door for a revelation if Shorty wants to talk. In this case, of course, Shorty is willing, and the humor of the situation is not lost on him, though he is the victim.

IT WAS SHORTY'S BALD-FACED HORSE ALL RIGHT. SLIM WAS SURE of that. But who could be riding him? The rider slumped in his saddle and wore no hat. Something white was tied about his head; must be an Indian. But as they came slowly up the wash, Slim saw that he held his hat in his hand. Slim spurred his horse across the wash, and where the trail heads into Bean Belly Flat he waited.

It was Shorty; both eyes were black, his nose was split, and the remnant of a silk shirt hung around his neck like a dicky. As he saw Slim his mouth cracked into a misshapen grin.

He hung his hat on the saddle-horn and rolled a cigarette.

"I've seen a few tenderfeet go bareheaded in the sun," said Slim.

"This hat's too small," says Shorty. "But it weighs a plenty."

A lump the size of a goose-egg extended from one eye to the roots of his hair. He touched it gingerly.

From *Men and Horses* (New York: Century, 1928; Lincoln: University of Nebraska Press, 1977), 123–129.

62

"This one's the biggest. But the one over my ear's shore tender."

"Things quiet in town, I s'pose," said Slim, "when a man ain't drinkin'."

"Nary a drop this trip," says Shorty. "I been on the police force."

"Must ha' been a race riot," said Slim. "But I ain't seen the papers lately."

"On the level, Slim, I never had a drink. Ya see there was a carnival in town. I hadn't any more'n landed when I met Bob. He's chief of police now, but we used to work together at the Diamond A's.

"I was huntin' a poker game, but stopped to auger him awhile. Finally he says they was puttin' on a few extra police durin' the carnival. He didn't expect any trouble, but would I help him out?

"Would I? I jumped at the chance. Pretty soft, I figured, seein' all the shows for nothin' and makin' wages besides!

"He goes up to his office and he pins on the badge. I didn't want to take the handcuffs, but he says I might need 'em.

"Then he offers me a gun.

"I never savvied an automatic, and besides I was wearin' old cedar in my shirt-front, so I figures one gun enough.

"My Levis was brand-new, but I stopped at the brown front and bought some new pants. After I got into 'em the shirt I was wearin' looked pretty tough, so I slides that dry-goods pirate twelve more pesos for this piece of silk."

Shorty eyed it ruefully.

"He tried to sell me a new hat and a pair of boots. But I was rearin' to look the layout over, so I eased out on the street.

"I took in two movies without payin'. The guinea at the second shows calls me 'mister' plumb respectful, and leads me to a seat. That night at supper I met Dogie Si.

" 'Beats flankin' calves and fightin' broncs,' says I, 'and spoon vittles every meal.' Dogie was plumb jealous.

"The carnival was at the ball-park, half a mile from town. I'd seen all the shows and was sittin' through that divin' act for the third time, when here comes a wild-eyed *hombre* yellin' for a cop. I was gonna help him hunt one when he spies my badge. I'd plumb forgot my dooty. But he reminds me in a hurry. A big Mexican was throwin' rocks at a stand full of glassware and crockery. The crowd was en-joyin' it, for that big Mex shore could throw. Every time he throwed somethin' smashed. At every smash that wild-eyed owner'd let out a squall, sort of like a dog a-howlin'.

" 'Look here, *hombre*,' I says, 'this ain't no babyrack! Ya got to cut it out and come with me. Ya can't act that-a-way.'

" '*Sí, señor*,' he says in a quiet voice, and come along plumb peaceful like. He wasn't a bit of trouble.

"We'd walked about a quarter when I rolled a cigarette. I was think-in' how soft this job was 'longside of punchin' cows, when I struck a light. Then it happened—I was gettin' up on all fours and had old cedar out when it happened again. A mule must have kicked me. About the time my head would clear a little, I'd get it again. Finally the whole remuda run over me and I went to sleep.

"When I woke up the Mexican was gone. I struck a few matches and found old cedar layin' in the dirt. Then I started figurin' it out. There wasn't no horse-tracks in the dust. Must have been that *hombre's* hob-nailed shoes. His tracks was everywhere. I struck more matches and cut his sign. He'd gone back toward the park. I was 'most there when I met Bob.

" 'What's the trouble?' he says.

" 'I'm lookin' for a big Mexican with hobnailed shoes.'

" 'Well,' says Bob, lookin' me over. 'He ought to be easy to find—if you put up any kind of a fight a-tall.'

"I didn't look like much. I had old cedar in my hand and shore was on the prod.

" 'Why didn't ya handcuff the bird?' says Bob.

" 'Lucky I didn't. He might have killed me if we'd been necked together.'

"The big Mex had gone straight back to the ball-park. The glass-ware was 'most gone when we found him, but he was throwin' rocks again. I itched to bore him through, but Bob says, 'No! Ya can't kill a man for throwin' rocks.'

" 'How come?' says I. 'Look what he done to me.'

"The big Mex acted plumb gentle when we gathered him again. '*Sí señor*,' he says in that quiet voice, as we led him down the road.

"About half-way in we caught a ride. The *hombre* sat between us, and everything went fine until Bob struck a match. Then it happens again with Bob on the receivin' end.

"Do somethin'!" he sputters.

" 'Ya can't kill a man for throwin' rocks,' says I.

"Bob's breath was gettin' short. I wasn't in shape for no more fightin.' So I lets the Mexican feel the butt of old cedar right where his hair was the thinnest. . . .

"When we got to town I quit."

Shorty rolled another cigarette.

"That divin' act shore was fine."

"What about the Mexican?" says Slim presently.

"Oh, him?" says Shorty. "He's still asleep, I reckon."

Old Fooler in Action

▼▲▼

Max Evans

Max Evans left his native Texas at the age of eleven and embarked on a varied career as cowboy, ranch owner, trapper, painter, and writer. *The Rounders* (1960) was his first big success. It was made into a motion picture and provided source material for a short-lived television series. In Evans's work, particularly in *The Rounders*, we begin to see the cowboy as victim, a trend that continued through the next two decades. Dusty and Wrangler are never going to get anywhere or be anybody, partly because of their own independent, improvident natures and partly because the system—society—is too much for them. At the same time they can be hilariously funny, so much so that most readers do not see the painful realities of their lives.

EVERYTHING WAS READY. THE SERIOUS WORK STARTED. ME and Wrangler was mighty earnest about that five-dollar-a-head bonus. It could be one hell of a big Fourth of July if we even made a 50 per cent gather.

First we jumped three mother cows and a four-year-old steer. They tore through the brush like a dose of salts. The broncs plowed right in after them, with me and Wrangler setting aboard ducking limbs, reining around boulders, feeling the brush pull and drag at us like the devil's own claws. That's why cowboys wear heavy leather chaps. Without them, there wouldn't have been enough meat left on our leg bones inside of ten minutes to feed a dying sparrow hawk.

When we couldn't see stock we could hear them. For a while it didn't look like we were going to get anywhere. The big steer cut back and I cut back with him. The brush was so thick and the rocks so big that I either had to let him go or risk losing the cows and calves. I turned back and went in after Wrangler. We had them headed downhill in a dead run. If we could keep them that way till we hit the flats we had a good chance. We made it.

From *The Rounders* (New York: Macmillan, 1960; Bantam edition, 1965), Chapters 5 and 6, pp. 33–48.

One old cow turned back again and again. The half-bronc sorrel I was riding didn't know what to do. I just had to whip him in the side of the head with my hat and spur hell out of him, all the time working them hackamore reins like they were a steering wheel to head that ornery cow.

Finally I got mad, and when she turned back for the tenth time I spurred up and dropped a loop around both horns. I kept spurring one way and she headed the other. It was quite a shock to her when all the slack pulled out of the rope. She came back and over and my little old bronc damn near went down. I threw my weight over on one side, ramming the spurs to him at the same time. He stayed up and held, turning to face down the rope like I'd been training him to do. It was all over quick-like. I had the rope off the cow's horns and was back on my horse before she got her wind back. From then on she headed the way I wanted her to.

There was no slowing up now. We came downhill in a long hard lope. Three cows, three calves—thirty dollars on the hoof. That's a lot of money to a working cowboy.

They hit that wing we had built and whirled around looking for an opening, but we crowded in just right and got them through the gate. I got down and slammed it shut, grinning all over. While the sweat dried on our horses, me and Wrangler had us a smoke and got a little clean, fresh pure mountain air into our lungs.

I said, "God a'mighty, thirty dollars in one day. This ain't never happened to me before."

Wrangler said, "Me neither."

I said, "I wish the Fourth of July was just next month."

Right then we figured we would have been the two richest cowboys ever to make a country rodeo. However, there was a whole long cold winter between us and the Fourth of July.

We went four more days before we penned another head. But little by little, one, two, three at a time, we gathered the stock out of the brush. We were sure enough doing what Jim Ed wanted. We were gathering his stock and putting sore backs and tender feet on the broncs at the same time.

The mother cows came first. They were easier to gather than the wild fat dry cows and the big, longer-legged steers. When we got to these last, things would really get wild on the mesa.

Finally, though, we had quite a bunch. We decided to pen what we had and hold a branding. These calves weighed in at between four and five hundred pounds and were as fat and slick as wagon grease on a peeled limb.

We penned them at the corral. Then we cut the mother cows out and checked the branding irons in the fire.

Wrangler said, "Just a little while more and they'll be ready."

I got the black-leg vaccine in the needle and sharpened my knife, getting ready to make a lot of little steers out of a lot of little bulls. Ever since I can remember I've liked a branding.

I remember when I was back home with Pa on his little leased outfit. We used to invite all the neighbors over for the brandings. The women brought something cooked, like chicken, hogside, pies and cakes. We made a real to-do out of it. There was plenty of hands to help. The women and little bitty kids watched from on the corral fence while the bigger kids like me and the old hands went to work.

There were two fires and always one old boy who was good at heelin' calves. He took great pride in this. A calf is lots easier to handle with the rope around his heels instead of his neck. Two of us would go down the rope just as the roper dragged the calf close to the fire. We jerked in opposite directions, one on the rope, the other on his tail. Down he would go. While one man jumped on his heels, the other gathered up a foreleg with his knee in the calf's neck. We would hardly get him down before a cowboy was there burning a brand on him and another was cutting his testicles out if he was a bull, and at the same time he would earmark him and reach for the needle to shoot the black-leg vaccine to him. The same thing would be going on at the other fire. We would brand a whole herd of calves in one day and have a big time doing it. After while everybody would eat and drink some water or something. You just couldn't beat it.

Me and Wrangler were going about it a little bit different. These were big calves—wild and mean. We were shorthanded and had only a bunch of raw broncs and an outlawed roan son of a bitch to rope off of.

Wrangler said the irons was ready. He went out and fit a loop on a big white-face calf. Then he fought his bronc around and started dragging him to the fire. I went down that rope and reached over his back with one hand in his flank and the other on the rope. The calf jumped straight up and kicked me in the belly with both feet. While he was up I heaved and down he went.

Wrangler bailed off his horse and came to help. In the meantime the calf had got one foot in my boot top and tore the bark off my shin. Then he kicked me in the mouth with the other foot. I had only one tooth in front that hadn't been broke, and now I didn't have that.

Wrangler pulled the calf's tail up between its kicking hind legs and held on while I tied all four feet with a four-foot piggin' string. Now, in rodeo they just tie three feet, but out here where we were you tied all four.

Wrangler went after the branding iron and started burning Jim Ed's J L brand on the calf's hip. I reached down and pulled the testicles as far out toward the front of the bag as I could. Then I split the bag and cut out the balls. I cut the fat off because that can cause infection, and swabbed the bag with pine tar. Then I cut a big chunk out of his ear called an earmark, which is part of a brand on every ranch. I cut off the little nubbin' horns and swabbed a little more pine tar on the holes. I shoved in the needle in the loose folds of skin at his neck and pushed the plunger. The hair was burning and getting in my eyes and up my nose, but I could see that redcolored brand would stay there as long as that calf hide was in this world.

Wrangler went back and got on his horse and rode him up to give me slack in the rope. I took the loop off his head, undid the piggin' string, and turned this young ex-bull loose into the world, all fixed up so the black-leg wouldn't kill him and branded so some cattle thief couldn't make off with him. He now belonged to Jim Ed Love for sure.

Well, we handled about three more like this and I had all the wind kicked out of me and half my hide was peeled loose here and there. My mouth was swelled up and I was already missing that broken tooth.

I said to Wrangler: "I wish we had a good heelin' horse. We could sure save lots of work and wear and tear."

I decided I would try Old Fooler. It was a crazy notion, but strangely enough it worked. I never rode a better heelin' horse in my life. Old Fooler had been to lots of brandings. Wrangler would throw his loop around a calf's neck and start toward the fire with him. Then I'd ease Old Fooler in close, riding in the other direction. At just the right spot I would let my loop drift slow and easy under the calf's belly, letting it lay up against his hind legs, then just as he moved out I'd pull it up around his heels, holding the slack out of the rope and riding on. The calf would hit the ground stretched out nice and tight between those two ropes. It made branding a lot faster and a lot easier.

I just couldn't believe that Old Fooler had ever tried to kill me. He really enjoyed this branding and settled down and did his job just like the rest of us. The way he worked that rope was a dream. He held it just tight enough but not too tight, and when you wanted slack he gave it to you. Those little short ears of his worked back and forth, and he watched every move out of those dark mean eyes. I still couldn't believe it when it was all over.

We turned the calves out to their mothers who were standing outside the corral. They trotted off together, all bawling, with the mother cows licking the calves like they had just been born.

I stared at Old Fooler standing out there looking so proud it showed right through the roan horsehair.

"I just can't figger that horse out," I said.

Wrangler said, "You never will. He's just like a woman."

"No," I said, "he may act like one but there is some little difference in the way they are built. How many mountain oysters we got?"

"Enough," he said, "for a good supper."

We went to the house and washed up. I brought in some wood for the cookstove. Wrangler set about mixing up a bunch of batter to cook them calf balls in. I got out the jug Vince Moore had left and we took a big slug apiece.

I said, "Wrangler, maybe I'm gettin' the best of that Old Fooler horse after all."

He didn't answer.

I hunted up an old stub of a pencil and sat down at the table to see how much our bonus was. It was just too much to add up in my head.

"Let's see, eighteen mother cows and calves, three dry cows and two steers." It took a lot of hard figuring, but I finally come up with the right answer.

I jumped up and took another slug out of the jug and yelled, "Wrangler, we've already made one hundred and fifteen dollars besides our regular wages."

"You don't mean it," he said, and sat down and figured it for himself. He never could get anything but a hundred and ten, but we decided as rich as we were that he was close enough.

I said: "Get back over to that stove. Them oysters is about to burn."

Pretty soon he took a pan of sourdough out of the oven browned just right. We poured us a big tin cup of coffee and sat down to consume a whole pan of crisp mountain oysters. It was the end of a hell of a fine day.

Everything was going along about as good as could be expected. We spent a lot of time, between runs on the mesa, trying to put a finish on some of the broncs. We kept three or four on a stake rope all the time. There is nothing better for a horse than that. Let an old pony get tangled up in that rope and peel all the hide from his hocks right down to the frog of his foot, and he learns not to fight a rope any more. First he gets respect for it, then he overcomes his fear. If a horse won't work with a rope, he ain't fit for a thing.

I was teaching them to turn at the slightest pressure of the knee and the feel of the rein on their necks. If you have to turn a horse by force and pressure from the bits only, you are going to ruin his mouth. He will get highheaded and start slinging his head. That kind of horse is a disgrace to any cowboy. I like to train a horse to back, too. There are lots of places you get with a cow horse that you will need to back out of. Another thing we worked hard on was stopping. A horse should stop with his hind legs well up under his belly and his tail jammed almost in the ground. This way is lots smoother, and leaves both the horse and rider ready to turn and move out. He has to be trained this way to keep him from overworking the livestock. I put a good stop on them by throwing my weight back in the saddle just as I pull up on the reins.

Jim Ed was not only going to have a lot of lost cattle found and gathered, he was going to have a top string of cow ponies by the Fourth of July.

Now maybe that's going too far. There was one big exception—Old Fooler. The thought caused my gizzard to cloud over. I felt a lot better about him after the branding, but I knew if I got overconfident the son of a bitch would try to kill me again. Just the same, I caught myself feeling pleased with him.

We had penned just about all the mother cows and calves. Now the rough part was starting. Those old thousand-pound steers and big fat dry cows were wilder than outhouse rats. We had jumped one huge steer about ten times, but we never even got him bent down the mountain toward the flats, much less had a chance to fit a loop over them long sharp horns.

We were riding along tracking him. I was on Old Fooler. Wrangler was on his favorite black. We saw where he had gone into a big thicket of oak brush and topped out on a steep point.

I said: "Wrangler, he's still in there. You stay up on this point so I can skylight you and I'll mosey over on the other side and go in after him."

"Whatever suits you just tickles me plumb to death," he said.

"Now if he comes out where you can get a run at him," I went on, "just yell and I'll know what you mean. If he comes out where you can't, but I can, just point at the spot and I'll go after him like Jim Ed does to money ."

I rode around and reined Old Fooler into the brush. He didn't like it but went in just the same. I heard something move. Then it sounded like a whole herd of hydrophobia buffalo had broke loose. It was just that one big steer.

I looked up and saw Wrangler pointing. He yelled, "To your left! There he goes!"

The steer had cut right back out not twenty feet away. I turned Old Fooler and that's all I had to do. Out of there he sailed with his head down and his ears laid back flat. I caught a glimpse of the steer and knew we had him going at an angle downhill It was up to Old Fooler now. He really put out. I could feel that smooth running power of his building up at every stride and pretty soon we could see that old steer's flying tail most of the time. Another half-minute and I was actually thinking about undoing my rope and getting a loop ready. *Cowboys, what a horse!* I said to myself. I was sure glad Vince had brought him back. I was going to have to figure some way to trade Jim Ed out of this fine steer-gathering old pony.

Well, the steer hit a bunch of scattered piñons. I could see a big opening just past. I jobbed the steel to Old Fooler and he gave it all he had. Things were looking up. The next thing I knew I was too, but I couldn't see much.

We had started around this piñon tree, and I had leaned over just enough so Old Fooler would know which side to go on. He acted like he was doing just what I wanted, but when we got to the tree he whirled back the other way at full speed. So there I was trying to go around one side, and him going around the other. My chest whopped into hard bark and off I went.

I was laying on my back trying to find the sky. My breath was gone and every move I made I could feel them busted ribs scraping against one another. It hurt so bad I tried not to breathe at all. I reckon that's why old Wrangler thought I was dead when he first rode up. But he soon found out different because as bad hurt as I was I could still think up new names for that double-crossing Fooler horse.

As soon as Wrangler figured I had at least a fifty-fifty chance of living, he rode on down and gathered Old Fooler and led him back. I would have taken a piñon limb and beat him to death right then and there but it was all I could do to hold myself together long enough for Wrangler to help me up on him. I couldn't have picked up a broken matchstick at that moment.

It was a long ride in. I laid around in my bedroll, for four or five days, moaning and groaning. Finally Wrangler took some strips of ducking canvas and tied them around me and it helped hold the ribs in place.

I asked him, "Ain't you got an old forty-four pistol in your warbag?"

Wrangler looked at me out of them pig eyes and pulled at his drooping britches.

"Yeah," he said.

"Will it shoot?"

"I don't know," he said. "I never shot it."

"Well, let me see it," I said. I pulled the hammer back and shot right up through the ceiling. It went off like a wet firecracker.

"Wrangler," I said, "if you'll go down and shoot that son of a bitch I will give you all my bonus from this wild-cow gather."

"Naw," he said.

"Why not?" I asked.

"Hell, he belongs to Jim Ed and we'll have to pay for him. Jim Ed will charge us double and be makin' a big profit."

Well, this thought hurt me just as bad as that tree did. I couldn't stand for Jim Ed to profit by that horse's death instead of me.

"Wrangler," I said, "there are times you amaze me. You actually show faint signs of intelligence once in a while."

Wrangler did not think this was funny and he made a noise like a fat bay mule that has just jumped a five-wire fence.

"I am goin' to stay here and get well and then I am goin' to go out and kill him in the line of duty."

When Wrangler asked, "How?" I gave him the same kind of answer he'd given me.

When my ribs healed to where I could take a deep breath, I told Wrangler, "Get that horse up for me, will you?"

"What horse?"

"You know what horse," I said.

He brought Old Fooler up. I limped out and stood and stared. Then I brushed him down nice and gentle-like, taking my time. I talked as sweet to him as I would to my old crippled grandmother. I bragged on that horse and told him that if only I had any sugar cubes I would give him a whole sack. I mean to say, I spread it on like honey on a hot biscuit. Then I got on him and rode easy and slow out toward the hills, not even touching him with my spurs and still bragging on him like he was my favorite animal in all the world.

I got off up there a ways and my ribs was aching to beat hell, but they still held together. Then I ducked my head like I had just found a fresh track. It was at least two weeks old. Then I threw my head up and made out like I had spotted a thousand head of unbranded steers. I didn't have to do anything but lean over, and away we went. You could build a fire on a jack rabbit's tail and he would look like he was going backward compared to the way Old Fooler ran. I could almost feel that rascal laughing plumb through the saddle leather. What a fool he thought I was. This time he would really get me.

The ground was rolling away under us so fast it made me dizzy. Right out ahead was another bunch of piñon. I spurred him straight at them, leaning over just like I did before. Old Fooler was already bunching his muscles to jump the wrong way and break my crazy neck once and for all. Just as he thought it was time, I straighened up and pulled one foot out of the stirrup, yanking my leg up behind the cantle of the saddle. Then I jerked him into that tree at full speed.

There must be a lot more wind in a horse than in a man. The air that came busting out of his lungs would have blown a Stetson hat around the world three times. That old horse staggered and fell. I stepped off, taking care not to make any sudden movements and snap a rib. A cowboy in my condition has got to be careful and not take any chances.

I hadn't killed him, though. He got up, and his eyes were rolling around in his head like a couple of gallstones in a slop jar. He wobbled on his legs.

I fancy-stepped all the way back to camp with Old Fooler stumbling along behind, just barely able to make it. That was the only time I ever took a walk I enjoyed.

Wrangler came out on the porch and asked, "What happened?"

I said: "You know what? That is the tree-lovingest horse I ever saw. He just can't pass one by without runnin' over it."

Partners

▼▲▼▲▼▲▼▲▼▲▼▲▼▲▼▲▼▲▼▲▼▲▼▲▼▲▼▲▼▲▼

Glendon Swarthout

Glendon Swarthout holds a Ph.D. from Michigan State University and has
been an English professor at Michigan State and Arizona State, but his academic record has not interfered with his becoming a successful novelist. His
rise began with *They Came to Cordura* (1958) and he did even better with *The
Shootist* (1975). Both were made into popular movies.

The Cadillac Cowboys takes a close look at a good old boy who falls from
grace when he becomes a high-pressure cattle buyer, accumulates a great
amount of easy money, and loses his way in the jungles of Suburbia (Scotts-
dale, Arizona).

We learn about him from Carleton Cadell, a fugitive from the East whose
great ambition is to meet some genuine Westerners. He is introduced to Eddie Bud Boyd, whose dress, personality, and conversation fascinate him, and
the next day he visits Eddie Bud and his ranch-girl bride at their Tahitian
hilltop palace. "Where," Cadell wants to know, "is the ranch?" In the pages
that follow, Eddie Bud, offers to show him his "herd."

W E LEFT CHRISTABEL AND HE LED ME INTO A DEN OFF THE LIV-
ing room furnished only with a leather-backed chair upon which was
the telephone. I stood transfixed by my own gullibility.

"Eddie Bud, you told me you were a cattleman."

"Ah'm a c'mission cattleman."

"What the devil is that?"

"It's a ex-pression. Theah's mebbe less'n a thousan' c'mission men
this side of Kansas City any more. We buy the critters an' sell the
critters but we don't brand 'em or finish 'em or eat 'em. In some ways
we don't even own 'em, excep' jes' long enough t' pass 'em on t'
somebody else for more'n we paid we hope."

"A middleman."

"Thet's right. In b'tween a bawl an' a bite. Makin' out on a half-
cent a poun' heah, cent a poun' theah, when the market goes up.
When it don't, whoooeee. Most times, at the end of the deal, the

From *The Cadillac Cowboys* (New York: Random House, 1964), 27–37.

c'mission man is the poor country boy standin' theah with 'is hand out. All's you need's a telephone an' a good car an' a mess of folks you trus' and who trus' you an' a carload of guts. Ah mean, you got t' have guts comin' out your ears. Sometime your office is like heah, sometime it's your car, sometime it's up in your think box. It's a lonesome bus'ness an' a risky, 'bout the riskies' theah is any more in the Wes'. You can lose your wipes before breakfast. But ah been in it ten years now an' it suits me like a pair of waddy britches. Ah have t' be my own boss. Carleton, men is jes' like cattle: the less they bunch, the easier they walk."

He could practically smell my ignorance of the cattle commerce, which ranged from rare to medium rare, but he was pleased as a boy with a firecracker to elucidate. His domain extended, roughly, from Little Rock, Ark., on the east, to the Imperial Valley, Calif., on the west; from Elko, Nev., on the north, as far south as Hermosillo, Sonora, Mexico. Between these points he drove 100,000 miles yearly, wearing out two automobiles. When he was not "on the circuit" he was on the telephone, and his bills averaged $600 a month. It was his discipline to know by name and character and location every stockman and feeder and broker and fellow commission man in this vast eight-state area, and by age and shape and breed and condition every pound of beef on the hoof. Acting on this knowledge, which was long and dear in the acquiring, it was his function to bring buyer and seller together, or actually the former's money and the latter's animals, and for this intermediary service to charge a commission. Buying sometimes outright, sometimes on contract, the term of his real ownership might be minutes or hours or days or even a few weeks, depending on the market. To pass the critters on to someone else at a higher price than he had paid was his livelihood and prayer, and the gods to whom he made obeisance, to whose mercies and moods he subjected himself, whose plaything, in the end, he verily was, were wind and rain and drought and disease and war and wallet and, of course, hunger.

"An' luck. Plain ol' aces-back-t'-back luck. Now ah s'pose all this's 'bout as clear t' you as a tender-hearted brand."

"Tender-hearted?"

"One thet ain't burnt deep enough. Well, reckon ah'll have t' show you. You jes' hunker down theah on the floor—ah'm sorry we don't have no furniture yet—an' watch an' ol' cowhand mount up."

I did as bade, though skeptically, while he picked up the telephone, sat down, put his boots to the wall and tilted himself on the chair's rear legs so far it seemed he must topple backward. Pushing up the brim of his hat he winked at me. "Carleton, right while you're lookin' ah'm goin' t' make me a thousan' dollahs. Ah feel right an' the market's right an' heah we go. First crack this mornin' ah called the feed lots over in Phoenix—we got us one of the bigges' pen-feedin' deals in the world right heah in Arizona—an' ah got me the fat market prices from Dodge 'n Amarillo 'n Gran' Junction an' so on an' they're strong as a big flea on a bitty dog." He grew serious. "Now. Ah'm goin' t' make me a couple phone calls. When ah set down like this, thet ain't no bare wall ah'm lookin' at, it's a map of this whole cattle country. Ah can see ev'ry town an' ev'ry road an' ev'ry feed lot an' ev'ry auction ground an' ev'ry ranch an' thet ain't but a start. Ah can also see, like on a tel-vision, ev'ry cattleman an' ev'ry one of his fam'ly an' also his herd, 'bout wheah they're at on his range an' how much they'll weigh out at, the big end, thet's the bes' ones, an' the little end, thet's the culls. So now, when ah put in a call, it's like ah was right theah, 'cause ah was theah myself not too long ago. Okeh, now."

He lifted the receiver from the cradle in his lap and dialed.

"Operator, this heah's Credit Card 2743311 . . . Ah'd like t' call me Buster Rutherford in Brawley, California. He'll be at the feed lot theah mos' likely . . . Now Carleton, Buster's a feeder. He buys him young cattle weighin' 400 t' 600 pounds an' feeds 'em out to a thousand, finishes 'em we say, then sells 'em to a packer. This time of year ah expec' he's lookin' t' buy . . . Hullo, thet you, Buster? . . . Eddie Bud Boyd. Yeh . . . Phoenix . . . Yeh. How you doin'? Gettin' richer? . . . Me? Oh, nothin' much, jes' gettin' ex-perience . . . You heard ah made me a mountain? You b'lieve ever'thin' you hear? . . . Well, ah ain't shinin' shoes . . . Say, ah did get married, though, las' month . . . Yeh, ah did . . . Oh, a lil' ol' Col'rado gal. Off a ranch . . . Oh, ah'll watch her. Ah plan t' keep her barefoot an' preg-ant . . . No, by myself, ah don't need no hep! How's the weather? . . . No grass, huh? . . . Well, we're dry, too, we got no desert. Talkin' with a ol' boy up in Raton, New Mex'co, yesterday, he said they had fros' . . . Yeh . . . Say, Buster, you buyin' any? . . . Yeh? . . . How's the quality? . . . Yeh? . . . Them little cattle ain't no-count, you right. Could you use you a thousand cattle ah was t' locate 'em? . . . Yeh? . . . Weighin' how much? . . . Yeh? . . . What'd you pay? . . . $24.75? Ah thought you wanted good cattle, not no dogs . . . $25? . . . Laid in. Well, ah might could. Ah'll thrash aroun' in the brush a little. What'd the Eas' do yesterday? . . . Yeh? . . . How's ol' Frank? . . . You don't mean it. Oh-oh. Them damn bankers. Well, listen, Buster, ah be talkin' to you . . . Yeh . . . So long."

He put down the phone. "Carleton, we got us a customer. Buster can use him a thousand head aroun' 500 pounds an' he'll pay $25 laid in, which means $25 a hundred pounds shipped t' him over in Brawley. So we jes' sold us $125,000 worth of beef."

"$125,000!" I gasped. "Sight unseen?"

"Why, shore. Ah've knowed ol' Buster a long time. He knows ah won't sell him no cripples or pink-eyes or locos or lump-jaws. We don't have t' sign nothin', neither of us. Carleton, this bus'ness is built on honor."

"But you don't have any cattle!"

"Not yet ah don't." Staring fixedly at the wall, he sat immobile for a while.

"What are you doing?"

"Studyin' my map. Tunin' in my tel-vision."

"To where?"

"Dalhart, Texis."

"Where's that?"

"Near Dumas."

"Oh."

He dialed again. "Operator, this heah's Credit Card 2743311 . . . Le's see if we can get us Pete Poteet in Dalhart, Texis . . . Yeh. At the sale barn, prob'ly . . . Now Carleton, ol' Pete's a c'mission man like me. Mebbe he can rustle us up somethin' in the line of critters. What say, Operator? . . . Well, try aroun' town, it ain't overpopulated . . . Pete an' me, Carleton, we been scratchin' each other's backs for years . . . Hey, Pete, you ol' bird dog? . . . Eddie Bud Boyd . . . Where you at? . . . In a mo-tel? You hidin' out? You

mean thet tax man ain't caught up with you yet? Heh-heh . . . Oh.
You sick. What from? . . . " He listened, grinning. "Heh-heh-
heh! Pete, he been down in Chi-wah-wah buyin' cattle an' ate some of
thet Mex-can food an' got him the trots! Heh-heh-heh. Say, Pete,
how's it look? . . . Yeh? . . . Me? Oh, ah been hittin' an' missin'—
mostly missin' . . . What? . . . You heard ah struck gold? Hell,
no. Ah feel like ah been shot at an' hit. Say, ah did get married,
though, las' month . . . Ah tell you true . . . Oh, a lil' ol' Col'rado
gal . . . Off a ranch . . . Oh, ah'll watch her. Ah plan t' keep her
barefoot an' preg-ant . . . No, by myself! You tell all them ol' gals
down theah t' stop cryin', heh-heh-heh. How's the weather?
. . . Yeh . . . They ain't got no grass in California, neither . . .
What's thet? . . . Cold front movin' in t' Amarillo, they said?
. . . Hum . . . You rollin' many cattle? . . . Yeh? . . . Say,
Pete, why ah called, ah'm not buyin' many, market's too warm for
me, but ah could use some good cattle weighin' aroun' five hundred if
they was even cattle, not up an' down, thet is . . . Yeh. You got any?
. . . How many . . . Four hundred? . . . Four. This damn con-
nection. Pete, are they the good shapey kind? . . . Will ah like
'em? . . . Yeh? . . . Well, ah might buy 'em long's they're in line.
How much? . . . Twenty-five dollahs? You mus' mean a head, not a
hundred! Now Pete. Now Pete." The buyer winked at me. "Pete, ah
don't mind losin' my own money, ah jes' don't want t' break you . . .
Yeh? . . . Heh-heh . . . Well, if them ol' boys is fightin' over 'em,
ah don't have t' have 'em. Pete, tell you what, you lay them cattle in t'
Brawley at $24.75 an' you got you a deal. Okeh? . . . Okeh. Say,
they strong enough t' ride? . . . Aw right . . . Buster Rutherford . . . Soon's you can. Pete, you get your guts in order an' stay
out of them mo-tels now . . . Yeh . . . Ah be talkin' to you. So
long. Say, Pete, you heard 'bout ol' Frank? . . . You know, over in
Brawley? . . . He bellied up . . . He shore did. Them damn
bankers . . . Yeh, you said it. Well, so long."

Dropping the receiver, he yawned resoundingly. "You savvy thet,
Carleton?"

"You bought four hundred head for Rutherford."

"Thet's right. At $24.75 a hundred pounds freight paid an' they'll av'rage five hundred. But Buster's payin' me $25. So how much did ah clear?"

"$1.25 per cow. Times four hundred."

"We're halfway t' thet thousand."

"Protein," I marveled. "And a party line connecting hundreds of people over thousands of miles. By the way, don't you do any business here in Arizona?"

"Hell, no."

"But you're a native. Where's your pride in your native state?"

"Same place as my ass. Well hid." The only cattlemen in Arizona who could be relied on, he said, were the Apaches; the white ranchers would pick the silver out of your teeth while you were biting on the gold. He'd discovered that early. "My first deal in Arizona, ah got wetlotted."

"What's that?"

"Ah bought me a truckload of cattle up north heah. They was t' be put in a dry lot thet night, no food or water, then weighed an' rolled in the mornin'. Thet way ah'd pay for true weight. But thet bastard lined 'em up at the water trough in the mornin' before weighin'. When they come off the trucks down heah, their bellies was so full of water they sounded like they was swimmin', not walkin'. Ah paid for about ten pounds of water in ev'ry critter. So ah learned me a lesson."

He closed his eyes. "Ex-cuse me, Carleton, time's a-wastin'." With eyes closed, while mapping and tuning, he performed the feat of rolling and lighting a cigarette before taking up the phone. "Operator? Credit Card 2743311 . . . Now Operator, ah want t' talk t' Eck Gowdy at the Gowdy Ranch east of Clovis, New Mex'co, don't know the number . . . Okeh . . . This heah's a real good rancher, Carleton. Raises him some of the best white-face yearlin's ah ever bought. What? . . . Well, lemme talk t' the gal over in Clovis . . . Hullo, honey. Now what's both'rin' you? . . . Don't fuss . . . Listen, it's about thirty miles east of where you settin' fussin'. Other side of the Flyin' O outfit, you know . . . Yeh, thet's the one. Eck Gowdy. You try, honey . . . This Eck is one of the damndes' funnies' ol' boys you ever met, Carleton, oh, he is a caution.

"Eck? . . . Eck, you ol' tarantula! Eddie Bud Boyd! . . . Shore is! Long time no talk to! . . . Phoenix . . . You still raisin' them plain cattle? . . . Say, how's thet good-lookin' wife of yours? Ain't run off? . . . Oh, no, not another. My, my . . . A boy? Why, you got you a truckload of kiddies now, you ought t' grass 'em fat an' roll 'em! . . . Me? Retired? Hell ah'm in such bad shape my frien's won't let me climb up an anythin' higher 'n a sidewalk for fear ah'll jump! . . . If ah had any . . . Why, frien's! . . . Ah did get married, though, las' month . . . Oh, a lil' ol' gal off a ranch. Col'rado. Not as good-lookin' as yours, though! . . . No, ah ain't passed out no ci-gars yet, you ol' buzzard! Say, how's the weather? . . . Yeh, no grass anywhere, been a bad year for stockers. Col' front movin' in t' Amarillo, ah heard . . . Yeh . . . Say, Eck, why ah called, you remember the las' time ah come by, we went up in your high country an' you showed me a herd on grass up in thet canyon, about three hundred head theah was? . . . Yeh. How much'd they weigh now? . . . You sold 'em? . . . What? . . . You didn't sell 'em? You was goin' to but you got throwed? Well, what happened?

The cattleman bent forward, offering himself entirely to mirth, his grin expectant and bright as a silver dollar. "You 'n Pedro got 'em hunted up an' in the pen . . . heh-heh . . . t' truck t' the Clovis sale in the morning', yeh . . . heh-heh-heh . . . then the goddam loadin' chute busted an' like t' broke Pedro's leg . . . heeh-heeh . . . then thet night you heard screamin' an' a goddamn bear was after them critters . . . heeh-heeh-heeh . . . an' they busted the pen an' the whole bunch took off for the high country again . . . heeh-heeh-heeh-heeh . . . hey, Eck, how'd you know it wasn't no bear but some ol' gal bein' raped? Heeh-heeh-heeh-heeh-heeh!" Guile snubbed his glee.

Squinting, he peered through the dust of his hilarity. "You still got 'em then, huh, Eck? . . . Yeh, somewhere? . . . Heh-heh. Listen, ah might jes' take 'em off your han's an' you be shet of 'em for good. They still uniform in flesh? . . . Yeh . . . Say, Eck, how much you want for the three hundred? . . . $25.25? You joshin' me. Ah couldn't go but $23.75, what with pork gettin' so popular . . . You got you a sight of cattle, Eck. They be sleepin' in bed with you an' your missus you don't sell some . . . $25. No, but ah might go

$24 . . . Them cattle been sweat, y'know, b'tween you an' ol' Pedro an' thet bear . . . $24.75? Well, now we gettin' somewhere. Say, you remember ol' Frank over in Brawley? . . . Yeh. Skunked out . . . Yeh. Them damn bankers. Eck, tell you what ah'll do. You got you another mouth t' feed now, so ah'll go $24.50 laid in t' Buster Rutherford, how's thet? . . . Okeh. Theah won't be much shrink on 'em, will theah? . . . No. Okeh. Say, Eck, ah shore en-joyed talkin' at you. You tell thet good-lookin' woman of yours ah be comin' by your place one of these days! Heh-heh . . . Okeh, Eck. So long."

He dropped his boots with a thump, leveling his chair, and banged down the telephone. "Whoooeee!"

"$24.50—" I began.

"Laid in!"

"Sold for $25. Fifty cents profit per hundredweight—"

"$2.50 a head clear!"

"Times three hundred—"

"$750!"

"And $500 on the other—"

"Twelve hundred fifty pesos U.S.! In twenty minutes, less ed-ucatin' you. An' Buster, he's still wantin' him three hundred more head! Told you ah could tail 'er!"

"Great Lord."

"How's thet for swingin' a wide loop!" He paced exuberantly before sitting again and rolling another cigarette. "Carleton, thet wasn't nothin', though."

"Steak," I murmured.

"Hell, thet was a ride down the road compared t' what ah done a little bit ago." I waited while he determined whether or not to con-tinue, vanity locked with the outdoorsman's natural reticence. The latter won, evidently, for letting his cigarette loll he exhauled smoke through his nostrils until his face was veiled from me. "Carleton, we're shy as a green hoss to a new water trough, Chris 'n me. We never had nothin' an' never been nowhere. Now we made our pile an' don't know how t' blow it proper. We're lonesome n' scairt 'n ig-orant. What ah'm sayin' is we need hep."

"In what way?"

"Ev'ry damn way. You 'n your missus, you b'long t' this heah country club, ain't thet right?"

"Camino d'Oro? Yes."

"Thet's what ah heard." He hesitated. "Carleton, ah don't know how t' say it. Howsomever. Carleton, could you mebbe get me 'n Chris in, too?"

So unexpected, so discrepant, so absurd was the request that it pained me, and I fought back with irony. "Sorry," I smiled, "but we've had to draw the line. You understand, I'm sure. We let one anachronism in and they'll all want in."

"No, Carleton, not for the golf! It's so we'd have us a place t' go an' meet folks an' have frien's. It's so we'd b'long t' somethin' in town. Please, Carleton?"

Suddenly a breeze cleared the smoke from his burnished, youthful countenance. I looked into eyes as trusting and supplicant as a captive deer's. For once in my life I met innocence cornea to cornea. The word has been debased. I mean innocence such as we associate with rosebuds, with babes in mangers, with graves and Grecian urns, with harps on high, with the most distant dewy dawnings of the earth. I mean innocence of such depth and rarity and truth that my heart literally turned within me, recoiled in shame that I had dared even for a moment to doubt its presence.

"Yes, Eddie Bud, I'll get you in the club, I'll help you, I'll do everything!" I said, the words springing from my mouth like frogs. "You didn't even have to ask!"

"Ah do thank you, Carleton. How come?"

"Because you're the genuine, indubitable article," I said. "Because in you the past still lives. Because in you I find all those qualities which have made the American character unique—daring, innocence, democracy, gusto, humor, cussedness, generosity, industry, vision, independence, horse sense, ingenuity, grit, sociability." I swallowed the lump in my throat. "Because you're the man I wish I had been."

"Partner," he said solemnly, extending his hand.

"Partner," I said.

Emotion, emotion. So overwhelmed was I by admiration and love for the man, by sheet natal joy in him, by recognitions and revelations which had come too swiftly, that I rushed from the room, undergoing as I left the house the raven gaze of his small, mustachioed retainer. "*Adios*, Titano!" I cried. Answer came there none.

Blood Of Spain:
A Humorous Image
for the Mexican-American

▼▲

Dorothy Pillsbury—"Little Piñon Fires"
(from *No High Adobe*)

Richard Bradford—"Life at Sagrado"
(from *Red Sky at Morning*)

John Nichols—"Joe Mondragón Defies the
Establishment."
(from *The Milagro Beanfield War*)

The Mexican-American
Moves Upward

▽▲▽▲▽▲▽▲▽▲▽▲▽▲▽▲▽▲▽▲▽▲▽▲▽▲▽▲▽▲▽▲▽▲▽▲▽▲▽

FOR A CENTURY AND A HALF THE MEXICAN-AMERICAN, LIKE THE
Mexican before him, has been swimming upstream. The Mexican
War established stereotypes that have not disappeared in the second
half of the twentieth century. Upper-class Mexican men were proud,
resentful, bigoted, and devious. Common men were dirty, cowardly,
cruel, and ignorant. Mexican women, on the other hand, were beautiful, gentle, and partial to American men. How such warm and attractive creatures could be the mothers, sisters, and daughters of Latin
males was a mystery. The whole country was thought to be backward,
and it was commonly believed that the only way Mexico would ever
prosper would be through a takeover by the United States.

The novels that reflected American interest in the Mexican and his
country took these ideas, in greater or less degree, for granted. As
time went on, however, a great reversal took place. Cecil Robinson
points out in *Mexico and the Hispanic Southwest in American Literature*
(1963, 1977), that in our time Americans have tended to find fault
with their own ways and traditions and regard Mexican and Indian
lifeways as superior. Mexicans are "a vivid, passionate, and spontane-
ous people, not acquisitive but endowed with a great capacity to enjoy the moment, communal in their use of land, responsive to the arts,
and devoted to ancient customs and impressive rituals which derive
from ancient tradition" (p. 211). In the 1960s the Chicano writers
branded the gringo with the same adjectives the gringo had once used
against them. The "Black Legend of Spain" was replaced by the
"Black Legend of the Gringos."*

*C. L. Sonnichsen, "The Two Black Legends" in *From Hopalong to Hud* (College Station: Texas A & M University Press, 1978), 83–102.

The selections that follow cast a beam of light on these developments. Alfred Henry Lewis's "greasers" begin to be replaced in the 1920s by more sympathetic characters. Harvey Fergusson (*Blood of the Conquerors*, 1921) showed how the acquisitive Anglos took advantage of the less-aggressive New Mexicans. Ruth Laughlin Barker (*Caballeros*, 1932), emphasized the refined manners and customs of even the humblest of them, supposedly inherited from the Spanish aristocracy and preserved through four centuries. Haniel Long (*Piñion Country*, 1941) analyzed the situation of rural New Mexicans, spotlighting such sad characteristics as illiteracy and disease. Dorothy Pillsbury in her sketches of Santa Fe Mexican-American families (*No High Adobe*, 1950) strikes a new note as she steps down of an afternoon into Mrs. Apodaca's kitchen and reports with gracious humor what is said and done there. It would be too much to say that her tone is condescending, but she offers a good illustration of the dictum of the late Arthur Campa of Denver: "Writers have not yet found a way to depict the Mexican-American as he is. They make him too quaint."

After Mrs. Pillsbury the Mexican-American in fiction become anything but quaint. A whole series of novels, some by Chicano authors, many by Anglos, paint well-rounded pictures of *paisanos, politicos, Tio Tacos* (who have sold out to the gringos), and many more. Edward Abbey, Richard Bradford, Frank O'Rourke, James Lehrer, and a few others, however, give their Mexicans special status and impact by looking at them through the glass of humor.

Little Piñon Fires

▼▲▼

Dorothy Pillsbury

There can be no doubt that Dorothy Pillsbury loved and enjoyed her
Mexican-American friends in the little adobe houses in Santa Fe. The question is, did she really understand them? She portrays herself as an accepted,
perhaps beloved, outsider who never quite comes down to the level of the
barrio, and she laughs kindly at their oddities. On the other hand, she injects
a much-needed note of appreciation into her little symphony, and she offers
her readers a green and shady nook on the edge of the thorny desert of Chicano belligerence which took root during the 1960s.

   Her sketches were originally published in the *Christian Science Monitor* and
were collected under titles using the word *adobe* as a leitmotif (*Adobe Door-
ways, Roots in Adobe, Star over Adobe*).

A BLUE CANDLE WAS BURNING BEFORE THE UNCURTAINED WIN-
dow of the Little Adobe House. Another candle, on the shelf of the
corner fireplace, coaxed piñon flames to higher soarings. White-
washed walls blushed Christmas red in the dim room.

   Suddenly Carmencita Apodaca's many-curled head appeared like a
ghost outside the square-paned window. Before I could open the door,
she was gone. But in a few minutes, there was her mother's shawl-
wrapped figure tapping to come in. A plate of little fried pies, bursting
with piñon nuts, was in her hand.

   "I say to Carmencita," Mrs. Apodaca explained, "run see if the
Señora has her lamp lighted. If she has, she is working and I will not
molest her. But, if the blue candles burn, the Señora will be sitting by
her fire doing nothing."

   Mrs. Apodaca settled herself in the big rocker and pushed her best
shawl back on her shoulders. From her ears dangled half circles of soft
old gold and on her brown index finger a big turquoise in a hand-
wrought, silver setting gesticulated with elegance.

   "The *muchacha* say," Mrs. Apodaca covered her smile politely with
a brown hand, " 'the Señora does *nada, nana.*' "

From *No High Adobe* (Albuquerque: University of New Mexico Press, 1950), 20–24.

91

"I was thinking," I replied, slightly on the defensive. "Nothing like a piñon fire for thoughts that sing."

"*Si*," nodded Mrs. Apodaca in complete understanding, "but it is strange that, being an Anglo lady, you can do it. Busy, busy, the Anglo ladies, the club, the PTA, the *teléfono*, the hair-drier, the book-of-the-month."

"I was thinking about Christmas here in Santa Fé," I explained, "simple and gay for the eyes and tender and warm for the heart, like our burning piñon pyres along the crooked snowy streets."

"*Si, es bueno,*" Mrs. Apodaca agreed, not overly impressed.

"Maybe it's because we are seven thousand feet nearer the stars than many other places," I elaborated. "Maybe it's because I know shepherds are watching their flocks in sheltered valleys. And little picture-book Spanish-American villages still keep ancient mellow ways."

Suddenly Mrs. Apodaca was thinking with me. Her big brown eyes were shining, her golden earrings danced, and the silver setting of her big ring focused a ray of firelight.

"Ah, Señora, the little villages! When a *muchacha*, I lived in one over by Truchas Peak. Cedar forests in the deep cañons! And snow burying the little houses! Goats' bells tinkling all night long. No one from outside came near us. Such processions around the windy plaza, where the piñon pyres lighted the whole place on *Nochebuena*. I can hear the fiddles and guitars even now, and the old Spanish songs.

"Once, Señora, I wore a blue cape and rode all over the village on a *burrito*. The wind blew my window-curtain veil straight out behind and I had to hold my tinsel crown on with both hands. Desiderio Dominguez (you have heard of him, Señora. He is a *politico* now) had a carpenter's box tied on his skinny *muchacho* shoulders. With all the village following us, we went from door to door asking lodging for the night.

"And once, you may not believe it, Señora, I played in the old play where Good and Evil battle and Good always wins. My *mamacita* taught me the words as her *mamacita* had taught her." Words in the old plays came down in families, like earrings of gold.

"And even in Santa Fé," continued Mrs. Apodaca, "there are many of the old ways left. No? I was sad, only a few years ago when the procession of the wood-haulers stopped. In those days all of the wood for Santa Fé came down from the mountains on burroback. Ah, being a wood-hauler was an honorable calling! Late on the afternoon before Christmas, the wood-haulers, in their best jackets and *pantalones*, and the *burritos*, brushed until their coats were as soft as kittens' fur, made a procession. Around the plaza they marched and all Santa Fé out in the dusk of *Nochebuena* to see them. And then a big piñon fire would be lighted in front of the cathedral. At that signal all the crooked, narrow streets would burst out with the flame from hundreds of other little piñon fires along the way."

Mrs. Apodaca slapped her shawl about her head. "Too long I molest you with my words. I go now to save the *muchachos* from a sea of tissue paper. They are wrapping gifts from the Five and Dime. No gifts in my day, Señora, not until Twelfth Night. Then we left straw in our shoes outside the door, for the camels of the Three Kings. It was always gone in the morning and in its place were sweets."

As I opened the door, we both exclaimed, "The first little piñon fire!" There it was up against the black mountain, lighting the way to some story-book village. "*Es bueno*," Mrs. Apodaca nodded, "*El Santo Niño* will find his way through the dark, bitter night."

Life at Sagrado

▼▲▼▲▼▲▼▲▼▲▼▲▼▲▼▲▼▲▼▲▼▲▼▲▼▲▼▲▼▲▼

Richard Bradford

Joshua Arnold, son of a prosperous Mobile, Alabama, boat manufacturer, has been spending summers at Sagrado, in the mountains north of Santa Fe, since he was a small boy. When World War II breaks out, however, his father decides to leave his family there for the duration while he goes off to war. Josh shows up with a mixed bag of students on the opening day at the local high school. Maximiliano "Chango" López and his superlatively endowed sister Viola create problems at once and life for Josh becomes not only complicated but dangerous. As time goes on Chango and Viola become part of Josh's circle of friends, but other trials and temptations come along without delay. He profits from a close acquaintance with the Montoya family, who live higher up in the mountains, and finds himself in tune with these country people. At the end he is on his way to enter the armed services, a much more mature young man.

Though he was born in Chicago and finished his education in Louisiana, Richard Bradford has taken New Mexico to be his province and his home. His two novels, *Red Sky at Morning* (1968) and *So Far from Heaven* (1973) are full of humorous insights into the life and people of his adopted state. He is particularly good with Mexican-Americans.

I HAD BEEN AWAY FROM SAGRADO FOR SEVEN SUMMERS, BUT nothing had changed. Nobody had built a defense plant there, or an Army base. There was talk of something warlike going on at Los Alamos, up in the Jemez Mountains, where there had once been a rustic boys' school, but we assumed it was just another boondoggle. "They're manufacturing the front part of horses up there," Dad suggested, "and shipping them to Washington for final assembly."

The streets in Sagrado were a little pockier than I remembered, and the few cars were fewer. While Mobile was growing and spreading out, raw, new and ugly, Sagrado protected itself, as it had for more than three hundred years, by being nonessential. That's the best way to get through a war: Don't be big and strong, be hard to find.

From *Red Sky at Morning* (Philadelphia: Lippincott, 1968), Chapters 4, and 5, pp. 34–50.

The Montoyas—Amadeo and his wife, Excilda—expected us. They had put fresh mud plaster on the house, swept the fine dust from inside, and put a polish on the welcoming job by thrusting sprigs of piñon through the door knocker and piecing out the message *"Bienvenidos a los Arnold"* with gravel on the doorstep.

They expected us, but they weren't there to greet us. Because they renegotiated their contract with Dad every summer that he came, it was their custom to wait a few days before the talks started. Mother had to cook during that period, and Dad had to irrigate and keep the place going. The work was tiring and the food was terrible. We were desperate for the Montoyas' help when they arrived.

Dad let me sit in on the negotiations this summer. He said I could learn some hard business sense from the bargaining, which began when he spread pink oilcloth on the big walnut outdoor table under the *portal*, set out ashtrays and Lucky Strikes, and pulled the cork on a gallon bottle of La Voragine Sweet Muscatel-Type Vino Fresno California A Family Tradition Of Gourmets Since 1934.

Amadeo and Excilda turned up in their truck on the afternoon of the third day. There were enormous greetings all around. I had grown *"casi una yarda,"* my mother was *"mas bella que antes,"* and my father was *"mas gordito y rico que nunca,"* a cunning opening shot which described him as richer than ever, and even rich enough to put on waistline.

Excilda went into the house with my mother, to tell her about the new *primos, nipotes* and *nietos*. Ordinarily, my mother loved talk of family; she came from a large and undistinguished family herself, notable for poltroonery and the seduction of minors, as it later turned out when her great-grandmother's diaries were published by the University of Alabama Press. But she always thought of them as being rich in Southern tradition. However, Excilda's family chatter annoyed her; there were never any grandchildren or cousins named Ashley or Lucinda; just Osmundos and Guadalupes, Alfonsos and Violas, all suffering from infant diarrhea.

My father and Amadeo Montoya and I sat around the walnut table, and the two men cracked the jug.

"How have you been, Amadeo?" It was plainly the wrong question.

"Well, Mr. Arnold, you remember that cold spell we had back

95

around Old Christmas. It got fourteen, fifteen below for almost a week. The Indians couldn't even open up the ditches 'cause the sluice gates were froze."

"It was nice and warm down in Mobile in January. Maybe you should have written me a letter about it. We don't get the Sagrado weather report down there."

"Well, this cold didn't hurt your house any, except for some windows cracked on the east side from some water got under the putty and froze, but up in. . . ."

"How many window panes?"

"Five or six, I forget. I got a receipt for glass from Roybal. It's somewhere in the *troca*; I can go get it in a minute."

"We'll come to that later."

"Up in Río Conejo there was this *chingao* wind that came straight out of Texas, killed two calves. They were gonna be fine calves."

"Where was that Archuleta boy that takes care of your stock in the winter? He's supposed to get your animals in the barn."

"You're right, Mr. Arnold. You're right about that, but that *cabrón* didn't show up. I think he got married."

"Married! He's only ten years old!"

"You're thinking about Epifanio. Epifanio went to live with his uncle in Arroyo Coronado. This was his brother Wilfredo, he's about seventeen. He didn't show up. He went to work for the Park Service over by Ute Mesa and had this girl with him. If it wasn't for that *chingadero* I wouldn't of lost two calves."

"You're not trying to blame me for those calves, are you? I told you to get winter help on the place in Conejo, and said I'd pay half your help's salary, didn't I?"

"Sure you did, Mr. Arnold. I didn't say it was your fault. How could you help what happens up there in Río Conejo when you're down there in Alabama on the beach watching those sailboats in the warm. . . ."

"Amadeo, wouldn't you like another glass of vino? I'm going to have one."

"*Un traguito, no más.*"

Amadeo and my father drank off a glass of wine, commenting on its smoothness and power, and silently prepared for the next round of negotiation.

"You have a real nice garden here, Mr. Arnold."

"Thank you, Amadeo. I owe much of it to you."

"Aw, well, I'm no gardener. My brother Esteban is the man who can make things grow. Me, I just slap a lot of manure on the plants and pray for a little rain in April. You know."

"A little rain in April is always a good thing, Amadeo."

"A gift from God. A true gift, because it doesn't rain much in April."

"How were the April rains this year, Amadeo?"

"There wasn't one. Not a drop. Dust blowing all the time. If you could have seen that *chingao* dust you'd have thought you were in Texas. I can still taste the dust."

"The rose trees look very good, in spite of all the dust. They should bud out very well in July. Did you water them?"

"Oh, sure. Your ditch was running sometimes. They got enough water. But it was the manure."

"The manure . . . ?"

"Sure. I put a lot of manure on the roses. You know Excilda's brother-in-law Cruz Gutierrez, got all those horses?"

"How much manure?"

"Four truckloads?"

"Are you asking me? I was down there on the beach in Alabama watching the sailboats go by."

"Make it two truckloads. Prime horse manure. Fresh. I had to wear a bandana over my face."

"Amadeo, we haven't even started on this wine. It's going to turn sour if we just sit here and look at it."

"*Una copita, nada más. Gracias.*"

"*Salud.*"

"*Salud, patrón.*"

"Now don't you start calling me *patrón*. I'm not your *patrón*. Those days are gone forever, thank God."

"You said it." They drank another glass of muscatel, and noted that several minutes in the sun had baked some of the impurities from it.

"I hear Excilda telling my wife all about the new grandchildren in Conejo. How many?"

"Four this winter. Three living. Margarita's little girl died. Named Consuelo."

"Oh, I'm sorry, Amadeo. I'm very sorry. How old was she?"

"Two and a half months. Pretty little girl, *rubia*, looked almost like a *gringa*. She died in April."

"What was the matter?"

"She had the shits. Goddamn, Margarita told all the kids to boil water before they gave it to the baby, but somebody forgot. Probably Francisco, that stupid *pendejo*, but he says it wasn't him."

"You had a doctor for her?"

"Sure. Old Anchondo. He couldn't do nothing for her, but he sure sent his bill to us."

"I think your glass is empty, Amadeo. There's plenty of wine left, and if you'd just pass your glass. . . ."

"I don't think I want any more just this minute, Mr. Arnold, thank you."

The preliminary negotiations were over.

"Would you and Excilda like to work here again this summer, Amadeo?"

Amadeo thought this over very carefully, and seemed doubtful. "Gee, I don't know about that, Mr. Arnold. Roybal offered me a job for the whole year, full time, driving his *troca*. No paperwork or anything. I just drive his machine."

"Roybal doesn't pay very well; he never has."

"No, well, but he offered me thirty-five to start, five days, a half Saturday, drive the *troca* home at night, he pays gas."

"Thirty-five! You know Roybal's never paid anybody thirty-five dollars a week in his life. Not even that dumb cousin of his that can't tell piñon from mahogany."

"He pays old Bernabe forty now. They're paying sixty up at Molybdenum, bucket man."

"Amadeo, that mine must be more than a hundred miles from Conejo. You want to drive a hundred miles twice a day?"

"No, Mr. Arnold. I don't want to, but man, sixty dollars, that's a lot of money."

"What about thirty for you, twelve for Excilda, I pay gas from here to Conejo, no Sundays? I'll let you use my gas coupons."

"I don't know. Excilda says she has to do a lot fancier cooking around here than up at home. She says it takes a lot out of her."

"Thirty-five for you, fifteen for Exilda, but by God we get *cabrito en sangre* at least once a month, from one of your own kids, and that goat better not be more than two months old."

"Thirty-five and fifteen. That only makes fifty a week, Mr. Arnold. Up at Molybdenum. . . ."

"Thirty-five and fifteen is all I can pay this year. I can always go talk to the Maldonados."

"Mr. Arnold," said Amadeo after reflection, "you think maybe your wife and my wife would like some of this good wine before it all turns to vinegar? Man, I sure hate to see this good wine go to waste."

That night, my father asked me if I'd learned any hard business sense, and I said I thought I had, but I wasn't sure.

But it was a good summer, the best summer ever, from June to August, 1944. My mother found lots of people to play bridge with at La Posta Hotel and almost forgot that she was living in a mountain town full of Catholics and dangerous people who felt, however vaguely, that Lincoln Was Right. Dad would have to report to the Navy in late August, and he said he took his commission seriously. "I'm out of shape," he said, shortly after we arrived. "They're going to run my fanny off with a bunch of callow college boys when I show up. I'd better take off some flab." We rode almost every day, or hiked—we didn't swim; there were no swimming pools in Sagrado; water was too precious—and once we made a two-week camp in the Cola de Vaca Peaks in the Cordilldera, carrying all the gear on our backs.

For an old man (he was forty-one) he did pretty well. I still didn't understand why he'd insisted on joining the Navy at his age. Mother didn't understand, and neither did Paolo Bertucci. The War Production Board didn't think it was a good idea; they had told him his patriotic duty was to stay in Mobile to build landing craft and small, fast tankers with shallow drafts; but he had scurried around and snapped at people, threatened bureaucrats and finally called the Secretary of the Navy in Washington—a man named Knox—and got his commission at the same time as the Normandy invasion, an operation which employed more than a hundred of his landing craft. "You see," he told Paolo one evening in Mobile, when he'd dropped by to argue, "they're fighting the rest of the war on land. They won't be needing Arnold-made craft any more. The yard can go back to making shrimp trawlers and garbage scows. You can handle that sort of thing yourself."

"I think you're just like a little boy playing sailor," Paolo told him.

"You're right," Dad said. "I am. And don't try to stop me, or I'll put a six-pounder into your poop deck. You swab."

In August, after running me around the mountains until my nose bled every afternoon, he declared he was fit to wear the uniform. On his last day with us, my mother forewent her bridge game at La Posta and stayed home. Excilda roasted a kid, we each had a glass of Harvey's Bristol Cream before dinner, and Dad cracked a bottle of Chambertin 1934, which had probably never been drunk with goat meat before. We toasted the President, John Paul Jones and Lord Nelson. My mother refused to toast David Farragut, but I went along with it. After dinner, he telephoned Paolo Bertucci in Mobile.

"Papa's off to the seven seas." he said. "Everything going all right down there, you loathsome wop?"

"I think so," Paolo said. "We're squirting boats like a machine gun. I'd say as many as twenty-five per cent of them stay afloat when they hit the water, although they don't all float right side up."

"That's a pretty good average for a Genoese landlubber."

"I do have one question, though," Paolo said. "Some of the men asked me, and I thought I ought to check with you. When you're standing at the back part of the boat, facing toward the front of the boat, what do you call the right-hand side? Is it starboard or larboard?"

"The right-hand side is called the mizzenmast," Dad said. "You call the left-hand side the fo'c'sle. I knew we'd have a language problem if we let a dago run the yard. Maybe I ought to resign my commission and get back there."

"We'll make do without you, Frank," Paolo said. "Hell, all you ever did was get in the way. I'm already saving twenty thousand a month by using oakum instead of rivets."

"The paper said some landing craft sank halfway across the Channel on D-Day. Any idea who made them?"

"Couldn't have been us," Paolo said. "Ours don't sink; they capsize. Well, keep your powder dry, Olaf. My respects to your family. Tell Josh we always have a job for him as ship's cat."

"I wish you wouldn't let him talk to you that way, Frank," my mother said, when he reported the conversation. "It wasn't too many years ago that he was a carpenter or something."

"I'll work on the dignity angle when I get back," he said. "Right now Paolo's building boats and keeping five hundred men occupied. If I want deferential language I'll hire a butler to run the yard."

He left the next morning, wearing his new suntans. "Practice your Spanish, you ape, and be nice to people," he said. "Make new friends. Get a haircut once in a while. Don't suck your thumb. And don't get cute with your mother. A little flippancy goes a long way with her." He set his suitcase down on the gravel driveway and gazed around him, sighing. "God, I'm going to miss this country."

"I'll try not to set fire to it," I said.

"Good-by, Hoss."

"Good-by."

He got into the car with Amadeo for the long drive to the train. I went into the kitchen, where Excilda was preparing lunch.

"Can I have a *burrito?*"

"Say it in Spanish."

"*Puedo yo* have *un burrito?*"

"That's the way they teach it in school down there in Mobile, huh? Your father ought to get his money back."

"*Dame un burrito, pues.*"

"*¿Por favor?*"

"*Por favor.*"

Excilda gave me a *burrito*. You have to work for everything.

The night before school started I did ten push-ups in my bedroom, and had to quit. With all the sky in Sagrado there simply isn't any air in it.

Next morning, when the home-room teacher called the roll, I listened for familiar names, but the only one that rang a bell was Stenopolous. There was a Doctor Stenopolous I kept reading about in *The Conquistador*, the Sagrado newspaper, who seemed to be the only obstetrician in the area and was constantly on the jump. When local

101

news was slow, and it generally was slow, the paper would run a baby story. "Woman Gives Birth in Mayor's Office," a headline would run, or "Baby Delivered in Wagon on Load of Melons."

At the recess break I introduced myself to William Stenopolous, Jr., a chunky, brown-haired boy who looked as Greek as Eric the Red. "Call me Steenie," he said. I asked him about athletics, and he said that Helen De Crispin High School had a track team, despite the lack of breatheable air.

"We're conditioned to it," he said. "Now, you take Swenson . . ." He pointed across the school yard to a tall, bulgy-looking brute surrounded by girls. "Swenson's a borderline moron and a prime horse's ass, but he has a forty-seven-inch chest. He's all lung, like those Peruvian Indians that carry grand pianos up and down the Andes."

"He seems to be in good shape," I said.

"Oh, he's got a good musculature on him," Steenie went on, "and some primitive bones to hang it on. Like all Scandinavians, he tends to run to calcium. I tried to get the calipers on him once, for some skull measurements, but he threatened to pound me. My guess is, his head's solid bone down to the center of it, where there's a cavity just big enough for his pituitary gland."

"I don't want to start off on the wrong foot," I said, "but my father's a Scandinavian clear back to Sven Fork-Beard. We're not *all* idiots."

"Don't take anything I say personally," Steenie said. "I have Sagrado-itis of the mouth." Sagrado-itis is the local name for violent diarrhea. "And there are exceptions about Scandinavians. I even heard once that Ibsen was a Norwegian. I doubt it, but that's the story." He backed away and looked at me searchingly. "You from the South?"

"Mobile, Alabama."

"There's a Negro in school here, in the tenth grade. Are you going to lynch him?"

"Not unless he tries to marry my sister," I told him. "As long as he stays in his place."

"And calls you 'Boss'?"

"Well, sure."

"All right, then. We don't want racial trouble out here. And don't call him a Negro. He thinks he's an Anglo. We only recognize three kinds of people in Sagrado: Anglos, Indians and Natives. You keep your categories straight and you'll make out all right. Do you have anything against your sister marrying an Anglo?"

"To tell you the truth, I don't even have a sister."

"Now, you see that girl over there by the cottonwood tree? The one with the knockers?" I saw her. She would have stood out in any crowd. "What would you say she was?"

"She looks like a Creole," I said.

"Arnold, you have a lot of work ahead of you. She's a Native. Her name's Viola Lopez. She speaks Spanish and English, and she's a Catholic. Don't ever make the mistake of calling her a Mexican. Her brother will kill you. Of course, if you call her a Creole she'll get confused as hell and think you mean she's part Negro—that is, part dark-skinned Anglo—and her brother will kill you again. So think of her as a Native, unless you're comparing her with an Indian. Then she's 'white.' Got it?"

"I think so," I said. "But what about the Negro?"

"I already explained that to you. He's an Anglo. That is, he's an Anglo unless you're differentiating between him and an Indian. Then *he's* 'white.' I admit he's awfully dark to be white, but that's the way it goes around here. You have to learn our little customs and folkways, or it's your ass. And if you've got any Texas blood in you, you'd better take 'spik' and 'greaser' out of your vocabulary. If there's a minority group at all around here, it's the Anglos. By the way, do you know any judo? I taught judo to a Commando class this summer."

"Aren't you a little young for that? You don't look any older than I do."

"Uncle Sam takes his talent where he finds it. There's a war on. Now, you be the Kraut and come at me with a knife." Steenie showed me some judo holds that I'd read about in *Life* magazine a year or so earlier.

"You'll learn," he said, afterward. "If the war turns against us, and we get invaded, this knowledge will come in very handy. My plan is to head up into the mountains and hold out, like Mikhailovich, harassing the enemy. I wish there was a railroad around here. I know how to blow up a railroad. You know anything about boats?"

"That's about all I do know anything about," I said.

"Do you know how to sink one?"

"Anybody can sink one. It's learning how to keep one afloat that's hard. My father told me once I'd foundered more catboats than anybody my age and weight. He said I hold the Southern Conference record in poor seamanship."

"Well," Steenie went on, "bad seamanship or not, it won't do you any good out here. That's the trouble. All this military talent going to waste. Sagrado is the worst place to fight a war I ever saw. You know, they've got people up there in La Cima"—he pointed to the mountains—"that don't even know there *is* a war. The last one they heard about was when the Spanish Armada got sunk. Second Punic, I think it was, or Jenkins's Ear."

"I think it was the War of the Roses," I said, "but I'm a little rusty on it myself."

"What does your old man do for a living?" he asked suddenly.

"Mine runs a chain of whorehouses in Juarez. I helped him pick the girls for it this summer. Exhausting work, let me tell you."

"I thought you said you were teaching judo to the Commandos."

"That was the early part of the summer. No, really, what does he do?"

"He's a Navy officer right now," I said. "Before that he ran a shipyard. He built the *Serapis*, the *Bon Homme Richard* and *The Golden Hind*."

Steenie thought that over. "I think you're crapping me," he said finally. "It's just what I deserve."

I had lunch that first day with Parker Holmes, leaning against a mud wall behind the school and eating from our lunch boxes. Excilda had packed mine, but Mother had supervised it: sliced ham between two slices of soggy bread, no mustard. A gangly boy with ears that reached out sideways for the most subtle sounds, Parker was munching something he claimed was elkburger, "cut off from around the brisket." His father was a game warden, and brought home lots of confiscated, illegally shot meat.

"This country," Parker said, grinding his sandwich, "abounds in game. Abounds. Elk, like this here, Rocky Mountain Mule Deer, bear, antelope, rabbit—both jackass and bunny—grouse, bandtail pigeon, snipe, rail, gallinule, *gallopavo merriami* and pea fowl. We also got the inedible, like feral dogs and pussycats, *zopilote*, fish-eating beaver and two-stripe skunk." He waved his arms to indicate vast populations of fauna. "A game biologist can go ape in this country. Ape."

In the afternoon, after a clumsy speech of welcome by the school principal, a small, pop-eyed man named Alexander who got tangled in the microphone cord and fell heavily, I found Steenie in the baked-mud school yard talking to a girl, medium-sized, slim with black hair and fair skin. Steenie appeared to be examining her face closely as I approached them.

"Not a blemish," she was saying. "You see? It worked."

"I still insist," Steenie said to her, "that acne is caused by psychiatric imbalance and not by chocolate malts. You could have drunk six a day and still not had a pimple. You deprived yourself for no reason."

"Well, how about this?" she said. She turned her back to him and pulled her skirt tight against her behind. "I didn't put an ounce of lard on it this summer. It's hard as a rock. No, don't touch it. Take my word for it." She saw me and smiled. "What do you think? Isn't that a pretty behind?"

"Turn around, Marcia, and I'll introduce the front part first," Steenie said. "Marcia Davidson, Jericho Arnold. Marcia's old man is rector of St. Thomas's Episcopal, but don't bother watching your language."

"It's Joshua," I said. "Jericho's where I fit the battle."

"That's a cute little scar you have," she said. "Are you sensitive about it?"

I noticed that she had dark circles under her eyes, like mice. "Did you get those shiners from asking rude questions?"

"No," she said. "They're functional. I've been getting them every month since I was twelve. Steenie's been giving me some exercises to help the cramps."

"How are they working, by the way?" he asked her.

"The cramps are better, but I still get that gicky feeling."

I knew I was beginning to turn red, and I started to get that gicky feeling myself.

"Couldn't we just talk about something else?"

"All right," Marcia said. "If it upsets you. But Steenie's my medical advisor." She said she was pleased to meet me, and walked away after shaking hands again. Her hand was cool and dry, and not gicky at all.

"Nice kid," Steenie said. "My only patient. She draws the line at examinations, of course. . . . Now, turn your back to me and bend your right arm as if you were carrying a rifle at shoulder arms. Ordinarily, I'd use a three-foot length of piano wire for this maneuver, if you were a real Kraut, but I'll let you off easy."

I turned my back and bent my arm, and he whipped his rolled handkerchief around my neck and assured me I was a dead Kraut.

When the bell rang for the last class of the first day, Steenie and I joined the herd and began to push through the double doors. There was the usual amount of shoving and bad manners and goosing and giggling; Point Clear behavior wasn't any more courtly. But in the middle of all this happy horseplay, somebody jammed an elbow into my ribs, a deliberate and painful jab.

I scanned the unfamiliar faces, most of them dusty from an hour spent on the grassless playing ground; Point Clear was lush and its grounds were closely covered in fine golf-course lawn. I saw a few faces that I recognized: Steenie, Parker, the white-haired look-alike Cloyd girls, and Viola Lopez, whom Steenie had pointed out to me because of her enormous, precocious bosom. None of these people had jabbed me in the side.

To my left, burning out of the sea of pink and tan faces, was the meanest-looking human pan I'd ever seen, a brown, flat face with hot black eyes, a mouth so thin and lipless and straight that it seemed like the slot in a piggy bank. The face was framed by rich, thick, black, shiny hair, long and carefully combed; it swept around the top half of the ears on its way to the duck's ass arrangement in back, and the side burns reached nearly to the bend of the jawbone.

By the time I saw this last face we'd all broken through the jam-up at the door and were pouring untidily down a corridor. Hate-Face fell into step beside me, shoving gently and insistently with his shoulder.

"Jew are a fahkeen queer," he said pleasantly. "I am goeen to bahss your ass."

I brought a right up from around my ankles, forgetting what science I knew, and landed it on his cheekbone.

His head rocked back perhaps half an inch, and a small spot of red appeared on the dark tan skin. He turned the lips upward, showing handsome teeth, and said softly, through the smile, "Jew heet like a fahkeen gorl. Now I am goeen to cot you estones off." He presented an upraised middle finger to me, said *"Toma, pendejo,"* and walked away toward music class, his long arms brushing against his thighs.

My legs were quivering, and I was having some trouble getting my breath as I followed him to class, wondering whether estones meant what I thought it did. Steenie was waiting near the door.

"I don't want you to think me crude," he said, "but may I perform the autopsy? I've never had a real cadaver to cut on, and what I really want to see is whether your brain is as small as I suspect."

"I guess I started school on the wrong foot," I said.

"Let's say you've just committed suicide," he said. "Why did you pick Chango? You got something against living?"

"Chango?"

"Maximiliano Lopez. Chango is his nickname, but don't use it to his face. No, in your case it's perfectly safe to call him Chango. You're going to die anyway. It means monkey; did you notice his arms?"

"Yes," I said, "they're long."

"That's only part of it. They're strong, too. I estimate he spends three hours out of every twenty-four hanging by his hands from a branch. Sometimes, the story goes, he hangs by only one hand, while he feeds himself bananas with the other." Steenie patted me tenderly on the shoulder, and sighed. "I don't think you've learned enough Commando to protect yourself."

"Why did he jab me? He damn near broke a rib for me when we were coming in."

"Did you by any chance stare at his sister's tits today? It's a natural thing to do, of course. I did it myself, once, and got off with a chipped incisor and some minor gum damage."

Joe Mondragón Defies The Establishment

▼▲▼▲▼▲▼▲▼▲▼▲▼▲▼▲▼▲▼▲▼▲▼▲▼▲▼▲▼▲▼▲▼▲▼▲▼

John Nichols

John Nichols lives at Taos, New Mexico, and specializes in the local Mexican-American population, with Anglo developers, pushers, thugs, and tourists not far behind in his cast of characters. In his first and most truly humorous novel (it is the first volume of a trilogy), *The Milagro Beanfield War*, the once-flourishing village of Milagro is a ghost town, the water rights having been acquired by Ladd Devine III, who lives on and operates a guest ranch, owns most of the business establishments in the new Milagro along the highway, and plans to put in a golf course where the bean fields used to be. Scrappy, battered Joe Mondragón, who has refused to sell out and still lives on his family plot in the old town, defiantly plants a small patch of beans and turns on the forbidden water, thereby touching off a wild series of skirmishes with Ladd Devine (called by the natives *El Zopilote*, the buzzard) and his minions, including the state police. The crisis unites the *paisanos* as never before, but their chances of beating the establishment seem remote at the end of the book.

Nichols's Mexicans stay on the comic side of the narrow line between humor and pathos. Most readers find them cute, quaint, and enjoyable. Others, who know Mexicans as well as Nichols, or better, are uncomfortable with what, for them, is caricature, and they have a feeling that Nichols's political convictions and lifestyle have rubbed off on his Latin neighbors. He "understands history from a Marxist point of view,"* in his own words, and he is really dramatizing the class conflict in his story. His raffish sense of humor conceals the party line.

*James Vinson and D. L. Kirkpatrick, eds., *Twentieth-Century Western Writers* (Detroit, Michigan: Gale Research, 1982), 571.

JOE MONDRAGÓN WAS THIRTY-SIX YEARS OLD AND FOR A LONG time he had held no steady job. He had a wife, Nancy, and three children, and his own house, which he had built with his own hands, a small tight adobe that required mudding every two or three autumns.

From *The Milagro Beanfield War* (New York: Holt, Rinehart & Winston, 1976), 19–33.

Joe was always hard up, always hustling to make a buck. Over the years he had learned how to do almost any job. He knew everything about building houses, he knew how to mix mud and straw just right to make strong adobes that would not crumble. Though unlicensed, he could steal and lay his own plumbing, do all the electric fixtures in a house, and hire five peons at slave wages to install a septic tank that would not overflow until the day after Joe died or left town. Given half the necessary equipment, he could dig a well, and he understood everything there was to understand about pumps. He could tear down a useless tractor and piece it together again so niftily it would plow like balls of fire for at least a week before blowing up and maiming its driver; and he could disk and seed a field well and irrigate it properly. "Hell," Joe liked to brag, "I can grow sweet corn just by using my own spit and a little ant piss!" He could raise (or rustle) sheep and cattle and hogs, too, and slaughter and butcher them all. And if you asked him to, he could geld a pony or castrate a pig with the same kind of delicate authoritative finesse Michelangelo must have used carving his *Pietà*.

Joe had his own workshop crammed full of tools he had begged, borrowed, stolen, or bought from various friends, enemies, and employers down through the years. In that shop he sometimes made skinning knives out of cracked buzz saw blades and sold them to hunters in the fall for five or six bucks. At the drop of a five-dollar bill he could also fashion an ornate Persian wine goblet from an old quart pop bottle. Then again, if the need arose and the money to pay for it was resting lightly on his main workbench like an open-winged butterfly taking five, Joe probably could have invented the world's tiniest dart gun, to be used by scientists for crippling, but not killing, mosquitoes. Just to survive there had to be almost nothing Joe couldn't or would not at least try to do.

The Mondragón house was surrounded by junk, by old engines, by parts of motors, by automobile guts, refrigerator wiring, tractor innards. One shed was filled with wringer washing machines, and when Joe had the time he puttered over them until they were "running" again; then he tried—and often managed—to sell them . . . with pumps that went on the fritz (or wringer gears that neatly stripped themselves) ten minutes after Joe's three-month warranty (in writing) expired. This presented no problem, however, because for a very small consideration Joe was more than willing to fix whatever broke in whatever he had sold you.

In a sense, Joe was kept perpetually busy performing minor miracles for what usually amounted to a less-than-peanuts remuneration. Still, when something, when *any*thing was wrong in town, when a pump was frozen or a cow was sick or the outhouse had blown down, the call went out for Joe Mondragón, who would defy rain, hail, blizzards, tornadoes, and earthquakes in order to skid his pickup with the four bald retreads and no spare to a stop in your front yard and have the thing or the animal or whatever it was temporarily patched up and functioning again. Reeking of energy like an oversexed tomcat, Joe was always charging hell-bent for election around town in his old yellow pickup, like as not with a beer clutched tightly in one fist— arrogant little Joe Mondragón, come to fix your trouble and claim your two bits, who didn't take no shit from no body.

But he was tired, Joe had to admit that. He was tired, like most of his neighbors were tired, from trying to earn a living off the land in a country where the government systematically gathered up the souls of little ranchers and used them to light its cigars. Joe was tired of spending twenty-eight hours a day like a chicken-thieving mongrel backed up against the barn wall, neck hairs bristling, teeth bared, knowing that in the end he was probably going to get his head blown off anyway. He was tired of meeting each spring with the prospect of having to become a migrant and head north to the lettuce and potato fields in Colorado where a man groveled under the blazing sun ten hours a day for one fucking dollar an hour. He was tired, too, of each year somehow losing a few cows off the permits he had to graze them on the government's National Forest land, and he was tired of the way permit fees were always being hiked, driving himself and his kind not only batty, but also out of business. And he was damn fed up with having to buy a license to hunt deer on land that had belonged to Grandfather Mondragón and his cronies, but which now resided in the hip pockets of either Smokey the Bear, the state, or the local malevolent despot, Ladd Devine the Third.

Usually, in fact, Joe did not buy a license to hunt deer in the mountains surrounding his hometown. Along with most everybody else in

Milagro, he figured the dates of a hunting season were so much bullshit. If he hankered for meat, Joe simply greased up his .30-06, hopped into the pickup, and went looking for it. Once a Forest Service vendido, Carl Abeyta, had caught Joe with a dead deer, a huge electric lamp, no license, and out of season to boot, and it cost Joe a hundred dollars plus a week in the Chamisa County Jail. In jail he half-starved to death and was pistol-whipped almost unconscious by a county jailer, Tod McNunn, for trying to escape by battering a hole in the cheap cinderblock wall with his head.

Joe had been in jail numerous times, usually just for a few hours, for being drunk, for fighting, for borrowing (and consuming) Devine Company sheep, and each time it had cost him fifteen or twenty-five dollars, and usually he had been manhandled, too. The corrections personnel laughed when they clobbered Joe because he was funny, being so small and ferocious, weighing only about a hundred and twenty-five pounds, kicking and hitting, trying to murder them when he was drunk, and when he was sober, too. Sometimes they tried to hold him off a little for sport, but Joe was too dangerous, being the kind of person—like the heralded Cleofes Apodaca of yore—who would have slugged a bishop. So they tended to belt him hard right off the bat and then let him lie. Joe had lost a few teeth in that jail, and his nose had been operated on by police fists, clubs, and pistol butts so as to conform to the prevalent local profile. Outside the jail Joe had broken fingers on both his hands hitting people or horses or doors or other such things. "I ain't afraid of nothing," he bragged, and thought he could prove it, although when he said that his wife Nancy hooted derisively: "Oh no, that's right, you're not afraid of *any*thing."

But Joe was tired of the fighting. Tired of it because in the end he never surfaced holding anything more potent than a pair of treys. In the end he just had his ass kicked from the corral to next Sunday, and nothing ever changed. In the end half his gardens and half his fields shriveled in a drought, even though Indian Creek practically formed a swimming pool in his living room. In fact, Milagro itself was half a ghost town, and all the old west side beanfields were barren, because over thirty-five years ago, during some complicated legal and political maneuverings known as the 1935 Interstate Water Compact, much of Milagro's Indian Creek water had been reallocated to big-time farmers down in the southeast portion of the state or in Texas, leaving folks like Joe Mondragón high and much too dry.

This situation had caused a deep, long-smoldering, and fairly universal resentment, but nobody, least of all Joe Mondragón, had ever been able to figure out how to bring water back to that deserted west side land, most of which, by now, belonged to Ladd Devine the Third and his motley assortment of dyspeptic vultures, who (not surprisingly, now that they owned it) had figured out a way to make the west side green again.

But then one day Joe suddenly decided to irrigate the little field in front of his dead parents' decaying west side home (which Joe still owned—in itself a miracle) and grow himself some beans. It was that simple. And yet irrigating that field was an act as irrevocable as Hitler's invasion of Poland, Castro's voyage on the *Granma*, or the assassination of Archduke Ferdinand, because it was certain to catalyze tensions which had been building for years, certain to precipitate a war.

And like any war, this one also had roots that traveled deeply into the past.

For several hundred years, and until quite recently, Milagro had been a sheepy town. Nearly all the fathers of Joe Mondragón's generation had been sheepmen. There was no man, however, and there had been no men for more than a hundred years, perhaps, who had truly made a living off sheep, the basic reason for this being that Milagro was a company town, and almost every herder, simply in order to survive as a sheepman, had been connected to the Ladd Devine Sheep Company. And being a sheepman connected to the Devine Company was like trying to raise mutton in a tank full of sharks, barracudas, and piranha fish.

For this, the people of the Miracle Valley had the U.S. Government to thank. Because almost from the moment it was drawn up and signed in 1848, the Treaty of Guadalupe Hidalgo, which not only ended the war between the United States and Mexico, but also supposedly guaranteed to the Spanish-surnamed southwestern peoples their communal grazing lands, was repeatedly broken. Shortly after the war, in fact, the U.S. Congress effectively outlawed their communal property, passing vast acreages into the public domain, tracts which then suddenly wound up in the hands of large American ranching enterprises like the Devine Company. Later, during Teddy Roosevelt's era, much remaining communal territory was designated National Forest in which a rancher could only run his animals providing he had the money and political pull to obtain grazing permits.

Hence, soon after the 1848 war, most local ranchers found themselves up to their elbows in sheep with no place to graze them. In due course the small operators were wiped out either from lack of access to grazing land or from trying to compete with the large companies that now dominated the public domain and Forest Service preserves. The sheepmen who survived did so only by becoming indentured servants to the large companies that controlled the range and the grazing permit system.

In Milagro, this meant that since the last quarter of the nineteenth century most sheep ranchers had been serfs of the Devine Company, which, during the seventies and eighties, in one of those democratic and manifestly destined sleights of Horatio Alger's hand (involving a genteel and self-righteous sort of grand larceny, bribery, nepotism, murder, mayhem, and general all-around and all-American nefarious skulduggery), had managed to own outright, or secure the grazing rights to, all the property on the Jorge Sandoval Land Grant in Chamisa County.

At the end of each year since this takeover, every sheepman, woman, and child in Milagro had discovered themselves heavily in debt to the Devine Company. In fact, after an average of ten years under the sheep company's tutelage, just about every man, including men like Joe Mondragón's father, Esequiel, had owed the rest of whatever resources he might accumulate in his lifetime to whichever Ladd Devine happened to be sitting on the family nest egg at that particular moment.

Of course, the Ladd Devine Company had not only been interested in land and sheep and its company (now Nick Rael's) store. It owned controlling interests in both the First National Bank of Chamisaville and its Doña Luz branch. The Dancing Trout Dude Ranch and Health Spa had been operating on the Devine estate up in Milagro Canyon ever since the early twenties. When the Pilar Café was constructed across from the company store in 1949, it was a Devine operation. And when, more recently, the Enchanted Land Motel was built on the north-south highway to handle the new breed of pudgy tourists who simpered by in their baroque apartment houses on wheels, it was a Devine-financed and Devine-controlled operation.

To be truthful, the Devine Company, which had gotten fat on sheep, was not dealing in wool anymore. The company had much more interest in a project called the Indian Creek Dam, a structure—to be located in Milagro Canyon—that was considered the essential cornerstone of a Devine development endeavor known as the Miracle Valley Recreation Area.

A dam in Milagro Canyon had been the dream of both Ladd Devine Senior and the present caudillo, Ladd Devine the Third, who took over the Devine operation when his grandfather (who was eighty-nine at the time) was caught alone and on horseback up beyond the Little Baldy Bear Lakes in an early autumn snowstorm back in 1958. Ladd Devine the Second, a profligate and playboy who married five times, put a bullet in one ear and out the other on the Italian Riviera at the age of thirty-nine, thus accounting for Ladd Devine the Third's early ascendancy to the throne.

The Ladd Devine Company had started drawing up plans for the recreation development about the same time people were losing their water rights and beginning a wholesale exodus from the hapless west side. The original Ladd Devine had not objected much to the unfair 1935 water compact shenanigans, which somewhat damaged his sheep operations by driving many of his herders elsewhere, because he was too busy buying up those herders' momentarily worthless land at bargain-basement prices. In this way, during the years immediately following World War II, when the water compact really began to be enforced, almost all the abandoned and apparently worthless land on the west side passed into Devine hands.

And now—*Que milagro!*—the Indian Creek Dam was conveniently going to restore water rights to the west side so Ladd Devine the Third could bless the few surviving small farmers of Milagro with a ritzy subdivision molded around an exotic and very green golf course.

The dam would be built across Indian Creek at the mouth of Milagro Canyon, establishing a mile-and-a-half-long lake whose easternmost shore would extend up to within hailing distance of the Dancing Trout's main lodge. And the dam—or paying for it, that is—would be made possible by creating a conservancy district whose boundaries, for taxation purposes, would incorporate almost all the town's largely destitute citizens.

Wherein lay a rather profound rub.

At least one person understood this rub. Hence, right after Ladd Devine the Third announced plans for the Miracle Valley Recreation Area (which would include the Indian Creek Reservoir, the Miracle Valley Estates and Golf Course, and the Miracle Mountain Ski Valley) by erecting an elaborate wooden sign on the north-south highway just below town, the old bartender at the Frontier, Tranquilino Jeantete, began telling anybody who would listen:

"You watch. The conservancy district and the dam is a dirty trick. Like the 1935 water compact, it's one more way to steal our houses and our land. We'll be paying the taxes for Ladd Devine's lake. And when we can't pay our conservancy assessments, they'll take our land and give it to Devine. And that fucking Zopilote will sit up there on his throne in his fucking castle putting pennies on our eyes as they carry us to the camposanto, one by one."

But most farmers, completely baffled by the complexity of a conservancy district, did not know what to do. Should they hire a lawyer and fight the vulture? Or should they just sit tight and let this terrible thing happen the way terrible things had been happening now ever since the 1848 war, trusting that, like Amarante Córdova, they could somehow, miraculously, survive?

In the end, after much talk and many heated arguments, the people shrugged, laughing uneasily and a little ashamedly. "That conservancy district and that dam," they philosophized, "will be as hard to live with as Pacheco's pig."

Pacheco being an enormous, shifty-eyed, hysterically lonely man who—in the time-honored tradition of Cleofes Apodaca and Padre Sinkovich—had been losing his marbles at a vertiginous rate ever since his wife died six years ago, and who owned one of the world's most ornery sows, an animal he could never keep penned. For years it had been a regular thing in Milagro to see unsteady, mammoth Seferino Pacheco staggering across fields or splashing through puddles in the dirt roadways, searching for his recalcitrant porker, which was usually inhaling a neighbor's garden or devouring somebody's chickens. Pacheco was forever knocking on front doors and back doors and outhouse doors, asking after his sow. And people were forever shouting at, and shooting at, and throwing rocks at Pacheco's gargantuan, voracious animal. Yet for a long time the pig had led a charmed life, nonchalantly absorbing high-powered lead lumps in its thick haunches, or else—it being also a rather swift pig—escaping on the run unscathed. "Maybe that marrana carries a chunk of oshá in her cunt that protects her from poisonous people," Onofre Martínez once giggled. And because the pig, with Pacheco gimping crazily after it, had become such a familiar sight all over town, sayings had grown out of the situation. Such as: "He's more trouble than Pacheco's pig." Or: "She's got an appetite like Pacheco's pig." And again: "It's as indestructible as Pacheco's pig."

And of course: "That conservancy district and that dam will be as hard to live with as Pacheco's pig."

Which is about where things stood when Joe Mondragón suddenly tugged on his irrigation boots, flung a shovel into his pickup, and drove over to his parents' crumbling farmhouse and small dead front field in the west side ghost town. Joe spent about an hour chopping weeds in the long unused Roybal ditch, and then, after digging a small feeder trench from Indian Creek into the ditch, he opened the Roybal ditch headgate at the other end so water could flow onto that fallow land.

After that Joe stood on the ditch bank smoking a cigarette. It was a soft and misty early spring morning; trees had only just begun to leaf out. Fields across the highway were still brown, and snow lay hip deep in the Midnight Mountains. Milagro itself was almost hidden in a lax bluish gauze of piñon smoke corning from all the fireplaces and cook stoves of its old adobe houses.

Last night, Joe recalled, the first moths had begun bapping their powdery wings against his kitchen windows; today water skeeters floated on the surface into his field, frantically skittering their legs.

The Trailways bus, with its lights still on, pulled off the highway to discharge and pick up a passenger. And the water just kept gurgling into that field, sending ants scurrying for their lives, while Joe puffed a cigarette, on one of the quietest lavender mornings of this particular spring.

About fifteen and a half minutes after Joe Mondragón first diverted water from Indian Creek into his parents' old beanfield, most of Milagro knew what he had done. Fifteen and a half minutes being as long as it took immortal, ninety-three-year-old Amarante Córdova to travel from a point on the Milagro-García highway spur next to Joe's outlaw beanfield to the Frontier Bar across the highway, catty-corner to Rael's General Store.

Back in 1914 Amarante had been Milagro's first sheriff. And he still wore the star from that time pinned to the lapel of the three-piece woolen suit he had been wearing, summer and winter, for the last thirty years. The only person still inhabiting the west side ghost town, Amarante lived there on various welfare allotments (and occasional doles from Sally, the letter-writing Doña Luz daughter) in an eight-room adobe farmhouse whose roof had caved into seven of the eight rooms. Until the year before Jorge from Australia keeled over with his mouth full of candied sweet potato, Amarante had gotten around in a 1946 Dodge pickup. But one summer day he steered it off the gorge road on a return trip from a wood run to Conejos Junction, was somehow thrown clear onto a ledge, and from that spectacular vantage point he watched his rattletrap do a swan dive into the Rio Grande eight hundred feet below. Since that day Amarante had been on foot, and also since that day, come rain or come shine, he'd walked the mile from his crumbling adobe to town and back again, babbling to himself all the way and occasionally lubricating his tongue with a shot of rotgut from the half-pint bottle that was a permanent fixture in his right-hand baggy suit pocket.

On this particular day, as soon as Amarante had safely landed his crippled frame on a stool in the huge empty Frontier Bar and fixed a baleful bloodshot eye on the owner, eighty-eight-year-old Tranquilino Jeantete, he said in Spanish (he did not speak English, or read or write in either language):

"José Mondragón is irrigating his old man's beanfield over there on the west side."

117

Tranquilino turned up his hearing aid, and, after fumbling in his pockets for a pair of glasses, he perched the cracked lenses on his nose, muttering, "Eh?"

"José Mondragón is irrigating his old man's beanfield over there on the west side."

Tranquilino still couldn't hear too well, so he muttered "Eh?" again. Neither man's pronunciation was very good: they had six teeth between them.

Ambrosio Romero, a burly carpenter who worked at the Doña Luz mine, sauntered through the door for his morning constitutional just as Amarante repeated: "José Mondragón is irrigating his old man's beanfield over there on the west side."

Ambrosio said, "Come again? When are you gonna learn how to talk, cousin? Why don't you go down to the capital and buy some wooden teeth? Say that once more."

With a sigh, Amarante lisped, "José Mondragón is irrigating his old man's beanfield over there on the west side."

"*Ai, Chihuahua!*" Ambrosio made his usual morning gesture to Tranquilino Jeantete, who slid a glass across the shiny bar, selected a bottle, and poured to where Ambrosio indicated stop with his finger. In silence the miner belted down the liquor, then belched, his eyes starting to water, and as he left he remarked: "What does that little jerk want to do, cause a lot of trouble?"

Ambrosio went directly from the bar to Rael's store where he bought some Hostess Twinkies for a midmorning snack at the mine, and also casually mentioned to Nick Rael, "I hear José Mondragón is irrigating over on the other side of the highway."

Nick's instinctive reaction to this news was, "What's that little son of a bitch looking for, a kick in the head?"

Four men and two women in Rael's store heard this exchange. They were Gomersindo Leyba, an ancient ex-sheepman who would, for a dollar, chauffeur anybody without wheels down to the Doña Luz Piggly-Wiggly to do their shopping; Tobias Arguello, a onetime bean farmer who had sold all his land to Ladd Devine the Third in order to send his two sons to the state university (one had dropped out to become a career army man, the other had been drafted and killed in Vietnam); Teofila Chacón, the mother of thirteen kids, all living, and

118

at present the evening barmaid at the Frontier; Onofre Martínez, a one-armed ex-sheepman who was known as the Staurolite Baron and also as the father of Bruno Martínez, a state cop; and Ruby Archuleta, a lovely middle-aged woman who owned and operated a body shop and plumbing business just off the north-south highway between Milagro and Doña Luz in the Strawberry Mesa area.

These six people scattered like quail hit by buckshot. And by noon, many citizens engaged in various local enterprises were talking excitedly to each other about how feisty little Joe Mondragón had gone and diverted the water illegally into his parents' no-account beanfield.

And by and large, the townspeople had three immediate reactions to the news.

The first: *"Ai, Chihuahua!"*

The second: "What does that obnoxious little runt want to cause trouble for?"

And the third: "I'm not saying it's good or bad, smart or stupid, I'm not saying if I'm for or against. Let's just wait and see what develops."

At two that afternoon an informal meeting convened in Rael's General Store. Attending this meeting were the Milagro sheriff; an asthmatic real estate agent named Bud Gleason; Eusebio Lavadie, the great-great-great-grand-nephew of Carlos the ringside-seat millionaire, and the town's only rich Chicano rancher; the storekeeper, Nick Rael; two commissioners and a mayordomo of the Acequia Madre del Sur—Meliton Mondragón, Filiberto Vigil, and Vincent Torres; and the town's mayor, Sammy Cantú.

The sheriff, forty-three-year-old Bernabé Montoya, had held his job now for nine and a half years. All four of his election victories had come by three votes—27 to 24—over the Republican candidate, Pancho Armijo. Bernabé was an absentminded, rarely nasty, always bumbling, also occasionally very sensitive man who dealt mostly with drunks, with some animal rustling, with about five fatal car accidents a year, and with approximately seven knifings and shootings per annum. He also reluctantly assisted the state police, once in the spring and again in the fall, during which raids they confiscated maybe five hundred marijuana plants that later mysteriously turned up in the pockets of Chamisaville Junior High School kids. Bernabé had arrested Joe Mondragón a dozen times, and had personally driven him down to the Chamisa County Jail twice. In earlier times Joe and Bern-abé had run together, and the sheriff still admired his former pal's spunk, even though Joe was a constant hassle to the lawman's job—a troublemaker, a fuse that was always, unpredictably, burning.

Bernabé had gloomily called this meeting because he sensed a serious threat in Joe's beanfield. He had understood, as soon as he heard about the illegal irrigation, that you could not just waltz over and kick out Joe's headgate or post a sign ordering him to cease and desist. Because that fucking beanfield was an instant and potentially explosive symbol which no doubt had already captured the imaginations of a few disgruntled fanatics, and the only surprise about the whole affair, as Bernabé saw it, was, how come nobody had thought of it sooner?

"So I don't really know what to do," he told the gathering. "That's how come I called this meeting."

Eusebio Lavadie said, "What he's doing is illegal, isn't it illegal? Arrest him. Put him in jail. Throw away the key. Who's the mayordomo on that ditch?"

Vincent Torres, a meek, self-effacing old man, raised his hand.

"Well, you go talk to him," Lavadie huffed. "Tell him to cut out the crap or some of us will get together and break his fingers. Or shoot his horses. I don't see what all the fuss is about."

A commissioner for the Acequia Madre, Filiberto Vigil, said, "Don't be a pendejo, Mr. Lavadie."

The other commissioner, Meliton Mondragón, added, "What kind of harm does anybody think this really might do, anyway?"

"It's a bad precedent," Lavadie said. "This could steamroll into something as unmanageable as Pacheco's pig. Any fool can see that."

"Are you calling *me* a pendejo?" Meliton Mondragón asked.

"Not you personally, no. Of course not. But it's obvious the question isn't whether to let this go on or not. The only question is, how do we stop it?"

There was silence. Nobody had a suggestion.

At length, Bernabé Montoya said, "If I go over and tell him to stop he'll tell me to shove a chili or something you know where. If I go over to arrest him he'll try to kick me in the balls. And anyway, I don't know what the water law is, I don't even know what to arrest him for or charge him with or how long I could hold him. I know as soon as we fined him, or he got out of the Chamisa V. jail, he'd go back to irrigating that field again. It seems to me it's more up to the water users, to the ditch commissioners and the ditch bosses here, to stop him."

"Well, have them talk to him, then," Bud Gleason said. "How's that sound to you boys?"

It didn't sound that good to the boys. The two commissioners and the mayordomo shrugged, remaining self-consciously silent.

"For crissakes!" Lavadie suddenly exploded. "What a bunch of gutless wonders we got in this room! If you all are too chicken to do it, I'll go talk to that little bastard myself. There's no room in a town like ours for this kind of outrageous lawlessness—"

Five minutes later Lavadie's four-wheel-drive pickup lurched into Joe Mondragón's yard, scattering chickens and a few flea-bitten hounds.

A cigarette lodged toughly between his lips, Joe emerged from his shop tinkering busily with a crowbar.

"Howdy, cousin," Lavadie said.

Joe nodded, eyes crinkled against the cigarette smoke. Nancy opened the front door and stood there, flanked by two big-eyed kids.

"I came over to talk to you about that field you're irrigating on the other side of the highway," Lavadie said.

"What interest you got in that beanfield?" Joe asked.

"I figure what's bad for this town, whatever stirs up unnecessary trouble, is bad for all of us, qué no?"

Joe shrugged, inhaled, exhaled, and replaced the cigarette Bogey-like between his lips.

"I just came from a meeting we had over in Nick's store," Lavadie said. "We decided that since it's illegal to irrigate those west side fields, we ought to tell you to quit fucking around over there."

Joe delicately flicked the head off a small sunflower with the crowbar.

"Well—?" Lavadie said.

"Well, what?"

121

"What's your answer to that?"

Joe shrugged again. "Who says it's me irrigating over there?"

"I guess a little birdie told somebody," Lavadie grunted sarcastically.

"Hmm," Joe comented.

"So what's your answer?" Lavadie demanded.

Joe spit the cigarette butt from his lips and, swinging the crowbar like a baseball bat, expertly caught the butt, lining it across the yard at his antagonist, missing him only by inches. "Maybe you better quit fucking around over *here*."

Lavadie flushed, but kept his cool. "Are you or are you not going to stop irrigating that field?" he asked.

Joe smiled blandly. "The real question is, are you or are you not gonna get off my property, Mr. Lavadie?" He advanced a few steps flexing the crowbar.

Lavadie hastily backed up to his truck. "What are you doing . . . are you threatening me?"

"This is my property," Joe explained matter-of-factly.

"Well, goddamn you . . ."

Lavadie slid behind the wheel of his truck and started it up. "I'll go over there myself and see that not another drop goes into that field," he threatened.

"You do and won't nobody show up for work at your place tomorrow, Mr. Lavadie," Joe said quietly. "Your hay and your corrals might get burned by accident, too."

Lavadie fumed silently for a full ten seconds before jamming the gearshift into reverse and bouncing backward out of the yard.

"And—?" Bernabé Montoya politely inquired several minutes later.

Lavadie, pacing around the sheriff's living room, shook his head nervously. "What do you think. Bernie? Could he really get people to stop working at my place? Would he have the guts to burn my hay?"

"Sure. Maybe. Who knows?"

"I'd be up the creek without a paddle if that happened." Lavadie picked his nose. "This is more complicated than I thought. That little shithead's got no respect, does he?"

"Nope."

Following an awkward pause, Lavadie said, "I think maybe I better back out of this, Bernie. I think maybe the best thing right now is I shouldn't get involved, qué no?"

"Suit yourself, Mr. Lavadie."

"It's just I didn't realize—I had no idea . . ."

After Lavadie had slunk off, Bernabé slouched out to his pickup, tuned the radio to mariachi music coming from KKCV in Chamisaville, and steered onto the highway, turning south. Like everyone else in town, he automatically fired an obscene gesture (known as a "birdie") at Ladd Devine's Miracle Valley Recreation Area sign. Almost immediately after that he shuddered going over a painted cattleguard on the road, muttering to himself, "It sure beats me how a handful of white stripes can fool cows like that." Then, smoking thoughtfully, he listened to the radio and allowed his eyes to drift half-assedly around the landscape as he drove the fifteen or so miles to Doña Luz. In a field some kids were flying kites. Magpies hunkered atop flattened prairie dog carcasses along the shoulder. A few miles farther, the sheriff had to stop for some cows stupidly milling around on the highway. After that he tried to think about Joe's beanfield, but quit because already it made him uncomfortable to confront this thing; he had no idea how to deal with it. It was a situation like this, in fact, that could cost him his job. If he blew it, which was more than likely, that three-vote margin over Pancho Armijo every two years could dissolve into a landslide victory for his opponent.

So he had decided to try and pass the buck.

Two men occupied the tiny cinderblock state police headquarters at Doña Luz: a crew-cut good ol' boy state cop, Bill Koontz, and a young good-looking radio dispatcher, Emilio Cisneros.

Bernabé leaned against the counter behind which the two men sat—Koontz reading a comic book, and Cisneros typing up some forms—and he lit another cigarette.

"What's new up in the boondocks?" Koontz asked lazily. "Who shot whose cow last night?"

Bernabé smiled tiredly. He disliked the state police; he was also slightly awed by them. They were well-equipped men with an organization to back up their actions, and he himself was a loner with one stupid deputy. Any difficult crime he always referred to the state police: in fact, they wound up processing most of his arrests. Accident victims always awaited state cars to take them to the medical facilities in the south. All the same, he disliked going to cops like Bill Koontz for help or advice because that usually meant he wound up siccing them on his own people. And although nothing much ever really came of that, it made him uncomfortable all the same.

Now he said thoughtfully, "I came down here because I got a problem."

Koontz smiled. "So what else is new?"

"This one is kind of funny."

"Shoot," Koontz said.

"Well, there's a guy up in my town, maybe you know him—Joe Mondragón—"

"Sure, I know that S.O.B. What's he up to now?"

"He's irrigating his old man's beanfield on the western side of the highway."

"So—?"

"None of the land over there that used to have irrigation rights has irrigation rights anymore. I don't know the whole complicated story of how it happened, but it's got to do with the 1935 water compact."

"Sounds to me like the ditch boss, the one you people call the major domo, ought to handle this kind of thing," Koontz said. "What could we do about it?"

"Maybe you don't understand." Bernabé scratched behind one ear. "It's not like he's just irrigating this little beanfield. There's a lot of people in Milagro, you know, who aren't too happy with the way things are changing there, or down in Chamisaville, or all around the north. Up in Milagro—you've been along the Milagro-García spur, haven't you? You've seen the houses people used to live in out there, the old farmhouses, and all those fields?"

"That's a ghost town, man. Only that crazy old fart—what's his name—the little waffle with the badge and the suit, lives in those ruins—"

"Amarante Córdova."

"Yeah. He's the only one lives over there."

Bernabé drifted away from the counter over to the door, where he stood, hands behind his back, staring at the highway. The thought crossed his mind that he ought to handle this thing himself, because after all he more or less understood and had sympathy for the situation. On the other hand, if he handled the situation himself, suppose he butchered the job (a likely supposition), what then? At least if he gave it to the state cops he was off the hook.

Facing Koontz and Emilio Cisneros again, he said, "The thing is, irrigating that field is symbolic, the way I see it. People are bitter over how they lost their land and their water rights. And this sort of act, small as it may seem, could touch off something bigger."

Koontz said, "What do you want us to do?"

"I don't know. Frankly, I don't know what to do about it. It's not like you can just go in and arrest him or fuck up the beanfield or something. I mean, this is too *close* to everybody—"

Koontz frowned. "I'm not sure I understand, Bernie."

"Why don't you talk with somebody else," the sheriff suggested. "Talk with Bruno Martínez when he comes in. Better yet, get in touch with Trucho down in the capital. This is his sector, isn't it? Tell him to call me."

"For what? For a little loudmouthed troublemaker who's trickling a couple gallons of water into a crummy beanfield?"

Bernabé mumbled, "Ah, screw it then, I guess I'll handle it myself," and walked out to his truck.

Emilio Cisneros said, "If I was you, Bill, I'd call Trucho."

"Why?"

"Because I think he'd want to know. I don't think you really understand what Joe Mondragón is doing."

"You honest to God think I oughtta call Trucho?" Koontz asked uncertainly.

"Sure. The least he might do is talk with the state engineer. You let Bernie Montoya go back up there and handle something as sensitive as this on his own and he's sure to blow it badly. That sheriff is so stupid his boots were on the wrong feet, did you notice?"

"Okay. So maybe I'll call Trucho, then . . ."

Xavier Trucho, the third highest ranking cop in the state, in charge of the entire northern sector, said, "Repeat the whole thing to me again, Bill. Slowly. I want everything you can remember that honky-tonk Cisco Kid told you."

125

"It ain't much," Koontz said, suddenly nervous about the bean-field. "There's just this little guy, Joe Mondragón, who's cutting water into some deserted field isn't supposed to have water rights on the west side of the highway, in that ghost town part of Milagro, that's all."

"I think what I'll do," Trucho said, "is talk with the state engineer. Seems to me his office ought to handle it. I'll get back to you—"

And when he got back Trucho said, "Listen, Bill, this thing could be a little antsy, but for the time being we're gonna steer clear of it. Bookman's—the state engineer's—office will handle it, or at least try to. So why don't you drive up to Milagro and tell that Montoya ape to keep his boots from getting muddy over there on the west side, okay? You might also stop up at the Devine place and let them know we're aware of the problem. And Bill—?

"Yeah?"

"The key word is tact, alright? The key thing right now is to play this cozy. I mean, lay off Joe Mondragón, and let's keep our uniforms as inconspicuous as possible up there. Be nice to Bernie Montoya. People start getting the bright idea something is cooking, Bookman feels it'll only aggravate the situation, and we're liable to find ourselves up to our ass in Mexican hornets. Okay?"

"Okay," Bill Koontz said, puzzled by the respect people seemed to be developing for Joe Mondragón and his puny beanfield. He turned, asking Emilio Cisneros:

"What does a little jerk like that want to cause this kind of trouble for?"

"I dunno," the dispatcher said, smiling faintly, curiously. "Let's just wait and see what happens."

PART TWO

▼▲▼▲▼▲▼▲▼▲▼▲▼▲▼▲▼▲▼▲▼▲▼▲▼▲▼▲▼▲▼▲▼▲▼▲▼▲▼

New Times, New Faces: Humor in Contemporary Western Fiction

Oh, wretched world, more rank each day
And ruled by lunatics.
The heroes all are gone away;
Where are you now, Tom Mix?

*Wallace Tripp**

Wurst Seller (Jaffrey, New Hampshire: Sparhawk Books, 1981)

Outlaws and Peace Officers:
A New Breed

▼▲▼▲▼▲▼▲▼▲▼▲▼▲▼▲▼▲▼▲▼▲▼▲▼▲▼▲▼▲▼▲▼▲▼▲▼▲▼

Thomas Berger—"The Real Wild Bill Hickok"
(from *Little Big Man*)

David Markson—"The History of Sheriff C.L.
Hoke Birdsill" (from *The Ballad of Dingus
Magee*)

Will Henry—"Tom Horn Meets Al Sieber"
(from *I, Tom Horn*)

The Decline and Fall of the Gunman

▼▲▼▲▼▲▼▲▼▲▼▲▼▲▼▲▼▲▼▲▼▲▼▲▼▲▼▲▼▲▼▲▼

IF ANYTHING WAS ESSENTIAL TO THE MYTHICAL WEST, IT WAS the badman–peace–officer complex. Without the desperado the law-man would have had no way to demonstrate his expertise and his ded-ication to the good of western society. Without the dedicated peace officer, the desperado would have had things his own way and the West would have been a shambles indeed.

Then there was the idea that the outlaws were really battlers for justice and right, in rebellion against a corrupt system dominated by greedy entrepreneurs, crooked officials, and predatory ranchmen. This view would seem to give the outlaw an unfair advantage until one remembers that outlaws and lawmen were often indistinguish-able from each other and in the habit of changing sides. In any case, they were taken seriously and despised or cheered accordingly.

There could also be considerable emotional response to a bandit who reformed or an outlaw who gave up his wicked ways for the love of a good woman, as Wild Bill Crowley almost did in Owen Camer-on's "Civilized Man."*

There was much good meat for a humorous writer in these roman-tic imaginings as disillusion about the Old West took hold, and sev-eral skeptics have made hearty meals out of such figures as Wild Bill Hickok in Thomas Berger's *Little Big Man* and Sheriff C. L. Hoke Birdsill in David Markson's *Ballad of Dingus Magee*. Several humor-ous novels feature more or less innocent bystanders who became he-roes in spite of themselves, like the unwilling impersonator of Black-jack Sam in Lee Hoffman's *Legend of Blackjack Sam* (1966) or Jason McCullough, the unwilling sheriff in Philip Ketchum's *Support Your*

*Bar 6 Roundup of Best Western Stories Ed. Scott Meredith. New York: Dutton, 1957; New York: Permabooks, 1959.

Local Sheriff (1968). Alan LeMay's *Useless Cowboy* (1943) and John Reese's *Sure Shot Shapiro* (1968) continue in the same vein. Our changing views light the way to a better understanding of this aspect of frontier life—if Leslie Fiedler is right about taking it as a joke.

The Real Wild Bill Hickok

▼▲▼▲▼▲▼▲▼▲▼▲▼▲▼▲▼▲▼▲▼▲▼▲▼▲▼▲▼▲▼▲▼

Thomas Berger

Though Thomas Berger has written twelve novels, well crafted and well reviewed, he is best known for *Little Big Man*, his only western. Jack Crabb, Little Big Man to the Cheyennes, is 111 years old when he comes on stage in an old folks home and tells his life story. He has been everywhere in the West, has known everybody who counted and many who did not. Adopted by the Cheyennes, he became an effective Indian warrior, in fact, a legend among them. Back with the whites, however, he degenerated rapidly. The Cheyennes—the "human beings," as they called themselves—come out far ahead in comparison with the whites. Among the famous Westerners encountered by Crabb are Wyatt Earp ("that mean man"), General Custer (portrayed as a madman), and Wild Bill Hickok, who comes in for some rather heavy satire. Among the debunkers of the western myth, Thomas Berger belongs in the front row.

I REACHED KANSAS CITY IN THE SPRING OF '71, WHICH HAD growed considerably since I had knowed it as Westport, and if you recall, Fort Leavenworth was nearby. No sooner had I hit town when I found that none other than the Seventh Cavalry itself had wintered there, General Custer commanding. He was often to be seen over in K.C., at his tailor's, at restaurants, and at theatrical performances, being extremely fond of the last, as might be supposed from his character. His Lady was ever by his side, and she was so pretty it was said both men and women turned around when she passed by. Of course, the General was right comely himself.

The man who told me the foregoing had long blond curly locks falling to his shoulders and a silken mustache of the same hue, was above six foot in height, slim in the waist and broad as to chest, and in clothing a remarkable dandy. He wore a black frock coat with velvet facings on the lapels, an embroidered vest, turn-down collar with a black string tie, and topped it off with a silk hat.

No, he wasn't Custer, but blonder, curlier, warmer blue of eye, and

From *Little Big Man* (New York: Dial Press, 1964; Fawcett, 1964), 290–99.

his face was softer, with a hooking nose and short chin. He was James Butler Hickok, so-called Wild Bill after he rubbed out the man who named him Duck Bill.

But back to Custer, for whom Wild Bill had scouted on the Kansas campaign a year before the Washita. He knowed him well, and liked him and vice versa, and had a harmless crush on his wife and let her believe much exaggeration concerning himself, which Custer also believed, and so everyone was friends, as big, pretty, handsome, and powerful people always are. For everything goes their way, until some wretched, crosseyed, broken-nosed bum shoots them in the back, as Jack McCall did to Hickok in Deadwood in '76, only two months after the Indians did in the other Long Hair.

However, that was five years into the future, and here we was on Market Square in K.C., and I was fully intending to find Custer before the week was out and do my duty. Let me say about Market Square that it was the hangout for buffalo hunters in the summer when the hides run poor, and scouts would come there when off a campaign, and mule drivers between trips, and it was where you'd go for news if you was my type of case rather than read the papers.

And this is how I met Wild Bill, who was one of the centers of attraction thereabout, having already got his reputation a year or two before as marshal of Hays City, Kansas.

During the day, Hickok generally set on a bench outside of the police station where his friend Tom Speers, the marshal in K.C., encouraged the frontier types to congregate partly because he knew and liked most of them, but also I believe because it tended to keep them out of trouble. They could palaver with one another and even hold target matches without bothering the respectable element in the better part of town, and being that Speers and his deputies was around, real fights was rare.

Not that celebrated gun-handlers ever fought each other much, anyway. Anybody who specializes in violence has the greatest respect for another such expert.

Now, as to my revenge against Custer. Well, you can go to the history books and read how he died fighting Indians on June 25, 1876, so you know I never killed him in Kansas City. If he had been a nobody, I could have kept up the suspense till the last minute, whereas the way it stands I got to admit it was near the first of April when I reached K.C., and the Seventh Regiment had been recalled from the plains in March, Custer going back East. I had missed him by a few days!

You might wonder why I did not follow him. After all, it wasn't that he had gone to China. I already come across the western half of the country expressly to shoot him down. The image of that deed was what I had been living on for two years, ever since my vow on the banks of the Washita.

All I can say is that there was something about the Missouri River that took my drive away. Old Lodge Skins felt the same about the Platte, and look what happened to him when below it: Sand Creek and the Washita. I hoped he had now learned to rely on his instincts rather than his pride, and gone up north to stay.

In my case, I stopped right there in Kansas City, where the Missouri takes its big bend for the run to St. Louie. I looked at its muddly swirl and thought: Well, Custer's anyway gone off the prairies; that's the important thing. Maybe it was me who scared him off, in a spiritual or medicine sense, for it was right queer the coincidence of our comings and goings. Anyhow, I didn't go East. I had a funny idea of that part of the country: I figured it to be cityfied from St. Louie right on to the Atlantic Ocean, and mainly slums at that, filled with poor foreigners from Europe who had pasty faces and licked the boots of powerful, glittering people like Custer. I would be at a peculiar disadvantage there.

In Kansas City I was not far from the place where the Pendrakes had lived thirteen years before, and probably were still residing, for people in their situation maintain it forever, and I thought about going over there and just riding down the street once and be done with it, but didn't have the stomach for even that much. I tell you this, I was still in love with Mrs. Pendrake as ardently as I had ever been, after all them years and battles and wives. That was the real tragedy of my life, as opposed to the various inconveniencies.

The subject came to mind now because with the news of Custer's departure I felt more let down, despondent, and bereft than at any time since I had left Missouri years before, and naturally, in such a mood, thought of Mrs. P. was inevitable.

135

Well, if Custer ever come West again, I would kill him. I swore to that, but rather mechanically, for I didn't have no hopes he would.

The central plains was all cleaned up now of hostiles. The summer after the Washita battle, troops under General Carr whipped the Cheyenne Dog Soldier band at Summit Springs, killing their chief, Tall Bull. That was the end of the Human Beings in Kansas and Colorado.

So what did I do? Well, I met Wild Bill Hickok, and knowing him become almost a profession in itself for a while. I had inquired around about Custer, and a fellow pointed out Wild Bill as having been sometime scout for the General. I had never heard of Hickok at that time, but he was the celebrity of Market Square, and I recall that when I come up to him for the first time he was showing to some other fellows a pair of ivory-handled revolvers he had been give by a U.S. Senator he guided on a prairie tour.

I pushed amidst the throng and says: "You Hickok?" He had been pointed out to me as such, but I had to say something for openers.

"I am," says this tall, lithe man with the long fair hair and gives me but a fleeting glance from his sky-blue eyes, and then lifts the pistol in his right hand and fires the entire cylinder faster than you could count the shots, at a sign upon the wall of a saloon a hundred yards and at a slant across the square.

This incident later went down in history, I understand—without any mention of my part—but standing there at the time, I was not impressed. I was intent on finding out about Custer, and the flowing hair of this specimen made me think he was another of the same ilk.

So when he had exhausted them five shots, I says impatiently: "Well, Hickok, if you can spare the time, I'll have a word with you."

He throws the fresh gun from his left hand into the right, while at the same time and in the same fashion transferring the emptied revolver from his right hand to his left. This maneuver was called the border shift, and constituted a neat-looking trick as both pistols traveled through the air for a second.

Following which Hickok fired five more shots at that sign, and then the whole bunch walked on across the square to see how good he did. One of them at the back of the crowd comes over to me and says:

"I reckon you must know Wild Bill purty well, to bother him at a time like this."

"Don't know him a-tall," says I, "and don't know as I want to. What makes him so important?"

This fellow says: "You never heard how he took care of the McCanles gang ten year ago at the Rock Crick stage station down in Jefferson County? There was six of them, I believe, and they come for Wild Bill, and he took three with his pistols, two with his bowie, and just beat the other to death with a gunstock."

I immediately reduced that by half in my mind, for I had been on the frontier from the age of ten on and knew a thing as to how fights are conducted. When you run into a story of more than three against one and one winning, then you have heard a lie. I found out later I was right in this case: Wild Bill killed only McCanles and two of his partners, and all from ambush.

"Yes sir," this fellow goes on, who belonged to the same type as Custer's striker, "that is what he done. And over in Hays City when he was marshal he had a run-in with Tom Custer, the General's brother, who he locked up when drunk and disorderly, and Tom come back with two soldiers to put a head on him, and Wild Bill knifed one and shot the other."

Now this interested me, so I asked how he got Custer's brother, with knife or gun.

"It was the soldiers he killed, not Tom."

That figured.

Hickok and the others now returned from looking at the saloon sign, and this suck-up who had been talking to me, he asked what happened and another man says: "He put all ten inside the hole of the O, by God!" And everybody was whistling and gasping at the wonder of it—well, not exactly everybody, for there was other scouts and gun-handlers around, people like Jack Gallagher, Bill Dixon, Old Man Keeler, and more who was well known in them days, and they looked thoughtful so as not to display jealousy. As elsewhere in life, there are specialists on one hand, and the audience on the other.

I steps up to Wild Bill again and says: "If you can spare the time—"

He is feeling good what with his performance and the adulation rising from it, and I guess it might have irritated him that I should be totally occupied with my own matters, and he says quite negligent to one of them men at his elbow: "Run him off."

So that fellow comes towards me with a contemptuous look on his ugly, hairy face, and he is right large, but then he stops abruptly. For my S & W .44 is on a dead line to where his belly sagged over his belt.

"Pull in your horns," Hickok tells him with a guffaw. "That little bastard has got the drop on you. . . . Come on," he says to me, "put aside your popgun and I'll buy you a drink."

So Wild Bill and me went over to the saloon and passed under the sign where he had put ten shots in the hole of the O at a hundred yards, and I glanced up at it and saw he sure enough had. Inside, we got us our whiskies and then he found the farthermost corner from the door and put his chair in the angle of it and pulled his frock coat back on either side to expose the handles of the pistols stuck into his waistband, and all the while we was there he was eying every individual who came and went without it making any difference in his attention to our talk, except once when the bartender dropped a glass, at which Hickok automatically responded like a cat, coming half out of the chair.

So that was where he told me about Custer's going East and all, and the stuff I related earlier.

"Why did you want to know about the General?" he asked, but of course I never told him of my true interest but some lie about hiring on as a scout, and then to cover up whatever emotion I might have showed, I says: "I understand you had some trouble with his brother Tom."

"Well," he says, "that is all over."

Now this is a good example of a point I want to make. Wild Bill Hickok was never himself a braggart. He didn't have to be. Others did it for him. When I say he was responsible for a ton of crap, I don't mean he ever spoke a word in his own behalf. He never said he put a head on Tom Custer, nor wiped out the McCanles gang, nor would he ever mention them ten shots inside the O. But others would be doing it incessantly, and blowing up the statistics and lengthening the yardage and diminishing the target. Until about thirty year ago, I was still meeting people who claimed to have been on Market Square that day when Wild Bill put ten shots one on top of another into the point of an *i* at two hundred yards.

It was just after this that the bartender dropped the glass and Hickok come out of his chair, hands ready at his gun butts.

When he sat back again, I says: "What are you so nervous about?"

"Getting killed," says he, as simply as that, and takes a sip of his red-eye. And then he looks at me, a little amusement crinkling his blue eyes, and says: "Maybe you figure to do it."

That just made me laugh, and I says: "It was you who asked me to have a drink."

"Look," says he, "tell me straight, was it Tom Custer who sent you here? For as far as it goes with me, that is over and done with. But if he wants to start it up again, he ought not to send a fellow around carrying a S & W American in a tight calfskin holster. I tell you that for your own good, friend."

I was insulted, being proud of that new piece of mine, and I also took it hard that I would be considered as working for anybody named Custer.

"Look yourself, Hickok," I says. "I ain't no man's flunky. If I got any killing to do, it'll be for myself and no other. If you want to fight, we'll drop the guns and I'll take you on bare-knuckle though you be big as a horse."

"Settle down," he says. "I didn't mean to hurt your feelings. Let me buy you another." He called the bartender, but that individual had gone into a storeroom in back and couldn't hear him, so Wild Bill asks me would I mind fetching the bottle?

Still sore, I says: "Are you lame?"

He answers apologetically: "I don't want to get shot in the back." Hastening to add: "I don't mean by you. I believe you, friend. But I don't know about these others."

Meaning the ten or twelve harmless persons who shared the saloon with us at the moment. It wasn't crowded, being the middle of the afternoon. There was a table of four, playing cards; another couple or three men was down towards the lower right of the bar. And I recall a person dead drunk at a table in the middle of the place. His head and shoulders was flat limp on the tabletop in a pool of spilled whiskey, sort of like a piece of harness dropped in some standing rainwater.

So I felt a contempt for this Wild Bill, thinking he was either batty or yellow if he couldn't walk across a peaceful room. Then it occurred to me that he might be putting on an act for my benefit. Maybe he was waiting for me to turn my back on him so he could drill me.

This is a good example of the suspiciousness which warps the minds of gunfighters. I had fell into it right quick, just being in Wild Bill's proximity. You feel like your whole body is one live nerve. At that moment one of them cardplayers, having just won a pot, let out a holler of triumph, and *both* Hickok and myself come out of our chairs, going for our iron—and he had been right about that tight calfskin holster of mine, which fitted the piece like a glove: the faster you pulled at it, the more it gripped the revolver.

I says: "Now you got me doing it."

"I never," says Hickok, "have held by a holster." Now that he seen my deficiency I reckon he finally did trust me. "Always carry my weapons in the waist. You have to get a tailor to make a real smooth band there, no excess stitching nor suspender buttons, and of course your vest ought to be cut so its points don't interfere. And," he goes on, "see how I had my coat designed so it swings away on the sides."

"The only thing," I says, "is I wonder that sometimes when walking, your guns just don't slip on through and run down your trouser legs."

"Ah," says he, "you open the loading gate and catch it onto your pants-tops."

He was warming up to me through this technical talk, a man generally being fascinated by his own specialty and the tools for it. Bill proceeded to lecture me on the merits of the various means of toting a pistol: silk sash, shoulder holster, hideout rig inside the vest, derringer harness along the underside of the arm, back pockets lined with leather, and so on. He even claimed to know a fellow who carried a small pistol in his crotch, and when cornered he would request to take a leak before dying, open his fly, and fire. The trouble was onetime he got overhasty and shot off his male parts.

I learned an awful lot that afternoon. I had thought I was pretty handy with a gun before reaching K.C., but I was awful raw alongside of Wild Bill Hickok. Of course, I could see he was a fanatic. You had to be, to get so absorbed in talk of holsters and cartridge loads and barrel length and filing down the sear to make a hairtrigger and the technique of tying back the trigger and earing the hammer to fire, etc., etc. He had forgot about that drink and even his suspicions and commenced to call me "partner" and "hoss," rather than that sinister "friend."

I got tired after a bit and reminded him we was going to wet our whistles again, and started up, but he says: "Sit down, old hoss, I'll get them." And makes for the bar, despite the fact that the saloonkeeper had sometime since returned from the storeroom and could have fetched the bottle over.

One thing that amused me: Wild Bill carried that silk hat of his with him rather than leave it behind. I figured this was the last bit of suspicion he held towards me, that maybe I would swipe that article. Or maybe it was just that he didn't want to forget and sit upon it when he come back.

Now he had got within six feet of the bar and was already in the process of giving his order, when that drunk I have mentioned at the middle table suddenly reared up, revealing a pistol at the end of the arm that had been crumpled under him, thrusts it purposefully in the direction of Hickok's tall, broad back, and pulls the trigger. I would estimate the range as fifteen feet. Now this was quick. I mean if you had sneezed you would never have knowed anything happened, for in the next instant the "drunk" was sprawled once again in exactly the same position he had just emerged from, the difference being that blood was leaking out of a small hole between his eyes, adding to that pool of liquor.

He had fired all right, only his bullet went into the ceiling, for in the time between his rearing up and pulling the trigger, Wild Bill had seen him in the mirror back of the bar, turned, flipped his silk hat into the left hand, revealing the pistol he carried under it in his right, and killed the man. Then he put the hat upon his head, went over, and inspected the corpse. The other fellows gathered around, and shortly in come Marshal Tom Speers, and Speers says: "Know him, Bill?"

"No," says Hickok, expelling the empty cartridge and replacing it with a new load. Then he shrugs, gets that bottle from the bar, and joins me again.

Somebody says: "That's Strawhan's brother."

Now I was some agitated by this event, being no stranger to violence but not having looked for it here. I gulped the drink Hickok poured me with his calm hand, and coughed, and says: "The name mean anything to you?"

He shrugs again, sips his whiskey, and his eyes is heavy as though he is going to fall asleep. Finally he answers: "I recall a man of that name in Hays."

"Have trouble with him?"

"I killed him," he says. "Now then, about that S & W you carry. It is a handsome weapon, but the shells have a bad habit of erupting and jamming the chambers. I'd lay the piece aside and get me something else: a Colt's, with the Thuer conversion. . . ."

Meanwhile, Speers had got two fellows to drag the body out and he says to Wild Bill: "Drop by the station later when you have a minute."

I reckon the marshal had to make a report. Hickok gives him a little wave of the hand—the left one, of course. I should have known something was up when I seen him carrying that hat in his right, which he reserved absolutely for his gun. Pointing, gesturing, scratching, going for money—think of everything you do with your right hand: he did none of these, but kept it totally free at all times. The one exception was shaking hands, in which case he barely touched your fingers before whipping his back.

Not that afternoon, but later on I asked Wild Bill if he had really suspected that apparent drunk or if he always crossed a room gun in hand.

"I did, indeed," he answered. "I suspect any man whose gun hand is out of sight, be he even dead. I am wrong ninety-nine times out of a hundred; but I am right once in that same space, which pays me for my trouble."

Hickok was a marvelous observer of anything which pertained to killing. He noticed now how I had been shaken by the incident, though otherwise I don't think he would have recognized me if I had gone off to the outhouse and come back. He was like an Indian in his single-mindedness. For example, he never reacted at all to the quality of the whiskey we was drinking, which was fairly rotten. And later I come to realize that he had talked about General and Mrs. Custer in that apparently interested way only because he suspected me of being out to get him and playing for time. Actually he did not care anything about them or anybody else as persons.

But he could be considerate, if it fell within the area of his obsession. So now he says to me: "It is always harder on a man to watch trouble than to be in it. Best thing for you to do now is go get yourself a woman. Come on, I'll show you the best place in town."

The History of Sheriff C. L. Hoke Birdsill

▼▲▼▲▼▲▼▲▼▲▼▲▼▲▼▲▼▲▼▲▼▲▼▲▼▲▼▲▼▲▼▲▼▲▼▲▼

David Markson

Novelist, anthologist, and teacher (Long Island University), David Markson made monumental fun of the sheriff-outlaw formula in the *Ballad of Dingus Magee*, which became well known to the public through the motion picture starring Frank Sinatra. Dingus is a baby-faced outlaw whose sharp wits get him out of all scrapes and enable him to take advantage of less perspicacious people, both men and women. Sheriff C. L. Hoke Birdsill is his comic foil, a lusty lackwit who is always losing control of his destiny. Chapter 2 traces Hoke's history and brings him to the summit of his career as the law in Yerkey's Hole, New Mexico.

> *"No, by heaven! I never killed a man without good cause."*
>
> —WILD BILL HICKOK, QUOTED BY HENRY M.
> STANLEY

As a normal thing, Sheriff C. L. Hoke Birdsill affected a cutaway frock coat, striped pants, and a vest with a chain from which the tiny gold star of his office was sported. He also wore a derby, usually brown.

It had not always been so. Indeed, Hoke was thirty-one, and if he allowed himself the vanity of such sartorial excesses it was because until less than one year before he had never owned much more than the shirt on his back, which smelled generally of cow. Nor had he been a sheriff then either.

But then one day he had awakened with a pain in his chest. He tried to ignore it, but when it persisted, and severely enough to keep him

From *The Ballad of Dingus Magee* (Indianapolis: Bobbs, Merrill, 1965), 20–31.

144

out of the saddle, meaning out of work as a trail hand, he visited a doctor in Santa Fe. The doctor diagnosed consumption and gave Hoke twelve months to live.

This staggered him, less because he did not particularly care to die than because he had no notion how to cope with his time until then (he had never been especially burdened with imagination). He drifted to Fort Worth, for no particular reason. He had very little cash, but he took to gambling anyway. So then an incredible run of luck was to dumfound him all the more. Within short weeks he had won eleven hundred dollars, more money than he had ever seen at one time in his life and certainly far more than he would need to get through the remaining days of it.

Perhaps he was conscious of the irony. In any case he decided he might as well live according to his new means, which was when he began buying the clothes. "At least I'll be buried in style," he told himself. He was a tall man with a long, leaden face who had always been rail-thin but now believed himself cadaverous, and he grew a mustache also, which came out orange (his hair was quite dark, almost black). He had sold his horse and saddle and virtually all the rest of his gear, save for a single Smith and Wesson .44-caliber revolver in its sheath that he infrequently wore. He took to strolling considerable distances about the town or sitting wordlessly on his hotel's porch. Probably he looked thoughtful. Possibly he was. He wrote the projected date beneath his signature when he made arrangements with a bewildered local mortician and paid the man full cash in advance.

Then one morning he sat bolt upright in his bed some hours before dawn, startled by a realization that should have come to him weeks earlier, even before he had arrived in Fort Worth. His room was chilly, but when he undid his long woolen underwear, clutching at his chest, he found he was sweating. By the time he reached the stairway beyond his door, wholly without regard for sartorial propriety now, he was running, sprinting down through the darkened lobby and into the street. The nearest signboard he could recall was two blocks away, on a quiet side road, and he achieved it in no more than a minute. It was a woman who finally opened, and had she not been the wife of a doctor for forty years she might reasonably have taken Hoke

Birdsill for mad. "Yes," she said, "all right, he's dressing, he won't be a moment, perhaps if you would tell me what it is—"

But he had already sprung past her. The doctor was in his woolens, climbing into his trousers. "I ain't got it," Hoke said, or rather sobbed. Only the sight of a second turned-down bed, the woman's, gave him pause. But if he hesitated long enough to catch his breath he made no move to back out again. "It's a month and I ain't," he gasped. "I got so used to thinking about dying from it that I reckon I forgot all about having to live with it first, because—"

The doctor had paused with one leg raised, gawking. "What? Live with—?"

"Not for a month. More than that. I can't remember when I had it last. Not when I sold my horse or won all that there money or went to the undertaker's or—"

"What? Listen now, I still don't . . . do you mean to say you've come barging in here at four o'clock in the morning to tell me about some pain you haven't got, haven't had since . . . what undertaker? Listen, are you all right? Do you feel—?"

The doctor had to throw him out, at the point of a Sharps buffalo gun Hoke did not notice until it finally materialized under his chin. So he waited until six o'clock for the next one, and then he saw three doctors in half as many hours. They all told him the same thing. If they weren't positive about what it had been in Santa Fe (two suggested indigestion, one ventured gas) they were unanimous about what it wasn't now. Hoke jumped a stage before noon.

He returned to Santa Fe first. He found the original doctor, in the same office. "That's a shame," he told the man, "you ought to have been gone." The man did not recognize him. "Birdsill," Hoke said. "C. L. Hoke Birdsill. I'm gonter die in ten months from the consumption." "Oh, yes, of course," the doctor said, "I remember now. Well, and how are you feeling, Mr. Birdsoak?"

"Fine," Hoke said, "and how do you feel, Doc?" "I?" the doctor said, "oh, I'm fine, fine, never sick a day in my life." "You know the date?" Hoke asked him, "today's date?" The doctor glanced at a calendar and read it off. "Remember it," Hoke said. The doctor was an unassertive soul, an Easterner, and he began to tremble the moment Hoke took hold of his shirtfront. "Keep it in mind good," Hoke said, "because on this same day next year, one full year from today, I'm gonter come back here and shoot you square between the ears." "But you'll be dead by then yourself," the doctor protested. "Then you'll be jest lucky," Hoke told him.

Yet the truth of the matter was that Hoke actually owed the man a debt of gratitude, a fact which dawned on him about now. He was through punching cattle, nor was it simply a matter of the clothes. During his stay in Texas he had also discovered he liked the feel of a bed.

The next coach he took was posted for California. He picked California mainly because he had no idea what was to come next in his resurrected life, and that appeared as good a place to muse on it as any. One notion that had crossed his mind was that he might open a saloon. Another was that he might serve as a peace officer somewhere, though he had no idea how one went about this last. He had some eight hundred dollars left.

But he was not to achieve the coast, and only in part because old habit had made him too frugal to pay for more than piecemeal passage. It was at a meal stop some hours shy of a place called Yerkey's Hole, which marked the limit of his current ticket, that nemesis entered Hoke Birdsill's life to alter it for eternity.

Hoke was the only passenger on the run, and he was eating without haste since the horses were likewise to be fed. So he was still at the table when the gelding cantered up outside the cantina and the youth dismounted. Hoke recognized the fringed red-and-yellow Mexican vest at once. "Why, howdy there, Dingus," he called.

"Well, will you look at Hoke Birdsill in the dude's duds. You come into some riches now, did you?"

"A middling piece of luck," Hoke allowed as the boy joined him. Hoke knew him only slightly from random saloons. He thought him a pleasant lad. "Jest passing by, are you?"

Dingus gestured vaguely with a hand that Hoke now saw to be bandaged, or rather it was the wrist. "Thought I'd mosey over west fer some sporting life, maybe. Like as not try some stealing here and there too, I reckon."

"I heard tell you'd gone bad," Hoke said. "What do you want to perpetrate things that ain't lawful for, now?"

Dingus removed his sombrero, fanning air across his merry face. "Hot, ain't she?" he said. "Tell you the truth, Hoke, I don't rightly approve on it much neither, but a feller's got to live, and that's the all of it." He indicated the damaged wrist. "Sort of trying, too, what with lawmen taking pot shots at you like they do."

"Honest Injun?" Hoke's own forty-four had never served to enter contest with more than an occasional rattlesnake.

"Weren't nothing, really," Dingus said.

But abruptly Hoke grew uncomfortable. "That sure is a handsome-looking derby hat," the lad was adding. "Always did want to git me one of those, and that's a fact. Let's try her, eh Hoke?"

"I reckon not," Hoke said hastily. "I shed dandruff pretty bad."

"Let me jest inspect how she's manufactured then. I won't put her on."

"I reckon not," Hoke said again.

"Well, now. And I always pegged you fer a accommodating sort of feller, too."

"A man's clothes is his castle, is all," Hoke said, abandoning his meal. He called the proprietor. Deliberately, he withdrew a billfold in which he carried some seven paper dollars, allowing Dingus full scrutiny as he settled his accounting.

"Don't look like much remaining of that there luck," Dingus speculated.

Still distressed, Hoke said, "I were ill a spell in Fort Worth. I had to go to four doctors in one morning, it got so bad." He arose all too casually and strolled toward the stage.

"Ain't gonter climb back aboard without a pee, are you?" Dingus inquired, idly walking with him. "Gets right shaggy in a feller's crotch, he sweats in a dusty coach all morning. Nice to air her out, like, even if she's only got a little trickling to do."

"I reckon you got a point," Hoke admitted. They accompanied each other to a rear wall, reaching to unbutton in tandem.

"Jest keep a good strong holt there, Hoke," Dingus suggested then.

"Huh—?"

But it was far too late. Jerking his head just enough to see a revolver in the hand he had trusted to be otherwise occupied, Hoke urinated on his boot.

"I'll jest take a loan of that there derby hat, I reckon," Dingus decided. "A desperado's a desperado, but I kin leave a man his final few dollars, seeing as how you was sick."

Terrified by the looming weapon, though heartsick over far more than Dingus knew, Hoke closed his eyes as the outlaw reached to the derby. He sobbed miserably as his eight hundred dollars fluttered from within it to the ground.

"Well, howdy do!"

"Aw now, Dingus. Aw now, Dingus—"

Dingus was already squatting. "Back off there a step like a good feller, will you, Hoke?" he requested. "You're dribbling on some of my new twenties—"

So when he found himself stranded in Yerkey's Hole there was no saloon to be opened—nor would there be a bed either, or not for long. But there was still the job of sheriff to think about, urgently now and with certain expectations as it developed also, since the local man had only then struck it rich in the nearby mines and headed back east. Hoke sought out the town mayor.

"Who're you?" the mayor said. "C. L. Hoke Birdsill," Hoke told him. "Never heard of you," the mayor said. "Is that important?" Hoke wanted to know. "Of course it's important," the mayor said. "What we do, we pick some outlaw with a real foul reputation for meanness, usually some killer's been drove out of some other town and decides to raise a ruckus here. Safest that way. How do you think they picked that Wyatt Earp, over to Tombstone?" "Oh," Hoke said, "well, no harm in asking." "No harm 'tall," the mayor said. "Go get yourself a reputation, like say that feller Dingus Billy Magee, you mosey on back and we'll make you sheriff in jig time. Right smart derby hat you got on there—"

And then it was the derby that saved him. Or rather the local madam did, once she had seen the hat.

Her name was Belle Nops. Hoke had met her on occasion through the years, although as a cowhand he had never spoken more than a dozen words to the woman, and those strictly business. She intimidated him, as she did virtually everyone else. No one knew where she came from, although she had been something of a legend in the territory for a decade or more. She might have been forty, and she admitted to having been married once, if obscurely. She had arrived in Yerkey's Hole with one covered wagon and two girls, both Mexicans, and had set up business in a tent near the mines. Now the tent had long since become a house of exceptional size and intricate design (evidently it had been built originally to accommodate six girls, with new rooms added haphazardly and askew as the six became twelve and fifteen and twenty; finally there were even additional stories) replete with saloon, parlors, and piano. Some of the girls were white these days also.

Not that Hoke could afford any of either classification in his present circumstances. So he was both confused and complimented when she propositioned him. "A manager?" he said. "Me? And anyways, what kind of a job is—?"

She was a bawdy, overwhelming woman built like a dray horse and homely as sin, almost as tall as Hoke himself, if with an astonishing bosom nearly as famous as her house. Hoke had been in the bordello itself perhaps three times during his first week in town, and then only to nurse a solitary glass of cheap Mexican *pulque* in its saloon each time, nor was he conscious that she was even aware of his presence until she appeared at his table peremptorily and without preliminaries on the third of those nights to say, "You, Birdsill, down on your luck, ain't you? Come on—" She led him to a large room at the head of the main stairway which he expected to find an office and did, with a scarred desk in one corner and with a safe, but which was her bedroom also. Beneath a canopy of a sort Hoke had never seen except in pictures was a bed of a size he had not dreamed imaginable. He could not take his eyes from it. "What kind of manager?" he asked.

"Them duds," she told him. "Listen, if there's one thing on this earth a frazzle-peckered cowpoke or a dirty-bottomed miner respects, it's somebody he instinctively thinks is better than he is. You hang around in those fancy pants and you won't even have to tote a gun half the time."

"Gun?" Hoke said. "Oh. What you mean, you want somebody to hold the drunks in line?"

"And to count the take and keep the bartenders from robbing me blind and to bash the girls around too, maybe, when they get to feeling skittish. It's got too big; I can't watch it all by myself. All you'd have to do, you'd be here nights. I'll give you sixty a month, room and meals too, if you want that—"

"So I get to be a law officer, all right," Hoke thought, "excepting it's only in a whorehouse." Aloud he said, "What I'm supposed to be, it's a Colt-carrying pimp—"

"And what you mean is, you're afraid the boys will call you that. All right, we won't let anybody know you're working for me at all then. I'll make you sheriff of the whole ragged-assed town. Hell's bells, I own nine-tenths of the sleazy place anyway. The official sheriff's job pays forty—"

"But I thought a sheriff had to be—"

"What?"

"Never mind." Hoke was only half-listening anyway. He kept glancing toward that bed.

"That forty, and twenty more from me," Belle went on. "All right, it's only money—leave it at the original sixty from the house. That's a hundred altogether and you can live in the back room of the jail, and if you spend your nights here it'll look legitimate because we get all the action anyway—" She was standing. Hoke arose also, holding his derby. "So it's all set. I'll talk to the mayor tomorrow. We—"

"Lissen," Hoke said then. "That bed. Could I—?"

"Bed? Well naturally it's a bed. What else did you think it would be, a—"

"No. I meant some night. Or some afternoon when you're not here. Kin I jest try it out once, to see what it—"

"Some afternoon *what*? When I'm not where?" Belle Nops was scowling at him. "What are you talking about? Or rather what do you think *I'm* talking about? Come on now, and get shed of them duds. If they're too fancy to throw over a chair you can use the closet there. It's—"

"What?" Hoke said. "Use the—"

Belle Nops had already bent to disengage her skirts.

"First man in the territory in half a year who looks like he's had a bath since the war ended. Well, come on, come on, you figure on doing it from where you're standing, maybe?"

"Oh," Hoke said. "Oh. No. I were jest—" He set down the derby. "So that's how a feller gets to be sheriff," he said, watching her emerge.

Tom Horn Meets Al Sieber

▼▲▼▲▼▲▼▲▼▲▼▲▼▲▼▲▼▲▼▲▼▲▼▲▼▲▼▲▼▲▼▲▼▲▼▲▼

Will Henry

Henry Wilson Allen, near the top as a writer of westerns and of novels that go far beyond conventional westerns, started his career in Kansas City, Missouri, and pursued it through many occupations until he came to Hollywood and a job with MGM. He began writing as a sideline, achieved modest success, and switched to full time. In the next thirty years he published fifty-three books, won the Wrangler Award from the Cowboy Hall of Fame, accumulated a Golden Saddleman and five Spur Awards from the Western Writers of America, and watched his production grow to fifty million volumes in print. He has not had the recognition he deserves, possibly because under his two pseudonyms (Will Henry and Clay Fisher) he shows a confusing variety in mood and message; possibly because his critics, mostly academics, brush him off as a writer of "formulary" westerns.

At heart he is a poet and handles the language with a poet's skill. There is a romantic streak in him, but there is also a healthy respect for fact and a recognition of human weakness and folly. His latest editor and biographer calls him "a truly gifted writer" with a special ability "to summon up lost times and places and people," to "reconstruct in fiction actual historical personages," to "convey his genuine love for the horseback Indians of the plains and deserts of the West," and to "evoke emotional responses from the reader."*

One thing needs to be added to this list—a fine sense of humor. It appears to good advantage in *I, Tom Horn*, perhaps his best work.

Will Henry's West, ed. Dale L. Walker (El Paso: TWC Press, 1984), p. xxi.

Hello Prescott

PRESCOTT LOOKED LIKE HOME TO TOM HORN.

I came to it over the Mingus Mountains by the pass above the mines at Jerome. Then down the long sweeps of that high-country grass, which was as fine a cow and antelope pasture as God ever made, into the Granite Dells. Once past the dells, the town lay before you in its cup of gray rock and green pine.

From *I, Tom Horn* (Philadelphia: Lippincott, 1975), 50–64.

Near on sat the unbelievable spreadout of buildings that was Whipple Barracks, the biggest army settlement west of Fort Leavenworth, Kansas. Whipple was where I was bound, only my luck or my chance or whatever you want to call it hadn't told me so yet. First, it sent me on into Prescott itself. And, once into that place, I saw what it was that made this main hub of Yavapai County rouse up my memories of old Missouri.

Prescott was built by middle westerners, not Mexicans. It looked more like Memphis, my hometown, than it did anything in New Mexico or what I had seen, so far, in Arizona. It had a town square and false-front Kansas City buildings all around it. The houses fanning away into the rocks back of the center of town could have been freighted in and reerected from Topeka, Saint Joe, Independence, Sedalia, Jeff City, why, just anyplace a body could name from back home. Hell, better even. The houses in Prescott were painted. And the hotels, like the Yavapai House, were full of brass spittoons and real-live palm trees planted in dirt, where you could stub out your cigar butts, handy as anything. It was a real town, Prescott.

The saloons began just beyond the stage office at Gurley Street and Mount Vernon Avenue and ran from there on. I had heard the rumor that there were other businesses than sour-mash mills in Prescott. But from what I could see, riding in at ten A.M. of the morning, it appeared from the sheer number of saloons that there would be more whiskey drunk in that one town that in all the rest of Arizona Territory. It was told about that Prescotters used whiskey to chase their water with. A man had to admit it was possible. There likely was more rotgut than good water available.

The only things natural that growed there was granite outcrops, rock dust, and red-bark bull pines. The creek that ran through town was said to be damp in certain years but mostly it ran to ragweed, rusty cans, chicken dusting puddles, and old bedsprings. It was therefore and desperately needful, the natives claimed, to drink bottled fluid so as not to dehydrate and die of thirst right spang in the middle of the big city. As far as I saw, even that early in the morning, a scant few of them were taking any chances on such a terrible end.

I decided it had been a long ride from Verde.

Besides, at the 5,600-foot altitude, the wind, just then on the rise, cut at a man like an Apache scalp ax. After a quick tour of the square and turn of the sights along Whisky Row and Tomcat Alley, with detours to see the old log Governor's Mansion and the site where they were aiming to raise up the new all-stone courthouse, the damn wind got sharper still. I reckoned I had seen enough of the tourist attractions to hold me till noon dinner.

What I needed was a shot of that antidehydrater.

I shanked a spur into the flank of the rangy bay I was riding and swung him for the hitchrail outside the Red Geronimo Saloon & Theatre of the Performing Artes.

At the time, I thought nothing of that place's name. But the day in my life was fast running up on me when *Geronimo* would mean the difference of live or die for Tom Horn. And I would remember back to that morning in Prescott, and the Red Geronimo.

For now, I only wanted a drink before setting out to find lodgings less splendid than the potted palm trees of the Yavapai House, yet still more accommodating than my high-cantle Mex saddle for a pillow and the bay's trail-sour horse blanket for coverlet. The need was imperative. Or at least the choice of common brains.

In late December in old Arizona it can freeze a man's nose-drips twixt nostil and mustache. Cold? You can break off your horse's breath and melt it in your mess-kit can for coffee water. It gets so cold at five thousand feet in north central Arizona that the snow won't fall but freezes in the air. You have to build a fire to thaw out enough of a hole in the flakes to move about and breathe. In Verde, I heard of a man up in Holbrook that froze his stream solid in a rainbow arch from his front-fly to the hole in the crapper seat. he couldn't bust himself loose, either, for fear of snapping off his pecker. So he set fire to the cob box on the wall next the seat, figuring to free up his stream from the heat. But somebody had soaked the dry cobs in bear grease to soften the swipe of them against the winter chafe. The smoke from the oily cobs clotted up the outhouse air so thick and fast the poor feller strangled hisself and wasn't found till the spring melt thawed his body and let it fall out the door.

So I needed that one glass of rotgut rye I had promised myself at the bar of the Red Geronimo Saloon.

As it turned out, one glass wouldn't do it. I ordered up one more.

Which called for a third to fortify with full safety against the storm that surely must be building up outside. Three good belts of course called for four. To which five is only one more. So I had that.

When I next looked around, I was laid out snug in the snow of an alley just off Gurley Street. From the nine-shaft blackness all about, it had to be way along in the night. Also, my pockets was all turned out, empty as a whore's hope chest, and I was right back where I started out in Kansas City in that other alley—flat-ass busted.

My bay horse was gone, my whole outfit with him, including my new 1873 model Winchester. My colt belt pistol was likewise lifted. Along with my money poke pinned inside my horsehide button-up vest, near some two hundred dollars saved up from the three months of wood camp bossing in Verde.

But it wasn't until I wiggled my toes to see if I was still working all of a piece that I discovered what I thought was the last straw; the sons of bitches, or some son of a bitch, had stolen my boots!

But it stayed for another, real son of a bitch, to apply the actual clincher, or drencher.

Down the alley came a mongrel stray dog. He was nosing into every trash barrel, sniffing out any crumpled paper or heap of horse dung that might give promise of something to eat, or at least carry off and bury. But when he got to me, he veered off. After a long stare and a spooky snort or two, he lifted his leg on my hat, wheeled about, scraped snow and grit in my face, and traveled on out into Gurley Street without so much as one good-bye woof.

I took that dog's opinion as a portent. He had been sent to do his work on me by *mi sombra*, my shadow.

The Mexicans say that a man's shadow not only follows him but goes ahead of him. It stalks his life but guides him too. It was the same thing as an Anglo like me saying his fate led him on. It was what I called "something strange," back when I had felt it push me along so strong in Santa Fe. And it was what had meanwhile come to make me understand that Tom Horn was an *hombre de sombra* for real and forever; a man not truly responsible for his misdeeds and wrong directions.

Most won't believe that a growed-up fellow could lay there in the freezing slush, peed on by a passing dog, and have such thoughts to parade through his aching head. But most won't believe anything of what happened to Tom Horn, either. God knows they proved that. So it's no point in trying to explain a cowpen Spanish saying like *hombre de sombra* to them. All a man can do is tell his life the way it truly went; and Tom Horn truly did ride his whole life with somebody else's hands on the reins of his horse.

What drew me away from Scotland County, Missouri? Lured me into that alley in Kansas City? Directed me onto that flatcar bound for Newton, Kansas, with Staked Plains Bronson aboard? What put me in the freight-wagon business with teamster Blades? Brought fat Mrs. Murray to make her skinny husband hire me on to drive the Overland Mail? Steered Pajarita Morena into my cell, and me to her red-lighted *casa numero tres* down old Calle Cantina?

I will tell you what; it was the same thing that got me out of the wood-chopping venture at Camp Verde and bent my tracks to Prescott where, as will be seen, my life took its first deep set from me meeting up with the one man who would change it all for me. The man my *sombra* had in secret store for me six months down the trail from that night the mutt dog peed me into getting up out of the snow behind the Red Geronimo Saloon, determined to once and for all give up hard liquor and take that fateful new direction in my life.

Hello, Prescott, and good-bye! Tom Horn was outward bound to find Al Sieber.

Seebie's Boy

Lucky for any damn fool to be caught sockfoot in December, I knew where I could totter to and at least be given shelter for the night. It was to the stage company I had spotted back out on Gurley, before the saloons began. I could tell them I drove for Murray and the Overland Mail people. There was a sort of comradeship mongst all stagers. Like with roundup crews in cattle country. Or old rodeo cowboys. They would take me in on trust. No question.

I began to suffer my first maybes when I drew up outside the place and spraddled back to gawk up at the company name. It took the whole of the front of the horse barn to spell out. My socks froze to the wagon-rut slush before I finished it:

THE VERDE VALLEY & MOGOLLON RIM, NORTH PHOENIX, BUMBLE BEE, OAK CREEK, COCONINO COUNTY & SOUTH FLAGSTAFF STAGELINE & LIVERY COMPANY, AMALGAMATED.

Christ Amighty, I thought. Might be that such a grand company would, after all, scowl at late-night shelter seekers from a puny outfit like Overland Mail. However, a man, like a gelded jackass, could at least try.

I walked out of my ice-stiff socks, leaving them standing side-by-each in the middle of Gurley Street. Barefoot, I hammered on the office door, still not quite sobered even with the half-mile hike up from the alley behind the Red Geronimo. Inside, I heard a lot of unfriendly language and wheezing coughs, and the office door was creaked open by an old man in his nightshirt, eyeshade, knee-high boots and carrying a 10-gauge messenger's shotgun, both outside hammers cocked.

This rheumy old rooster sized me up with one squint.

"Git," he said. "If one more drunk wakes me up at three A.M. of the morning, I am going to increase his heft by four ounces of DuPont double-ought buck right square in both apples of his goddamn ass."

For emphasis, he triggered off the left barrel over my hat about three inches. I caught a part of the hot wad and some black powder chunks in my face. If that was the old coot's idea of where my butt was, there would be little telling where he might plant that right-hand barrel. In accordance, I did not take the time to ask any more of him, but took off and ran like a rabbit.

Once around behind the horse barn, I held up.

I was in the back corral, or "yard" of the place, where the line kept its busted-down and out-of-service equipment. Ah, yonder was the repair shed, a lean-to ramada, housing at the time the run's road-service wagon. This was actually a big toolbox on wheels and, shivering fit to loosen my rear teeth with the black cold, I figured that toolbox would do to spare my life from freezing. It took no more than ten minutes to chuck out the tools and bust a bale of hay open and dump it into the box. When I'd pulled shut the lid over my head behind me and snugged down into that softfine native hay, I was better off than a lost dog in a dry barrel full of butcher-shop sawdust. The hell with that old grouch and his 10-gauge. I was toasty as a tickbird on an old bull buffalo's rump.

When I woke up, it was to a jarring squeal of wagon axles and jolt of iron rims. By the time I could recollect where I was, the road-service wagon had hauled to a stop and its crew pried open the top of their toolbox. When they found me inside, rather than their rim irons, spoke wrenches, hub spanners, and the like, they were not happy. I tried to make up for their gloom.

"Why," I said, bright as brass, "where at ever can we be? This here surely ain't where I purchased my ticket for. This *ain't* North Phoenix, is it?"

The crew boss pulled a rim-springing bar out from under the driver's box. "No," he said, hefting it in my direction, "it ain't North Phoenix, it's South Prescott. This here is the wagonyard at Whipple Barracks, and we got a contract to maintain their ambulances and other rolling stock. Except that some young smart aleck done pitched all our handtools out'n the toolbox and filled it full of fresh hay. Which same half-growed, whiskey-pickled s.o.b. is right now going to get this here spring bar bent into a size-eight horseshoe square over the back of his cowboy hat. Up and out of thar, you damn bum!"

Whether or not he and his two mean-looking helpers meant to murder me was never contested. Just then, a herd of cavalry remount horses, leastways three, four hundred of them, came thumping through the yard on the whoop-and-holler run, hazed along by four riders. On the instant, I seen real trouble shaping.

At the back of the wagonyard at Whipple, there was an arroyo about twenty feet deep and sharp-filled with outcrop rock, sides and bottom. If those idiots driving those high-grade remounts didn't get the point of the bunch turned hard right in the next thirty seconds, Fort whipple and the Fifth Cavalry was going to be out about fifty head of replacement stock.

There wasn't any time for debate.

The boss herder was sweeping by the repair wagon even as I saw the danger. I just bailed out of the toolbox and onto his horse's rump behind him without thinking it over any longer than to wind up and make the jump.

Next thing, I barred one arm over the boss herder's throat from behind, lifted him wide of his damn saddle, and dropped him like throwing off the mailsack at Bacon Springs or Crane Ranch without slowing the stagecoach. Into the empty saddle I went. That poor horse must of thought he'd been mounted by a six-foot cougar. I put the spur rowels into him to their shanks and nearly broke his ewe-neck turning him in full stride to his right. But he didn't fall, and we did get the point of the running bunch headed short of the sharp-rock arroyo. And by *we*, I mean me, Tom Horn, and that skinny-necked mustang I'd appropriated by long-jump from the tool wagon of the Verde Valley & Mogollen Rim Stageline Company. Those blasted other herders never even knew why their big remuda swerved so hard. In fact, one of the bastards kept right on going and wound up in the bottom of the arroyo himself. In further fact, I was still sitting my borrowed plug up on the rim of the gully and yelling down at this dim-brain that, if his horse had to be shot, he could figure to get the same medicine, and I would be just the doctor to give it to him, when up puffs no less than an oak leaf, or "light" colonel of the cavalry, on foot and mad as a dog-bit badger. He proved to be on my side.

When he had added his sentiments to mine in the direction of the banged-up herder down in the rocks, he wheeled about on me.

"Colonel," I said in hopeful haste, "I'm right sorry I let him get by me. But it was all I could do to get the herd turned."

"I saw it all," the officer said. "How much do they pay you down at the stageline?"

I started to come up with some offhand yarn, then realized he thought I was working with the repair-wagon crew, out from Prescott. So I changed to a better lie.

"Seventy-five per, and found, colonel. But—"

"Don't but me. The army will pay you a hundred, no keep. Come on."

He started off and I held back only long enough to see the boss crewman coming our way on the quick-trot, still swinging the rim-spring bar.

"Yes sir!" I saluted the bowlegged little officer, and that's how I got to be chief herder for the U.S. Cavalry remount station at Fort Whipple, Arizona, in January of eighteen and seventy-six.

Early in '76, when I went to work for the Quartermaster herding the remount stock at Fort Whipple, all the horses came overland from California. They came in big trail herds of some four hundred head each. I was the boss of watching them all until the various posts throughout the territory sent and got their due consignments. Since Prescott was headquarters for the Department of Arizona, I handled every head that went into service the first six months of that year. It was some job of work.

There was but three of us to do it, too. Me and two Mexicans. One of them was half Apache, his mother's half, and he talked more Indian than Mexican. Neither one of them spoke English. Whatever I had yet to pick up of Mex or Apache lingo, I surely came by most of it in those five, six months handling horses by the thousands with Julio Vasquez and Tagidado Morales.

Morales was the half blood. Because I could speak his tongue and was so dark of hide myself, he thought I had to be part Indian of some kind. From that, he trusted me. When it came time, along early in July, for the three of us to say *adiós*—the last horses for the year was allotted the Fifth Cavalry and we was out of work—Tagidado hung back when Julio rode away.

He was an older man, ugly as sin or, as his friend Julio said, as his Apache mother. "*Niño*," Tagidado said, touching my shoulder, "I want to give you something." He reached up and took off the turquoise earring he wore in his left lobe. I had marked it many a time as a most curious piece, but I had never asked him about it. That it was of Indian design was evident. But it looked terrible old too, and I knew it wasn't just Arizona Indian. Now he reached and put the bauble in my hand, closing my fingers over it mighty careful. "Keep it," he said, "but a condition goes with it; a prayer really, *Comprende?*"

"*De seguro*," I answered, "go ahead."

He told me I was a young man and that he knew I was spiritbound to the *Indios* and would one day go and live among them. He meant the Apaches, of course, and not the tame ones. "I had a son," he said.

"The people of Mangas Coloradas took him as a small child. We heard they traded him to the Warm Springs people, but he was never returned, nor was it even known if he lived. When he was taken, he wore upon a circlet chain about his small neck the mate to this turquoise earring of the feathered serpent. Perhaps today, should he have lived, there somewhere rides a young Apache of your own tender years who will wear that earring in his right lobe. If you ever see him, show him your earring and tell him its story. The rest I will leave to God."

I didn't think too much of the story, as Mexicans are not to be believed except at considerable risk. I assured this old man, however, that I would be faithful to the trust and would wear the earring when it came to pass that I should go among the wild Apache.

"Remember to do it," old Tag said. "It will preserve your life one day. That sign has medicine power."

He got on his runty Sonora mule and started off.

"Hey!" I yelled after him. "*Alto!*"

He waited, and I loped my horse up to him. "Listen," I said, "I am a shadow man, you understand?"

"Yes, of course," old Tag eyed me noddingly, "I knew that you were. We all are. But only some of us know it. Most do not. What do you want, *joven?*"

"Well, you are right, you see. I have always dreamed of *los Indios*. The *broncos*, the wild Indians, you understand, not the *reducidos*, the tame ones. Yet until this moment that you spoke of going to live with them, I had never thought of that. That was my shadow telling your shadow, eh?"

The old half-breed shrugged. "*Pues*, perhaps. But one does not require his sombra to inform him of your feeling for my mother's people. What is it, now?"

"I want to know what is the best way for a white man to find the *broncos?* I mean, without getting killed doing it. What should I do if I want to go and live with the wild Apache?"

"Easy," said old Tag. "Go and find Seebie."

"Seebie? *Quién es?*"

"Al Sieber."

He said it as though I would at once say, Oh! of course, Al Sieber! Now why didn't I think of that?

But I just frowned in my special dense way, and old Tag said, "What? You do not know Sieber? You never heard of the name?"

"Never. Not till this moment, *anciano.*"

Later, men would say that I couldn't possibly have failed to hear of Al Sieber working at Camp Verde and then Fort Whipple all those months. Whipple and Verde were important posts. Anyone hanging around them must have heard of Sieber. The only alternative was that Tom Horn was a damned liar (again!) and never set foot in either place. He couldn't have it both ways.

Well, he did.

People forget that in 1876 Al Sieber wasn't of the same renown he was by 1886. You might as well say that anybody in that day who hadn't heard of Tom Horn was a damned liar and never lived in Arizona Territory. But who was Tom Horn in 1876? Nobody. And Al Sieber wasn't that much more of a somebody either.

Except to the Apaches.

And, ah! that was the difference.

Old Tagidado knew it.

"Well, *hijo mío,*" he said patiently, "now you have heard the name. And it is the one you must know if you are a white man thinking to find the true *broncos.*"

"All right," I replied, "can you then tell me, *tio*, where I may find this Al Sieber? A *dónde está, amigo?*"

Old Tag gave me a mixed Indian and Mex look.

"Your *sombra* served you well in sending you to ride after me and ask this question," he said. "It so happens that Seebie has been in Prescott ten days, and what do you suppose he has been doing? Looking for someone to work with him. He has been given a big promotion to chief of scouts and requires an assistant now. *Qué tal!* And do you know what else, *chico?* No, you don't. Well, I will tell you; he is leaving today and he did not find anyone. If you hurry, you may catch him still."

"*A dónde?*" I repeated. "*Nombre Dios, a dónde?*"

"You know of the place called *Geronimo Rejo?*"

"Uncle," I said, wheeling my horse, "I know it well. *Adiós. Vaya con Dios. Wagh!*"

And I lit out on the flat gallop for Prescott and the Red Geronimo Saloon, not even thinking to say *mil gracias* to old Tag for his information.

Well, that was all right.

He would understand.

We were both *hombres de sombras.*

It wasn't our faults the way things happened to us, or that we got directed into doing them to others.

You didn't worry if you were a shadow man.

You just lit out.

You did, anyway, if fate had just tapped you on the shoulder to be Seebie's Boy.

Miss Pet

I had a good horse and outfit under me once more. I had earned myself back into a decent state, had money in my pocket, and a purpose in my mind. If I was out of a job, it was by hard work, not by prowling Tomcat Alley or drinking Whiskey Row dry. Moreover, I had good references. Matter of fact I was riding past one of them on my way into Prescott. This was the firm of Tully, Ochoa, & DeLong, beef contractors and general freighters for the military. Between horse herds from California coming in to Whipple, I'd filled in delivering beef herds for them to local Indian agencies. They were mighty good people, but I just waved at them now riding past on my classy blood bay gelding. The work paid cheap and wasn't steady. Nothing like good enough to compare with going to live with the wild Indians. *Wagh!*

Ah! that was a grand morning to be sixteen years old, yet grown tough and smart as a desert-bred mustang. There is not time in a man's life so glorious as that minute when he figures the boy in him has at last haired over, making him full-grown and ready to growl.

Not unless it's that other minute old Tag told me about, where a man is truly growed old but feels one brief day like he was a boy again and could pee his mark as high on the wall as any *macho* youngstud in Mexico.

Well, naturally I couldn't speak to that. I just reckoned nobody had better challenge Tom Horn to any wall-wetting contests that particular sunfresh July morning of eighteen and seventy-six.

Wasn't I about to find the great Al Sieber down at the Red Geronimo Saloon? Hadn't my *sombra* sent me to him by way of old Tag? Wasn't I as good as hired by the new chief of scouts for the whole Fifth Cavalry, at San Carlos the main Apache Indian reservation in the territory? Well, wasn't I?

No, as a matter of fact, I surely was not.

I never even got to the Red Geronimo Saloon. I was stopped on my way to it, going by Madame La Luna's New Orleans House, taking the shortcut through Tomcat Alley. Madame came stomping out into the street just as I drew up. She spooked hell out of my hot-blooded red bay gelding, and it was plain she was mainly unsettled about something. "Here, you," she said, spotting me. "You look like you had more muscle between your ears than compis mentis. Get down off that damn horse and come along. I've got a chore for you. Pays quick cash and no questions. Come along in, didn't you hear me? Don't just sit up there gawking with your mouth hung open fit to trap flies. Ain't you never seen a woman in a nightgown before?"

"No ma'am," I said, touching the brim of my hat, polite. "Not so close to high noon, I ain't."

She wasn't young but she had a body like she was, and she saw me admiring her splendid lines and she mellowed down a bit from that. Fact is, I swear she blushed a tinge.

"Goddamnit," she said, "foller me, boy."

Well, I went into her whorehouse with her and sure enough she did have a job of work for somebody laid out in there. It was a fellow built like *the* prize herdsire Hereford bull of the whole cow business. Big and blocky and thick-strong all over, and mean-looking like he would charge you on or off your horse. He was passed out cold drunk snoring on a tapestry settee in the red plush lobby of the place. And, saving for his stovepipe riding boots and Mexican cartwheel spurs, complete with pure silver jinglebobs, he was naked as a new-hatched nest-bird. "Jesus H. Christ, ma'am," was all that I could think to say.

"Yes," she agreed. "And I will give you five dollars to haul this drunk son of a bitch out of my decent house without waking him up or scratching my hardwood floors. Here are his clothes, and when he comes alive you tell him he owes me for Clara, Bonnie May, Charlene, and Pet. And tell him Pet says if he ever again tries to bed her with his boot-irons on, she will cut off his cajones and mail them to his C.O. at San Carlos in a plain paper bag. Now get!"

I thanked the lady for the work, taking pause only to struggle on the man's pants for him and to ask Madame La Luna to please donate my five-dollar fee to Miss Pet so she might see the doctor about her spur cuts.

"You're a nice lad," Madame said to me. "Don't ever take up with the likes of this *lunático*. You would do better to join up with the Apache Indians."

That's remarkable," I said, admiring her again. "How ever did you guess I aimed to do that?"

"Do what, boy?" she snapped. "Don't fret me."

"No ma'am," I said, tipping my wide hat again. "I wouldn't never do that to any lady. I just purely was wonering how come you to know I was bound to join up with the Apache Injuns?"

"Oh, my God!" she cried, clapping hands to head. "*Two* lunatics!" Then, addressing herself to the half dozen disclad young females now peeking into the lobby at all the fuss. "Here, you, Pet. This young jackass won't take my five dollars for dragging this dead piece of meat out of here. Wants you to have the money for the doctor to tend your spur gashes. Ain't that rich!"

She commenced to laughing like a loon, but Miss Pet hipswung her way over to me with a sober face. And, oh but she was something! The most slimmest and beautiful blonde girl—and I mean all of her blonde—that I had ever dreamed to see in that life. She sidled up to me with a downglance look and murmured husky-voiced, "I want to thank you, mister. Truly I do." After which she eyed me up and down and in the middle, and she stopped there and sort of stared at me and added, "You can take it out in trade anytime, tall boy. Just put it on my bill, Madame," she said to the La Luna woman. "Oh, my!" With that, she touched me where she oughtn't to have, and all the girls giggled and I just grabbed up the Hereford bull man off the settee and drug him out into Tomcat Alley, sweating some thing fearful.

And that is how, of course, I met Al Sieber.

It surely may not seem a proper way, nor moment in a man's time, that he would choose to see printed of himself in the history books. Not neither for Sieber nor Tom Horn. But when you set out to tell of your life and have promised to put it down in a true way, then you don't stand short with your story.

That *was* the way that the Missouri farm boy ended his long journey to the West and came at last to live with the wild Indian horsemen of his rainy night dreams.

167

PILGRIMS: HUMOR OF THE WEST ON THE MOVE

▼▲▼▲▼▲▼▲▼▲▼▲▼▲▼▲▼▲▼▲▼▲▼▲▼▲▼▲▼▲▼▲▼▲▼▲▼▲▼

Pilgrims in the West

▼▲▼▲▼▲▼▲▼▲▼▲▼▲▼▲▼▲▼▲▼▲▼▲▼▲▼▲▼▲▼▲▼▲▼▲▼▲▼

HUMOROUS WRITERS HAVE ALWAYS LIKED TO PUT THEIR
people in motion. Oddballs and eccentrics exist in every community
and a man on the move sees more of them than stationary people do.
The chance for bizarre adventure is also increased, and when one
escapade is concluded, the pilgrim can move on to another.

Down through the ages travelers have been especially interesting to
readers: Ulysses in his wanderings, Marco Polo on his way to Cathay,
Lazarillo de Tormes, Gil Blas, Moll Flanders, Tom Jones—there is
no end to the list of wanderers, many of them humorous.

Much of our own literature has been about people on the move.
They journeyed westward in wagons of Santa Fe traders, Conestogas
of emigrant trains, steamboats on the western rivers. They piled their
goods into Mormon pushcarts. They drove cattle and sheep and even
turkeys westward. They traveled on trains after the Civil war and used
the automobile when Jack Kerouac made his pilgrimage. American
storytellers have used these travelers from the beginning to comment
on life and its vicissitudes.

Examples are easy to come by. Rambling cowboys are standard fare
in popular westerns. Some have been fugitives like Booger Jones in
John and David Shelley's *Hell-for-Leather Jones* (1968) or Clay Calvert
in H. L. Davis's *Honey in the Horn* (1935). Some have been crime
busters like Sheriff Henry Harrison Conroy in W. C. Tuttle's *Wild-
horse Valley* (1938). John Reese kept the rangeland detective going
later in the person of Jefferson Hewitt (*A Pair of Deuces*, 1978).
Westward-migration epics were with us even before Emerson
Hough's *The Covered Wagon* (1922), and they enjoyed a new birth of
freedom as the Bicentennial came up on the calendar in 1976. Unusual characters appeared in the leading roles. There was Uncle Ned
Oldcastle in Lee Hoffman's *The Truth about the Cannonball Kid*
(1975), a charming but conscienceless con man, always good for a
laugh; Wilson Young, the holdup man in Giles Tippette's *The Bank*

Robber; Corcho Bliss, the bibulous gunrunner for Pancho Villa in Austin Olsen's *Corcho Bliss* (1972); Indian convert Peter Hermano McGill in Edwin Shrake's *Blessed McGill* (1968). They are all amusing and would be introduced in these pages if there were world enough and time.

A favorite device of the storytellers is to view the kaleidoscope of the West through the eyes of a teenage boy who sees and reports more than he understands while his natural shrewdness keeps him alive and moving. Andy Adams used this device in *Wells Brothers* (1911), as did Weldon Hill in *Lonesome Traveler* (1970) and Benjamin Capps in *The True Memoirs of Charley Blankenship* (1972). Two good examples, excerpted in the following section, are Robert Lewis Taylor's *The Travels of Jaimie McPheeters* (1958) and David Wagoner's *The Road to Many a Wonder* (1974). These cousins of Huck Finn add a special dimension to the humorous view of western history.

Sir Harry Flashman is a different breed. He is a blue-blooded, globe-girdling picaro, *avec peur et avec reproche*, whose abysmal villainy is relieved, though not removed, by his self-deprecating sense of the ridiculous. He adds a new dimension to the humorous view of the American West, its stereotypes, and its history.

Jaimie Meets Jim Bridger

▼▲▼▲▼▲▼▲▼▲▼▲▼▲▼▲▼▲▼▲▼▲▼▲▼▲▼▲▼▲▼▲▼▲▼▲▼▲▼

Robert Lewis Taylor

Illinois-born and educated, Robert Lewis Taylor got his start as a writer as a newspaper reporter and later wrote for the *New Yorker*, the *Saturday Evening Post*, and other magazines with national circulation. He has also done some important biographies, but he is best known for the first of his four novels, *The Travels of Jaimie McPheeters*, which won a Pulitzer Prize for fiction in 1958. With his father, a Louisville doctor given to dreams and purple rhetoric, Jaimie sets out for the California gold fields and has some astounding adventures en route. At Independence, Missouri, they join a wagon train guided by an extraordinary frontiersman named Buck Coulter and are part of a group that includes a waif named Jennie and the Kissel family, farmers who hope to own a few fertile acres in California. Chapter 28 brings them to South Pass and an encounter with Jim Bridger, the famous mountain man and epic liar.

F ROM WHAT I'D HEARD OF THESE MORMONS, I DIDN'T CARE TOO much about them. Besides, we were supposed to be off adventuring after gold and not holed up with a bunch of mule-headed religious nuts. My father always claimed that people who took on about being pious would bear watching. "I wouldn't trust one for a second," he said. Back home, he was barely civil to the Reverend Carmody, and when we left church each Sunday, he'd take his watch and slip it into his trousers pocket before shaking hands on the way out. He was only having fun, but my mother said it was irreverent and pointed up his deficiencies before God. But the preacher they'd had before Carmody sat up praying with the wealthiest old man in the parish when he was down sick of malnutrition, being something of a miser, and finally prayed so hard that when the man died, they came to find out he'd changed his will. And right after the burial, the preacher collected his inheritance, turned in his stole, and moved to Philadelphia. He'd been popular around Louisville, but nobody heard from him again until two years later, when he got into the news from being shot. So I

From *The Travels of Jaimie McPheeters* (Garden City: Doubleday, 1958), 270–83.

don't intend to dwell on that winter with the Mormons, but will just hit the high spots—there *were* a few—then get right on to California.

After the fight with the Crows, we reorganized and moved on fast to Fort Bridger. Within a few days, we'd left the Platte forever. Nobody was sorry. It seemed we had been within view of this sluggish nuisance for as long as we could remember.

We followed the Sweetwater, within sight of the Wind River Mountains, over a country a-swarm with mosquitoes, and finally began the long rocky climb toward the snow ridge that "divides the Continent." That is, the rivers change directions here; the ones on the East flow toward the Eastern sea, and those on the West empty into the Pacific.

For several days in a row, there was little grass, but the ground was carpeted over with thistles, on which the oxen and mules fed, though without much appetite. Food for the immigrants was scarcer. Mostly people still were refreshed from Laramie, but Coulter kept trying to bag game, which could often be seen on these rocks up above. Twice he shot antelope, but the wolves moved in and devoured them before we could get there.

Several women came down with fever, so my father and Dr. Merton were hopping again. The upward pull was affecting both people and beasts. Part of it, my father said, was anxiety, fear of the summit we were approaching, which they called South Pass. But when we arrived, it was no worse than the road before, and was nineteen miles wide. We hardly knew we'd got to the top, but if you ran or moved fast, you knew it well enough, for they said the altitude here was over seven thousand feet high.

From the top we went along a level road two or three miles, then started a gentle descent to a gushing fountain known as Pacific Spring, very cold and good, being the last water for a long time. And after this we passed over a dry brown plain with what they called buttes—reddish-brown knobs of sandy rock—standing straight up like mushrooms. My father said they were once islands in a great inland sea, but he got into an argument with two other men about it, and was kept busy all afternoon.

Camped beside the Big Sandy, and started on a stretch of twenty miles without water or grass. Everybody was in a grouchy humor when we reached the Green River, which was nearly three hundred feet wide, and the fording was done to considerably more cussing than had formerly been noted on the train. People were so tired out I almost felt glad that our bunch was calling it off for a while.

On October twelfth we rode into sight of Fort Bridger, where we were to part, and of course there was some sniffling and carrying on. People went around shaking hands, and wishing good luck, and I honestly think we nearly backed out. But Mrs. Kissel now had to spend part of the day lying down, and my father, to do him credit, was bound and determined to get her back to health.

Coulter was going on with the train. "I hired out to deliver it to California, and that's where I'll deliver it," he told us. He waited a bit after we'd said everything, then followed Jennie to the tail of Brice's wagon. Having a little free time on my hands, I crawled underneath to rest up.

It was funny; Coulter had quit being so sarcastic with us, but he still spoke to Jennie with a kind of joky ragging.

"I'll be back, once I've got the sheep in the corral," he said.

"Indeed, you don't mean it. And leave all that gold behind?"

"I'm not much of a hand to go scratching in the ground like a squirrel."

Jennie gave a sniff. Now she was beginning to recover a little, she was handsome and lively. And since she'd been married, she was different, somehow. She had lost her sharp look and was softer and rounder. But there wasn't much improvement in her manner toward Coulter. He got her back up, no mistake, but I thought she liked him, too. It was a different kind of liking than what she'd had for Brice. I heard one of the men say she hadn't any mroe use for Coulter than a Jenny had for a Jack, but I didn't know what he meant.

"I hear gold-mining's hard, back-weary work," she said. "I don't doubt you'd shy off. Gallivanting's more your style."

"If a man's without ties, he might as well roam. A man, that is, not a doddering mooncalf—"

"You say anything against Brice and I'll slap your Indian's face."

"I wasn't talking about Brice, so maybe I'll give you a real excuse."

He grabbed her shoulders and kissed her hard, pushing her up against the tail gate so that she went limp, leaning over backwards, with her legs apart.

When he let go, she caught her breath and hissed, "You vulgar roughneck. You ought to be ashamed. Leave me be." But when he turned half around, she said, "Where are you going?"

"California—remember?"

Jennie began to cry, she was so mad, and said, "Go ahead. And don't come back, hear?"

"You want me to kiss you goodbye again, just for luck?"

"No, I don't! You catch me letting you. Not ever! Just once, then—not that way—all ri—"

Then she broke loose, hanging on a second, and gasped, "You'll have to stop. Damn you—I'd like to kill you!"

"I'll be in Salt Lake City by Christmas."

"I won't be there."

"You'd better."

"I'll marry a Mormon."

"I'll make you a widow."

When he left, she put her head down against the board, breathing sort of hard, but she took it up again in a minute and kicked the wheel. She was an interesting case. Still, I couldn't make out what was bothering her, and anyhow I was rested up, so I left.

Before the train rolled on for California, Coulter took the men of our group to meet Jim Bridger, who he said was an old friend. If my father was right, Coulter'd only had a handful of friends since his childhood, and these were such hardened old geezers they wouldn't care whether he murdered his brother or not. Being friends, they'd simply have figured he had a good reason.

One was this Bridger, and another was a scout named Carson that Coulter said was somewhere on the Oregon Trail this year. He hoped to see him soon.

Coulter told us that Bridger's Fort, where the Mormon route to Salt Lake splits off from the California-Oregon Trail, was on Black's Fork of the Green River, where it took the fresh waters from the Uintah Mountains. He said Bridger himself was one of the toughest birds alive. "In 1834, he came out of a fight with the Blackfeet at Powder River with two iron arrowheads in his shoulder," Coulter said, "and a Doctor Whitman removed them while Bridger sat on the grass, smoking a cob pipe and playing mumbledy-peg with a soldier. Injuns carried the story all over the West. In appearance he's as mild as soup, but don't be surprised at his stretchers. He ain't any bad hand at story-telling; fact is, he's famous for it."

The train had camped on one of the three river forks surrounding the Fort, and we walked on in, Coulter and my father leading the way, Kissel and Coe behind them, me bringing up the rear. The first thing you noticed was how foxy Bridger had been in his location. The Fort was plopped down on an island in the middle branch of that stream, and we had to get to it by flat-bottomed boat, though we could have waded, they said. When we reached the island, the Fort wasn't any beauty, but it seemed solid for defense, being encircled all around with a strong stockade that had a heavy gate in the middle. The construction was picket, with the lodging apartments and offices opening into a hollow square, like Laramie. On the north side a corral was full of animals—mules, horses, oxen, ponies, and the like—and Bridger's house stood in a southern corner—a long cabin of very ordinary appearance for a man so well known, calling himself a military Major to boot.

We observed that the proprietor of this seedy dwelling was now within view on his doorstep, and I'll copy down what my father said in the Journals: "A man of middle stature, lean, very leathery of countenance, wearing a fringed buckskin shirt in indifferent repair, also a low black hat, and on his face a look both of deeply ingrained mischief and studied innocence; small eyes, close together but incredibly sharp and black, nose beaky, neck wattled, mouth set as if determined to avoid laughing at some epic jest."

At the time of our arrival, he was lugging a big brass spyglass, which we understood later was with him most always. He knew everything going on in that area, and the Indians never understood how he managed.

His meeting with Coulter was somewhat out of the common, as such formalities went. It departed from custom.

177

As he stood there, in an easy slouch, holding his telescope, we could see two fat Indian women in the doorway behind, and at their feet a number of copper-colored brats.

Bridger lifted his glass, though we were now only twenty or thirty yards away, and fixed it rather rudely on Coulter's face. Then he gave every appearance of alarm, as if the Fort was under attack. It set my father and the others back a notch, especially Coe, who had a pretty stiff notion of manners, even after all these weeks on the trail.

"Get the children back!" cried the proprietor to the Indian women. "Shut and bolt the doors—bury the silver." He stepped spryly aside and whisked the telescope out of sight behind the door, coming up with a very long rifle instead. His attitude was concerned, if not downright menacing.

Coulter, for his part, fell into this nonsense as if he'd done it before, and called, "I wonder if you could direct us to the person in charge of the Fort. We understood old Bridger was killed by a couple of Arapahoe children."

"Keep back," said Bridger to the women, who had yet to move a muscle in obedience to his commands. "Don't show yourselves. It looks like Coulter."

"Put down that rifle."

"Come up, Coulter, but come slow, and don't move your hands."

Coulter now grinned and said, "By God, if you aren't the worst-looking sight I ever run across. Have they quit sewing buttons on shirts?"

"What's happened to your hair?" asked Bridger.

"It got singed."

"You haven't a particle of business outside the Fort without a guide. I've told you before, only you won't listen."

"These are friends," said Coulter, introducing us. "They want to make serious talk, so cut out the piffle."

At this odd point in their reunion, they shook hands, but each did it as though the other was an object of miserableness almost past belief.

"I didn't figure on seeing you again," said Bridger, "wandering around unattended."

Inspecting him with an air of pity, Coulter said, "I'd almost forgot what an ugly old squirrel you are. It's always a shock. Why in hades don't you shave? It might help some."

"Come in, gentlemen," said Bridger, "make yourselves to home. I'm starting a new house next month, of imported Vermont marble, but the workmen aren't quite ready to go."

I found out later this was a lie; in fact, the proprietor of Fort Bridger practically never told the entire truth, if there was an opportunity to make up a better story. Coulter said that was the way he got his amusement, and my father added later that what he was, at heart, was "a first-rate working humorist, a rose wasting his fragrance on the desert air."

When we went inside, Kissel stooped over to avoid striking his head and Bridger introduced two Indian women as his wives, saying their names were "Durn Your Eyes" and "Drat Your Hide." None of our group had the impoliteness to inquire if he was joking, but these were the authentic names, according to Coulter, thought up by their husband several years before. The women were proud of them.

We got down to business and explained that we wanted to go to Salt Lake City for the winter. Then my father suggested that we would never make it without a guide. "He'll do it," said Coulter, addressing us, although Bridger was sitting at his elbow. "Once in a while there's work to be done around here, so he gets away and hides whenever he can."

"I'm not in good with Brigham Young right now," said Bridger, in a serious vein. "He says I've been selling firearms to the Utes; what's more, he'd admire to annex my Fort. It so happens I was meaning to go over and have a talk with him; you can ride along and welcome."

This was wonderful news. He would be leaving the day after to-morrow, when his partner, Vasquez, returned from a trading trip. Meanwhile he said we might enjoy seeing the local sights. Then he promised to take us, women and all, to a stream up in the mountains that he said had the fastest current in America, but he cautioned us beforehand not to stick our foot or hand in, so that we wouldn't be scalded. "Water running that fast works up a power of friction against the bottom and sides," he said, eyeing us with a kind of squint. "During the spring thaw, the temperature's close to biling."

Walking us down to the ferry, he rode over with us. A number of Indians were camped on the far bank, as well as the remnants of another train—three wagons altogether. "They're stopping here," Bridger said. "They like the country and mean to settle. They're a mighty smart bunch—got everything they need right in their own crowd, butcher, baker, blacksmith, cobbler, and all like that. They didn't pick a single man unless they needed him for a purpose."

Sitting beside the nearest wagon, sunning himself on a stool, was a gray-bearded old man so ancient and rickety you'd have thought he might fall apart any minute. I could see my father trying to fight down the question.

"What'd they bring the old fellow for?"

"To start their graveyard with."

On the way back to camp, Coe said, "Did you hear what he said about that stream? I don't believe it for a minute; it doesn't stand to reason."

"That man Bridger," replied my father, about to burst, "is the most preposterous humbug and liar I've met in the course of a lifetime devoted to the study of such creatures. I don't believe anything about him. I don't even think he's an Indian fighter."

"Well," observed Coulter, "you can't say I didn't warn you. But you corner him, and I wouldn't be surprised if he'd fight."

All of us except Jennie stood beside the train as it pulled out, waving handkerchiefs and calling our last goodbyes. We had exchanged names and addresses, the way people do, and made vows of keeping in touch later on in the gold fields, knowing in our hearts that we weren't apt to meet again, ever. The passing of time eases the best intentions; it's sad but true.

Coulter would return to Salt Lake City. When he said so, I believed him. But not Jennie. "That's the last we'll see of that critter," she said, angrily fighting back the tears. "He's purely worthless." Standing apart, she turned around when he grinned and waved, riding by. "You performed me a service," he had said to my father. "I'll be along back to see you through to California."

Then he offered one last piece of advice. "A word about Bridger, now. Never mind his yarn-spinning. Trust him as you'd trust your mother. You wouldn't know it, but he's guiding you because I asked him. So keep this in mind; never forget it. Trust him absolutely. There's just about nothing he can't do. And now—goodbye, all."

My father spoke up with real affection. "Coulter, we regard you as a member of the family. It'll be a happy day when we see you back." Kissel crushed some of his bones with a handshake, and Mrs. Kissel broke down and sniffled; even Coe looked distressed to see him go.

So we split up. It was a mournful pass to come to. I found myself holding Po-Povi's hand, with a good-sized lump in my throat. It was like watching all our hopes and plans go fading off in the distance. Would we really get to California? I didn't much think so any longer.

Led by its owner, we pulled out of Fort Bridger before dawn on the day promised, prepared for a hard passage to the Great Salt Lake, much of it over scorched desert and soda flats.

Major Bridger was in a cheerful humor, but he cautioned us that the country was humming with Indians and that we must keep a sharp lookout.

He placed Coe's wagon, still mule-drawn, in the front, the Brice wagon with children and Mrs. Kissel next in line, and our new pack mules, Kissel's and my father's, in the rear. The men were supposed to go on a kind of sentinel duty, roaming the flanks and dropping behind but never getting out of eyeshot. I trotted on Spot up forward near our guide, who rode an Indian pony as raggedy and careless as himself.

By dawn we were well beyond sight of the Fort, keeping to the eastern fringe of the mountains. This route, a short cut by the Great Salt Lake, was coming into use by the bolder of the California immigrants, but the majority still clung to the old trail that continued to Fort Hall and the Humboldt River.

It was October, now, but it was a blistering hot day. Before us stretched an empty waste as forlorn as the eve of creation—no trees, no water, no grass, no growth except artemisia, or sagebrush, and I didn't care if I never saw that wiry shrub again.

When it was full light, and the sun broiling down from about fifty yards high, we began to see the same old thrown-away furniture and wreckage. And before the day was out, dead oxen again, along with graves. "E Pritchard, died July 28, 1849." My father picked up a

181

novel called *The Forger*, by a man named G.P.R. James, and read it walking along, occasionally laughing at something funny, but when Bridger pointed in his dry, squinted-up way at a file of Indians that had taken up the march beside us, scavenging, he put it hurriedly away.

The Indians were Utes, all but naked, so ratty and poor they made the Pawnees seem elegant by comparison. In the afternoon, at a time when the trail lay close to the hills, we passed a village of Diggers—outcast Utes—a breed so low they acted more animal than human. Bridger stopped to show a few dwellings; they were nothing but holes in the ground, a fox's den, with a crude lean-to over the weather side. My father made a hasty sketch of one; I have it now: a shallow pit in which a stark-naked woman crouches, eyes wide and frightened; beside her a bowl of roasting crickets; and hung against a pole, in a skin pouch laced to a board, a papoose wrinkled and shrunken. One of the scavengers now came up with hand thrust out, saying, "Chreesmas gif, Chreesmas gif," but Bridger shooed him away.

"They beg in Brigham Young's city," he said. "They ain't dangerous unless they got an advantage, and then they'll kill you with pleasure."

The scout had been businesslike and silent, considering his reputation for talking, and I think my father was relieved. Bridger placed a strain on him. He never knew how to act when the tall tales began. Only twice during the day did our guide pull any nonsense, and as Mr. Coe said, these two made up for everything. Once, rolling along a perfectly straight, well-marked trail, in what seemed like the middle of the desert, Bridger stopped and glanced to the right and left, as if checking his bearings. Then he uncorked his spyglass and had a careful look around. After this, he wheeled his horse off the trail and began a wide, bothersome detour, finally ending up back on the road.

"I durn near made that same mistake again." he said with a chuckle. "I've bashed up me and my horse twicet already."

"What is it? Why'd we leave the trail?" demanded my father, as the others rode up, sweating in the sun.

Bridger pointed back. "It's that pesky road-block—a mountain of pure glass. You can't see it unless you get right on top, almost."

"Where?" cried my father. "Surely you can't be serious. I can't see a thing."

The trouble with this fellow was, his departures from normal were so crazy and unexpected he caught everybody flat-footed. That's what made my father so mad.

"First time I encountered it, I fired at an antelope and didn't ruffle a hair. I laid down a regular bombardment until I found out what was the matter. He was standing on the other side."

"A mountain of transparent glass," said my father, with heavy scorn.

"You'd better have a last look. You don't see them often. There ain't more than a handful in the entire West."

"No, I expect not," said my father, about to blow up again. "How do you like it, Coe? Pretty, don't you think?"

Falling in with the humor, Coe shook his head. "You couldn't convince me it's glass. If I know anything about gems that mountain's solid blue-white diamond."

"You don't say," said Bridger, studying Coe with new interest. "Well, now, you may be right. Next trip out, I'll bring a jeweler with an eyeglass and have him look her over. Be worth a fortune, if it wasn't flawed."

"Get up," cried my father, swatting one of the mules. "We've got a journey to finish." But in an hour, he'd forgotten the mountain and made the mistake of asking Bridger what he knew about California.

"I've got a fair knowledge of it," said Bridger. "I've been out three times, and enjoyed it, but wouldn't care to live there."

"Why not?" demanded my father, bridling slightly.

"Well, sir, I'd in nowise relish the longevity. No, when my three-score and ten's up, as they say in the Book, I'll be ready to call her off."

"What do you mean? What the deuce has longevity got to do with it? California's just like every place else."

"Not exactly. There's a difference in that respect," said Bridger. "A few die on schedule, give or take a couple of decades, but the majority'll go right on without a hitch. You never know they've aged. It's the climate. Take the case of a man I know out there, name of Psalter, living north of Sacramento. If I remember right, he'll be two hundred and fifty-five in November. He's a tragic example, but there don't seem to be any help for it. When he got to be two hundred, he was plumb wore out, wanted to die and get some rest. But he couln't make it, no matter what. He went to the priests and begged permission to commit suicide, but they thumbsed down on it—said there wasn't any scriptural precedent.

"Then his youngest sister—she couldn't have been over a hundred and fifty and hadn't been paid any attention to before, being the baby—came up with a fine idea. 'Why don't you move away, get out of the state, maybe that'll work?' she said. Well, sir, he was tickled pink. He arranged all his affairs and journeyed over into Nevada, and sure enough, he died, within a month. But he'd left in his will he wanted to be buried in California, so they plopped him down, after a beautiful service, in the Sacramento graveyard, with a marble slab to seal the bargain: 'Horace E. Psalter. 1594-1794. Rest in Peace.'

"However—" Bridger paused and squinted sideways at my father.

"Yes, of course. I quite understand," said my father in disgust, as if he was talking to an idiot.

"Yes, sir," said Bridger. "The climate was too much for him. He wouldn't stay dead. He came back to life, and being a husky sort of fellow, he busted the box and pushed right out. He was perfectly resigned, last time I saw him. Says he don't aim to make any more tries—he'll stay on and die in California if it takes till Doomsday."

My father looked at him steadily for about a minute. "I want to thank you for the anecdote, Major Bridger," he said at last. "You've cleared up a good deal of confusion in my mind about California."

"Any information I've got about it, you're more than welcome. Situated where I am on the trail, I'm apt to hear more than most. I'll try to think up some other points by and by."

"Pray don't bother," said my father stiffly. "There couldn't possibly be anything else of importance."

The third day out from the Fort, we crossed the Wasatch Mountains and then came within view of Salt Lake, an eighty-mile sea with a number of very high islands thrusting up from its calm, silent waters. Thousands of waterfowl—geese, ducks, gulls and bigger birds on the surface—but they made little or no noise. Along with the fact that not a solitary tree, not so much as a two-foot bush, rose from the land nearby, it gave the region a feeling of being more dead than alive.

Before supper, Po-Povi and I walked to the shore and tasted the water, which was brackish and bitter, puckering up your mouth, but in appearance it was as clear as a spring. You could see the bottom sloping down a long way out.

Before we left camp, Major Bridger stated that a person couldn't drown in this lake, unless they fell in upside down, but he said it used to be a lot saltier, and more buoyant. Then he began a story about trying to drive a stake in it with a maul, back in '32, but my father interrupted. I don't think he could of stood any more, not right now.

Ike Bender's Indian Scare

▼▲▼▲▼▲▼▲▼▲▼▲▼▲▼▲▼▲▼▲▼▲▼▲▼▲▼▲▼▲▼▲▼▲▼▲▼▲▼

David Wagoner

Ike Bender is almost eighteen, big and strong and full of dreams. His brother Kit has run off from the family farm in Nebraska to the Colorado gold mines and has sent a letter inviting Ike to join him. After a final battle with his father, Ike leaves for the West, pushing a homemade wheelbarrow, constructed in secret at the home of Tom Slaughter, a neighbor with an attractive fifteen-year-old daughter. Millie Slaughter speaks correct Victorian English (she and Ike have been to school to Miss Wilkerson) and loves Ike with all her heart and vocabulary.

Ike has pushed his wheelbarrow as far as Fort Kearney, Nebraska, when Millie, traveling by stagecoach, catches up with him. A girl who Gets Things Done, she bullies the post chaplain into marrying them and they experience connubial bliss under a tarpaulin attached to the wheelbarrow.

Dangers and difficulties beset them and a fine array of humorous frontier characters pass in review as they trudge westward, but with luck and gumption they finally reach the infant city of Denver and find a way to make their fortune.

David Wagoner, an Ohio-born professor of English who lives in Seattle, has written four novels, using in each an adolescent who attains maturity as he travels through the West, meeting and surviving the pitfalls and perils of the frontier world. The chapter that follows, from *The Road to Many a Wonder*, is typical of their experiences.

WALKING IS A SURE WAY OF GETTING SOMEPLACE IN MOST kinds of country because there don't seem to be much to taking a step or two and, while you're at it, taking a couple more and, once you get going, taking a couple dozen more. And pretty soon you don't notice how many you're taking (unless you're pacing off miles like I done sometimes), and you don't have nothing to wear out or break down except you and what you stand up in. And walking's an interesting way to get someplace because you don't miss much of what's going on like you do when you're memorizing the rear end of an ox or a mule and wondering which fly is bothering it the most. And with walking you never lose track of how far one place is from another, the way you

From *The Road to Many a Wonder* (New York: Farrar, Straus & Giroux, 1974), 133–46.

can in a wagon or a boat if you doze off and start learning the inside of your eyelids by heart.

But one thing you have to say about walking is it takes time. Yet it didn't seem like ordinary time with Millie along, but some new kind, with more room in it sideways, fuller, thicker, and more noticeable. It wasn't just her talking though she done plenty of that, and me too, mostly answering. It was the way I *looked* at everything because I knew she was looking at it too, feeling it out and feeling it through, and I become more alert about everything under the sun because of her. There wasn't a minute of the walking day, with me wheelborrowing and her leading Mr. Blue, when something didn't catch my eye or seem to wake up some new part of my head, and I come to think of it as one of the best parts of love. (I wasn't afraid to think the word no more nor say it neither.)

Day after day and night after night, instead of catching myself napping or going dull-hearted, I'd catch myself breathing and waking up for the sheer wonder of something most folks wouldn't of noticed, including me back before Dogtown—the shape the current makes turning aside at the head of an island; the plain, miserable pleasure a hostler can get out of being mean to strangers at a mail station; the way rain turns all colors falling through sunshine; how fearful it is to listen to somebody else's heart beat and know yours is doing likewise and they'll both stop someday; the way a burro goes about appreciating oats, turning his lips in tight and bulgy like an old man gumming his mush; the feel of your own hams touching the ground when you haven't set on them but once or twice all day; how proud you feel when you make a fire in a place where it didn't look like there was nothing left to burn for miles around; how many different sounds a coyote can make when he settles down to it and has a little neighborly help; the way the moon can turn so bright some nights, you can't look at it no longer than if it was the sun; the way a girl's face can be fifty faces a day, all different, and all enough to make you ache for her; and on and on like that, forever if you've got a mind to.

We seen and heard more folks coming back from the gold fields without having stayed there but overnight, glum and burning mad and some even raving about all the gold being in the storekeeps' teeth, about wanting to lynch the liars back on the Missouri River that had

187

set them on the road to ruination, and we seen old wrecks like Hotchkiss setting theirselves up at trading posts, waiting for the huge flow of new springtime fools, which we was among the first of, and it's certain sure it would of been enough to discourage us if we hadn't been so happy to start off with.

And since we'd already come more'n halfway, it didn't make no difference which direction we kept walking but might's well keep on going and see for ourselves. People would lean out of wagons and yell at us and call us idjits and fall to cussing, and some had crossed off the "Pikes Peak or" on the sides of their wagons and left "Bust" by itself, maybe adding a "By God!" But them people didn't even like where they stood or set *right now*. And we did. They didn't see or feel what we seen or felt *right here*, so how could we trust them about someplace we hadn't laid our eyes on or set foot?

Many a time Millie says to me, "Isn't this beautiful, Mr. Bender?" walking along a barren stretch of road. And it was. She was right. And half an hour later some lunkhead would be jawing and blaspheming at us about the godforsook valley we was in and the sonofabunching Platte and all like that. (I had long since give up defending Millie's ears from foul language, since it would of took too much time to fight a thousand men.)

People see what they believe, I spose, or see what they're set to believe. And me and Millie done a lot of looking at each other in the meantime, when we wasn't bumping into other wonders.

One day she says, "Do you think I'm too tenderhearted, Mr. Bender?"

"No," I says, but it was one of the subjects I'd worried about because I didn't want her getting heartbroke or heartsick over some of the miseries we'd seen and was bound to go on seeing.

"I believe it's one of my many faults," she says. "At least I'm not tender-*footed* any more, but how can I get over the other without turning *hard*hearted?"

"I don't know," I says. "Maybe you better not try."

"I have always believed it was a good idea for all of us to cultivate *feelings*, but now I'm not so sure," she says. "I want to be the most useful kind of wife to you and not a drawback."

For the life of me I couldn't figure out why she wanted to be any kind of wife of mine, but I didn't say so because there's no fit answer to a remark like that when you're already stuck. "You're no drawback," I says. "And it was true what you told me about that Wedded Bliss."

"I'm very glad to hear it," she says, smiling and blushing and giving Mr. Blue an extra twitch on his rope.

Which made me blush too but the same time I wished it was sundown already and us setting by the wheelborrow tent waiting for it to get dark enough to slip inside. Then, like I done most every day, I says, "Are you sure it's not going to be too far for you? You can still catch a mail wagon or stagecoach part ways."

And as usual she says, "Mr. Bender, I'm getting stronger every day, not weaker."

And truth to tell, she seemed to be. She wasn't losing weight and getting scrawny and hollow-eyed like many another I seen on the road. I didn't have no idea what *I* looked like, but she didn't seem worried about me.

If I'd had a mind to it and the muscle and the wagon space and a couple yoke of oxen, I could of set myself up as a blacksmith in the gold fields: by the time we begun the long curve southwest on the South Fork, where there was a couple good fording places for wagons aiming at Fort Laramie and on to Oregon, we'd passed six or seven good-sized anvils laying on the ground and tongs and pinchers and a box full of horseshoes and a stack of rusty sheet iron and plowshares and scythes and bar iron and grindstones and a bellows, all thrown overboard along the way to lighten the loads or maybe just out of disgust with that line of work. The stuff just laid there, and nobody had room to pick it up. Or maybe lots of people done what I done: they'd see something heavy they liked and pick it up and cart it along for a spell, even a day or two, then chuck it away again as too blame heavy. Probably some of them tools had been picked up and flung down again dozens of times and might make it to Denver City by relay in a year or two. The only things I hung on to and tied them alongside my wheelborrow was a two-handled whipsaw that had a beautiful set of teeth and hardly rusty at all and an ax.

"What do you intend to use the saw for?" Millie says.

"I expect I'll saw something with it," I says. "It don't look much good for digging gold."

She give me a peckish frown and says, "I was merely wondering why you'd want to weight yourself down any more than you already are."

I kept it anyway and two big pocketfuls of two-inch nails out of a heap that must of been from a keg but somebody had burnt the keg for firewood. And one night we camped by a cookstove somebody had tossed out, and we got it set upright and built a fire in it and baked some pretty near real bread and biscuits and then set beside it a long time, even after dark, enjoying the comfort like we was in our own kitchen except for the wind and the coyotes. When we left it behind the next day, Millie kept looking back at it, but even if I'd tossed out the whipsaw, ax, pickax, spade, and quicksilver and give up all thought of striking it rich, I don't think I could of brung it along without spraining my back or breaking down the *Millicent Slaughter*.

We seen our first pine trees mixed in with the cottonwood out on the river islands, and I knew we was getting onto higher ground. Every step had been a fraction of a fraction of an inch uphill, and the country was beginning to change. And then late one afternoon on a deserted stretch where nobody was catching up with us and there wasn't nobody up ahead—just some traces of smoke from campfires on the other side of the river, which was still near a mile wide, even though it'd been halved back at the fork—a party of eleven Injuns on horseback come over the low valley rim and rode straight down at us, coming pretty fast like they meant business, and I got my gun into my belt and stood in front of Millie and Mr. Blue and commenced worrying as hard as I could without showing it.

"Are the savages hostile around here?" she says.

"I hope not," I says, keeping my voice calm, like she had asked was the chokecherries ripe yet.

I don't know too much about Injuns, not having got friendly with none back home who'd tell me what *they* knew (such as how to live on the prairie without dirt farming, which dang few white men can do), but I thought I could reckonize a war party when I seen one, and that's what this was. When they come up close and reined in, using their thin little woven horsehair or rawhide hackamores that didn't look like they'd control a newborn calf, let alone a wild-eyed skittery paint without no bit in his mouth nor stirrups nor saddle, I seen they wasn't much older than me and some younger. But they had painted for war and carried bows and arrows and coup sticks and a couple old rifles and looked fierce and joyful and full of vinegar.

The leader—I didn't have no trouble picking him out—was an uncomfortable sight and not just because he was taller and stronger-looking and had a bad wound down the side of his neck and was going bare-chested under his blanket even in the chilly weather: what bothered me most was the way he set still and stared while the others let their ponies do shifty, tight-footed little dances and laughed and chattered at each other. His pony didn't lift a hoof, and he looked like he'd growed up there on its back, and he was wearing his hair all swooped around on one side and down in a single braid, and behind the one ear showing he'd stuck a small blue bird with its beak pointing forward, dead, I guess, but maybe not. And to make it worse, he was staring at me like he'd just found the man who'd give him that half-healed wound.

"I don't believe we're going to be able to cover this matter with a twenty-five-cent-piece, Mr. Bender," Millie says.

"Don't do nothing," I says. "Not yet."

A smaller and younger-looking Injun with two big feathers sticking up out of the back of his head jumped down off his pony and come toward us hunched forward and smiling. Some of the others was cackling at him and saying words, and he looked back a couple times at Blue Bird (which is how I thought of the other one right off) to see if he was doing something wrong and getting no sign one way or the other far as I could see. He had a bowie knife and a feather-tipped coup stick and a loose buckskin shirt with a narrow kind of bib down the front of it made out of skinny bird or critter legbones and streaks of white paint all aiming out from his nose and mouth, and hanging around his neck on a strip of rawhide like a necklace, he had a pair of gold-rimmed specs with one lens busted out.

He stopped within arm's reach of me and straightened up and

begun acting puffed up and solemn and pursing his lips, which must of been what I looked like because all the others except Blue Bird laughed and howled to egg him on.

I didn't do nothing, since being mocked at is no worse than a little bad weather and a considerable improvement on going hungry.

Then this Specs started clowning around bowlegged, and imitating me pushing the wheelborrow with arms pulled down stiff and straining, and while he was staggering off in a circle and getting some more cackles, I moved three or four steps forward to give me some elbow room away from Millie in case there was going to be fisticuffs or worse, which I prayed not, eleven opponents being no fit number for a sane man with a wife to protect.

He seemed a bit surprised when he seen I wasn't in the same place no more, and he come back acting crazy and teasy but a little annoyed too. Some of the others was giving him advice now, it seemed like, and he didn't want none of it. He dubbed me quick on the shoulder with his coup stick and sobered up a few seconds to see how I'd take it. I reckoned that to be a kind of insult, a way to score off of me, but I didn't mind. I didn't have no stick of my own, but I tipped my hat to him and give him a little bow and a smile just like he was a nice old lady who'd said Good Morning.

He frowned over that and got some more advice from the other nine and nothing but that same long stare from Blue Bird.

"How much money would you suggest I give them, Mr. Bender?" Millie says.

"None," I says. "Just wait."

I was scairt bad, mostly for Millie and Mr. Blue and the Future and Wedded Bliss, but some for me myself in my personal skin too. "Does anybody talk English?" I says.

But there was no sign from any of them, no change. I'd heard tell a lot about the way Injuns fight, and I felt pretty sure if they'd been feeling really smoky, they'd of done their killing and scalping at the first swoop. This was more like bullyragging back home where a lot of kids will pick on one or two that's different and torment them a while, then go off and think up something better to do. The only one that didn't fit was this Blue Bird, who looked man enough to face down eleven white men if the situation had been turned inside out. Seemed like I only had two choices: I could try to be as big a clown as Specs or I could try to be as steady and dignified as Blue Bird, and the trouble was I didn't think I could handle either one of them parts very good.

So then I had an inspiration, and I spread my arms out solemn and used the best voice Miss Wilkerson had learnt me how to get down in my chest, and I says:

> *"O sweet and strange it seems to me, that ere this day is done,*
> *The voice that now is speaking, may be beyond the sun—*
> *Forever and forever,—all in a blessed home—*
> *And there to wait a little while, till you and Effie come—*
> *To lie within the light of God, as I lie upon your breast—*
> *And the wicked cease from trouble, and the weary are at rest. "*

That seemed to shake them up a little. Specs backed up and forgot to make faces, and the others talked it over a bit like they'd just heard the first part of a Peace Treaty.

"How can you possibly expect savages to appreciate Lord Tennyson?" Millie says.

But I wasn't trying to get them to appreciate nothing but our right to keep on walking (in case we had any right), and I says, "In about a minute, they may take everything we own, Millie, including our scalps, so I might's well try giving them something that don't cost nothing first."

They'd begun to stir at the sound of my normal voice, and I seen Specs maneuvering to get his audience back: he begun to stalk me, circling a bit like I was a strange dumb animal, gliding his moccasin along the ground and feeling out each inch of foothold, so I spread my arms again and says,

> *"I grieve for life's bright promise, just shown and then withdrawn;*
> *But still the sun shines round me, the evening bird sings on,*
> *And I again am soothed, and, beside the ancient gate.*
> *In this soft evening sunlight, I calmly stand and wait. "*

Which wasn't any too appropriate or even true but was all I could remember offhand from Miss Wilkerson's elocution lessons, where even when I done my best I embarrassed myself something awful.

Specs had pulled back a ways and was scowling like he was scairt I might be making medicine, and I *was*, the only kind I knew how, because I didn't want nothing of mine or Milie's to wind up decorating their necks like whoever had brung them gold-rimmed eyeglasses this far west and was now having a hard time reading fine print—wherever he was—or maybe even breathing.

Spreading his arms out like I'd done and puffing up his chest, Specs tried mocking my voice, but he wasn't any too good at it. And after just a few words, which I think was neither Injun nor English but made up, Blue Bird stopped him cold and silenced him with one little grunt. Then we all just stood there for a spell, the other nine leaving off their joshing and joking and me not remembering no more poems, and Millie commenced singing.

From behind me come her thin, clear, high voice, and she sang:

> *"Though our way is dark and dreary,*
> *And we toil from day to day,*
> *While the heart is sad and weary,*
> *At our home there shines a ray.*
> *Kindly words and smiling faces,*
> *Gentle voices as of yore,*
> *Loving kisses and embraces*
> *Ever wait us at the door."*

Which I hadn't heard before and sure didn't sound like no home of mine, but the Injuns was listening hard and quiet, and even Specs held still like he might learn something.

She sang:

> *"Here we turn when all forsake us,*
> *Here we never look in vain*
> *For the soothing tones that wake us*
> *Back to joy and peace again."*

Then she loudened it up a good bit and poured on the chorus:

"Kindly words and smiling faces,
Gentle voices as of yore,
Loving kisses and embraces
Ever wait us at the door. "

Well, there wasn't a smiling face in the bunch, and I'd sooner been kissed by Mr. Blue than one of them, but when she quit, nobody was scowling neither, not even Specs, who had backed off near the others.

Then Blue Bird come to life and slipped off his horse and held his rust-colored blanket close around him and took his slow, sweet time coming straight at me. So I took my hat off, partly out of respect and partly to hold it over my waist so's I could get hold of the revolver handle, but even then knowing I didn't have no use for one bullet. He'd seen the gun already, and it must not of worried him, and I was in a total fluster inside my head, wondering what to do, but I didn't let none of it get to my face. There still wasn't nothing on *his* face but that dead, deep stare and a white circle painted on his forehead.

I let my hat slip down to my side so's he could see the gun again if he felt like it, but his eyes didn't turn that way, just kept boring into mine. He'd been hit bad on the neck, where the jagged cut was all crusty with blood and something that looked like dry leaves crumbled up, and now he let his blanket fall open, and I seen he didn't have a gun but a knife the size of mine and a stone ax with a stick handle wrapped in thongs and an old deerskin pouch the size of a goose egg tied around his neck. And hanging down from his waist was two long clumps of black hair with bloody patches at one end, and they hadn't grown on no trees.

He was near enough to touch now, and I was hoping he'd decide to bump foreheads like the buffalo Injun and we could call it a day, but instead, without no change of expression, he took his ax out of where it was stuck under the drawstring of his deerskin leggings and lifted it up high in the air aimed right at the top of my skull. He was an inch or two taller than me and had an arm on him as thick as most legs, and it looked like my hour had come.

In the smidgen of an instant I had thought up all the things I could do: knife him and offer to fight the rest one at a time, start bargaining off our goods, shoot him and pretend the gun was full of bullets, recite another poem even if I had to make it up as I went along, beg for mercy, and so on—the only thing that never occurred to me was to shoot Millie, which I had heard of being done by others to spare their spouses a Fate Worse Than Death, it being my opinion that nobody can decide what's worse than death for somebody else. Meanwhile, I done absolutely nothing but stand there, and when I thought it over later, I figured out I didn't *believe* Blue Bird was going to do nothing bad. There was just something too manly about him, and I think that's what he was looking for in me.

He put on a good show of raising that ax over my head and starting to bring it down hard right on top of my skullbone, which would of taught me a lesson not to trust no dignified-looking Injuns, and raised the start of a shriek out of Millie, who, I believe, was about to tackle him. But he stopped it a few inches short, while still staring deep and fixed into my eyes and me staring back and not flinching (though I say so, as shouldn't) because I *knew* everything was going to be all right. How could I have a grand Future if it wasn't?

He stood holding that ax over me, then just barely touched the crown of my head with it, and let a little smile come at the edges of his broad, thin lips. He stuck the ax under his drawstring again (all the other Injuns was keeping dead still, and Millie had shut off her squeal before it hit full pitch) and nodded at me. Then he spoke in a deep, slow voice and touched hisself between the eyes and on the crown of his own head and touched along his scar. The other Injuns made a noise like an agreement, and he took the bird from behind his ear and kissed its beak, and I was scairt for a minute he was going to give it to me (what would I of done with something like that?), but he stuck it behind his own ear again like a storekeep with a pencil.

Well, I didn't know quite what to do to show my appreciation and sympathy and whatever else he wanted, so I just picked the nearest thing and took out my revolver and handed it over. It wasn't mine anyway, and I didn't like guns, and it saved me chucking it into the river like I'd planned.

Millie says, "Mr. Bender," like she was beginning to protest, but I shushed her, which I wouldn't ordinarily do, believing in free speech. The Injun looked the gun all over, smiling broad now, and the other Injuns made them approving sounds again, and I seen Specs climb back on his horse like he knew this little game was over.

Blue Bird took the pouch from around his neck and put it around mine, backed off and says something ceremonial-sounding to me and waited, I guess expecting me to do likewise, so I says,

> *"God is great, God is good.*
> *Let us thank Him for our food.*
> *By His goodness we are fed.*
> *Give us, Lord, our daily bread."*

Which was the only other poem I could think of offhand besides "Mary Had a Little Lamb" and "Little Jack Horner" and like that. But he seemed to like it fine, and if it was good enough for him, it was good enough for me, and when he swooped back up onto his pony (they make mounting up without stirrups look easy, but try it sometime wearing a blanket) and galloped off, me and Millie stood there waving till they was gone out of sight, and we didn't have to explain to each other why we was going to camp right there on the spot and not move another step in what was left of daylight: our knees just wouldn't of behaved.

Flashy and Sonsee-array

▼▲▼▲▼▲▼▲▼▲▼▲▼▲▼▲▼▲▼▲▼▲▼▲▼▲▼▲▼▲▼▲▼

George MacDonald Fraser

George MacDonald Fraser, the creator of Sir Harry Flashman and his global adventures, served in a Scottish regiment in India, Africa, and the Middle East, accumulating background that he put to use when he retired to the Isle of Man to pursue Flashman through his battles and betrayals.

Flashman first appears as a cowardly bully in Thomas Hughes's once-famous *Tom Brown at Rugby*. Fraser picks him up as a young officer, already dedicated to duplicity and dissipation. He admits that he "never had a decent feeling in his scandalous, lecherous life." His son, a Sioux Indian with a Harvard degree, sums it up: "You're a yard-wide son-of-a-bitch, aren't you, Papa?" He is, nevertheless, a dashing figure, irresistible to women, and his frankness, wit, and British *sang-froid* are engaging.

The story begins in New Orleans, where Flash is in trouble as usual. With the help of Suzy Willinck, madam of a fashionable bordello, he escapes and engages to shepherd her and her young ladies across the plains to Santa Fe. He marries her en route and helps her set up in business. When he finally deserts her and heads for Mexico, he is forced to join a party of scalp hunters who raid a sleeping camp of Mimbreno Apaches. The men proceed to rape the Indian women, but Flashy treats his prize with forbearance, and when her people, led by the mighty Mangus Colorado, ambush the ambushers, she saves Flashy's life and eventually marries him.

Her name is Sonsee-array, recalling the heroine of Elliot Arnold's *Blood Brother*, and the whole episode is a takeoff on Tom Jeffords's courtship and marriage. Fraser's Sonsee-array, however, is no demure Apache maiden. She is a spoiled brat who goes after what she wants, and when she instructs Flashman the morning after their marriage, "Make my bells ring again, white man," Flashy has to give his all.

POSSIBLY BECAUSE I'VE SPENT SO MUCH TIME AS THE UNWILLING guest of various barbarians around the world, I've learned to mistrust romances in which the white hero wins the awestruck regard of the silly savages by sporting a monocle or predicting a convenient eclipse, whereafter they worship him as a god, or make him a blood brother, and in no time he's teaching 'em close order drill and crop rotation and generally running the whole show. In my experience, they know

From *Flashman and the Redskins* (New York, Alfred A. Knopf, 1982), 203–20.

all about eclipses, and a monocle isn't likely to impress an aborigine who wears a bone through his nose. So don't imagine that my tent-pegging hand impressed the Apaches overmuch; it hadn't. I was alive because Sonsee-array fancied me and was grateful—and also because she was just the kind of minx to enjoy flouting tribal convention by marrying a foreigner. I'd come creditably out of the Vasco business—nobody mourned him, apparently—and Mangas had given me the nod, so that was that. But no one made me a blood brother, thank God, or I'd probably have caught hydrophobia, and as for worship—nobody gets that from those fellows.

They were prepared to accept me, but not with open arms, and I was in no doubt that my life still hung by a hair, on Sonsee-array's whim and Mangas's indulgence. So I must try to shut my mind to the hideous pickle I was in, recover from the shock to my nervous system, and play up to them for all I was worth while I found out where the devil I was, where safety lay, and plotted my escape. If I'd known that it would take me six months, I believe I'd have died of despair. In the meantime, it was some slight reassurance to find that however unreal and terrifying my plight might seem to me, the tribe were ready to take it for granted, and even be quite hospitable about it, white-eye though I was.

For example, the Yawner made me free of the family pot and a blanket in the wickiup which he shared with his wife Alopay, their infant, and her relatives; it stank like the nation and was foul, but Alopay was a buxom, handsome wench who was prepared to treat me kindly for Sonsee-array's sake, and the Yawner himself was more friendly now that he'd saved my life—have you noticed, the man who does a good turn is often more inclined to be amiable than the chap who's received it? He'd evidently been appointed my bear-leader because although he wasn't a true Mimbreno, he was related to Mangas, and trusted by the chief; he was as much jailer as mentor, which was one reason it took me such a deuce of a time to get out of Apacheria.

Having taken me on, though, he was prepared to make a go of it, and that same evening he inducted me into a peculiar Apache institution which, while revolting, is about the most clubbable function I've ever struck. After we had supped, he took me along to a singular adobe building near the fort, like a great beehive with a tiny door in one side; there were about forty male Apaches there, all stark naked, laughing and chattering, with Mangas among them. No one gave me a second glance, so I followed the Yawner's example and stripped, and then we crawled inside, one after the other, into the most foetid, suffocating heat I'd ever experienced.

It was black as Egypt's night, and I had to creep over nude bodies that grunted and heaved and snarled what I imagine was "Mind where you're putting your feet, damn you!"; I was choking with the stench and dripping with sweat as I flopped on that pile of humanity, and more crowded in on top until I was jammed in the middle of a great heap of gasping, writhing Apaches; I felt I must faint with the pressure and atrocious heat and stink. I could barely breathe, and then it seemed that warm oil was being poured over us from above—but is was simply reeking sweat, trickling down from the mass of bodies overhead.

They loved it; I could hear them chuckling and sighing in that dreadful sodden oven that was boiling us alive; I hadn't even breath enough to protest; it was as much as I could do to keep my face clear of the rank body beneath me and drag in great laboured gasps of what I suppose was air. For half an hour we lay in that choking blackness, drenched and boiled to the point of collapse, and then they began to crawl out again, and I dragged my stupefied body into the open more dead than alive.

That was my introduction to the Apache sweatbath, one of the most nauseating experiences of my life—and an hour later, I don't know when I've felt so splendidly refreshed. But what astonished me most, when it sank in, was how they had included me in the party as a matter of course; I felt almost as though I'd been elected to the Apache Club—which in other respects proved to be about as civilised as White's, with fewer bores than the Reform, and a kitchen slightly better than the Athenaeum's.

I had a further taste of Apache culture on the following day, when with the rest of the community I attended the great wailing funeral procession for the deceased Vasco, and for the victims of Gallantin's massacre, whose bodies had been brought down from the valley in the hills. That was a spooky business, for there were two or three of my own bagging on those litters, each corpse with its face painted and scalp replaced (I wondered who'd matched 'em all up) and its weapons carried before. They buried them under rock piles near the big hill they call Ben Moor (and that gave me a jolt, if you like, for you know what big hill is in Gaelic—Ben Mhor. God knows if there's a tribe of Scotch Apaches; I shouldn't be surprised—those tartan buggers get everywhere). They lit purification fires after the burial, and marked the place with a cross, if you please, which I suppose they learned from the dagoes.

Speaking of scalps, I discovered that the Mimbrenos had no special zeal for tonsuring their enemies, but they brought back a few from those of Gallantin's band they'd killed, and the women dressed and stretched them on little frames, to brighten up the parlour, I dare say. One scalp was pale and sandy, and I guessed it was Nugent-Hare's.

Meanwhile, no time was lost in bringing me up to scratch. After the funeral, the Yawner told me I must take my pony to Sonsee-array's wickiup and leave it there—so I did, watched by the whole village, and madam ignored it. "What now?" says I, and he explained that when she fed and watered the beast and returned it, I had been formally accepted. She wouldn't do it at once, for that would show unmaidenly eagerness, but possibly on the second or third day; if she delayed to the fourth day, she was a proper little tease.

D'you know, the saucy bitch waited until the fourth evening?—and a fine lather I was in by then, for fear she'd changed her mind, in which case God knows what might have happened to me. But just before dusk there was a great laughter and commotion, and through the wickiups she came, astride my Arab, looking as proud and pleased as Punch, with a crowd of squaws and children in tow, and even a few menfolk. She was in full fig of beaded tunic and lace scarf, but now she was also wearing the long white leggings with tiny silver bells down the seams, which showed she was marriageable; she dropped the Arab's bridle into my hand with a most condescending smile, everyone cheered and stamped, and for the first time I found Apache faces grinning at me, which is a frightening sight.

There was even more grinning later, for Mangas held an enormous jollification on corn-beer and pine-bark spirit and a fearsome cactus tipple called *mescal*; they don't mind mixing their drinks, those fellows, and got beastly foxed, although I went as easy as I could. Mangas punished the *tizwin* something fearful, and presently, when the others had toppled sideways or were hiccoughing against each other telling obscene Apache stories, he jerked his head at me, collared a flask, and led the way, stumbling and cursing freely, to the old ruined fort. He took a long pull at the flask, swayed a bit, and belched horribly; aha, thinks I, now for the fatherly talk and a broad hint about letting the bride get some sleep on honeymoon. But it wasn't that; what followed was one of the strangest conversations I've ever had in my life, and I set it down because it was my introduction to that queer mixture of logic and lunacy that is typical of Indian thought. The fact that we were both tight as tadpoles made it all the more revealing, really, and if he had some wild notions, he was still a damned shrewd file, the Red Sleeves. What with the booze and his guttural Spanish, he wasn't always easy to follow, but I record him fairly; I can still see that shambling bulk, his blanket hitched close against the night cold, like an unsteady Sphinx in the moonlight, clutching his bottle, and croaking basso profundo:

Mangas: The Mexicanos built this fort when they still had chiefs over the great water. The Americanos build many such . . . is it true that even Santa Fe is a mere wickiup beside the towns of the *pinda-lickoyee* where the sun rises?

Flashy: Indeed, yes. In my country are towns so great that a man can hardly walk through them between sunrise and sunset. You ought to see St. Paul's.

Mangas: You're lying, of course. You boast as young men do, and you're drunk. But the *pinda-lickoyee* people are many in number—as many as the trees in the Gila forest, I'm told.

Flashy: Oh, indubitably. Perfect swarms of them.

Mangas: Perhaps ten thousand?

Flashy (unaware that ten thousand is as far as an Apache can count, but not disposed to argue): Ah . . . yes, just about.

Mangas: Huh! And now, since the Americanos beat the Mexicanos in war, many of these white-eyes have come through our country, going to a place where they seek the *pesh klitso**, the *oro-hay*. Their

*Gold; literally "yellow iron."

pony soldiers say that all this country is now Americano, because they took it from the Mexicanos. But the Mexicanos never had it, so how can it be taken from them?

Flashy: Eh? Ah, well . . . politics ain't my line, you know. But the Mexicanos *claimed* this land, so I suppose the Americanos—

Mangas (fortissimo): It was never Mexicano land! *We* let them dig here, at Santa Rita, for the *kla-klitso**, until they turned on us treacherously, and we destroyed them—ah, that was a rare slaughter! And *we* let them live on the Del Norte, where we raid and burn them as we please! Soft, fat, stupid Mexicano pigs! What rule had they over us or the land? None! And now the Americanos treat the land as though it were theirs—beause they fought a little war in Mexico! Huh! They say—a chief of their pony soldiers told me this—that we must obey them, and heed their law!

Flashy: Did he, though? Impudent bastard!

Mangas: He came to me after we Mimbreno rode a raid into Sonora with Hashkeela of the Coyoteros, who is husband to my second daughter—she is not so fair as Sonsee-array, by the way. You like Sonsee-array, don't you, *pinda-lickoyee* Flaz'man? You truly love my little gazelle?

Flashy: Mad about her . . . I can't wait.

Mangas (with a great sigh and belch): It is good. She is a delightful child—wilful, but of a spirit! That is from me; her beauty is her mother's—she was a Mexicano lady, you understand, taken on a raid into Coahuila, ah! so many years ago! I saw her among the captives lovely as a frightened deer, and I thought: that is my woman, now and forever. I forgot the loot, the cattle, even the killing—only one thought possessed me, in that moment—

Flashy: I know what you mean.

Mangas: I took her! I shall never forget it. Uuurrgh! Then we rode home. Already I had two wives of our people; their families were enraged that I brought a new foreign wife—I had to fight my brothers-in-law, naked, knife to knife! I defied the law—for her! I ripped out their bowels—for her! I tore out their hearts with my fingers—for her!

---

*Presumably copper, since this was mined at Santa Rita. *Kla-kitso*, literally, is "night-iron."

I was red to the shoulders with their blood! Do they not call me the Red Sleeves—Mangas Colorado? Uuurrghh!

Flashy (faintly): Absolutely! Bravo, Mangas—may I call you Mangas?

Mangas: When my little dove, my dear Sonsee-array, told me how *you* had fought for *her*—how you sank your knife in the belly of the *pinda-lickoyee* scalp-hunter, and tore and twisted his vitals, and drank his blood—I thought, there is one with the spirit of Mangas Colorado! (Gripping my shoulder, tears in his eyes.) Did you not exult as the steel went home—for her?

Flashy: By George, yes! That'll teach you, I thought—

Mangas: But you did not take his heart or scalp?

Flashy: Well, no . . . I was thinking about looking after her, you see, and—

Mangas: And afterwards . . . you did not uuurrghh! with her?

Flashy (quite shocked): Heavens, no! Oh, I mean, I was in a perfect sweat for her, of course—but she was tired, don't you know . . . and . . . and distressed, naturally . . .

Mangas (doubtfully): Her mother was tired and distressed—but I had only one thought . . . (Shakes head) But you *pinda-lickoyee* have different natures, I know . . . you are colder—

Flashy: Northern climate.

Mangas (taking another swig): What was I saying when you began to talk of women? Ah, yes . . . my raid with Hashkeela six moons ago, when we slaughtered in Sonora, and took much loot and many slaves. And afterwards this Americano fool—this pony soldier—came and told me it was wrong! He told *me*, Mangas Colorado, that it was wrong!

Flashy: He never!

Mangas: "Why, fool," I told him, "these Mexicanos are your enemies—have you not fought them?" "Yes," says he, "but now they have yielded under our protection, at peace. So we cannot suffer them to be raided." "Look, fool," I told him, "when you fought them, did you ask our permission?" "No," says he. "Then why should we ask yours?" I said.

Flashy: Dam' good!

Mangas: It was then he said it was his law, and we must heed it. I

204

said: "We Mimbreno do not ask you to obey our law; why, then, do you ask us to obey yours?" He could not answer except to say that it was his great chief's word, and we must—which is no reason. Now, was he a fool, or did he speak with a double tongue? You are *pinda-lickoyee*, you know their minds. Tell me.

Flashy: May I borrow your flask! Thanks. Well, you see, he was just saying what his great chief told him to say—obeying orders. That's how they work, you know.

Mangas: Then he and his chief are fools. If I gave such an order to an Apache, without good reason, he would laugh at me.

Flashy: I'll bet he wouldn't.

Mangas: Huh?

Flashy: Sorry. Wind.

Mangas: Why should the Americanos try to force their law on us? They cannot want our country; it has little *oro-hay*, and the rocks and desert are no good for their farmers. Why can they not leave us alone? We never harmed them until they harmed us—why should we, with the Mexicanos to live off? At first I thought it was because they feared us, the warrior Apache, and would have us quiet. But other tribes— Arapaho, Cheyenne, Shoshoni—have been quiet, and still the *pinda-lickoyee* force law on them. Why?

Flashy: I don't know, Mangas Colorado.

Mangas: You know. So do I. It is because their spirit tells them to spread their law to all people, and they believe their spirit is better than ours. Whoever believes that is wrong and foolish. It is such a spirit as was in the world in the beginning, when it was rich and wicked, and God destroyed it with a great flood. But when He saw that the trees and birds and hills and great plains had perished with the people, His heart was on the ground, and He made it anew. And He made the Apache His people, and gave us His way, which is our way.

Flashy: Mmh, yes. I see. But (greatly daring) He made the *pinda-lickoyee*, too, didn't he?

Mangas: Yes, but He made them fools, to be destroyed. He gave them their evil spirit, so that they should blunder among us—perhaps He designed them for our prey. I do not know. But we shall destroy them, if they come against us, the whole race of *pinda-lickoyee*, even all

205

ten thousand. They do not know how to fight—they ride or walk in little lines, and we draw them into the rocks and they die at our leisure. They are no match for us. (Suddenly) Why were you among the Americanos?

Flashy (taken aback): I . . . told you . . . I was a trader . . . I . . .

Mangas (grinning sly and wicked): An Inglese trader—among the Americanos? Strange . . . for you hate each other, because you once ruled their land, and they were your slaves, and rose against you, and you have fought wars against them. This I know—for are there not still chiefs among the Dacotah of the north who carry *pesh-klitso* pictures of the Snow Woman's ancestors, given to their fathers long ago, when your people ruled? Huh! I think you were among the Americanos because you had angered the Snow Woman, and she drove you out, beause she saw the spirit of the snake in your eyes, and knew that you do not speak with a straight tongue. (Fixes terrified Flashy with a glare, then shrugs) It does not matter; sometimes I have a forked tongue myself. Only remember—when you speak to Sonsee-array, let it be with a straight tongue.

Flashy (petrified): Rather!

Mangas: Ugh. Good. You will be wise to do so, for I have favoured you, and you will be one of the people, and your heart will be opened. When we fight the Americanos, you will be glad, for you are their enemy as we are. Perhaps one day I shall send you to the Snow Woman, even as the *pinda-lickoyee* of Texas sent messengers to her, with offers of friendship. Fear not—the anger she bears you will go out of her heart when she knows you come from Mangas Colorado, huh?

Flashy: Oh, like a shot. She'll be delighted.

Mangas: She must be a strange woman, to rule over men. Is she as beautiful as Sonsee-array?

Flashy (tactfully): Oh, dear me, no! About the same build, but nothing like as pretty. No woman is.

We were sitting among the ruins by now, and at this point he toppled slowly backwards and lay with his huge legs in the air, singing plaintively. God, he was drunk! But I must have been drunker, for presently he carried me home in one hand (I weighed about fourteen stone then) and dropped me into my wickiup—through the roof, not the door, unfortunately. But if my final memories of that celebration was confused, I'm clear about what he said earlier, and if it sounds like drunkard's babble, just remark some of the things that supposedly simple savage knew—along with all his fanciful notions.

He'd heard of Spanish and British colonial rule, and of the American wars of '76 and 1812; he'd even somehow got wind of Britain's negotiations with the old Texas Republic before it joined the States in '46. At the same time he'd no idea of what Spain or Britain or the United States or even Texas really *were*—dammit, he thought the whole white race was only ten thousand strong, and obviously imagined Queen Victoria living in a wickiup somewhere over the hills. He probably thought the American troops he'd seen were some sort of tribal war party whom the 'Pash could wipe up whenever they chose. And yet, he could already read with uncanny wisdom the minds of a white race he hardly knew. "Their spirit tells them to spread their law . . . they believe their spirit is better than ours." Poor old Red Sleeves; wasn't he right, just?

No, he wasn't an ordinary man. I knew him over several months, and can say he had the highest type of that lucid Indian mind which can put the civilised logician to shame, yet whose very simplicity of wisdom has been the redskin's downfall. He was a fine psychologist—you'll note he had weighed me for a rascal and fugitive on short acquaintance—an astute politician, and a bloody, cruel, treacherous barbarian who'd have been a disgrace to the Stone Age. If that seems contradictory—well, Indians are contrary critters, and Apaches more than most. Mangas Colorado taught me that, and gave me my first insight into the Indian mind, which is such a singular mechanism, and so at odds with ours, that I must try to tell you about it here.

Speaking of Apaches in particular, you must understand that to them deceit is a virtue, lying a fine art, theft and murder a way of life, and torture a delightful recreation. Aha, says you, here's old Flashy airing his prejudices, repeating ancient lies. By no means—I'm telling you what I learned at first hand—and remember, I'm a villain myself, who knows the real article when he sees it, and the 'Pash are the only folk I've struck who truly believe that villainy is admirable; they haven't been brought up, you see, in a Christian religion that makes much of conscience and guilt. They reverence what we think of as evil; the bigger a rascal a man is, the more they respect him, which is why the likes of Mangas—whose duplicity and cunning were far more valued in the tribe than his fighting skill—and the Yawner, became great among them. This twisted morality is almost impossible for white folk to understand; they look for excuses, and say the poor savage don't know right from wrong. Jack Cremony had the best answer to that: if you think an Apache can't tell right from wrong—wrong him, and see what happens.

* * *

The morning after Mangas's *tizwin* party I was rousted out at dawn by a foul-tempered Yawner, who took me miles off into the hills, both with our heads splitting, to prepare for my honeymoon. We must find a pretty, secluded spot, he snarled, and build a bower for my bride's reception; we lit on a little pine grove by a brook, and there we built a wickiup—or rather, he did, while I got in the way and made helpful suggestions, and he damned the day he'd ever seen me—and stored it with food and blankets and cooking gear. When it was done he glared at it, and then muttered that it would be none the worse for a bit of garden; he'd made one for Alopay, apparently, and she'd thought highly of it.

So now I sweated, carefully transplanting flowers from the surrounding woods, while the Yawner squinted and frowned and stood back considering; when I'd bedded them around the wickiup to his satisfaction, he came to give them a final pat and smooth, growling at me to go easy with the water. We got it looking mighty pretty between us, and when I said Sonsee-array would be sure to like it, he shrugged and grunted, and we found ourselves grinning at each other across the flower-bed—odd, that's how I remember him, not as the old man I saw last year, but as the ugly, bow-legged young brave, all Apache from boots to headband, so serious as he arranged the blooms just so, cleaning the earth from his knife and looking sour and pleased among the flowers. A strange memory, in the light of history—but then he's still Yawner to me, for all that the world has learned to call him Geronimo.

The wedding took place two days later, on the open space before the old fort at Santa Rita, and if my memories of the ceremony itself are fairly vague, it's perhaps because the preliminaries were so singular. A great fire was lit before the old fort, and while the tribe watched from a distance, all the virgins trooped out giggling in their best dresses and sat round it in a great circle. Then the drummers started as darkness fell, and presently out shuffled the dancers, young bucks and boys, dressed in the most fantastic costumes, capering about the flames—the only time, by the way, that I've ever seen Indians dancing round a fire in the approved style. First came the spirit seekers, in coloured kilts with Aztec patterns and the long Apache leggings; they were all masked, and on their heads they bore peculiar frames decorated with coloured points and feathers and half-moons which swayed as they danced and chanted. They were fully-armed, and shook their stone-clubs and lances to drive away devils while they asked God (Montezuma, I believe) for a blessing on Sonsee-array and, presumably, me.

It was a slow, rhythmic, rather graceful dance, except for the little boys, whose task seemed to be to mock and tease the older men, which they did with great glee, to the delight of all. Then the drumming changed, to a more hollow, urgent note, and all the girls jumped up in mock terror, staring about, and cowering as out of the darkness raced the buffalo-dancers, in coloured, fearsome masks surmounted by animal heads—scalps of bison and wolf and deer and mountain-lion. As they leaped and whooped about the fire, all the virgins screamed and ran for their lives, but after a while, as the drumming grew faster and faster, they began to drift timidly back, until they too were joining in the dance, circling and shuffling among the buffalo-men in the fire-glow. All very proper, mind you, no lascivious nonsense or anything like that.

Then the drums stopped abruptly, the dance ceased, and the first spirit-dancer took his stance before the fire and began to chant. The Yawner tapped me on the shoulder—I was in my buckskins, by the way, with a garland round my neck—and he and another young brave called Quick Killer conducted me forward to stand before the spirit-chief. We waited while he droned away, and presently out of the darkness comes Mangas, leading Sonsee-array in a beautiful long white robe, all quilled and beaded, with her hair in two braids to her waist. She stood silent by me, and Mangas by the spirit-chief, whose headdress barely topped the Mimbreno giant. Silence fell . . . and here's a strange thing. You know how my imagination works, and how at the hitching-rail with Susie I reviewed my past alliances—Elspeth and Irma and Madam Baboon of Madagascar . . . well, this time I had no such visions. It may be that having Mangas Colorado looming over you, looking like something off the gutters at Notre Dame, concentrates the mind wonderfully; but also, it didn't seem to be a very *religious* ceremony, somehow, and I didn't seem to have much part of it. What was said was in Apache, with no responses or anything for poor old Flash, although Sonsee-array answered three or four times when the spirit-chief addressed her, as did the Yawner, grunting at my elbow. I suppose he was my proxy, since I didn't speak the lingo, and while it's a nice thought in old age that Geronimo was your best man—well, there was something dashed perfunctory about the whole thing. I don't even know at what point we became man and wife; no clasp of hands, or exchange of tokens, or embracing the bride, just a final wail from the spirit-chief and a great yell from the assembly, and then off to the wedding-feast.

There, I admit, they do it in style. That feast lasted three days, all round the fire, stuffing down the sweet roasted agave leaves from the mescal-pits, and baked meats, corn bread, chile, pumpkins and all the rest, with vast quantities of a special wedding brew to wash it down. And d'you know, they don't let you near your bride in all that time—we sat on opposite sides of the fire, in a great circle of relatives and friends with the lesser mortals pressed behind (I suppose we must have left off feasting from time to time to sleep or relieve ourselves, but I swear I don't remember it) and she never looked in my direction once! Myself, I think they're damned cunning, the Apaches; you may know that in Turkey at wedding feasts they have a plump and voluptuous female who writhes about half-naked in front of the groom to put him in trim for the wedding-night; it's my belief that the Mimbreno are far subtler than that. Maybe there's something in the drink, maybe it's the repetition of the dancing that goes on during the feast, with those bucks in their animal heads chasing (but never catching) the young females, who flee continually (but never quite out of reach); perhaps it's just the three days' delay in getting down to business—

whatever it may be, I found myself eyeing that white figure through the flames, and starting to sweat something frightsome.

I know she was no great beauty—not to compare with Elspeth or Lola or Cleonie or the Silk One or Susie or Narreeman or Fetnab or Lakshmibai or Lily Langtry or Valla or Cassy or Irma or the Empress Tzu'si or that big German wench off the Haymarket whose name escapes me (by Jove, I can't complain, at the end of the day, can I?)—but by the time the third evening was reached if you had asked me my carnal ideal of womanhood I'd have described it as just over five feet tall, sturdy and nimble, wearing a beaded tunic and white doeskin leggings, with a round chubby face, sulky lips, and great slanting black eyes that looked everywhere but at me. God, but she was pleased with herself, that smug, dumpy, nose-in-the-air wench, and I must have been about to burst when the Yawner tapped me on the shoulder and jerked his head, and when I got up and panted my way out of the firelight, no one paid the least notice.

Possibly I was drunk with liquor as well as lust, for I don't remember much except riding into the night with the Yawner alongside and the shadowy form of Quick Killer ahead; the nightwind did nothing to cool my ardour either, for it seemed to grow with each passing mile through the wooded hills, and by the time we dismounted, and they and the ponies had faded tactfully into the darkness, I could have tackled the entire fair sex—provided they were all short and muscular and apple-cheeked. Through the trees I could see the twinkle of a fire, and I blundered towards it, disrobing unsteadily and staggering as I got my pants off, and there was the little wickiup, and no doubt the flowers were flapping about somewhere, but I didn't pause to look.

She was reclining on a blanket at the door of the wickiup, on one elbow, that sturdy little brown body a-gleam in the fireglow as though it had been oiled, and not a stitch on except for the patterned headband above the cinnamon eyes that gleamed like hot coals, and the tight white leggings that came up to her hips. She didn't smile, either; just gave me that sullen stare and stretched one leg while she stroked a hand down the seam of tiny bells, making them tinkle softly. My stars, I thought, it's been worth it, coming to America—and that's when I remember the pine-needles under my knees, and the smell of wood-smoke and musk, and deliberately taking my time as I stroked and squeezed every inch of that hard, supple young body, for I was damned if I was going to give her the satisfaction of having me roar all over her like a wild bull. I'd been teased and sweated by her and her blasted tribal rituals too long for that, so I held off and played with her until the sulky pout left her lips, and those glorious eyes opened wide as she forgot she was an Apache princess and became my trembling captive of the scalp-hunters' camp again, and she began to gasp and squirm and reach out for me, with little moans of *querido* and hoarse Apache endearments which I'm sure from her actions were highly indelicate—and she suddenly flung herself up at me, grappling like a wrestler, and positively yowled as she clung with her arms round my neck and her bells pealing all over the place.

"Now, that's a good little Indian maid," says I, and stopped her entreaties with my mouth, while I went to work in earnest, but very slowly, Susie-fashion, which was a marvel of delightful self-restraint, and I'm sure did her a power of good. For as the warm dawn came up, and I was drowsing happily under the blanket and deciding there were worse places to be than the Gila forest, there were those little lips at my ear, and those hard breasts against me, and the tiny whisper: "Make my bells ring again, *pinda-lickoyee.*" So we rang the changes for breakfast.

Crusaders:
The Humor of Real
and Imitation Reformers

▼▲▼▲▼▲▼▲▼▲▼▲▼▲▼▲▼▲▼▲▼▲▼▲▼▲▼▲▼▲▼▲▼▲▼▲▼▲▼

Don Imus—"Reel 11"
(from *God's Other Son*)

Larry L. King—"Spotlight on Cullie Blanton"
(from *The One-Eyed Man*)

Edward Abbey—"Seldom-Seen Smith"
(from *The Monkey Wrench Gang*)

Evangelists, Politicians, and Conservationists

▼▲▼▲▼▲▼▲▼▲▼▲▼▲▼▲▼▲▼▲▼▲▼▲▼▲▼▲▼▲▼▲▼▲▼

OUR COUNTRY WOULD BE A MUCH LESS INTERESTING PLACE without the people who want to make it over. These include charismatic evangelists who want to clean up our lives and save our souls, political pied pipers who believe they can bring in the millennium by remodeling the government, and ecologists who would save the species by saving the environment. These types attract humorists as a lightning rod attracts lightning.

Religious reformers have come in for specially caustic analysis in the second half of our present century, following the path marked out by Sinclair Lewis and Flannery O'Connor and building on the foundation laid by Aimee Semple McPherson. The spirit of these spellbinders is strong and the flesh is conspicuously weak. These flawed Billy Grahams are exposed by a variety of novelists with triumphant irony and bitter amusement.

Examples are many. Darby Foote in *Baby Love and Casey Blue* (1975) dissected a "prophet" in the Texas cotton fields, a rustic charlatan who held his congregation in practical captivity. Max Crawford paid his respects to country preachers in *The Backslider* (1976). In 1981 Ben Bradlee and Dale Van Atta published *Prophet of Blood*, a "docudrama" or work of "faction" (fact plus fiction) following the career of a cult leader in Utah and Old Mexico. In 1982 the procession was joined by no less a figure than Harold Robbins with *Spellbinder*, the story of a magnetic young religious leader who, with the help of a Texas oil billionaire and modern communications gadgets, sets out to evangelize the world. A year later Edward Swift's *Principia Martindale* featured Corinda Cassy and her Cowgirls for Christ.

Such antics ignite revulsion in the souls of contemporary novelists, as seen in the chapter quoted in this section from Don Imus's *God's*

Other Son—a scene that seems wildly overdone until one remembers that religious people can do, and have done, wild and incredible things.

Political leaders are not far behind the preachers in combining visions and vices. Novelists did not have to wait for Watergate to become aware of the divided nature of *homo politicus*, and satiric humor has been a favorite weapon in their arsenals. A pioneer work—a non-humorous one—in the field was Robert Rylee's *The Ring and the Cross* (1947), which dealt with the abuses of power in Texas. The good guys won.

A more realistic stance was taken by William Brammer in *The Gay Place* (1961), which cut to the bone in dissecting Texas politics. Lyndon Johnson was considered to be a model for Governor Arthur Fenstemacher, in whom idealism and political realism struggled for mastery. A year later Francis Rosenwald published *A Big Man in Saludas*, a thinly disguised portrait sketch of Archie Parr, the ruthless political boss who was said to have given Lyndon his start. Larry King's *The One-Eyed Man* (quoted here) and Al Dewlen's *The Session* (1981) follow the same path. Dewlen's excellent novel takes a revealing look at law and lawmakers in Texas.

It is interesting to note that Texas seems to have a virtual monopoly on evangelists and politicians with divided souls. Conditions can't be all that different in Utah and Montana, but the humorists and satirists have been slow in getting around to other western states.

A third type of crusader is waiting in the wings—witness Edward Abbey, a fierce conservationist, a Jeremiah thundering, "Woe unto thee, Arizona," as he surveys the wreckage of the desert, the diminishing water supply, the mindless mining and building and destroying that must eventually lead to ruin of the Sunbelt states. In *The Monkey-Wrench Gang* a great cast of characters, led by half-mad Vietnam veteran George Hayduke and Seldom-Seen Smith, the peripatetic polygamist, plan to blow up Glen Canyon Dam. They might have succeeded.

Reel 11

▼▲▼▲▼▲▼▲▼▲▼▲▼▲▼▲▼▲▼▲▼▲▼▲▼▲▼▲▼▲▼▲▼▲▼▲▼
Don Imus

Like the other novels about phony men of God, *God's Other Son* might have been titled *Bawdy and Soul*. It traces the career of Billy Sol Hargus, father unknown, who is abandoned by his waitress mother and reared, after a fashion, by Elroy and Edna Hargus of Del Rio, Texas, owners and operators of a roadside diner. His practical education is conducted by Otis Blackwood, who manages the filling station next door, with the help of Otis' black friend Tyrone. Edna Hargus, "Step Edna," efficiently takes charge of Billy Sol's sex education.

In spite of these earthy ties Billy Sol becomes a teenage evangelistic sensation under the tutelage of a fabulous exhorter and money raiser named Dr. Boone Moses. In the pulpit a shining spiritual star, at home down-to-earth, greedy, and profane, Moses is typical of the sons of Elmer Gantry, and by the time Billy Sol attains maturity, he has outstripped his mentor in all departments. His fame grows, and with the help of a Madison Avenue public relations firm, he becomes nationally known. His success, however, is his undoing. He decides that his birth was the result of an immaculate conception, that Jesus is his brother, and that God is his father. He refers to the latter as "Dad." It all comes to an end with his spectacular death, and we learn the "facts" from tapes made in his final hours, clarified by the insertion of pertinent newspaper stories, and released fifteen years later.

Reel 11 (Chapter 11) begins as Billy Sol is preparing to make his first appearance before a national radio audience. Boone Moses is now functioning as his chief adviser. Otis and Tyrone are handymen. The rest of the characters speak for themselves.

Editor's Note—The following is a verbatim transcript of Dr. Billy Sol Hargus's first national radio broadcast, aired February 23, 1958, a Sunday. The program originated in the Hargus Crusade, Incorporated, studios, KSOL, Tulsa, Oklahoma. Over three thousand radio stations contracted to carry the initial program, and eighteen hundred more joined the Hargus network in the following week. (Ed.)

From *God's Other Son* (New York: Simon & Schuster, 1981), 240–53.

Announcer: Ladies and gentlemen, the *Jump For Jesus* Show is on the air! And now, here's your host, the original *Jump for Jesus* man himself . . . the RIGHT REVEREND DOCTOR BILLY SOL HARGUS!

Hargus: Thank you! Thank you, Boone Moses! Thank you! Well, hi, friends!

Choir: HI, BILLY!

Hargus: Yes, friends, it's Billy Sol Hargus here on behalf of the Discount House of Worship comin' to you live and direct from Del Rio, Texas . . . for the salvation of your soul! We're glad tonight! We're happy! We're filled with joy! We're just bubblin' over! And you know why? I just can't keep my little secret here another second. I gotta surprise guest with me here tonight for our initial show, who you are *not* going to believe. You know who's with us here in the studio tonight?

Choir: Who, Billy? Who you got? Tell us!

Hargus: All right, all right. Just settle down. Are you ready? You got hold of somethin'? Friends, our special guest tonight is . . . JESUS CHRIST! THAT'S RIGHT! JESUS CHRIST IS HERE TONIGHT AND WHAT'S MORE, HE'S COMIN' TO SEE YOU! WE ARE GOING TO SEND JEE-ZUS INTO YOUR HOME THIS EVENING! CHOIR? SOLETTES? HELP ME HERE A MINUTE NOW! CAN I GET A WITNESS? GREAT GOD!

Choir/Solettes:
   Jesus Christ is here tonight!
   Ain't no reason to be uptight!
   Everything's gonna be all right
   'Cause Jesus Christ is here tonight!

Hargus: PRAISE GOD AN' PASS IT AROUND AGAIN!

Choir/Solettes:
   Said Mr. J. C., Th' Man Hisself, is our guest!
   You know He's better than all th' rest!
   Comb your hair an' shine your shoes,
   Tell the old man to lock up the booze,
   And maybe you should show a little remorse,
   'Cause tonight we're sendin' Jesus from our house to yours.

Hargus: Thank you, Choir! Thank you, Solettes! Yes, friends, it's true. Jesus is with us here tonight, and we're gettin' ready to send Him out to each and every one of you. We pray there is love and charity wherever you are this night . . . and we thank you for allowin' us to visit with you for awhile. And right now, are you ready? Huh? You want *Him* to come into your home? You want Him to come into your heart? Have you prepared His room? Well, okay then! I want everybody out there to put your hands on your radio! Put your hands on your radio and close your eyes! Choir, tell 'em!

Choir: Here comes Jesus!

Hargus: When?

Choir: Here comes Jesus . . . NOW!

Hargus: FEEEEL YOUR RADIO! AIN'T IT WARM? YES, IT IS! THAT'S HIM! THAT'S JEE-ZUS! THAT'S THE WARMTH OF JESUS CHRIST SEEPIN' INTO YOUR HOUSE! DON'T HE FEEL GOOOOOOOD?

Choir: HALLELUJAH!

Hargus: Friend, you better go set an extra place at the table there . . : because you asked for Him an' you got Him! Jesus is right there in your house with you. Oh, I know you can't actually see Him, but, PRAISE GOD, HE'S THERE! OHMIGOD!

Choir: OHMIGOD!

Hargus: Shall we pray?

Choir: Say it on, now!

Hargus: Lord, we want to thank You for sendin' Your Boy out there into the homes and hearts of each and every person lissenin' to this broadcast tonight. Yessir, that was right white of You an' we 'preciate it. Amen.

Choir: Amen!

Hargus: Friends, now that we've sent you Jesus I want to tell you about the rest of our show. We got a wonderful lineup for you this evening. The choir's here as you know; the Solettes are standin' right over there lookin' snappy, and right now I want to introduce 'em to you 'cause they're lookin' and soundin' so fine. Come on over here, girls. Don't be bashful, now. Just step right up an' say "hi" to all our friends. Who's gonna go first? Thelma. Come on over here, honey. Folks, this here's Thelma!

219

Thelma: Hi, everybody!

Hargus: And Bethea? Say hi, sugar.

Bethea: What it is, y 'all!

Hargus: And Tina? Tina, folks!

Tina: Uhhhh-HUH, now!

Hargus: Ain't she ju' somethin'? Now, that's a package, ain't it? Praise the Lord! An' last, but far from least, specially if you could see 'er, folks, meet . . . Big Mama Bobbie Mae Morton!

Bobbie Mae: Woooowee, sugar!

Hargus: Woooowee yourself, baby doll! That's them, folks, and they're ready to sing for you and Jesus! . . . .

Now, then. Friends, from time to time here on the *Jump for Jesus* Show we're going to be suggesting to you ways for you to get closer to the Lord, ways that'll make it easier for you to maintain your relationship with Jesus Christ. Because once you got Jesus in your heart, you don't want Him sneakin' off someplace, do you? Of course not. Once you got Jesus in your heart, you wanna lock Him up in there. Well, friends, each item, each service, we'll be offerin' to you will help you do just that. So get out your paper and pencil now . . . 'cause we have an item for you tonight that you're not going to want to be without if you really are a Christian and love Jesus. Solettes? What's tonight's FAITH DEAL?

Bethea: Well, Billy, tonight we have for the folks a plastic Jesus!

Hargus: You mean our little Jesus that goes up on the dashboard of your car?

Bethea: That's the one, Reverend. He's cute, too !

Hargus: OHMIGOD! FALL DOWN ON YOUR KNEES AND PRAISE JESUS WITH ME! A PLASTIC JESUS FROM OUR AUTOMOTIVE NOVELTIES DIVISION FOR YOU TO AFFIX TO THE DASHBOARD OF YOUR OWN PERSONAL AUTOMOBILE! TURN THAT THING FROM A CHRYSLER . . . INTO A *CHRIST*-LER! THAT'S RIGHT! SOLETTES? WHY DON'T YOU TELL 'EM, IN SONG?

Solettes:

I don't care if it rains or freezes,
Long as I've got my plastic Jesus,
Ridin' on the dashboard of my car.

I can go a hundred miles an hour,
Long as I've got the almighty power,
Glued up there by my pair
Of fuzzy dice.

Hargus: ALL RIGHT! Thank you, Solettes! Mighty fine. Yes, friends, it's absolutely true. You can actually have Jesus Christ keepin' you company on the road. He's tiny, but strictly lifelike, with little bitty eyes that light up when you hit the brakes. The eyes of Jesus, lookin' down the road for you . . . checking for that unseen hazard or lead-footed heathen. Jesus Christ will see them and say to you, "Better get on the binders, before we hit the business end of that bridge abutment, bub."

And the best part is, it's absolutely free. It doesn't cost you a penny to be able to drive around with this kind of divine intervention just waitin' there to warn you before you get turned into mucilage on the front of some semi or somethin'. Just send me a prayer pledge, anything over twenty-five dollars and ninety-five cents, and we'll get your little Jesus in the mail to you this very day.

And, friends, when you write to us here in Del Rio, Texas, I want you to tell Billy how much Jesus has done for you in your life. I want to hear your testimony so that we might be able to share it in the future with everybody over these microphones. Just take a page and make a list. Say, Billy, these are the things Jesus has done for me. Then, on the other side of that page, I want you to make another list and say, Billy, these are the things I've done for Jesus. Then, add 'em up. Are they a little outa whack? Of course they are. Jesus has done everything for us—and we can't never fill up that balance sheet under the "What-I've-Done-for-Him" headin'. I want you to ask yourself this question. Say, Billy, have I done enough for Jesus? Am I doing enough after all He's done for me? Am I fallin' down on my end of the bargain here? Well, friends, why don't you make sure you're covered in His eyes. Why don't you, when you write to me, bump that prayer pledge up to fifty, seventy-five, a hundred dollars and SHOW THE LORD JESUS CHRIST HOW GRATEFUL YOU REALLY ARE! SAY, JESUS . . . HERE'S A LITTLE SOMETHIN' TO HELP OUT. I KNOW IT AIN'T MUCH, BUT I PROMISE YOU I'LL SEND ALONG SOME MORE REAL SOON.

221

Then, friends, you might want to have each member of your family help you help Jesus. Why, you might want to organize your neighborhood to help th' Lord by helpin' our ministry here. This ain't no bed of roses, friends; we have missionaries in every country in the entire world that we must support with your prayer pledges and blessing vows.

Hell, you might just wanna organize your entire town or city to help in this vital work. Say, Jesus, here's 250,000 dollars, JUST TO SAY THANKS! Get it together, wrap it up, and send it to the Right Reverend Doctor Billy Sol Hargus, care of the Discount House of Worship, Del Rio, Texas. I'll just tell you what. You get us 250,000 dollars and I'll PERSONALLY see to it that you get TWO plastic Jesuses for your automobile. Choir, say thank you to Jesus!

Choir: THANK YOU, JESUS!

Hargus: My Gawd, ain't it wonderful to be in th' land of opportunity. Say it, Choir!

Choir: IT'S TH' LAND OF OPPORTUNITY!

Hargus: PRAISE TH' LORD! YES, SIR! All right, Choir, time now to sing one of our favorite hymns—it's an original, penned by Reverend Billy hisself and available to you for a nineteen-ninety-eight Faith Promise from the Discount House of Worship's Audio Branch—"Oh, Billy Sol, Won't You Please Heal Us All!" Let's hear it now!

Choir:

Oh, Billy Sol, won't you please heal us all.

Oh, say, Billy Sol, won't you please heal us all.

Grandma's ticker's gettin' weaker,

She's got her hands up on the speaker.

Oh, say, Billy Sol, won't you please heal us all!

Hargus: Let me jump in here, Choir!

Late last night, Mama took a fever,

Little Tommy killed the kitty with Pop's meat cleaver,

Sister came home with a social disease,

Even our dog's got terminal fleas.

Oh, Billy, Sol, won't you please heal us all.

Choir: OH, BILLY SOL, WON'T YOU PLEASE HEAL US ALL!

Hargus: Praise Jesus! Yes, it's true. Billy Sol does have that healin' hand, the gift of settin' right that what's wrong with you and those you love. For I can feel out there that many of you tonight, all over this great land, are burdened. You have troubled hearts and minds tormented by worry. You're sayin', "Billy, I'm powerful unhappy. I'm miserable. I don't know what to do with my life, because nothin's workin' out for me, Billy! I'M SICK, BILLY! I'M LAAAAAME, BILLY! LORD, BILLY! I NEED YOUR PRECIOUS HELP!" CHOIR? I WANT YOU TO SAY IT NOW! SAY, "BILLY?"
Choir: BILLY!!
Hargus: "I need your HELP!"
Choir: I NEED YOUR HELP!
Hargus: Say, "BILLY!!"
Choir: BILLY!!
Hargus: "I NEED YOUR HELP!"
Choir: I NEED YOUR HELP!!
Hargus: Yes, say, "Billy, I want you to help me tonight!" Say, "Reverend Hargus, I want you to come into my heart." Friends, somewhere in America right now, in some small, sleepy little town or some bustlin' big city, there is a poor, or perhaps even some wealthy, soul cryin' out in despair! Beggin' for guidance, for some one to show them the direction in which they oughta be pointin' their lives. Friends, praise Jesus, that help is available to you right now. For we have here at the Discount House of Worship a wonderful and truly holy item that can point you to that Righteous Path! Never again shall ye waver! For you can carry with you, every day, our St. Peter's Compass—yes, the very same compass the Apostle Peter used to navigate his frail craft on the storm-tossed Sea of Galilee. This is it! The same exact instrument! Isn't that wonderful? Write to me here in Del Rio, Texas. Say, Billy, send me the compass. And guess what? It'll come to you completely free of charge. All we ask is that YOU remember Jesus when you write your order . . . and include a Bible bestowal. Anything over sixteen-ninety-five will do. For you don't want to stray from the path that guarantees you your reservation in Paradise, do you? Of course not. You want to prepare yourself now, here, while you're in this mortal life, for your day of IMMORTALITY! The day when you'll be able to step right up to JESUS HISSELF and say,

223

"Jesus, I raise my cup to You!" But, but . . . just a minute. There's nothing *in* your cup. It's dry! It's empty. And you, standin' before the Son of God with nothin' to give Him. Why? Why, because they told you back on Earth that "You can't take it with you"! And sure enough, you listened and you got "there," and sure enough, YOU'RE BROKE! OH, THE SHAME OF IT! Let me ask you somethin', friends. Who *knows* that you can't take it with you? Huh? WHO KNOWS THAT INDEED YOU CAN'T TAKE EVERY SINGLE LAST STINKIN' PENNY WITH YOU? HUH? WHO? WELL, DR. HARGUS IS HERE TO TELL YOU RIGHT NOW THAT YOU *CAN* TAKE IT WITH YOU!! ALL OF IT!! EVERYTHING!! YOU CAN OPEN A BANK ACCOUNT IN HEAVEN WHILE YOU'RE STILL RIGHT HERE ON EARTH!! SOLETTES? LET 'EM IN ON THIS ONE!!

Solettes:
Wooooweee!
Save a nickel or a dime,
Think of all that peace of mind.
Send it now while you're alive.
It'll be in heaven when you arrive.
Don't be dead and caught out on a limb,
Deposit now in Billy's First National Bank of Him!

Hargus: You heard it right, folks. Billy's First National Bank of Him. Send me all your money now, and I'll arrange for it to be waitin' for you in heaven after you're gone! Isn't that divine?

Solettes:
Yes, a check will be okay.
Get it in the mail today.
Why have the folks who love you so
Fightin' for it when you go?

Hargus: Isn't it the truth, friends? You work your whole life and leave whatever you made for your relatives to gouge eyeballs over. All that money, suddenly in the hands of heathens. Heathens who will not help Jesus! Who won't help Billy! Here you got that nice little nest egg sittin' someplace where it's not helpin' Jesus, and it won't be helpin' Jesus then, after you're dead, unless you can get it to me RIGHT THIS INSTANT, so I can get it into the First National

Bank of Him AT ONCE! You'll help Billy, you'll help Jesus, and you'll be helpin' yourself. Helpin' us while you're alive, and waitin' for you in Paradise when you arrive! OHMIGOD! Let's have an amen from the Choir on this deal!

Choir: AMEN!

Hargus: Thank you, Choir. Now, before we close for tonight . . . remember, ol' Billy Sol's gonna be in your town in person, to see you in person, sometime soon . . . somewhere. Because I want to MEET YOU! Don't forget, now, send for your plastic Jesus, don't go through another day without your St. Peter's Compass, and send me those bank deposits *immediately*. You never know!

And remember: For the Lord thy God loves you, Jesus loves you, and, yes, Billy Sol Hargus loves you. Thank you, Choir! Thank you, Solettes! Little Bobby? Bobby? Where are ya? Oh, there you are, boy. Thank you! And . . . THANK YOU, JEEEEEE-ZUS! See ya next week! Write to me now, Billy Sol Hargus, Del Rio, Texas. Goodnight y'all.

Announcer: You've been listening to the *Jump for Jesus* Show. A weekly presentation of the Doctor Billy Sol Hargus Crusade, and this station. If you would like any or all of the holy items Doctor Hargus was privileged to offer to you during this program, call us right now at this number: 512-GO-JESUS. That's right. 512-GO-JESUS. It's the same as dialing 512-465-3787. Or write to us here at the *Jump for Jesus* Show. The address: Billy Sol Hargus, Del Rio, Texas. Write or call now. Operators are standing by to take your order. This is Boone Moses saying Billy will see you next Sunday when we all join together and *Jump for Jesus*.

Editor's Note—This concludes the broadcast transcription of the first *Jump for Jesus* radio program. The following resumes the Hargus narrative as transcribed from the Hargus Tapes. (Ed.)

Spotlight On Cullie Blanton

▼▲▼▲▼▲▼▲▼▲▼▲▼▲▼▲▼▲▼▲▼▲▼▲▼▲▼▲▼▲▼▲▼▲▼▲▼▲▼

Larry L. King

Larry L. King (*The Best Little Whorehouse in Texas*) is a Texas farm boy who made it, struggling and panting, in New York. Like most exiles, however, his heart could not help turning homeward, and with very mixed feelings: nostalgia on the one hand and outrage on the other. The outrage, as William T. Pilkington points out, is against "present-day Texas—the vulgarity of its burgeoning cities, the provincialism of many of its people, the relative poverty of its art and literature."*

One area he knew inside and out was Texas politics, having served as administrative assistant to a Congressman from West Texas. This knowledge served him well when he wrote *The One-Eyed Man* (1966). The title comes from a Spanish *dicho*, not quite accurately remembered by King: "In the land of the blind, the one-eyed man is king." The one-eyed man in this case is Cullie Blanton, governor of an unnamed state (obviously Texas), whose feet of clay extend upward to his knees but not to his heart, which is at least semipure.

The crucial political fact Cullie has to deal with is his approval of the admission of the first black student to the state university. This step is hysterically opposed by every "redneck" and "peckerwood" from the outlands, by a mob of students, and by most members of the state legislature. His most dangerous opponent is a rabble-rousing ex-Marine general who wants Cullie's job. The odds seem insuperable, but Cullie is a mighty politician, a remarkable human being, and a great humorist with fantastic verbal and metaphorical resources. Almost as impressive is the narrator Jim Clayton, "the swamper, the lackey, the pale shadow of a slightly mad governor—who wants to do good and build monuments to dwarf the goddam Sphinx." His narrative is a devastating and sometimes hilarious exposé of politicians and of the people who elect them to office.

*William T. Pilkington, *My Blood's Country* (Fort Worth: TCU Press, 1973), 164.

WE CAME SWOOSHING ACROSS THE FAULT LINE OF THE ROCK-dotted hills and burst out of the pine thickets into the falling flatlands without slowing down or looking back, like maybe something howling and hairy was gaining on us fast. Soon the black limousine was rolling through the canebrakes where the air was heavy and faintly

From *The One-Eyed Man* (New York: New American Library, 1966), 1–19.

jasmined, as perfume on a nocturnal lady of the streets. The highway was smooth and flat and broad. Rows of sugar cane mottled by grape-colored blotches marched to the edges of the slab of raised concrete, pressing in God-close on each side.

The Governor slouched in the back seat, wallowing in the feel of good leather, smacking meaty lips over a slice of salted watermelon. His mouth moved up and down as if running the scale on some juice-laden harmonica. The single white line dividing the dazzling pavement rammed straight at the car, boring in from the burnt-orange globe of late-afternoon sun. Bo Steiner, the back of his neck like a sun-blistered tree trunk sticking up from the gingerbread-brown coat of the State Highway Patrol pulled tightly across his bull shoulders, hunched over the wheel.

"Bo," the Governor said suddenly.

The trooper's eyes sought the Governor in the rear-view mirror and he spat his answer like a soldier at roll call: "Hassah!"

"Melon runs through me like shoats through a hog wallow," Cullie Blanton said. "Find a place fit for a good governor to pass water."

Bo Steiner wrinkled his forehead with the rare ache of thinking. His thick lips pursed in an agony of concentration. He cleared his throat and ran his tongue in and out like a frog catching flies.

"Now?" the trooper asked. "Now, Governor?"

"Hell, no," the Governor snorted from around a juicy hunk of watermelon. "A week from Thursday. I just wanted to get on the god-damn waitin' list." He glowered, legs crossed Buddha-like in the wide, plush seat—a great, profane god awaiting the bearer of bad tidings. The trooper opened his mouth a time or two like somebody had pulled his string before he was ready. Finally he choked it past his teeth: "I mean . . . uh . . . right this here second, sir?"

"Godamighty," the Governor said, "why would I want to piddle into the wind at seventy miles an hour? To help the goddamn pants-pressin' industry?"

"Nossah," the trooper said unhappily.

"Sweet Jesus!" the Governor said in supreme disgust. He worked his jaws over the watermelon. "Just hang loose. *I'll* say when."

Bo turned thankfully to the task of driving. And that was something he could do. He could make the big car do everything but card tricks. If you had the heart and the stomach for it, and good kidneys that didn't flush easily, and if you could give up dwelling on how it would be with the car flipping across the canebrakes if ever it broke out of control, and how mere mortal flesh would tangle with ripping hunks of splintering iron and steel and twisting chrome, all you had to do when Bo went lickety-splitting down the highway, finding room enough to caper in the islands of space between the creeping mule-drawn wagons and the whizzing sedans and old pickup trucks, was hang on and whoop silent prayers begging deliverance. And he would get you there.

The Governor must have been thinking of Bo's genius at the wheel. "What the hell," he said abruptly, "all Mozart could do was write music."

Cullie Blanton ate watermelon with a relish. His head was bent into the sweet, pulpy heart of it like maybe he was gnawing through to reach the answer to some woolly riddle. Now and again he pulled his broad face out of the red pulp and blew the black seeds into one hand. The other, cupped so that the dark green rind of the melon rested in his palm, he thrust over toward me. I zeroed in on the pulpy part with a miniature box of Morton's salt and dive-bombed until Cullie Blanton grunted gubernatorial satisfaction, and I wondered what the other members of my graduating class might chance to be doing right at that crossroads junction in Time.

It was food for thought, and I chewed it.

Cullie Blanton had hired me eight years earlier to get a monkey off his back. And I was the monkey.

Yeah, I had been the monkey, and had been well trained and knew my act. Which was to write in *The Morning Star* of the unmatched virtues of a corpulent then-incumbent governor with buttermilk-white skin, deep pockets, and sticky fingers, who never in his life was justly accused of rattling the bushes in the name of the people. But *The Morning Star* was not people. It was a newspaper equally dedicated to elevating profits and to keeping down corporate taxes and new ideas.

The fat boys had grabbed the state a long time before, back when the flop-hat Big Daddies of the plantations called the turn of the wheel. And so the Governor, being the type of high-minded fellow that could barely read or write but could count sufficiently to see that all the brothers of the lodge got a fair split, was crowned with printed laurels and named "statesman." It figured that if the do-nothing Governor was such a grand prize, then only foul fools and crass knaves could oppose him. So the nabobs in the front office decided over whisky highballs and four-bit cigars that Cullie Blanton should be named public fool. And it fell my lot to do the christening.

The nabobs in the front office rigged a little ceremony and commissioned me the ace political writer of *The Morning Star*. They rationed me one of the four-bit cigars and grudgingly poured out a whisky highball, moving their doughy jaws over words like "states' rights" and "creeping Socialism" and "right thinking." And I nodded sagely to show I got the message. I got it, all right. Loud and clear. It said I should compare the incumbent favorably with Jesus Christ and Jeff Davis and jolly old Saint Nick. And I should measure Cullie Blanton against the suspect standards of Genghis Khan, with maybe Judas Iscariot and a little bit of Jack the Ripper tossed in on the side. I was a trained monkey and I did what I had to do in order to earn my peanuts.

Cullie wasn't the governor then, of course, but he was getting there. The race is not always to the swift. Cullie kicked and gouged his way up the ladder from that rung which nestles closest to the common dirt, and the closer he got to the rarefied atmosphere at the top, the more the fat boys felt uneasy in the region of their swollen pocketbooks. For Cullie was an unreasonable man to their way of thinking. He was always wanting to put crooks in jail, and he had a radical notion taxes ought to be returned to the people in manifest ways.

You could have gathered gloom in the plush clubs like it grew on bushes the night Cullie knocked off one of the house men for the office of state commissioner of utilities. Men of sober mien got glass-eye drunk, and the infidel called on God. It was like somebody had let the stealing license get chewed up in the washing machine, and maybe no more would be printed. And sure enough, that turned out to be the case. Within six months he had the moneybag hoarders wailing over the wire at each other through the lonesome hours. He caused the telephone company, who, Cullie held, had knocked the rates up past that point the law said was permissible, to rebate a whole hunk of money to subscribers. A commissioner of utilities who enforced the law was a poor sport indeed. Panic got to galloping through the financial community. They swore the people were up in arms. But out there among the great unwashed, what they were up in was not arms but cashier's checks. Big, lovely, retroactive checks dating back over four solid years of overcharge.

And the people knew where the money came from. Cullie saw to that. He had it fixed so the phone company had to furnish him a list of every manjack who owned a black instrument and how much the fellow would get back. He sent a form letter to each of them, detailing how he fought the good fight for them and won, and in an underscored spot on the letter was typed in the amount of money each particular taxpayer would soon get courtesy of the state commissioner of utilities.

Cullie hit the gas boys on the same ploy, and busted some heads in electric-power circles for conspiring to fix prices against the common good. He stirred up the biggest clamor since the burning of Atlanta and upped and announced for governor after two terms.

I followed Cullie all over the state. I dogged him like he was possum in the brush. I was his shadow and I bayed for his blood. When he leaned into the crowds with his eyes standing on stems and his gums beating promises, it sounded better than the call to eat the barbecued goodness of the golden calf. But I would knock the sharp edge off their appetite by taking to the typewriter to accuse Cullie of tampering with the truth, or else being guilty of very bad arithmetic. Once I wrote that he would have to tax the doorknobs off every building in the state to pick up the tab for his assorted schemes. Later, after I'd switched sides, I told him he couldn't come close to carrying out the programs he'd put upon the tongue of a promise.

"I can make a run at it," he said.

"But you can't do it."

"Boy," he said, "do you dispute the state needs all the things I've been whoopin' for?"

"No," I said. "But you just add up the cost of your binge of goodie pledging and see if it won't break the back of reason. It's plain poor mathematics."

"It may be that," he said. "But it is also somethin' else. It is damned excellent politics. It is grade-A, pure, uncut, government-inspected and genuinely certified politics, of the type's been endorsed by every-body from Duncan Hines to the Prince of Peace. They vote for names on that ballot, not a bunch of goddamn numbers."

Once, when I was hounding Cullie for *The Morning Star*, he got careless. We had bounced into this decaying town in the deep boon-docks, a collection of antique shacks jammed together in at the roots of a red-clay hill, and Cullie had ordered the driver to pull in because he had a hankering for a cold Nehi Cola. I jolted over the dirt road trailing Cullie's car, eating the dust from his wheels, and plaguing him like the past of a repentant scarlet woman. Cullie had coughed up his dime and I was fishing for one before either of us realized we were in as black an order as you could find on the Gold Coast. Cullie began to josh the Negroes and they took up the habit of grinning. He got the cold feel of the Nehi laying good on his tongue, and he got careless. He got careless enough to confide to the awed gawkers that he sus-pected God of loving all men. Even those with black skins. The way it came out of my typewriter, and the way it read on the front page of *The Morning Star*, was that Cullie had bootlegged a courting visit to the land of the bogeymen, where he had told the ebony natives they were God's chosen children. That was water on our paddle, for you yell "nigger" in the boondocks and all you've got to do it is get out of the way of the trampling herd.

That was the bit of chicanery, it turned out, that caused the ball of yarn between me and the nabobs in the front office to unravel. But we didn't know it at the time. It was a week later that our little association fell apart at the seams.

Cullie had come from out of the brush to campaign in King's Port, where *The Morning Star* rolled off the presses in the black hours before dawn. He came for a round of rafter-shaking speeches and baby-kissing, and the requisite number of meetings in smoke-filled rooms. He came like a hill-country circuit rider hell-bent on driving the in-fidel out of the sinful city, quoting liberally of the Bible, cautiously of Shakespeare, and boldly of Edgar A. Guest. After sitting mesmerized through one of his lung-bursting performances one evening, I took to typewriter and cut him a new one. Cullie must have picked up one of the first papers that hit a door stoop the next morning, for by noon he had sent a lackey round to summon me.

It was late in the evening when I showed at Cullie's hotel room, and it was not one of the best hotels. It was the kind that still had potted plants in the lobby, and no air conditioning, and it was about six blocks too close to the railroad tracks. Cullie was alone in his hotel room except for a bottled friend named Jack Daniel's. After he'd introduced me to that gentleman, he sat on the edge of his bed and watched me a few minutes as if he might be visiting the zoo and had been told my species was fast becoming extinct. He cocked the big mop of white hair over to the right and squinted his eyes at me, grinning like he was in a contest.

"Boy," he said by way of openers, "how you fixed for principles?"

"I reckon I got just barely enough to get by," I said.

"You ain't plumb eat up with high principle, are you? It ain't malignant? It don't gnaw on you like cancer in the dead of the night?"

"It hurts some," I said. "But I never needed transfusions for it."

He nodded and tipped a bit more of his spirited friend into my glass. "It's like the goddamn typhoid fever," he said solemnly. "Some folks carry it and some don't."

"I'm not a carrier. Maybe I never was exposed."

He grunted and gladdened the insides of his own glass. "You hate me?" he asked abruptly. "I ever wrong your stepsister or kick your hound dog . . . anything like that?"

I shook my head.

"Boy," Culie Blanton said easily, "this here is just between you and me and Almighty God. And me and Him will swear a paralyzed oath this little meetin' never happened if you ever indicate to the contrary."

Cullie walked to a switch on the wall and flicked on an old-fashioned ceiling fan. Its *swish swish swish* sliced the air up in little pieces.

"You're hurtin' me," he said. "You been stickin' me with needles like I was one of them goddamn voodoo dolls. Why, when you hit a sour note on that typewriter of yours I know it if I'm three hundred miles away. For it is like a kick in the goddamn privates. Like that mishmash you wrote the other day about how I went courtin' the black brethren in the bush. I stop and have one little ole pissant Nehi Cola because my tongue's growin' hair, and you make it sound like I appoint two dozen Mau Mau campaign managers."

I didn't say anything. Cullie ambled across the room in a slow lope, sucking at his whisky glass. "Yeah, you got a gift for muckrakin'. You got a natural flair. A regular goddamn knack. And you lay it on the line in three-cent words the woolhats and rednecks and the peckerwoods can get in their heads easy as sniffin' snuff. Boy, you write like your pen's been dipped in bile and boiled in lye water. You are a regular goddamn assassin."

I mumbled thanks for the compliment. Cullie was at the double window at the end of the room. He pulled aside the faded drapes and tugged at his undershorts. He turned around several times like a dog inspecting a potential resting place, and he whistled between his teeth and breathed a neutral "goddamn."

"I got the itch to be governor," he said with his back to me. "I want it like a hog craves slop. You ever want anything till it ached you clean to the bone?"

"No," I said.

"Count your blessin's. With some folks it's whisky and with some it's threshin' around in the bedsheets and with others it's smokin' dope. But with me it's wantin' to be governor. You got any notion why?"

"I reckon," I said, "that you just naturally lack ambition."

He turned from the window to face me, and there was a hazy look fogging up his ice-blue eyes.

"I want to be the winged ram," he said in a hoarse voice. "The winged ram with golden fleece. The political Holy Ghost. I want to walk on the goddamn water. Yeah, and I want to build healin' temples for the sick and give alms to the blind. Put free textbooks in the schools and drive away the dark angels of ignorance. Pave the loblolly roads out in the backwoods. Give the mule-drivin' snuff-dippers a pension. Levy taxes like King Tut. Get reelected and build monuments to dwarf the goddamn Sphinx."

I didn't say anything. I just thought that he carried a burdensome load of ambition for a potential governor in our state. In those days, a progressive in our part of the country favored debtors' prison and wavered on use of the rack. Cullie Blanton cocked the big white head a bit more to the right and studied me like maybe I was the Mona Lisa and he was Leonardo da Vinci trying to decide what was wrong with my smile.

"And you are goin' to help me," he said softly.

"Yeah," I said, "and as soon as I sprout wings I'm going to fly non-stop to the West Coast."

"Boy," he said. And he grinned. "Boy, I see the nubs sproutin' now. How'd you like to go to work for me?"

"Jesus Christ!" I said, and spilled some Jack Daniels.

"Naw," he said. "Wrong fellow. But now you mention it there is a passin' similarity."

"Good God! *I* don't know anything about politics!"

"Yeah," he said, still grinning. "Yeah, and that is a natural fact. But you know about somethin' else. You know about gut-shootin'. You musta been born mean and never outgrowed it. You got the instincts of a goddamn black widder spider. And let's say I'm in the market for poison."

"Hell," I said, "I don't know . . . I hadn't thought about it."

"Well, think about it. You make it on a couple of hundred a week? And expenses?"

"I'm making it on a damn sight less."

"You got a goddamn job," he said. "Congratulations." He reached out and grabbed my hand in one huge paw, giving it three shakes in a pump-handle motion.

I was lost in a fog. "What the hell?" I asked. "I don't even know what I'm supposed to do."

"You got a bright mind," Cullie Blanton said. "You figure it out. Wash my socks. Chant my praises. Make me a statesman. Gut-shoot that goddamn pirate I'm runnin' against."

"I don't even know what it's *like*."

"It won't be as classy as sellin' reefers to kindergarten kids," he said with a grin slicing his broad face. "Maybe more on a par with playin' backup piano in a Cajun cat house. But we will call the goddamn tunes."

234

So I had gone to work for him, and that had been long ago as a man measures his little demitasse of Time. I had learned to dance to the secret music of politics; Cullie had indeed called the tune, and I'd found that I liked the tempo. Only now and again was there a sour note turned up on the piano. Now and again there was watermelon to be salted . . .

The Governor shoved the watermelon over again and I dive-bombed it dizzy. Cullie was relaxed, almost cherubic. He worked his way down to the light green coating between the red of the meat and the darker green of the rind, took one final bite, and rolled down the window and tossed out the remains. Licking the last sugary traces of juice from his fingers, he looked back at the splatter the melon had made on the highway.

"Broke the state law," he said, as if greatly pleased. "You feel a twitch to do your duty, Bo?"

The trooper tried to smile.

"Hundred-dollar fine for throwin' crap on the highway," the Governor said smugly.

"Hassah," the trooper mumbled.

"Corruption and evil-doin' all around," the Governor boomed. "Half the world in rubble and the other half bound for hell in a paper sack. Heathens in the pulpits and love for sale on sinful streets. Knaves and fools violatin' the sacred temples of public trust. Nation's goin' bankrupt shootin' rocket doodads at the moon. Jaded police officers winkin' at the high crime of litterbuggin' the public's paved primrose path. Shameful, *sinful*, goddamn thang! How long, America? O, how long?"

Cullie Blanton closed his eyes and leaned back in the cool blue leather of the seats. The air conditioner purred like a contented cat breathing across a bowl of ice. The Governor's face began to fold into frowning lines. Little dark pockets of worry bunched up under the eyes and in the shaded hollow of his high cheekbones.

"Talk to me of wondrous goddamn things," he said. "Tell me what you divine. Bend your tongue to knowledge and let wisdom have its way."

"They're not scaring," I said.

"Wrong. Wrong as shortchangin' blind men."

"No," I said doggedly. "No more scared than Frank Buck would be of a garden snake."

"They're scared," the Governor said, "and that is the unflyblown Gospel. That's the jawbreakin' truth." He opened his eyes and grinned. But it was not a happy grin. It was the kind of cynical grin a man might grow after he has looked too long into the putty faces, midget minds, and tar-black hearts of creatures made in His image, and maybe had wondered and despaired at what in hell He could have had on His celestial mind that He could have botched the job so.

"Pull over, Bo," the Governor ordered. "I got a urgent message from my kidneys."

The trooper eased off the gas and hit the brake in one smooth motion. The Governor, his hand on the door handle, motioned with his head that I should follow. He plunged into the canebrakes fumbling with the zipper of his trousers. Walking a dozen steps behind, hearing the whisper of the wind among the dry stalks, I realized that the box of salt was still in my hand.

The Governor searched the sky as if looking for hostile airplanes and watered the earth with a mighty splash.

"Yeah," he affirmed for the third time. "They're scared. For I have come stalking upon the knowledge of fear. I have found it in the dark bullrushes of Time. And they are afraid, all right. They're so scared they're nothin' but pus and custard."

"Some maybe," I said. "But just the born cowards."

The Governor sighed at the sky. He said, "Jim, you have been off to college and studied how to find X in algebra and maybe learned the name of the doctor discovered a painless cure for clap. You got a diploma with your name on it in writin' so fancy it's hard for an ignorant peckerwood like me to read it. But by God, Jim! Sometimes I wonder if you got sense enough to be coached for a crooked quiz show. Hell, you oughta know by now *all* men are born cowards. And most of 'em don't ever outgrow it."

Cullie Blanton zipped up his trousers. He wiggled massive hips to settle more comfortably in his underwear. Standing ten paces behind the Governor, I was assaulted by the thought that the opposition camp would cough up many gold dollars for a film clip of the Governor rolling his hips and apparently dry-humping the air in a lonesome cane field. Bayonet Bill Wooster would scream to hosts on high about such a vulgar, immoral display. The picture of the former general screening the film for his angry, evangelistic superpatriots in some flag-bedecked hall, touching the blown-up image of the Governor's grinding hips with a Marine-officer's wooden swagger stick itself quaking with righteousness, white mustache snapping in hate and the dark frustrations that seemed to motivate the man, was more than I could conjure up and keep a sober face. I half turned to hide a smile.

When the Governor had finished his chore to the accompaniment of satisfied sounds, he buckled his belt and sniffed the air with raised head. "Smell rain," he said. "Looks like a gully washer comin' up. Put out a press release takin' credit for it."

Bilious thunderclouds boiled low on the horizon. Forked spears of lightning kindled the distant sky, bringing quick touches of color to the cheerless strands of Spanish moss out in the swamps. Soon drops of water would tremble on the yellow leaves in the pine thickets. The earth would smell cool and freshly bathed.

We marched out of the canebrakes. The Governor debouched massively, the great white head inclined as if alert for the drumming hoofbeats of horses. At the highway he paused and stomped his feet on the pavement, responding to some silent signal. Little clouds of dust spiraled from his shoes. The Governor, mired in the deep bogs of private thought, plowed toward the limousine with his head down.

"Scared past the point of passin' water," he mumbled. "Scared like the great woolly mastodon was runnin' after 'em through the shinnery. Jack-rabbit scared."

"Sullen," I said. "They're more sullen than afraid."

The Governor acted as though he hadn't heard. He said, "Take a bunch of rabbits caught in a beam of light. All they can do is freeze and listen to their poundin' hearts throb fit to bust the fur. They're scared. God on a white mule, they're scared! But they don't know what of. You know, Jim?"

I didn't feel the need to play guessing games. I was weary from the day's drive and the series of political pop meetings. By night we would be back in Capitol City and it would be necessary to try to deal again with the personal hairshirt of life. To bring order out of chaos. I decided to take the easy way out.

"No," I said.

"Boy," the Governor said, "sometimes I wonder how you passed anything in school but the Wassermann test. What they're scared of is fear."

We climbed back into the limousine, the Governor lowering his bulk into the seat with the aid of a mighty, hydraulic grunt. Bo pulled the car away smoothly.

"Man," Cullie Blanton breathed. He waited, and there was the deep well of silence. "Man is born into trouble as the sparks fly upward, like it says in the Book of Job. Brought into this mortal coil full of fear and tremblin'. Pulled from the warmth of the womb, hung up by his heels like a side of beef, and smacked on the backside until he takes one shudderin' breath of shock and gaseous surprise. So the first sound he makes and the first sound he hears is the awful sound of fear. And he never gets over it, for there is always so goddamn much to spook him."

The Governor lowered his eyelids as if to shut out both sight and sound, and maybe even to still the rushing train of thought rattling through his mind. It struck me that he looked old, old as the devil's grandfather. The ruddy skin, normally flushed pink with good health like Eisenhower had exuded in his best days, seemed suddenly flabby and sallow. Lines marking the corner of his eyes and running like plowed furrows in the forehead were now etched too deeply into the flesh, as if seared by a branding iron.

"Life is a race against the hairy hounds of horror," the Governor said. "A race run from the swaddling cloth of the cradle to the dark folds of the shroud. Death and war and taxes . . . creditors and vile bossmen and wrathful gods . . . tongues of serpents and cold-hearted lovers and the bu-damn-bonic plague. . . ."

"Falling dandruff," I offered.

". . . and a fiery place called Hell."

The Governor opened his eyes and the sleep went out of them. They were at once hard and bright like round blue marbles. "And

238

around here," he said, "there is something else. The mark of the goddamn beast. The curse of Ham's wife."

He held out a hand and snapped his fingers. I dug into the coat pocket of my wrinkled drip-dry suit for a pack of cigarettes and shook one into his upturned palm. The Governor inserted it between his lips and leaned forward to accept a light. He inhaled and eased back, releasing the smoke with a gusty blow approaching a bellow. Twin streams of smoke poured from his nostrils, and for a moment he was a fire-breathing dragon. Eyes squinted against the wisp of smoke that wafted upward in a slow spiral, he inspected the empty air as if he'd found at long last which shell the pea was under.

"Fear is big and black and wool-headed," he said. "And you wouldn't want your sister to marry one." He stared out of the car window, darkly brooding.

The sun had dropped suddenly behind the flat curve of the horizon, and infant shadows toddled along the cane rows. Cullie bored his eyes into the shadows like he was peeking behind the final veil, glimpsing the Last Secret. The cane fields blurred and bridge abutments faded into vague, ill-defined humps huddled by the highway. Mist lay heavy on the land and cuddled against the edges of the concrete slab, and Bo flicked a switch to mar the completeness of night. Cullie was lost in the steep canyons of the muse. The miles passed and the wheels turned in the Governor's head.

"And that's the shape of the hobgoblin," he said. "That is the craven nature of the spook."

I stirred and blinked my eyes and plotzed back toward the land of the living.

"What do you think the Court's likely to do?" I asked.

"You read the papers," Cullie Blanton said. "I take it you get past Chester Gump once in a while. You know what the courts have done in other places."

"Yeah," I admitted.

"Gonna split this state from hell to breakfast. And the bare bones and tough gristle and most foul innards are goin' to be laid out like somethin' dead on the highway. Gonna order that blackbird admitted to the university and march in a Coxey's Army of Feds to see nobody breaks his wings. And it will be hell among the yearlings."

"Well, if the cookie crumbles that way . . . what then?"

"Boy," the Governor said, "if I had the answer to that one I'd send off for a patent and retire on the profits."

"Hell," I said, "you got to have a plan."

He looked at me like I had something that belonged to him and wouldn't give it back. "You think you're the only one with brains hooked up to figger that out? You think I just got to town on the goddamn Greyhound?"

"No," I said.

"Then quit talkin' like I'm somebody's goofy cousin home for the weekend from the funny farm." He huffed and puffed at his cigarette butt. "*I* know I got to do somethin'. I saw those jake-leg pols today same as you did. Turnin' up their noses like the wind had changed so they sniffed a passin' gut wagon. And I know what that pensioned-off Marine's gonna do. Yeah, with the election waitin' in ambush just around the goddamn bend, Bill Wooster's gonna scream like I'd violated the unsullied maiden aunt of the Virgin Mary. And ever' wool-hat who owns a bedsheet's gonna bust a clavicle rippin' it off the mattress and wrappin' up in it. They'll wave the bloody shirt, hoot the rebel yell, and whistle up the departed ghost of ole Jeff Davis."

"They might not," I said.

"Boy," he said, "it is as certain as sex on a honeymoon. You can't stop the unstoppable."

"You might if you put your foot down. You've done it before. You don't hold the indoor record for being bashful."

The Governor birthed a growing sigh. "Boy," he said, "about the time I think you're housebroke and got control of all your marbles, you go spoilin' my illusion by pissin' down your leg. There's a slag heap of difference in squashin' a ladybug and steppin' on a mad rattler. That's just a natural law of physics."

He mashed his cigarette in the ashtray hollowed out in a padded armrest and flicked grains of tobacco from his fingers. He pulled at his nose, cleared his throat, and scowled. In the eerie green light from the dashboard he took on a murderous look.

"All those speeches by Adlai Stevenson up at the U.N.," he said sourly. "All those high-blown words about equality and the eternal brotherhood of man and love ye one another. Red and yellow, black and white. Hell yes, they *sound* good—up at the U.N. But you got to remember I'm governor down here in the fruit-jar-whisky backwoods. In the potlikker and poke-bonnet and pellagra belt. And down here a liberal's somebody don't hold with lynchin' on Sunday. Listen . . . you recollect how I had to go around the goddamn horn to get colored nurses on at the state hospital? You remember that?"

"Yeah," I said.

For I remembered, all right.

And he hadn't done it with high-blown speeches. He had done it in a very different way. Which started with receiving a delegation of hat-in-hand Negroes who had broken the spine of custom by the mere act of calling on the state's biggest political poobah for the purpose of asking for something. They had stalked into Cullie's office joint-locked with unease, mummering their way across new ground, and they had made their pitch. Which in any other league might not have been a high, hard one like Bob Feller used to throw, but which in the magnolia loop where the pitch was made was about as radical as nose bobbing for sharecroppers' daughters. They said how they paid taxes to support the state hospital. They said how they were the last to get a bed and the first to get a bill. They said how the only colored employees were held to the low level of the mop and the pushbroom. They said they didn't want the moon. They didn't ask the favor of black hands poking around the insides of white bodies with the cold steel of surgery. All they asked was a few nurses of their kind. And they stood in a brave little knot, waiting like they had invented waiting, expecting to be turned down.

Cullie had listened them out. He had grunted and nodded and frowned and once in the middle of their pitch he had locked his eyes on an invisible Something, picking his teeth with great sucking sounds. He had toyed with a clay bust of Robert E. Lee and had idly fluttered the folds of a miniature Confederate flag. And when the fellow who'd been tapped finally came down with a tired tongue, Cullie sat as if he'd been stricken with a painful case of lockjaw. Finally, about the time they had begun to figure he had dropped off for a nap, he glanced up from under the forest of frosty eyebrows.

"You want the nurses or you want somethin' to yowl about?"

They had wanted the nurses.

241

"All right," he promised. "You got 'em. Only don't go out of here hoo-hawin' about a batch of social progress. Any of those newspaper boys go pokin' around askin' questions, lie about it. Say you came to see the goddamn Governor about voter registration for colored folks and I read you the riot act and threw you out."

They nodded and shuffled in confusion.

"You won't like the way I do it," he said, "but it is the only way it can be done. You got to trust my judgment. I'll go out and kill your woolly bear, but don't ask me to do it with a switch. Leave me to my own bear trap . . . Jim, Fix these folks somethin' to cool parched throats."

And he had pumped their hands and plunged off on some urgent errand of mystery.

So a week later I hied myself up marble steps leading to the neo-antebellum front entrance of the state hospital, which Cullie had sprung out of the barren loins of the clay bogs and hammered out of a reluctant legislature in his first ten months in office, possessed of a clear view of Cullie's buttocks ham-hocking it on the double toward the top. The two of us led a sweating coterie of photographers whose suit pockets bulged with flashbulbs, and a panting swarm of reporters fatally bent on recording the Governor's first eyeball inspection of his prized healing temple. By that time the Capitol correspondents knew that Cullie could make more news at a country goat-roping than most pols could make by breaking wind for a new airport, so we didn't want for daily attention. Everybody had the idea they were trailing around in the indelible tracks of History.

The key hospital staffers were starched to the gills and stiffly smiling, circled back from the door at a distance calculated to give the Great Man room, and the place had been mopped and scrubbed and disinfected until you could drink out of the bedpans. The administrator was a timid soul with the kind of face that must have been made from the mold God Almighty uses when He's behind in His work. It was a mass-production face, with two eyes in the right place and a nose popped out in the middle like a bump on a pickle and a mouth cut into the face about where you'd expect to find it. He owned just two expressions: scared and worried. He alternated between the two as Cullie Blanton padded down on him like a gay grizzly bear, pawing the air and happily pressing flesh, growling some great, practiced glee.

The administrator, propelled along by mobile fear, quivered at the Governor's heels. He squeaked of recovery rooms and blood plasma and out-patient clinics, and for a while it looked like he would get around to quoting a price on salve for bedsores. Cullie nodded and mumbled a great benediction, beaming benign approval of the healing arts. The Governor got his picture made pressing a Snicker bar on a six-year-old boy who had his hips hiked up in traction. The flashbulbs froze him tenderly reading a page of *Chicken Little* to an emaciated little girl in an iron lung, and caught him handing a bouquet of yellow roses to a senile old woman who bared her gums like a chimpanzee, drooled on her nightgown, and announced in a cracked cackle that she had an urgent need to pass water.

When we tooled into the wing where they kept the colored patients, the Governor shook the hand of an old granny and wisecracked at two little giggling girls. He moved across the hall to the colored men's ward and stopped inside, running his eyes over the scene carefully as if inspecting for ticks. He watched a plump blonde nurse take the temperature of an ancient Negro man. He moved over close to me and mumbled in my ear, frowning. He stalked on down the line of beds and put the glim on another nurse, tense and nervous under the all-seeing eye of the Mighty, while she changed the bed linens for an expressionless Negro of indefinite age.

All at once the Governor whirled on the administrator like he hoped to catch him picking his nose, eyes popping.

"What the hell's goin' on here?" he demanded.

The administrator couldn't have jumped higher if he'd been prodded with a pry pole. He clasped his hands in prayer, then he wrung them like a limp dishtowel, and turned the color of Swiss cheese.

"I want to know what the ding-dog devil you think you're *doin'* here," the Governor thundered.

The reporters began to scramble for elbow room, running around in tight little circles and braying the beginning of questions that sounded like barks, acting like they might bite somebody in the leg.

The photographers reverted to knee-jerk reaction. They pointed their souped-up Kodaks and caught the paralyzed image of the Governor conjuring up an historic wrath.

"Godamighty," the Governor roared. "You got *white* nurses waitin' on *nigger* men? Carryin' out their bedpans and givin' 'em sponge baths! For Christ sake, you lost your goddamn mind?"

The administrator couldn't believe it was happening to him, after all that scrubbing and scouring of the bedpans. It was simply more disaster than his pea brain could conceive of in one dose. He was beyond the form of words. He just made sounds without any recognizable shape.

"You think this is a charity hospital in New York City?" the governor shouted. "You some kind of damn trouble-makin' carpet-bagger come to take us in?"

The administrator choked it out that he was from Ospalosso, which was just a catbird's call down the road, and laid claim to a grandfather who had ridden with Jeb Stuart.

"Jeb Stuart would spin in his grave," the Governor howled. "They didn't teach you this down at Ospalosso! They sure-God don't go around down there teachin' folks to put white women lookin' after the creature comforts of a passel of field niggers!"

And he was off. He screamed and stomped his foot and if he had been Shirley Temple he would have ripped loose from his curls. He walled his eyes like a steer down with the blackleg. He thundered of the unmatched glories of Southern womanhood and called up obscure passages of Scripture. He was Jesus driving the money-changers from the temple and Samson among the thousand swinging the jawbone of an ass. He scared the nose warts off the administrator by threatening to fire him on the spot he'd violated.

"Tomorrow mornin' . . . ," he shouted, with his forefinger pinioning the administrator against a wide expanse of guilt, ". . . tomorrow mornin' I wanta see black nurses in here waitin' on black men. You don't know where to find any, look in the Yellow Pages."

He wheeled around and moved off down the hall in a running lope, leaving behind him a sort of instant polio, a quick and sudden paralysis, and it was a while before the news boys could recover enough to scurry after him, braying questions. And they had splashed it all over the papers, from the piney woods to the sparkling seashore, in Second Coming headlines. The woolhats moved their lips over the print out in the brush and blessed him by name. The professional haters walked with a spring in their step and started a move to fire the hospital administrator, who, they said with double dead-dog certainty, was from Perth Amboy, New Jersey, and had nigger blood in his veins. The magnolia-scented editorial pages across the state for the first time hauled off and paid Governor Cullie Blanton a sort of cautious homage, and the Daughters of the Confederacy passed a resolution commending him for his vigilant protection of Southern Womanhood.

Nobody seemed to notice that he had sullied the lily-white staff of the state hospital.

Later on I would tell him that he'd had the luck of the Irish. He never should have been able to pull it off. Because, I said, it was pure corn.

"Boy," he had said with a chortle, "there is corn and then there is corn. You put corn in a can and ship it across the distant miles and it gets the taste of the tin in it and loses a lot in the translation. You open up the can in New York or Chicago and dump it in a servin' dish and the tongue quickly knows it has been tainted by the despoilin' hand of man. You can't taste the warmth of the sun in it, or hear the cool wind singin' among the tall stalks, and the spring-green goodness is gone from the cob."

I waited a while, hoping he would develop the theme. But he just clammed up with a look of rich-man smugness and said no more. "So," I said after a respectable wait, "what does that prove?"

"Somethin' ever' backwoods politician ought to write in his hatband and read as regular as the Ten Commandments," he had said with a pleased grin. "It proves corn tastes better where it grows. . . ."

So now, all these years later, we plunged on into the night and Bo qualified for witchcraft at the wheel. We had outlasted the cane fields and now scooted through a tangled jungle of reedy marshlands where weeping willows bent to whisper to the grass of some vague personal sorrow. Rain tumbled down in the beam of the headlights like strands of clear, wet rope.

Cullie Blanton rummaged in his shirt pocket and found a cigar. He lifted it to his bulbous nose and rationed it one suspicious sniff through the wrapper. "What you got to remember," he said, "is that I don't happen to be Adlai Stevenson and this don't happen to be the U.N. And it ain't New York or California. Hell, it can't even lay claim to bein' *Mars*. It's the deep boondocks. Yeah, and it is the land of the blind. And if Bill Wooster and his mob of nutty hangmen runnin' around with flags stickin' from their bungholes get control of this state . . . well, if they get it, it will be the blind leadin' the blind."

"All I hope," I said, "is that you try to see the full picture. And I'm afraid you're looking at it through just one eye.".

"In the land of the blind," he said, "the one-eyed man is king." He leaned forward abruptly. "Haul ass, Bo. You think I want to paint a still life scenery?"

So Bo let out the last notch and we screamed through the swamps like caterwauling witches. Cullie looked past the drawn curtain of night and swept the hidden landscape with a strange pride in his eyes like he loved it all.

Cullie stared, and Bo stepped on the horses, and the night flashed by, and I sat in the darkness dwelling among mock shows.

"Boondock country," the Governor snorted in the ear of night. "Coon-ass country, by God. Fit for nothin' but raisin' billy goats and eatin' beans. The land is haunted and the hills are bloody and the wind is full of guilt. . . ."

Seldom-Seen Smith

▼▲▼▲▼▲▼▲▼▲▼▲▼▲▼▲▼▲▼▲▼▲▼▲▼▲▼▲▼▲▼▲▼▲▼▲▼

Edward Abbey

Edward Abbey, a Pennsylvanian, converted to the Southwest when he became a student at the University of Arizona. He has spent much time since then with the Forest Service and the Park Service protecting the wilderness and is a high-ranking apostle of conservation, an enemy of ugliness, waste, and urban sprawl. Until 1975, when he published *The Monkey Wrench Gang*, he seemed fierce rather than funny. In that book he proved that he could be fierce *and* funny.

The chapter that follows describes Seldom-Seen Smith, one of four conspirators who act out Abbey's revulsion against technological society. Smith, a Mormon, joins Vietnam veteran George Hayduke, Albuquerque doctor A. K. Sarvis, and Sarvis's friend Bella Abzug in sabotaging road-building machinery and bridges, and when the law catches up with them, they are preparing to blow up the great Glen Canyon Dam on the Colorado River—to Abbey the ultimate obscenity.

Abbey's second chapter, on the antics of half-paranoid Hayduke, should have been quoted here, but his gargantuan pleasure in Hayduke's character and antics makes for length, and George's happy, high-pressure obscenities could have sunk this subdivision like a bulldozer toppling into Lake Powell (see p. 115). The risk was too great.

Abbey predicts the eventual demise of the desert cities, thanks to the crush of immigrants and the inanities of developers. Phoenix will be ruined and occupied by terrorists (*Good News*, 1980), and "the sand dunes will block all traffic on Speedway in Tucson and the fungoid dust storms will fill the air." It is worth noting that Abbey was living in the Tucson area in 1985. His telephone, however, was unlisted.

Prologue: The Aftermath

WHEN A NEW BRIDGE BETWEEN TWO SOVEREIGN STATES OF THE United States has been completed, it is time for speech. For flags, bands and electronically amplified tech-industrial rhetoric. For the public address.

The people are waiting. The bridge, bedecked with bunting,

From *The Monkey Wrench Gang* (Philadelphia: J. B. Lippincott, 1975), 11–16, 35–43.

streamers and Day-Glo banners, is ready. All wait for the official opening, the final oration, the slash of ribbon, the advancing limousines. No matter that in actual fact the bridge has already known heavy commercial use for six months.

Long files of automobiles stand at the approaches, strung out for a mile to the north and south and monitored by state police on motorcycles, sullen, heavy men creaking with leather, stiff in riot helmet, badge, gun, Mace, club, radio. The proud tough sensitive flunkies of the rich and powerful. Armed and dangerous.

The people wait. Sweltering in the glare, roasting in their cars bright as beetles under the soft roar of the sun. That desert sun of Utah-Arizona, the infernal flaming plasmic meatball in the sky. Five thousand people yawning in their cars, intimidated by the cops and bored to acedia by the chant of the politicians. Their squalling kids fight in the back seats, Frigid Queen ice cream drooling down chins and elbows, pooling Jackson Pollock schmierkunst on the monovalent radicals of the Vinylite seat covers. All endure though none can bear to listen to the high-decibel racket pouring from the public address system.

The bridge itself is a simple, elegant and compact arch of steel, concrete as a statement of fact, bearing on its back the incidental ribbon of asphalt, a walkway, railings, security lights. Four hundred feet long, it spans a gorge seven hundred feet deep: Glen Canyon. Flowing through the bottom of the gorge is the tame and domesticated Colorado River, released from the bowels of the adjacent Glen Canyon Dam. Formerly a golden-red, as the name implies, the river now runs cold, clear and green, the color of glacier water.

Great river—greater dam. Seen from the bridge the dam presents a gray sheer concave face of concrete aggregate, implacable and mute. A gravity dam, eight hundred thousand tons of solidarity, countersunk in the sandstone Navajo formation, fifty million years emplaced, of the bedrock and canyon walls. A plug, a block, a fat wedge, the dam diverts through penstocks and turbines the force of the puzzled river.

What was once a mighty river. Now a ghost. Spirits of sea gulls and pelicans wing above the desiccated delta a thousand miles to seaward. Spirits of beaver nose upstream through the silt-gold surface. Great blue herons once descended, light as mosquitoes, long legs dangling, to the sandbars. Wood ibis croaked in the cottonwood. Deer walked the canyon shores. Snowy egrets in the tamarisk, plumes waving in the river breeze. . . .

The people wait. The speech goes on, many round mouths, one speech, and hardly a word intelligible. There seem to be spooks in the circuitry. The loudspeakers, black as charcoal, flaring from mounds on the gooseneck lamposts thirty feet above the roadway, are bellowing like Martians. A hash of sense, the squeak and gibber of technetronic poltergeists, strangled phrase and fibrillated paragraph, boom forth with the hollow roar, all the same, of AUTHORITY—

. . . this proud state of Utah [*bleeeeeep!*] glad to have this opportunity [*ronk!*] take part in opening of this magnificent bridge [*bleeeeeet!*] joining us to great state of Arizona, fastest growing [*yiiiiiiiiiinnnnnnnnnng!*] to help promote and assure continued growth and economic [*rawk! yawk! yiiiinnnng! niiiinnnnnnng!*] could give me more pleasure, Governor, than this significant occasion [*rawnk!*] of our two states [*blonk!*] by that great dam. . . .

Waiting, waiting. Far back in the line of cars, beyond reach of speech and out of sight of cop, a horn honks. And honks again. The sound of one horn, honking. A patrolman turns on his Harley hog, scowling and cruises down the line. The honking stops.

The Indians also watch and wait. Gathered on an open hillside above the highway, on the reservation side of the river, an informal congregation of Ute, Paiute, Hopi and Navajo lounge about among their brand-new pickup trucks. The men and women drink Tokay, the swarms of children Pepsi-Cola, all munching on mayonnaise and Kleenex sandwiches of Wonder, Rainbo and Holsum Bread. Our noble red brethren eyeball the ceremony at the bridge, but their ears and hearts are with Merle Haggard, Johnny Paycheck and Tammy Wynette blaring from truck radios out of Station K-A-O-S—*Kaos!*— in Flagstaff, Arizona.

The citizens wait; the official voices drone on and on into the mikes, through the haunted wiring, out of the addled speakers. Thousands huddled in their idling automobiles, each yearning to be free and first across the arch of steel, that weightless-looking bridge which spans so gracefully the canyon gulf, the airy emptiness where swallows skate and plane.

Seven hundred feet down. It is difficult to fully grasp the meaning of such a fall. The river moves so far below, churning among its rocks, that the roar comes up sounding like a sigh. A breath of wind carries the sigh away.

The bridge stands clear and empty except for the cluster of notables at the center, the important people gathered around the microphones and a symbolic barrier of red, white and blue ribbon stretched across the bridge from rail to rail. The black Cadillacs are parked at either end of the bridge. Beyond the official cars, wooden barricades and motorcycle patrolmen keep the masses at bay.

Far beyond the dam, the reservoir, the river and the bridge, the town of Page, the highway, the Indians, the people and their leaders, stretches the rosy desert. Hot out there, under the fierce July sun—the temperature at ground level must be close to 150 degrees Fahrenheit. All sensible creatures are shaded up or waiting out the day in cool burrows under the surface. No humans live in that pink wasteland. There is nothing to stay the eye from roving farther and farther, across league after league of rock and sand to the vertical façades of butte, mesa and plateau forming the skyline fifty miles away. Nothing grows out there but scattered clumps of blackbrush and cactus, with here and there a scrubby, twisted, anguished-looking juniper. And a little scurf pea, a little snakeweed. Nothing more. Nothing moves but one pale whirlwind, a tottering little tornado of dust which lurches into a stone pillar and collapses. Nothing observes the mishap but a vulture hovering on the thermals three thousand feet above.

The buzzard, if anyone were looking, appears to be alone in the immensity of the sky. But he is not. Beyond the range of even the sharpest human eyes but perceptible of one another, other vultures wait, soaring lazily on the air. If one descends, spotting below something dead or dying, the others come from all directions, out of nowhere, and gather with bowed heads and hooded eyes around the body of the loved one.

Back to the bridge: The united high-school marching bands of Kanab, Utah, and Page, Arizona, wilted but willing, now perform a spirited rendition of "Shall We Gather at the River?" followed by

"The Stars and Stripes Forever." Pause. Discreet applause, whistles, cheers. The weary multitude senses that the end is near, the bridge about to be opened. The governors of Arizona and Utah, cheerful bulky men in cowboy hats and pointy-toe boots, come forward again. Each brandishes a pair of giant golden scissors, flashing in the sunlight. Superfluous pop, TV cameras record history in the making. As they advance a workman dashes from among the onlookers, scuttles to the barrier ribbon and makes some kind of slight but doubtless important last-minute adjustment. He wears a yellow hard hat decorated with the emblematic decals of his class—American flag, skull and crossbones, the Iron Cross. Across the back of his filthy coveralls, in vivid lettering, is stitched the legend AMERICA: LOVE IT OR LEAVE IT ALONE. Completing his task, he retires quickly back to the obscurity of the crowd where he belongs.

Climactic moment. The throng prepares to unloose a cheer or two. Drivers scramble into their cars. The sound of racing engines: motors revved, tachs up.

Final word. Quiet, please.

"Go ahead, old buddy. Cut the damn thing."

"Me?"

"Both together, please."

"I thought you said . . ."

"Okay, I gotcha. Stand back. Like this?"

Most of the crowd along the highway had only a poor view of what happened next. But the Indians up on the hillside saw it all clearly. Grandstand seats. They saw the puff of smoke, black, which issued from the ends of the cut ribbon. They saw the flurry of sparks which followed as the ribbon burned, like a fuse, across the bridge. And when the dignitaries hastily backed off the Indians saw the general eruption of unprogrammed fireworks which pursued them. From under the draperies of bunting came an outburst of Roman candles, flaming Catherine wheels, Chinese firecrackers and cherry bombs. As the bridge was cleared from end to end a rash of fireworks blazed up along the walkways. Rockets shot into the air and exploded, Silver Salutes, aerial bombs and M-80s blasted off. Whirling dervishes of smoke and fire took off and flew, strings of firecrackers leaped

251

through the air like smoking whips, snapping and popping, lashing at the governors' heels. The crowd cheered, thinking this the high point of the ceremonies.

But it was not. Not the highest high point. Suddenly the center of the bridge rose up, as if punched from beneath, and broke in two along a jagged zigzag line. Through this absurd fissure, crooked as lightning, a sheet of red flame streamed skyward, followed at once by the sound of a great cough, a thunderous shuddering high-explosive cough that shook the monolithic sandstone of the canyon walls. The bridge parted like a flower, its separate divisions no longer joined by any physical bond. Fragments and sections began to fold, sag, sink and fall, relaxing into the abyss. Loose objects—gilded scissors, a monkey wrench, a couple of empty Cadillacs—slid down the appalling gradient of the depressed roadway and launched themselves, turning slowly, into space. They took a long time going down and when they finally smashed on the rock and river far below, the sound of the impact, arriving much later, was barely heard by even the most attentive.

The bridge was gone. The wrinkled fragments at either end still clinging to their foundations in the bedrock dangled toward each other like pendant fingers, suggesting the thought but lacking the will to touch. As the compact plume of dust resulting from the catastrophe expanded upward over the rimrock, slabs of asphalt and cement and shreds and shards of steel and rebar continued to fall, in contrary motion from the sky, splashing seven hundred feet below into the stained but unhurried river.

On the Utah side of the canyon, a governor, a highway commissioner and two high-ranking officers of the Department of Public Safety strode through the crowd toward their remaining limousines. Stern-faced and furious, they conferred as they walked.

"This is their last stunt, Governor, I promise you."

"Seems to me I heard that promise before, Crumbo."

"I wasn't on the case before, sir."

"So what. What're you doing now?"

"We're on their tail, sir. We have a good idea who they are, how they operate and what they're planning next."

252

"But not where they are."
"No sir, not at the moment. But we're closing in."
"And just what the hell are they planning next?"
"You won't believe me."
"Try me."
Colonel Crumbo points a finger to the immediate east. Indicating
that thing.
"The dam?"
"Yes sir."
"Not the dam."
"Yes sir, we have reason to think so."
"*Not* Glen Canyon *Dam!*"
"I know it sounds crazy. But that's what they're after."

Meanwhile, up in the sky, the lone visible vulture spirals in lazy circles higher and higher, contemplating the peaceful scene below. He looks down on the perfect dam. He sees downstream from the dam the living river and above it the blue impoundment, that placid reservoir where, like waterbugs, the cabin cruisers play. He sees, at this very moment, a pair of water skiers with tangled towlines about to drown beneath the waters. He sees the glint of metal and glass on the asphalt trail where endless jammed files of steaming automobiles creep home to Kanab, Page, Tuba City, Panguitch and points beyond. He notes in passing the dark gorge of the master canyon, the shattered stubs of a bridge, the tall yellow pillar of smoke and dust still rising, slowly, from the depths of the chasm.

Like a solitary smoke signal, like the silent symbol of calamity, like one huge inaudible and astonishing exclamation point signifying *surprise!* the dust plume hangs above the fruitless plain, pointing upward to heaven and downward to the scene of the primal split, the loss of connections, the place where not only space but time itself has come unglued. Has lapsed. Elapsed. Relapsed. Prolapsed. And then collapsed.

Under the vulture's eye. Meaning nothing, nothing to eat. Under that ultimate farthest eye, the glimmer of plasma down the west, so far beyond all consequence of dust and blue, the same.   .   .   .

Origins III:
Seldom Seen Smith

BORN BY CHANCE INTO MEMBERSHIP IN THE CHURCH OF JESUS Christ of Latter-Day Saints (Mormons), Smith was on lifetime sabbatical from his religion. He was a jack Mormon. A jack Morman is to a decent Mormon what a jackrabbit is to a cottontail. His connections to the founding father of his church can be traced in the world's biggest genealogical library in Salt Lake City. Like some of his forebears Smith practiced plural marriage. He had a wife in Cedar City, Utah, a second in Bountiful, Utah, and a third in Green River, Utah—each an easy day's drive from the next. His legal name was Joseph Fielding Smith (after a nephew of the martyred founder), but his wives had given him the name Seldom Seen, which carried.

On the same day that George Hayduke was driving up from Flagstaff to Lee's Ferry, Seldom Seen Smith was driving from Cedar City (Kathy's) after the previous night in Bountiful (Sheila's), on his way to the same destination. En route he stopped at a warehouse in Kanab to pick up his equipment for a float trip through Grand Canyon: three ten-man neoprene rafts, cargo rig, oars, waterproof bags and warsurplus ammo cans, tents, tarpaulin, rope, many many other things, and an assistant boatman to help man the oars. He learned that his boatman had already taken off, apparently, for the launching point at Lee's Ferry. Smith also needed a driver, somebody to shuttle his truck from Lee's Ferry to Temple Bar on Lake Mead, where the canyon trip would end. He found her, by prearrangement, among the other river groupies hanging around the warehouse of Grand Canyon Expeditions. Loading everything but the girl into the back of his truck, he went on, bound for Lee's Ferry by way of Page.

They drove eastward through the standard Utah tableau of perfect sky, mountains, red-rock mesas, white-rock plateaus and old volcanic extrusions—Mollie's Nipple, for example, visible from the highway thirty miles east of Kanab. Very few have stood on the tip of Mollie's Nipple: Major John Wesley Powell, for one: Seldom Seen Smith for another. That blue dome in the southeast, fifty miles away by line of sight, is Navajo Mountain. One of earth's holy places, God's navel, *om* and omphalos, sacred to shamans, witches, wizards, sun-crazed crackpots from mystic shrines like Keet Seel, Dot Klish, Tuba City and Cambridge, Massachusetts.

Between Kanab, Utah, and Page, Arizona, a distance of seventy miles, there is no town, no human habitation whatsoever, except one ramshackle assemblage of tarpaper shacks and cinder-block containers called Glen Canyon City. Glen Canyon City is built on hope and fantasy: as a sign at the only store says, "Fourty Million $Dollar Power Plant To Be Buildt Twelve Miles From Here Soon."

Smith and his friend did not pause at Glen Canyon City. Nobody pauses at Glen Canyon City. Someday it may become, as its founders hope and its inhabitants dream, a hive of industry and avarice, but at present one must report the facts: Glen Canyon City ("No Dumping") rots and rusts at the side of the road like a burned-out Volkswagen forgotten in a weedy lot to atrophy, unmourned, into the alkaline Utah earth. Many pass but no one pauses. Smith and girl friend shot by like bees in flight, honey-bound.

"What was that?" she said.

"Glen Canyon City."

"No, I mean *that*." Pointing back.

He looked in the mirror. "That there was Glen Canyon City."

They passed the Wahweap Marina turnoff. Miles away down the long slope of sand, slickrock, blackbrush, Indian ricegrass and prickly pear they could see a cluster of buildings, a house-trailer compound, roads, docks and clusters of boats on the blue bay of the lake. Lake Powell, Jewel of the Colorado, 180 miles of reservoir walled in by bare rock.

The blue death, Smith called it. Like Hayduke his heart was full of a healthy hatred. Because Smith remembered something different. He remembered the golden river flowing to the sea. He remembered canyons called Hidden Passage and Salvation and Last Chance and Forbidden and Twilight and many many more, some that never had a name. He remembered the strange great amphitheaters called Music Temple and Cathedral in the Desert. All these things now lay beneath the dead water of the reservoir, slowly disappearing under layers of descending silt. How could he forget? He had seen too much.

Now they came, amidst an increasing flow of automobile and truck traffic, to the bridge and Glen Canyon Dam. Smith parked his truck in front of the Senator Carl Hayden Memorial Building. He and his friend got out and walked along the rail to the center of the bridge.

Seven hundred feet below streamed what was left of the original river, the greenish waters that emerged, through intake, penstock, turbine and tunnel, from the powerhouse at the base of the dam. Thickets of power cables, each strand as big around as a man's arm, climbed the canyon walls on steel towers, merged in a maze of transformer stations, then splayed out toward the south and west-toward Albuquerque, Babylon, Phoenix, Gomorrah, Los Angeles, Sodom, Las Vegas, Nineveh, Tucson, the cities of the plain.

Upriver from the bridge stood the dam, a glissade of featureless concrete sweeping seven hundred feet down in a concave façade from the dam's rim to the green-grass lawn on the roof of the power plant below.

They stared at it. The dam demanded attention. It was a magnificent mass of cement. Vital statistics: 792,000 tons of concrete aggregate; cost $750 million and the lives of sixteen (16) workmen. Four years in the making, prime contractor Morrison-Knudsen, Inc., sponsored by U.S. Bureau of Reclamation, courtesy U.S. taxpayers.

"It's too big," she said.

"That's right, honey," he said. "And that's why."

"You can't."

"There's a way."

"Like what?"

"I don't know. But there's got to be a way."

They were looking at only the downstream face and topside surface of the dam. That topside, wide enough for four Euclid trucks, was the narrowest part of the dam. From the top it widened downward, forming an inverted wedge to block the Colorado. Behind the dam the blue waters gleamed, reflecting the blank sky, the fiery eye of day, and scores of powerboats sped round and round, dragging water skiers. Far-off whine of motors, shouts of joy. . . .

"Like how?" she said.

"Who you workin' for?" he said.

"You."

"Okay, think of something."

256

"We could pray."

"Pray?" said Smith. "Now there's one thing I ain't tried. Let's pray for a little *pre*-cision earthquake right here." And Smith went down on his knees, there on the cement walkway of the bridge, bowed his head, closed his eyes, clapped hands together palm to palm, prayer-wise, and prayed. At least his lips were moving. Praying, in broad daylight, with the tourists driving by and walking about taking photographs. Someone aimed a camera at Smith. A park rangerette in uniform turned her head his way, frowning.

"Seldom," the girl murmured, embarrassed, "you're making a public spectacle."

"Pretend you don't know me," he whispered. "And get ready to run. The earth is gonna start buckin' any second now."

He returned to his solemn mumble.

"Dear old God," he prayed, "you know and I know what it was like here, before them bastards from Washington moved in and ruined it all. You remember the river, how fat and golden it was in June, when the big runoff come down from the Rockies? Remember the deer on the sandbars and the blue herons in the willows and the catfish so big and tasty and how they'd bite on spoiled salami? Remember that crick that come down through Bridge Canyon and Forbidden Canyon, how green and cool and clear it was? God, it's enough to make a man sick. Say, you recall old Woody Edgell up at Hite and the old ferry he used to run across the river? That crazy contraption of his hangin' on cables; remember that damn thing? Remember the cataracts in Forty-Mile Canyon? Well, they flooded out about half of them too. And part of the Escalante's gone now—Davis Gulch, Willow Canyon, Gregory Natural Bridge, Ten-Mile. Listen, are you listenin' to me? There's somethin' you can do for me, God. How about a little old *pre*-cision-type earthquake right under this dam? Okay? Any time. Right now for instance would suit me fine."

He waited a moment. The rangerette, looking unhappy, was coming toward them.

"Seldom, the guard's coming."

Smith concluded his prayer. "Okay, God, I see you don't want to do it just now. Well, all right, suit yourself, you're the boss, but we ain't got a hell of a lot of time. Make it pretty soon, goddammit. A-men."

"Sir!"

Smith got up off his knees, smiling at the rangerette. "Ma'am?"

"I'm sorry, sir, but you can't pray here. This is a public place."

"That's true."

"United States Government property."

"Yes ma'am."

"We have thirteen churches in Page if you wish to worship in the church of your choice."

"Yes, ma'am. Do they have a Paiute church?"

"A what?"

"I'm a Paiute. A pie-eyed Paiute." He winked at his truck driver.

"Seldom," she said, "let's get out of here."

They drove from the bridge up the grade to the neat green government town of Page. A few miles to the southeast stood the eight-hundred-foot smokestacks of the coal-burning Navajo Power Plant, named in honor of the Indians whose lungs the plant was treating with sulfur dioxide, hydrogen sulfide, nitrous oxide, carbon monoxide, sulfuric acid, fly ash and other forms of particulate matter.

Smith and friend lunched at Mom's Café, then went to the Big Pig supermarket for an hour of serious shopping. He had to buy food for himself, his boatman and four customers for fourteen days.

Seldom Seen Smith was in the river-running business. The back-country business. He was a professional guide, wilderness outfitter, boatman and packer. His capital equipment consisted basically of such items as rubber boats, kayaks, life jackets, mountain tents, outboard motors, pack saddles, topographic maps, waterproof duffel bags, signal mirrors, climbing ropes, snakebite kits, 150-proof rum, fly rods and sleeping bags. And one one-ton truck with stock rack and this legend on magnetic decals affixed to the doors: "Back of Beyond Expeditions, Jos. Smith, Prop., Hite, Utah."

(Twenty fathoms under in a milky green light the spectral cabins, the skeleton cottonwoods, the ghostly gas pumps of Hite, Utah, glow dimly through the underwater mist, outlines and edges softened by the cumulative blur of slowly settling silt. Hite has been submerged by Lake Powell for many years now, but Smith will not grant recognition to alien powers.)

The tangible assets were incidental. His basic capital was stored in head and nerves, a substantial body of special knowledge, special skills and special attitudes. Ask Smith, he'll tell you: Hite, Utah, will rise again.

His gross income last year was $44,521.95. Total expenses, *not* including any wages or salary for himself, ran to $34,010.05. Net income, $10,511.90. Hardly adequate for an honest jack Mormon, his three wives, three households and five children. Poverty level. But they managed. Smith thought he lived a good life. His only complaint was that the U.S. Government, the Utah State Highway Department and a consortium of oil companies, mining companies and public utilities were trying to destroy his livelihood, put him out of business and obstruct the view.

Smith and his driver bought $685 worth of food, Smith paying in warm soiled cash (he didn't believe in banks), loaded it all in the truck and headed out of town for the rendezvous at Lee's Ferry, into the westerly wind across the sandy red-rock wastelands of Indian country.

WELCOME TO NAVAJOLAND the billboards say. And, on the reverse side, GOOD-BYE COME AGAIN.

And the wind blows, the dust clouds darken the desert blue, pale sand and red dust drift across the asphalt trails and tumbleweeds fill the arroyos. Good-bye, come again.

The road curves through a dynamited notch in the Echo Cliffs and from there down twelve hundred feet to the junction at Bitter Springs. Smith paused as he always did at the summit of the pass to get out of the truck and contemplate the world beyond and below. He had gazed upon this scene a hundred times in his life so far, he knew that he might have only a hundred more.

The girl came and stood beside him. He slipped an arm around her. They pressed together side by side, staring out and down at the hazy grandeur.

Smith was a lanky man, lean as a rake, awkward to handle. His arms were long and wiry, his hands large, his feet big, flat and solid. He had a nose like a beak, a big Adam's apple, like the handles on a jug, sun-bleached hair like a rat's nest, and a wide and generous grin. Despite his thirty-five years he still managed to look, much of the time, like an adolescent. The steady eyes, though, revealed a man inside.

They went down into the lower desert, turned north at Bitter Springs and followed Hayduke spoor and Hayduke sign (empty beer cans on the shoulder of the road) to the gorge, around a jeep parked on the bridge and on toward Lee's Ferry. They stopped at a turnoff for a look at the river and what was left of the old crossing.

Not much. The riverside campgrounds had been obliterated by a gravel quarry. In order to administrate, protect and make the charm, beauty and history of Lee's Ferry easily accessible to the motorized public, the Park Service had established not only a new paved road and the gravel quarry but also a ranger station, a paved campground, a hundred-foot-high pink water tower, a power line, a paved picnic area, a motor pool with cyclone fence, an official garbage dump and a boat-launching ramp covered with steel matting. The area had been turned over to the administration of the National Park Service in order to protect it from vandalism and commercial exploitation.

"Suppose your prayer is answered," the girl was saying in the silence. "Suppose you have your earthquake at the dam. What happens to all the people here?"

"That there dam," Smith replied, "is twelve miles upriver through the crookedest twelve miles of canyon you ever seen. It'd take the water an hour to get here."

"They'd still drown."

"I'd warn 'em by telephone."

"Suppose God answers your prayer in the middle of the night. Suppose everybody at the dam is killed and there isn't anybody left alive up there to give warning. Then what?"

"I ain't responsible for an act of God, honey."

"It's your prayer."

Smith grinned. "It's His earthquake." And he held up a harkening finger. "What's that?"

They listened. The cliffs towered above. The silent evening flowed around them. Below, hidden deep in its dark gorge, the brawling river moved among rocks in complicated ways toward its climax in the Grand Canyon.

"I don't hear anything but the river," she said.

"No, listen. . . ."

Far off, echoing from the cliffs, a rising then descending supernatural wail, full of mourning—or was it exultation?

"A coyote?" she offered.

"No. . . ."

"Wolf?"

"Yeah. . . ."

"I never heard of wolves around here before."

He smiled. "That's right," he said. "That's absolutely right. There ain't supposed to be no wolves in these parts anymore. They ain't supposed to be here."

"Are you sure it's a wolf?"

"Yup." He paused, listening again. Only the river sounded now, down below. "But it's a kind of unusual wolf."

"What do you mean?"

"I mean it's one of them two-legged-type wolves."

She stared at him. "You mean human?"

"More or less," Smith said.

They drove on, past the ranger station, past the pink water tower, across the Paria River to the launching ramp on the muddy banks of the Colorado. Here Smith parked his truck, tailgate toward the river, and began unloading his boats. The girl helped him. They dragged the three inflatable boats from the truck bed, unfolded them and spread them out on the sand. Smith took a socket wrench from his toolbox, removed a spark plug from the engine block and screwed in an adapter on the head of an air hose. He started the motor, which inflated the boats. He and the girl pulled the boats into the water, leaving the bows resting on the shore, and tied them on long lines to the nearest willow tree.

The sun went down. Sloshing about in cutoff jeans, they shivered a little when a cool breeze began to come down the canyon, off the cold green river.

"Let's fix something to eat before it gets completely dark," the girl said.

"You bet, honey."

Smith fiddled with his field glasses, looking for something he thought he had seen moving on a distant promontory above the gorge. He found his target. Adjusting the focus, he made out, a mile away through the haze of twilight, the shape of a blue jeep half concealed beneath a pedestal rock. He saw the flicker of a small campfire. A thing moved at the edge of the field. He turned the glasses slightly and saw the figure of a man, short and hairy and broad and naked. The naked man held a can of beer in one hand; with the other hand he held field glasses to his eyes, just like Smith. He was looking directly at Smith.

The two men studied each other for a while through 7×35 binocular lenses, which do not blink. Smith raised his hand in a cautious wave. The other man raised his can of beer as an answering salute.

"What are you looking at?" the girl asked.

"Some kind of skinned tourist."

"Let me see." He gave her the glasses. She looked. "My God, he's naked," she said. "He's waving it at me."

"Lee's Ferry is gone to hell," Smith said, rummaging in their supplies. "You can't argue that. Where'd we put that goddanged Coleman stove?"

"That guy looks familiar."

"All naked men look familiar, honey. Now sit down here and let's see what we can find to eat in this mess."

They sat on ammo boxes and cooked and ate their simple supper. The Colorado River rolled past. From downstream came the steady roar of the rapids where a tributary stream, the Paria, has been unloading its rocks for a number of centuries in the path of the river. There was a smell of mud on the air, of fish, of willow and cottonwood. Good smells, rotten and rank, down through the heart of the desert.

They were not alone. Occasional motor traffic buzzed by on the road a hundred yards away: tourists, boaters, anglers bound for the marina a short distance beyond.

The small and solitary campfire on the far-off headland to the west had flickered out. In the gloom that way Smith could see no sign of friend or enemy. He retreated into the bushes to urinate, staring at the gleam of the darkened river, thinking of nothing much. His mind was still. Tonight he and his friend would sleep on the shore by the boats and gear. Tomorrow morning, while he rigged the boats for the voyage down the river, the girl would drive back to Page to pick up the paying passengers scheduled to arrive by air, from Albuquerque, at eleven.

New customers for Back of Beyond. A Dr. Alexander K. Sarvis, M.D. And one Miss—or Mrs.?—or Mr?—B. Abbzug.

Humor of the
Towns and Cities

▼▲▼▲▼▲▼▲▼▲▼▲▼▲▼▲▼▲▼▲▼▲▼▲▼▲▼▲▼▲▼▲▼▲▼▲▼

H. Allen Smith—"The Founding of Caliche"
(from *The Return of the Virginian*)

Dan Jenkins—"Janet and Her Songs"
(from *Baja Oklahoma*)

William Brinkley—"Freight Train"
(from *Peeper*)

And Finally . . .

Urban Laughter

▼▲▼▲▼▲▼▲▼▲▼▲▼▲▼▲▼▲▼▲▼▲▼▲▼▲▼▲▼▲▼▲▼

TWO FACTS STAND OUT IN HUMOROUS WESTERN FICTION AFTER 1930: It has tended to move to the towns and cities, though there is plenty of country and rangeland humor left; and with the move came a deepening of disillusion, a sharpening of satire.

The scalpel has been applied to frontier towns that existed only in the imagination of the author. H. Allen Smith's account of the origin of Caliche is outwardly cheerful but his brush is tipped with acid. Another example that might have been used is John Seelye's history of the hamlet of Invincible in *The Kid* (1972). Like Leslie Fiedler, both men seem to believe that "to understand the West as somehow a joke comes closer to getting it straight."

Contemporary novelists likewise cherish no illusions. Lorna Novak of Amarillo, Texas, is not bitter, but she has no illusions about middle-class female society in a city like her own. Dan Jenkins pays his respects to the saloon-and-cocktail-bar stratum of the Fort Worth population, raking it with light artillery. The pace changes with William Brinkley's *Peeper*, which probes the soft underbelly of a prosperous town in the lower Rio Grande Valley.

Some kind of climax is reached in a few sharp-edged satires that tend to move outside the bounds of decency, for example Edwin Shroke's *Peter Arbiter* (1973), which covers in detail the activities of a bisexual interior decorator in the Dallas area. One chapter, devoted to an incredible dinner party at the home of oil billionaire Roy Eanes, has its roots in the banquet scene from the Roman writer Petronius Arbiter. Had the anthologist possessed a little more courage, he would have included this incredible performance.

The Founding of Caliche

▼▲▼▲▼▲▼▲▼▲▼▲▼▲▼▲▼▲▼▲▼▲▼▲▼▲▼▲▼▲▼▲▼

H. Allen Smith

H. Allen Smith abandoned a career as a newspaperman to engage—or, perhaps better, to indulge—in full-time writing. His material is Texas and Texans, seen through a distorted glass darkly. He speaks Texan and enjoys the metaphorical style supposed to characterize Texan common speech, but his formal manner and frequent literary allusion contrast humorously with the colloquialisms of his zany characters and with the peculiar pickles he puts them in. What he produces could be called farce with a purpose. Much can be deduced about his attitudes toward the good Christian people he lives with from the following brief selection from *The Return of the Virginian*. His comments on life in West Texas become, by a slight extension, comments on life in America.

His story focuses on the grandson of Owen Wister's Virginian, who comes to Texas looking for the son of the Virginian's enemy Trampas ("When you call me that, smile!"). The action takes place at Caliche, a town suspiciously like Alpine, Smith's home community. The narrator is Forsythe Grady, the local newspaper editor. A central character is Emily, an intelligent pig who starts a local feud by witching water wells. The final chapters take the reader far beyond the bounds of reason and probability, but the Virginian's grandson falls in love with Trampas's granddaughter and all ends well for almost everybody.

CALICHE IS AN OLD TOWN, ANTEDATING THE CIVIL WAR BY AS many as two years. It once bore the name of Ochiltree, and the story of its founding by a man of that name is an inspiring chapter in Texas history, a moving episode with deep tragic undertones—a tale of courage on the one hand and hateful intolerance on the other—little known even to Texans because it cannot be told without use of the word *tit*.

I have never dared to set down the true account of the town's origin in this newspaper, and I chose not to outline it for Jefferson Cordee during our brief tour of the downtown area. In the course of that stroll amidst the canyons of lower Caliche, he mentioned the Bible at least

From *Return of the Virginian* (Garden City: Doubleday, 1974), 56–61.

three times. People who mention the Bible that often would not care to hear about Charles Ochiltree's valiant war with the Four-Tit Baptists, except perhaps in private.

Long decades ago there was a town in Texas named Snow Hill, situated in flat country about twenty miles north of Dallas, in Collin County. It was a small community and could support no more than one church, and that church, to be sure, was Baptist. Among the upstanding citizens of Snow Hill were Coley Brewster and Charles Ochiltree, and both of these good men were deacons in the church.

One day in the late 1850s Brother Coley Brewster, who had a houseful of young'uns, found himself needing a good milk cow. He mentioned this need to Brother Charlie Ochiltree, who had cows to throw away, and Brother Ochiltree said, wye of course, he'd be happy to sell one of his herd to his fellow deacon.

Said Brother Brewster: "You understand, Charlie, that I got to have me a cow that's a prime milker."

Said Brother Ochiltree: "The cow I got in mind, Coley, is a cow that'll dern near drown you in milk. I will garrantee you that she will give you one gallon of milk per tit."

(Please, kind reader, keep in mind that this account of the happenings in Snow Hill is unleavened history, and keep in mind, too, that the events took place in a long-gone era; the temptation is strong upon me to give Brother Ochiltree's milk cow a suitable semi-comic name, but in the interest of historical truth and scholarly integrity, let us be content in the knowledge that no cow name, such as Bossy or Bessie or Fern, has been handed down to us from those ancient days.)

Brother Coley Brewster was pleasured no end that the cow in question was warranted to furnish him with four gallons of milk per day. Jehoshaphat! He'd be able to submerge his kids in milk and have some left over to sell to the neighbors. Judas Priest! A truly Christian blessing!

A price was agreed upon, the money changed hands, and Brother Ochiltree delivered the cow to the Coley Brewster home.

Within thirty seconds Brother Brewster had discovered that a monstrous fraud had been perpetrated. He always had been in military parlance, a tit man—even unto cows—and thus he was quick to detect that this animal as a sport, a mutant, a dad-burn freak. She

269

THE LAUGHING WEST

possessed an udder of standard size and shape, but depending from
that udder was just one single tit. Right in the middle.

There were witnesses to what happened next. Brother Brewster lost
his Christian cool. To keep himself from busting Deacon Ochiltree a
good one right in the beezer, he began picking up fallen tree limbs,
breaking them in pieces, hurling the pieces to the ground, and jump-
ing up and down on them in irreverent rage. All the while he was
uttering parts of speech that are normally strange and unpleasant to
the ears of churchy people. He charged his fellow deacon with lying
and larceny and jactitation of marriage and arson, and Brother Ochiltree responded with the patience of the Savior, as follows:

"Fetch me a milk bucket."

Someone brought the bucket and Brother Ochiltree seized the
cow's single spigot and milked her, and true enough she gave a gallon.

"All I said," he declared, "was that she'd give one gallon per tit.
That is what she has just give. The Good Lord is my witness."

"I demand my money back!" cried Brother Brewster, but Deacon
Ochiltree insisted that there had been no deception on his part, that a
deal is a deal and this particular deal would remain a deal.

Brother Brewster took the matter straight to the hierarchy of the
Snow Hill Baptist Church. A conference was summoned, patterned
after the Diet of Worms, and the purchaser of the one-titted cow told
his story. His opponent stood firm. After a while the church leaders
said they would take the matter under advisement, but Brother Ochiltree noted that they were casting dark looks in his direction. He
smelled real trouble. It seemed clear to him that he was in danger of
being unchurched—canned out of the flock. In those days being unchurched was a serious and degrading affair, almost as serious and
degrading as being hanged. Nowadays it means you get to be an
Episcopalian.

Up to this point we have been dealing with straight history. The
story of the quarrel is substantially true. As for subsequent events, it is
possible that the legend makers have taken a hand—yet the basic details have to be true. Caliche is a solid fact, and the sandstone statue of
Charles Ochiltree is on the courthouse lawn.

Rather than submit to the stigma of being unchurched there in
Snow Hill, Brother Ochiltree called together a group of his friends

270

and supporters who had stood beside him throughout his ordeal. He had them all kneel down and pray for guidance. Later that same day he told them that while they were kneeling with heads bowed, a seagull came out of the clouds and perched on his shoulder.

"He spoke to me," Brother Ochiltree told his people.

"What did he say?" they wanted to know.

"He said we should go to *The Place*."

"Did he mean you should go to The Bad Place?"

"Of course not. I don't know what he meant, but the Lord will surely give me a fill-in."

"You said, Brother Ochiltree, that he was a seagull. What in tarnation was he a-doin' in Collin County? A seagull is supposed to hang around the sea, and the only water we got here is Crippled Toad Creek, and it's dry as a gourd."

"God's seagull don't need no water," said the Leader.

There were, as always, a couple of dissenters.

"What language did this seagull use?" asked wise old Deacon Travis.

"It was halfway between Missouri Ozark and Tex-Mex," said Brother Ochiltree.

"I ain't goin'," said Deacon Travis.

Brother Willie Jim Grimes chipped in his quibble. "Did he say anything, this here seagull, in regards to one-tit cows versus four-tit cows?"

"Seagulls don't bother talkin' cow-talk," Deacon Ochiltree responded.

"I ain't goin'," said Brother Grimes.

"Then get lost," said the Leader. "The Lord go with you and the devil take the hindmost."

"A . . . men!" chorused the great throng of thirty-one loyal Single-Titters.

The following day these faithful ones loaded their belongings into their wagons and pushcarts and departed Snow Hill forever. As their sorry little caravan moved away from the town they were showered with rotten vegetables by the Four-Titter adherents of Coley Brewster, who lost their sense of balance so completely that they began shouting hard-core pornography at the apostates.

There was no welcome for the Single-Titters anywhere along the way. Early in their epochal trek they arrived at the thriving hamlet of Dallas, with a population of 775—Methodists, Cumberland Presbyterians, and Fulminant Pentacostal Christians. Not a Baptist in town. The Dallas folks would have nothing to do with the Ochiltree wagon train, refused to sell them supplies, offered them no jerky (the basic foodstuff of Dallasites then as now), and told them to mosey. For this, on July 8, 1860, a week after the caravan had departed, a mysterious wonder was performed: the whole damn town of Dallas caught fire and burned to the ground.

At Waco to the south, the Single-Titters tried to get some converts, since they had a desperate need of manpower, and they set up a baptismal ceremoney at the Brazos River, but nobody showed up except a few rowdy children, who shouted taunts at the visitors, and the Waco Water Commissioner, who said he would pour carbolic acid and paregoric in the river if the pilgrims didn't hitch up and get moving. No provisions. No jerky. Brother Ochiltree appealed to the body politic, but the people told him they were busy trying to get up a college, a Baptist school which they planned calling either Cowper Brann State Normal or Baylor U. They made it clear to Brother Ochiltree that the institution would be nondenominational Baptist, meaning neither one-titted nor quadri-titted. Mosey, said the God-fearing people of Waco, and our friends from Snow Hill did so. Ever southward. Ever westward. Ever weary.

On a Sunday morning they straggled into the little German settlement of Fredericksburg. The untidy, limping, hungry train moved along Main Street and came to the Vereins Kirche, where services were in progress. Pastor Ochiltree (for now he was so denominated) spoke to his weary flock, telling them that their fortunes would change now, that the Lord would smile upon them, that he had heard tell of this community, that the people here were kind and generous Teutons, quick to embrace the wayfaring stranger.

The door of the Kirche opened and people began coming out, disturbed by the noise the Pilgrims were making and led, no doubt, by old John Meusebach himself. The Fredericksburghers wanted to know what all the damn *Radau* was about, and Pastor Ochiltree stepped forward. He spoke of their long and harrowing journey, of the schism in the Snow Hill Baptist Church, of the dire need his people were suffering. The Fredericksburg leaders asked for details of the church trouble in Snow Hill and Charlie Ochiltree stated them, concealing nothing.

The elders of the German community then withdrew into their tabernacle to gnaw on Bratwurst and say Gott-in-Himmel and debate the thorny question before the house. At length they returned to the street. We do not know if John Meusebach, the colony's founder, was present as spokesman but if he was he extended his right arm, pointed south, and intoned:

"Du verdammter Kerl, mach dass Du raus Kommst aus unserum County mit Deiner verruckten Ein-Titten Religion!"

English translation:

"Verdammt noch mal! Raus mit you und your crazy Tittenreligion aus unser Gilleppisie Coundy und taken mit you zee dumbkopf undder-shtoopid Theorie!"

Alas! Head hanging, bellies empty, spirits at their lowest yet, the Pilgrims moved off toward the Pedernales River, and a gang of boys followed in their train, howling insults in Low Dutch and hurling rancid potato dumplings at the tormented wanderers.

At Uvalde the guileless travelers were set upon by Lipan-Apache Indians who had just captured the settlement. One Single-Titter was scalped, two were wounded, and four lit into the forest and are probably still running. At Del Rio the Pilgrims found the community beset by a plague of rattlesnakes; thousands upon thousands of the venomous vipers were wriggling around in the streets, chasing dogs and cats and iguanas and snapping at citizens, rich and poor alike. The invasion was so serious that the Town Council had imported Mexican bandits to fight the serpents, it being already a well-established fact in Texas that a rattlesnake will run from a Mexican every time.

Pastor Ochiltree surveyed this dreadful scene and felt a sickness in his heart; then he squared his shoulders and spoke to his people.

"It couldn't be any wussen it's been," he said, and forthwith led his disciples out of this snake-town, heading his caravan upriver and into the mountain country. Then one afternoon around four o'clock the wagons reached the crest of a rocky eminence and Charlie Ochiltree looked into a verdant vale, where there was no sign of a rattlesnake, a

Neiman or a Marcus, a Lipan-Apache, or a single platter of *Kartoffel-kloese*. The Founder raised himself off his wagon seat, swept his eyes across the glorious prospect, flung his arms Himmelward, and cried out:

"This here is The Place!"

And so they descended with a bang and a clatter into the valley, which was no way near as verdant as it had looked from the cliffs, and they set to work building their church and their town and all hands were as happy as larks.

Thus the story of how Caliche was founded. Most of it, as I have stated, is solid history—Texas history, that is. Some bits and fragments are reckoned by local scholars to be fabricated out of folklore and myth, especially the account of the Hegira itself. No one in present-day Caliche is able to sort out fact from legend. In any case, a dozen years after Patriarch Charlie Ochiltree was gathered to his fathers, the name of the town was changed to Caliche.

A lovely name, Caliche. It means dirt.

Janet and Her Songs

▼▲▼▲▼▲▼▲▼▲▼▲▼▲▼▲▼▲▼▲▼▲▼▲▼▲▼▲▼▲▼▲▼▲▼

Dan Jenkins

Dan Jenkins of Fort Worth seceded from Texas when he moved to New York to work for *Sports Illustrated* (he became senior writer), but the germs remained in his system. His satiric novels are tough and funny displays of the Heart of Texas, beating on his hand like freshly detached sacrificial organs in the palm of an Aztec priest. The word most commonly used in describing these novels is "raunchy," *and it is with some trepidation that an anthologist selects a chapter for inclusion. *Baja Oklahoma* (Texas is referred to as Lower Oklahoma) was a bestseller and a fine example of the western humorous novel in an urban setting.

Focus is on Juanita Hutchins, who tends bar at Herb's, said to resemble Herb Massey's Café in Fort Worth. Juanita has not made a conspicuous success of her life but she owns a good Martin guitar and composes, if one uses the term loosely, country and western songs. Her idol is Willie Nelson, and by the end of the book, she has moved up into the firmament in which he shines.

Chapter 7 finds Juanita with a new friend, known as Slick, at a restaurant called The Wandering Squid near L'Atrium Plaza, Dallas's "newest, biggest and fully enclosed shopping mall." The waiter's name is Evan. He brings a white-wine spritzer for Juanita and imported beer for Slick. The beer comes in a "cologne bottle with three umlauts, two slashes, and a backward letter in the name." After three spritzers Juanita wants to talk about her past and begins with Weldon Taylor, her first husband. Slick feels the urge also, and revelations follow.

*Kent Biffle, "Hops and Scotches: Dan Jenkins celebrates his newest book deep in the heart of "Baja Oklahoma," *Dallas Morning News*, November 15, 1981.

Sᴌɪᴄᴋ ᴄᴀᴜɢʜᴛ Eᴠᴀɴ ɪɴ ᴛʜᴇ ᴍɪᴅᴅʟᴇ ᴏꜰ ᴀ ᴅᴇᴀᴛʜ ꜱᴘɪʀᴀʟ ᴀɴᴅ ᴏʀ-dered four more umlauts for himself and a bottle of white wine for Juanita. It would save Slick the trouble of having to use semaphores between drinks. Any wine would be satisfactory. Slick said to the waiter, as long as it weren't a Chateau-le-S44.50.

"Pinot Chardonnay is a nice wine," said Evan.

"So is Gallo."

From *Baja Oklahoma* (New York: Atheneum, 1981), 114–29.

"I rather imagined you'd say that." Evan simpered, reaching for an overburdened ashtray.

Juanita rescued her cigarette.

Slick then settled back and confessed to Juanita that both of his ex-wives, like Weldon Taylor, had been crackerjack comedians.

The wife to whom Slick had returned from the army was Janet, his old high school sweetheart. Rather curiously. Slick had said good-bye to a Senior Class Favorite but had come home to find a metal-shop teacher.

Janet had done a darn funny thing back in their neighborhood in Tulsa. Almost single-handedly, she had popularized fat arms and screaming over the dinner table.

Slick's parting words to his first wife had been: "Damned if you haven't got me interested in loud voices, Janet. I'm goin' to the opera."

Nothing Janet ever did, however, was as hilarious as the stunt Bonnie pulled, which consequently made Bonnie, Slick's second wife, the wittier of the two women. In only twelve years of marriage, Bonnie fancifully transformed herself from Rita Hayworth into Joseph Stalin.

Bonnie deserved all the credit for driving Slick to a unique psychological discovery, the unearthing of Mankind's Ten Stages of Drunkenness, which were:

- Witty and Charming.
- Rich and Powerful.
- Benevolent.
- Clairvoyant.
- Fuck Dinner.
- Patriotic.
- Crank Up the Enola Gay.
- Witty and Charming, Part II.
- Invisible.
- Bulletproof.

The last stage was almost certain to end a marriage.

Slick had missed Bonnie's roll call one night in Tulsa because he drank himself Bulletproof and became involved with a persuasive home-wrecker who vowed he would not have to remove his socks.

Slick limped home about seven o'clock the next morning. His plan was to sneak into the house through the back door before anyone awakened and curl up on a couch and pretend to have slept there.

But Bonnie was already in the kitchen cracking eggs for her sister and mother, both of whom lived there—another of Bonnie's jokes.

"Where in the holy hell have you been all night?" Bonnie had bellowed.

Slick gingerly solved the riddle. He had worked past midnight on the transmission of a Chevrolet. He hadn't wanted to disturb anybody when he came home. That's why he had slept in the hammock in the backyard.

"I'll have mine over easy," he said.

"You lyin' bastard!" Bonnie exploded. "I took that hammock *down* three weeks ago!"

"Well," Slick had murmured sleepily, wandering off. "That's my story and I'm stickin' to it."

Juanita's second husband was Vern Sandifer.

Vern, as a figure in her past, was almost as distant as Weldon Taylor now, which was why Juanita could entertain thoughts of Vern without a return of the old combat fatigue.

In the five years between Weldon and Vern, Juanita lost the grandparents who raised her. Her grandfather died of a coronary as he sat in the swing on the front porch. He had been sitting there resting, smelling cotton seed from the elevators towering over the freight cars in the distance, and listening to the plaintive sound of beams falling at North Texas Steel up the road. Juanita's grandmother had died a year later because she missed him.

It was during these years that Juanita became adept at tracking down new clinics and sanitariums to keep Grace occupied. She nursed Candy through everything from mumps to anthrax. And she launched her career in Herb's Cafe as a waitress.

Vern Sandifer sold mud.

Juanita did not understand his line of work immediately, but she was nonetheless attracted to him. Vern was polite, well-groomed, very tan, and had tassels on his loafers. A hundred-dollar bill covered the one-dollar bills in his money-clip.

They met in Herb's when Juanita served him a BLD, the breakfast, lunch and dinner. The BLD was a hamburger steak with melted cheese, scrambled eggs and ketchup on top.

The mud Vern sold was something nobody could drill an oil well without. Mud was pumped into the hole to cut down on the friction as the drilling bit churned away at the rocks and roots to get at the dinosaurs.

Vern's job kept him outdoors in an enchanted land where long-horns rumbled across the purple sage, and lovable old ranch hands sat around campfires telling stories about Wyatt Earp and the Clanton brothers. Vern insisted he worked closely with the independent oil operators themselves, his good friends H. L., Clint, Sid, R. E., Monty, Arch and Hugh Roy.

Juanita envisioned herself lounging in the leather chair of a Petroleum Club watching Candy bouncing around on the knee of Uncle H. L. Hunt.

Herb Macklin gave Juanita fifty dollars for a wedding present. The other waitresses chipped in on a shortie satin nightgown that revived her memory of the Vargas Girl.

And Juanita moved to Wander, Texas, as Mrs. Vern Sandifer.

One thing Vern left out was the trailer.

The Sandifers had to fold up something before they could sit down on something. Candy slept on their backs.

In Wander, Texas, Juanita quickly volunteered a scheme that would make Vern rich: sell shade trees instead of mud. She met no wives or other women around the prefab drilling compounds who had bathed since the Apaches staked them to the ground. Juanita yearned for a paved road, a newspaper, or a valid passport to San Angelo.

The Sandifers got a big break in the second year of their marriage. Vern was transferred to another part of the state, to an encampment somewhere between the Gulf Coast and the Big Thicket. It was, in any case, the humidity core of the universe. Days were described as sunny if the sky looked like cardboard.

But the Sandifers were near a real town with houses for rent. Their own home at last. Juanita planted a ground-cover which conquered most of the oil slick in the yard. Candy had numerous insects to play with. For two years, it was the happiest Juanita had been as a married lady.

Juanita went to work in a diner, not realizing it would be her training ground for a return to Herb's. In the diner, she amused herself by asking the customers if they wanted French, Thousand Island, oil and vinegar or petrochemicals on their salad.

Vern started drinking heavily in the swamp. He got depressed about his job. His associates were being promoted and moving to Houston, but he was standing still. The drinking led Vern into escapades with women.

Juanita forgave him the phone call she received at home, the one from a girl who left the message for Vern to meet her at the same motel after she got off work at the roller rink.

Juanita forgave him the lipstick smudges she discovered on his boxer shorts as she sorted through things to put in the wash.

But she didn't forgive him the poetry.

One morning Juanita was on her way to work at the diner. She was going to pick up the cleaning that day so she went to the dresser to take some money out of Vern's wallet. Vern was sleeping off another hangover. Candy was feeding her dead goldfish.

The wallet lay on a cocktail napkin, a memento from Vern's previous evening. There was hand-writing, undeniably Vern's, on the cocktail napkin. A ball-point pen.

Vern's poem began, "How do I love thee, Donna Jean? Let me count the ways, you little sport-fucker . . ."

That was all Juanita read.

After the suitcases were packed, Juanita went to the bed, put her foot in Vern's back, and pushed him onto the floor.

Glowering down at him, she said, "I believe if me and my little girl try real hard, we can think up something better to do than watch your liver get to be the size of a moving van. I'm narrowing all my problems down to one, buddy. Arithmetic! I'm gonna see how many freeway off-ramps I can count between here and Fort Worth! It hasn't been all bad with you, and I mean that. You've got some good qualities. I'm grateful for the things you've done for Candy. But all in all, Vern, you could fuck up a nigger rent house!"

Juanita went back to Herb's Cafe. She returned to a hometown that was growing and changing. Suburbs were springing from Suburbs. New bars were opening in cellars, on rooftops, with pianos, with dart games, with red velvet walls and aquariums.

Which was why Herb Macklin made Juanita a barmaid.

"I need me a pretty lady behind my bar," Herb had said. "Pretty ladies attract men and sell lots of beer and setups if they don't look at theyselves in the mirror too much."

There were no big secrets to tending a bar, Herb had promised. "Keep your limes close to your tonics," he said. "You'll learn soon enough how to grab the mix with one hand and a beer with the other. You'll learn how to open them lower supply doors with your toe and close 'em with the back of your foot. Bend down from the knees. Don't stoop. If you stoop over a lot, your back'll go on you quicker than a sick dog. Measuring whisky in a hurry ain't nothin' but a feeling you acquire. Smile at folks. Learn everybody's name. That's how you get them tips. I say in no time at all you'll be an out-and-out mercenary."

Juanita had consented to take the job if it wasn't mandatory she wear a low-cut peasant blouse.

Herb had added. "I got me something better than a pretty bartender. You done got worldly, Juanita, if you don't mind me saying so. I can tell by looking in your eyes. I bet you can smell a load of bullshit a hundred miles this side of the state legislature."

Juanita had not been all that interested in the further adventures of Vern Sandifer, but she was kept up to date by Vern's sister in Sulphur Springs. Twice a year, Vern's sister called to tell Juanita about Vern making peace with God and becoming a new man.

Vern remarried. A good woman named Irene. Vern had met Irene in a Bible-study group. Vern had left the mud business and had taken up God's work on behalf of a Christian radio station in Laredo. Irene owned the radio station.

One night in Nuevo Laredo, however, God made the mistake of leaving Vern on his own for a few hours. Vern had been killed when his Mercury Cougar plowed into the front of a combination tamale factory and costume rental company.

Vern was found in the car wearing only a sport coat and socks. An empty bottle of tequila was locked in his hand. There was a cocktail napkin stuffed in his coat pocket on which Vern had apparently begun to write a poem. Scribbled on the napkin was:

"How do I love thee, Dolores and Consuelo? Get thee over here and sit down on my face, you little bandits . . ."

The check at The Wandering Squid was $147.39.

Juanita laughed out loud when she saw it. Slick said it was a bargain. Now he knew, once and for all, he never had to eat anything in Texas again but Mexican food, barbecue, chicken-fried steak and country sausage.

"You didn't like your rubber bands?" Juanita couldn't hide a smile. "You should have ordered the little sponges."

"I tried your little sponges. They tasted like my rubber bands."

"No, they didn't. Your rubber bands were dipped in Almaden and chicken broth. My little sponges were dipped in Campbell's Hot Dog Bean before they stuck them back in my seashell."

"What do you suppose it was they splattered on my square spaghetti?"

"I'm not sure. It had basil in it."

"Basil served it."

"Basil leaves," Juanita said, rising, pulling on her Paris policeman's cape.

"I imagine if we look around in here we can find us a greyhound named Basil."

Juanita stopped to speak to the maître d' as they were leaving *Le Strange Voyage du Grand Foule Poisson.*

"Excuse me," she said. "We want to come back again real soon. But do me a favor. I've written my Fort Worth address on this matchbook. Would you be kind enough to drop me a postard whenever you think your catch-of-the-day might be a can of Bumble Bee tuna?"

Slick took the road home that was still known as the turnpike although there were no longer any toll booths on it. The Turnpike was a thirty-five-mile laser beam connecting a cluster of downtown Dallas banks holding mortgages on the entire South to a reduced Fort

Worth skyline, which, when the buildings were outlined in Christmas lights, looked as if it ought to be sitting on top of a cake.

Between the two skylines were a thousand Dairy Queens and Self Serv islands calling themselves the Metroplex.

Juanita woke up from her nap when Slick stopped at a full-service Exxon in Fort Worth to get gas. He handed a twenty-dollar bill to a plump girl servicing the windshield.

"You got the real time of night?" Slick asked the girl.

"Sir, I don't," she said. "We was all down at Lake Granbury the other day when it was warm. An old boy shoved me off the dock. He knew I couldn't swim, too. Friend of mine fished me out before I drowned. My watch came off in that dirty water. Nobody ever did find it. I could have killed Olin Milford. He's the reason I can't tell you what time it is. I'm sorry. Here's your change."

Juanita lit a cigarette as Slick drove away.

"I love Texas, Goddamn it." she laughed. "It's the only place in the world where you can ask somebody a question and get back a plot."

"You love all of Texas?"

"Everything but the S's."

"You don't love the Panhandle."

"Sure I do. Old Amarillo High nicknamed its football team the Golden Sandstorm—on purpose. You have to love *that*."

"Isn't Wander in the Panhandle?"

"South Plains. I say Abilene's pure West Texas. Lubbock's the South Plains. Amarillo's the Panhandle. Are the High Plains the same as the South Plains?"

"You're the Texan."

Juanita dwelled on how many varied regions there were in Texas, of how abruptly the land could change, of the sprawling scrubby flatlands where it never seemed to change.

The person who had never seen Texas had been educated to think of it as a land where every home was designed in the conventional architecture of Hoss Cartright's hat and rhinestone oil derricks passed for shrubbery. That was Hollywood's lie. But Texas was simply a place where God had conducted a broad geographical experiment and merely forgot to paint half of it.

"Let's see," Juanita said. "There's West Texas . . . South Plains. Panhandle. Gulf Coast. Houston . . . which is its own place."

"King Ranch," Slick said.

"Austin and the Hill Country."

They were playing a game. Regions of Texas.

"Padre Island," said Slick.

"Big Bend."

"East Texas. Or Piney Woods. Whatever you call it."

"The Big Thicket."

"Cotton Belt."

"The Border."

"Edwards Plateau."

"The Valley "

"Mexiplex," said Slick.

"What?"

"San Antonio."

Letting that pass without a laugh, Juanita said, "It's amazing. You can go from a desert to a mountain . . . to rolling hills . . . a forest . . . wind up in an ocean. And never leave Texas."

"Yeah, I guess so," Slick said. "Of course, if you start out on the other side of that old Red River where I come from, you ain't goin' nowhere but Baja Oklahoma."

"Is that a fact?" Juanita bristled, blowing cigarette smoke at the driver. "Listen, friend. I've spent my whole life in Texas. Most of the time, I couldn't go to Baker's Shoe Store without matching funds from H.E.W. *That's* when you're living in Baja Oklahoma!"

Slick invited himself into Juanita's apartment and wondered aloud if he was going to get laid for the $147.39 dinner he bought.

Juanita thought not.

She had no moral hangups about it, and it wasn't as though she had to answer to a big sister in Pi Phi. In fact, Juanita said, under other circumstances perhaps, assuming Slick was not acting interested just to make her feel feminine, she might have to show him one of these nights that she could still go three miles over brush and timber. But right now, quite frankly, she had a song on her mind.

Juanita tossed her Paris policeman's cape on the sofa and went to the bedroom to get her Martin.

The maplewood flat-finished Martin had represented the most outrageous luxury of her life when she bought it in 1971 for four hundred dollars. But Lonnie Slocum assured her the Martin was a good investment, even if she never learned to play it better than an acid head who was into heavy metal.

The Martin was worth maybe $1,000 now. There were other good guitars, Gibsons, Ovations, Guilds, Yamahas, but an old steel-string acoustical Martin was like picking air compared to the others. And the clincher was that Willie Nelson's guitar was a Martin.

Juanita went to the sofa with her guitar. The yellow legal pad and Pentel were on the coffee table.

Slick reclined in the chair with the ottoman. He was asleep before he turned two pages in a current issue of *Sports Illustrated* with a family of Nigerian joggers on the cover.

About an hour and a half later, Slick was jolted out of his sleep by Juanita shaking him, saying, "Sit up."

Juanita arranged herself on the ottoman in her sweater, skirt and boots. She strummed the Martin.

"What's going on?" Slick stammered.

"Be quiet."

Juanita then picked an original melody and sang "Baja Oklahoma" for him in a voice that was one third Loretta Lynn, one third Tammy Wynette, and one third ragweed allergy.

> *It's in the schoolyards on the faces*
> *Of the children playing games.*
> *It's a pasture looking greener*
> *In the spring and summer rains.*
> *It's a highway going nowhere*
> *As far as you can see.*
> *It's a cowboy singing songs*
> *About his craving to be free.*
> *It's a river flowing gently*
> *Through an older part of town.*
> *It's a sky that's all around you*

Touching every patch of ground.
It's a prairie where the wind
Can't ever tell which way to blow.
It's our heroes getting taller
In that tiny Alamo.
It's the laughter you can carry
Through the years that turn you old.
It's "Baja Oklahoma,"
But it's Texas in your soul!

Juanita was radiant. This was a performance.

It's a skyline swiftly rising
And poking at a star.
It's a thicket's tangled branches
Turning daylight into dark.
It's the breeze along the beaches
Where the gulf is at your feet.
It's a lonely town imprisoned
By the dust and the mesquite.
It's a drive across the border
To the music and and the sin.
It's the blue that's in a norther,
It's football games to win.
It's a roundup stirring mem'ries
Of the rough-and-tumble days.
It's a detour off the freeway
To see where you were raised.
It's the laughter you can carry
Through the years that turn you old.
It's "Baja Oklahoma,"
But it's Texas in your soul!

Slick got out of his chair. "That almost makes me like Texas." He began to walk around the room. "Seriously, that's not half bad. Can I have a cup of instant?"

"I knew you'd like it." Juanita said, glowing.

"I didn't say I liked it."

"Yes you did. You just didn't say it out loud."

Slick looked at her, then started for the kitchen-breakfast room-den. "I *did* say I wanted a cup of coffee. I remember that part."

Juanita followed him, saying, "This is the song for Lonnie's album, Slick. I can feel it. If I get a song published, will you carry me off the field on your shoulders? Tear down the goal posts? Do some American thing like that?"

She turned on the fire under the kettle.

Slick was reaching for a cigarette when he said, "Well, I know one thing. Lonnie Slocum never said anything he couldn't take back."

"What do you mean?"

"Nothing."

"Yes do you."

"Aw, I don't know," he said. "I just wouldn't count on Lonnie too much, that's all."

"Lonnie's my friend, Slick. He wouldn't get my hopes up about something like his album if he weren't serious. He knows how much it means to me."

Slick said he was sure Lonnie wouldn't. Provided Lonnie remembered the definition of serious. A good part of the time Lonnie's brain was darker than the inside of a wolf's mouth.

Juanita struck a kitchen match to a Winston.

Slick said, "There's something else you ought to consider. Even if Lonnie likes your song—this one, or another one—he's got all those Nashville folks to deal with. Music executives and producers. What if they don't like your song? I doubt if that'll keep Lonnie from going ahead with the album."

"You really know how to make a lady feel good, you know that?"

"I've got another idea. It's been on my mind."

"What? Be happy tending bar?"

"I think you ought to take your songs over to Old Jeemy at KOXX. He knows everybody in the industry. If your songs are any good, he'll know it. He'll know what to do with them. If Old Jeemy likes your songs, he can get 'em published while Lonnie's sniffing up dust on furniture."

"You must be joking."

Slick wasn't joking.

"I can't tell you what a dumb idea that is."

Slick didn't think it was a dumb idea.

"It's not even insane. It's just dumb."

Slick said, "All I know is, Old Jeemy's got influence in the business, and Lonnie Slocum can't remember what yesterday was like."

Juanita flicked ashes on her floor and kicked at the dark red vinyl tile.

"What the hell would I do if I went to see Old Jeemy?" she said. "I've never met him. I've never even *seen* him. Do you know how many stupid people do that kind of thing? Do you really? Twice a day somebody goes up to Old Jeemy and says, 'You don't know me but my name's Juanita Hutchins and I've written this song. Everybody says it's real good. It's a song about my husband's hemorrhoid operation when he was in prison and my Momma was dying in the rain. I think Tanya Tucker could make a hit record out of it.' Old Jeemy says, 'Happy to meet you, little lady. Who have you been writing songs for up to now?' The stupid idiot—that's me—says, 'Oh, I've written songs for Slick Henderson . . . Doris Steadman . . . Herb Macklin . . . almost anybody you can name.' Old Jeemy smiles and says, 'I'll sure take a hard look at your material.' The stupid idiot thanks him and leaves, and Old Jeemy throws the songs in the wastebasket."

Juanita drenched two coffee mugs with boiling water. A river ran across her countertop. She handed a mug to Slick and ripped a wad of paper towels off a roller attached to the wall. Slick retreated to the butcher-block table.

"How do you know that's what happens?" Slick said, putting the mug down. "You've never tried it. Might be one reason you're still working in a bar."

Juanita's eyes flashed, and she said, "I work in a bar because Prince Charles broke the engagement!"

Slick said, "Okay. Take it easy."

"And by the way," she added. "I don't need to be reminded about what I've done with my life by the king of the unleaded gas pump!"

"Whoa," Slick said. "Hold on! I didn't mean to make you hot. I think more highly of a good bartender than I do a good songwriter."

He went to her and put his hands at her waist. He drew her close to him. He kissed her on the forehead politely, a brotherly kiss. Then on the cheek.

"I was only trying to be helpful, babe," he said with unrestrained affection. "I was thinking it couldn't hurt to go see Old Jeemy. Give yourself more than one chance. If Lonnie doesn't come through in Nashville, well . . . maybe Old Jeemy could do something. That's all I had in mind. I'm rooting for you, don't you know that?"

"I'm not really mad," she said, truthfully.

Slick kissed her on the cheek again, not so brotherly.

He gathered her up more firmly.

"You okay?"

"Yes," Juanita said softly. "I know you care about me."

She hugged him and put her head on his shoulder and he kissed her on the neck, the ear.

"I can think of a couple of things we can do right now . . . this time of night," Slick said, his tone more honeyed, his hand caressing her back. "You could let me hear that old song of yours again . . . if you want to. Or . . . we could stroll on in there to your bedroom. Maybe get to know each other a little better. That, uh . . . that would sort of get my vote."

Juanita voted for the song.

She eagerly led Slick into the living room and cuddled up with her guitar on the sofa and sang "Baja Oklahoma" three more times before he went home.

Freight Train

▼▲▼▲▼▲▼▲▼▲▼▲▼▲▼▲▼▲▼▲▼▲▼▲▼▲▼▲▼▲▼▲▼▲▼

William Brinkley

Like Daniel Baxter, his central character in *Peeper*, William Brinkley is a
newspaperman and a fugitive from the East. Both these scribes have settled in
the lower Rio Grande Valley, sixty miles upriver from Brownsville. Their
town is called Martha, but it sounds suspiciously like Edinburg or McAllen.
It is an *ambiente* they love and laugh at.

Brinkley paints a masterful, and funny, picture of the region, its landscape,
its industries, its folkways and prejudices, its big people and little people.
Martha is a place where everyone is an outsider unless his grandfather pio-
neered in the region. Life runs in deep and well-worn grooves and nothing
unusual happens until a clever and resourceful peeping Tom begins spying
on the town's most personable women, who dress and undress, unanimously,
without drawing their curtains. He is a gallant voyeur and leaves a charming
present on the window ledge after each episode. Husbands are outraged, but
not so their wives—or their daughters. Women who have not been peeped
feel somehow put down, and some of them pretend to have been peeped when
they have been passed over. Women who have been singled out for peeping
walk more proudly and their husbands, like it or not, regard them with new
respect and interest. The book is almost a celebration of the voyeur's art, a
treatise on the Joy of Peeping.

Directing the fruitless hunt for the clever peeper is police chief Claude
"Freight Train" Flowers, who is humorously introduced in the following
chapter. Jamie Scarborough is the twenty-two-year-old journalism student
from SMU who is editor Baxter's assistant.

SHE HAD BEEN HERE A MONTH.

When I got back from the island Monday after my traditional three
days away, I dropped by the paper and was at once confronted.

"I have to talk to you," she said in cross tones. "I have something
urgent to discuss."

She always wants to talk, and "urgent" is her only classification.

"Why don't we have supper tonight at the Bon Ton?" I said. "And
we'll talk. It'll help us digest our beef stew."

"The Bon Ton? Gee, are you sure you can afford it?"

From *Peeper: A Comedy* (New York: Viking Press, 1981), 20–30.

"I can afford mine. I'll be at the Cavalry Post if anything happens."

"Are you kidding? Jesus, I wish *something* would."

She is quite young.

I went over to see Freight Train Flowers. The first thing I always do on getting back to town is call on the chief of police, and then the mayor, to find out what has been going on in our metropolis during my absence.

The town government is situated in the old Cavalry Post—"the Cavary," as everyone in town calls it. The place still seems to have a ghostly smell of horses and saddle leather and harness. The inside is dark and cool. I went up the stairs and down the hallway. Both could have taken three horses abreast. I walked through the open door into the chief's office. It's a marvelous place for an office. It opens onto a wide veranda—"piazzas," as the Cavalry ladies called them—with a high ceiling and overhead fans. The Cavalry knew about these things, and those piazzas are the coolest place in town in summer. From them you look across the parade ground where Union horse mustered before setting forth to look for Comanche. Lt. Col. Robert E. Lee once commanded the Department of Texas from this office. It was empty now. A yard-long sign in letters three inches high hung across the wall: ONE AGGIE EQUALS TWO ORDINARY MEN. A moose, a deer, and a bear, all taken by the present occupant, looked down in bug-eyed moroseness at the desk. The desk has dents all over it from the cowboy boots parked there by that occupant.

I like visiting with the chief. He has a natural shrewdness and integrity that make him a good chief of police for a town that scarcely needs one. The town means everything to him. His dedication to its welfare is total. He knows where every scrap of power lies and exactly how to deal with it. I always felt the chief stood to the Town Council like a good chief petty officer to commissioned officers. The CPOs really run the Navy. The officers only think they do, because the chiefs astutely permit them to take the bows.

The chief of police is an Aggie, a graduate of Texas A&M University. Aggiehood is a very special state of mind, and being an Aggie is a lifetime undertaking. For example, if San Jacinto Day, the Aggie holy day, finds an Aggie in Paris, France, he will stop everything he is doing to search out other Aggies who may be in that city in order to be with them. It's called "Aggie Muster." The Aggie creed has guided the chief's life from college days, and it has never let him down. The thing about the chief is that he kids about being an Aggie more than anyone. Most of the Aggie jokes I've heard were told me by the chief, always followed by a detonation of laughter. Nonetheless he knows that nothing in life is so important as being an Aggie.

From the fact that the gun cabinet was open and a weapon missing, I knew where he was. The cabinet houses two rifles, a Remington .30-06 and a Weatherby 300, and an over-under 12-gauge Winchester. None of the weapons has ever been fired at a man, but the chief is a great hunter. I walked through the office and out onto the piazza.

He was standing by the railing with his back to me, the Weatherby 300 in firing position. It's a beautiful thing, its stock covered with rich filigree. He was drawing a bead on the statue of Lee which commands the center of the parade ground.

"Be right with you, Ace," he said without turning around. The chief always knows when I am there, even when his back is to me. Instinct, I guess. When you mix that with a kind of fine slyness, you have a formidable human being. It's a visceral combination, indigenous, a Texas thing. Something you're born with or learn very early on your own. I don't think you can teach it. "Soon as I get off a couple."

Martha not being a violent town, the chief's job gives him little opportunity to polish his eye and trigger finger for his hunting. He handles this problem by dry-squeeze practice on the piazza. He squeezed the trigger slowly.

"Got the Colonel," he said happily. "Right between the eyes."

The chief always refers to Lee by the rank he held when he occupied the chief's office. It is as if Lee had never made it to general and nothing he did after commanding Texas was of much importance. Using him for target practice was in no way against Lee. Actually the chief liked Colonel Lee a lot and certainly was the authority on everything he did in Texas. He lowered the Weatherby and stood a moment, gazing out over the prospect.

It had rained during the night, and there was a freshness and sweetness to the air. A few big snow-white clouds stood high in the clear blue sky. A bright March sun flooded down onto the parade ground, sown now in rich green Saint Augustine grass, and washed the old white-board Cavalry buildings standing neatly and cared for around it. You could almost hear the distant bugle call and see the dim columns of horse troops marching out in column line, their guidons fluttering before them.

"Nice place, ain't it?" the chief said. "That's the double truth. When you get down to it, I reckon this job wastes the talents of a fine police officer like myself. Let's take a load off."

We went back inside, and the chief sat at his desk beneath the stuffed animal heads and the Aggie sign. He overflowed the chair on all sides. He pulled open the top drawer, reached in, scooped up a handful of peanuts, and threw his head back and the peanuts in, all in one movement like an adept elephant. *Crunch-crunch.* He once told me that he thought better while chewing peanuts. He keeps a large supply in the drawer, not in any container but loose there, using the drawer itself as a huge bowl. They are cheap but of splendid quality. The chief buys them in number 10 cans across the Rio Grande in Las Bocas, nine miles away. He parked his Justin cowboy boots on the desk with a solid clump to add a new dent to it. *Crunch-crunch.*

"Got a new Aggie joke. This Aggie is up at Port Aransas, and he walks in a bait store and sees this sign, 'Special, all the worms you want, one dollar.' The Aggie reads the sign, thinks a moment, then looks at the proprietor and says, 'I'll take two dollar's worth.' "

The roar hit me like a blast from a cavalry cannon, the chief's big belly shaking like a run of sea waves. Aggies aren't really dumb. It is their conceit to pretend stupidity, and that pretense is their biggest edge.

"Well, Ace," he said when he had recovered, "here we are. Monday morning. Bright-eyed and bushy-tailed. How was the three-day pass this time?"

Why the chief calls me that I've never asked, but I assume it's for ace reporter and is his form of humor.

"Never lovelier," I said. "The sun was shining and the water was blue."

"Hail, if I didn't know better, I'd say you was running Mexican

brown down there, 'mount a time you spend. The drugs boys tell me
they's more of it comes in by sea than by land nowadays."

"Yeah. I hear the same thing."

"I don't know how you do it. Sure sounds like a winner. I wish I
could spend my life screwing off at the beach."

"Why don't you? There's nothing to keep you here."

He sighed. "They's something in what you say."

We passed the time of day, and he told me there had been a speeding
ticket on Cavalry Street after the Bloomer Girl Ball and a fight in the
Here-Tis bar. He had solved the fight by holding the two combatants,
one in each hand, and having them kiss and make up.

"I think they liked that part," he said.

"I didn't realize we had anything like that in Texas."

The chief gave me a sly look. "You didn't?" *Crunch-crunch.* "Well,
it ain't generally known, but between you and me, Texas has always
had its share of queers. I don't find that so peculiar. From my experience on the subject, I'd say they's a direct connection between being a
queer and being a macho, and we surely got our share of machos."

"I'm shocked. I'll have to watch my step. Someone as pretty as I
am. You ever try it, Chief?"

"Yeah. When I was five. Didn't relish it too much."

I sighed. "You mean there's nothing else you can give me to fill the
columns of the *Clarion*? A speeding ticket and a bar fight?"

The chief gave a minor belch. He belches fairly often, on various
decibel levels, some almost inaudible, like a baby's burp, some like a
clap of thunder exploding right above you. I blame it on the peanuts.
Actually the chief's belch is one of his friendliest traits. It's nice and
warm, a sign that he likes you. He never does it in front of strangers.

"Naw, I reckon that's it," he said. "Our usual week of high crim-
inal activity. Sometimes I do wake up in the short hours with a night-
mare that the Town Council fired me, figuring this town don't require
a chief of police. Not that I'm complaining, you understand."

The chief looked at me thoughtfully. He has large ears with long
lobes, a prominent nose, and keen brown eyes. You feel they don't
miss anything. But it is Freight Train Flowers's voice which identi-
fies him. It has a decided rhythm and pace to it, ritualistic, as if lan-

guage were an important thing, not to be hurried over. It takes him about the same amount of time to say ten words that an ordinary person would take to say twenty. I have always found it a soothing voice. I have never heard him raise it or even alter its mensural cadence. At the most he will emphasize words during moments of conviction, like italicizing them on a written page. He is characteristic of a type in this part of the world. He can talk quite grammatically when he wishes—that is, speak the language learned during schooling—but usually he speaks another, preferred language, learned and burnished outside the confines of the classroom.

"They was one other thing," he said. "Something a little different for Martha. We had us a Peeping Tom."

"Well, *that's* something anyhow. Who'd he peep?"

"The Carruthers girl. Sally Carruthers."

I whistled low. "A nice choice. You catch him and have them kiss and make up?"

The chief gave a medium belch. "The offender has not been apprehended."

"Sally Carruthers," I reflected. "Any idea who'd want to do that?"

Crunch-crunch. "Well, if you talking about *want*, I'd say just about every man in Martha over twelve."

The chief told me it had happened an hour or so before the Bloomer Girl Ball.

"Probably some Mexican drifter wanting to see some Anglo nooky," he said in that slow-motion voice. "They like it too, you know."

"Yeah, I've heard somewhere they do."

"Maybe he figured it was turn about. After all, we go to Boys' Town."

"Yeah, you're probably right. Some Mexican." I waited a moment and looked at the chief. "Mexican drifters know all about when the Bloomer Girl Ball is. Come on, it had to be some high school kid, Chief."

The chief recrossed his Justins and looked at me. "Hailfire, I've thought of all that, boy. I don't need no *former* big-city, Washington, D.C., newspaper reporter to tell me that. You probably right. Kids sure know about the Bloomer Girl Ball."

He chewed some peanuts and spoke thoughtfully.

"In my tenure in office we never had nothing like a Peeping Tom in Martha. Damn serious business. A felony, I'm sure. I'll have to look it up."

"What so serious about a kid looking through a window at Sally Carruthers?"

The chief reached in the drawer, scooped up a fresh feeding of peanuts, tossed his head back, and threw them in. *Crunch-crunch.* He spoke solemnly.

"Well, pussy is private property, for one thing. I reckon it's about the most private property we got."

I looked up at the big Aggie sign. "Well, maybe. I don't think Peeping Toms are taken that seriously anymore. All this liberation. You've got these magazines and everything and they show it all. I doubt if anyone anywhere gets that excited now if someone gets a quick peek at a little fur."

The chief gave me that shrewd look of his. "Well, for one thing, we not talking about magazines. We talking about *live* pussy. For another, we not talking about anywhere. We talking about Texas. And we talking about *Martha*, Texas."

The chief pulled his Justins off the desk and stood up. When he stands, Freight Train Flowers dominates any room. He is a big man in every way, six feet one inch and a beefy two hundred and thirty pounds. An acre of belly overhangs his Mexican-silver belt buckle, which weighs two pounds and is engraved with Quetzalcoatl, the sacred Toltec bird-serpent. Someone seeing him for the first time might think of the word "fats," but this would be misleading, as younger and supposedly stronger men have realized on occasion from a position flat on their backs. What looks like pure lard is as solid as a Santa Gertrudis bull. He has arms like ham sides and hands that could hide a cantaloupe. His skin is the color and texture of rawhide and his hair the color of nails left out in the rain. His uniform is gabardine "summer serge," a heritage of his undergraduate days in the Aggie Corps. Like that of any good Aggie, the chief's hair could be mistaken for a pair of military bristle brushes laid side by side, though it is seldom seen, since he keeps his Resistol kicker hat on virtually all the time, especially indoors. It was off now only because of his target practice. As if to correct this oversight in manners he stepped over to the filing cabinet where he had left it and put it on.

"You been away too long, boy," he said, looking down at me from all that bulk. "For all I know, in Washington, D.C., the women, they walk down the street shaking their tits and the men playing with themselves. But we ain't in Washington, D.C., are we?"

The chief opened a drawer of the filing cabinet.

"Yeah, like you said, Ace, it was some kid. No class, these kids today. I'd never a dreamed of just looking. No, sir, that's not the Aggie way."

"The way I hear it, any way is the Aggie way."

The chief paused over the cabinet drawer and gave me a solemn look. "Well, they's something to that. Anywhere they'll let an Aggie in, an Aggie's likely to go."

I could see the faded football just beyond him. The bookcase contained only four books, but resting on it, atop a kicking tee, was the football that was involved, twenty-four years back, in one of the most famous plays in the annals of Texas sports. The game was the historic Thanksgiving Day meeting with the hated "University," whose students are referred to as "tea-sippers" by Aggies. It had been played in a virtual monsoon on a field so muddy the players at times seemed submerged in it. With A&M trailing by a score of 3-0, and with the University punting from its own fifteen against a clock which showed but twelve seconds remaining, tackle Claude Flowers had broken through the two linemen prudently assigned all afternoon to block him, slid savagely toward the kicker, and not merely blocked the kick but, leaping high, caught it on the fly in his gut as it came off the kicker's toe—thereby completing perhaps the rarest of all football plays, an intercepted punt. Despite a gait which permitted half the Texas team to catch up with him, he dragged four tacklers across the goal line as the gun sounded. In the Friday papers, the prose of the Dallas sports editor had taken flight and rechristened the Aggie tackle. The yellowed clipping was preserved under glass in a picture frame hung above the football: "On a dying Thanksgiving afternoon in Austin, a freight train named Claude Flowers roared out of South Texas to geld the proud Texas Longhorn, raise high over the slop and slime of Memorial Stadium the A&M maroon and white, and blazon

his name into Aggie immortality. . . ." The sportswriter wrote in
Old Style. That play was surely the biggest moment in the chief's life,
so far.

From the file drawer he got out one of those enormous cans of Mexican peanuts, brought the can back to his desk, got a can opener out of
his middle desk drawer, opened the can, and emptied the contents
into his peanut drawer with a sound like a dump truck discharging a
load. He threw the can in his metal wastebasket with a crash that
would have awakened the Second Cavalry had it still been quartered
below. He sat, parked his Justins on the desk, and shoved back his
Resistol.

"How did Miss Sally and the Carrutherses take the desecration?" I
said. "Are they hospitalized?"

He gave me a crafty look and pulled at one of his long ears. I knew
something was coming. Though I have always found Freight Train
Flowers to be a man of integrity, this is not to say he is above cunning.

"Well, Miz Carruthers, her and I had a little talk and she waxed
my ass. Said she considered it a serious breach of our law-and-order
atmosphere. She's the only cow I know don't know what tits is for.
Asked me what the town was coming to. You know how parents are.
But Sally was pretty cool. She hasn't had a collapse or anything like
that. Of course she didn't know she'd been visited till the next day."

"How did she find out?"

"She thought she heard this noise. Wasn't sure. Except that next
morning she found these tennis shoe tracks outside her window. Also
a cigarette butt in the grass. But the main way she knowed was she
found something else."

The chief paused. I felt he was deliberately drawing this out. As if
he had a case, for a change, and meant to make the most of it.

"Found what, for God's sake?" I said.

"Take a even strain, boy. She found a little present on her window-
sill."

"A present?" I said in exasperation. "What do you mean, a present?"

"A little box wrapped neat as can be. Carruthers Mercantile
couldn't a done it better."

I sighed. "All right, Chief. What was inside?"

"A strawberry."

"A strawberry?"

"A red enamel strawberry. Right pretty thing," the chief said in his deliberate tones. He slumped back in his chair. "I don't know why we talking about it. You can't print any of this nohow, that's sure and certain. I don't think the mayor or my employers the Town Council would relish any story in the *Clarion* about a Peeping Tom in Martha. No, sir."

He was right. It doesn't bother me, except now and then. I knew it when I bought the paper. I'm not down here to win any Pulitzer prizes. I gave all that up. I'm in Texas. Not that it amounted to anything anyhow. If I had been living in a free society I probably would have given it two paragraphs, without the strawberry. You couldn't print that anyhow, and it was the best part. Still, I would have a little talk with the mayor about running *something*. I had to keep a few principles, just for the principle of it. Screw it. All I really wanted was to get through my four days and back to my boat. The one just made the other possible.

"One thing they do in Washington besides walk down the street and play with tits, they have something that vaguely resembles a free press." I sighed and got up. "Well, I've got to drop in on his excellency. Thanks for so much news, Chief. I'm not sure we'll have room for all of it in one issue."

The chief's eyes held a far-off look. "Imagine seeing that like God made it. Musta been mighty nice. I always felt Sally Carruthers had about the prettiest red hair I ever seen. If nothing else comes of this, it's reassuring to know finally it's for real. Somehow makes you believe they's some honesty left in this world."

He came out of it.

"Yeah, it was a kid all right." He was pleased with his little triumph. "A kid would think up a gift like that, get a box, wrap it real neat. Just like you said, Ace. Some kid."

"All right, Freight. One for the Aggies."

I started out, then waited.

"You know something? Anybody who would leave a present like that for Sally Carruthers, that shows a touch of class."

"Yeah. Well, we got a couple a those around too. You looking at one of 'em." He gave a minor belch. "You behave, now."

He's probably right about that. I went out of the building with its cool shadows, into the warm sun of the parade ground, and back to the paper and phoned the mayor to tell him I was on my way out for our regular Monday session. Holly Ireland answered and said they'd had an unexpected "dressing" and Brother Ireland couldn't be disturbed.

"Mrs. Byram crossed over Jordan this morning," she said. "Why don't you drop out after supper and I'll give you a piece of fresh rhubarb pie? I know you relish rhubarb pie."

I also relish seeing Holly Ireland. I said I'd be there and would look forward to the pie. I reminded myself to skip dessert at supper and told my employee to telephone the Byrams and get some material for a story on Mrs. Byram's crossing. I told her she could write the story herself, an assignment which did not provoke the enthusiasm you might reasonably expect from a recent journalism student.

And Finally . . .

The trail leads back to its starting point—to the oneness of humor and character. As in the times of Aristotle and Henry Fielding and Mark Twain, the unusual human being is the focus of interest and amusement. He is the prime mover in most of the narratives in this volume, but his appearances barely suggest the richness of the field.

There should have been room for so many more of these original geniuses—for Happy Jack, the melancholy horseless cowboy facing the world naked on the banks of a Montana river in B. M. Bower's *The Happy Family* (1910); for Ruggles, the English butler, who exchanges snobbery for democracy in Wyoming in Harry Leon Wilson's *Ruggles of Red Gap* (1915); for Dr. Lao, the subtle Chinese showman who brings the Medusa to Tucson, Arizona, in Charles Finney's classic *The Circus of Dr. Lao* (1935); for General Maximilian Rodriguez de Santos, the fat little patriot who captures the Alamo for Mexico in James Lehrer's *Viva Max* (1966); for John Reese's spellbinding auctioneer, invincible in salesmanship, combat, and love in John Reese's *Singalee* (1969).

Over there is the Reverend Praxiteles Swan, equally persuasive with tongue and fists, in John W. Thomason's *Lone Star Preacher* (1941). Closer at hand is Colonel William Patten, gambler, entrepreneur, and sexual athlete, in Richard Condon's *A Talent for Loving*. Still closer, Larry McMurtry's mobile mountebank, *Cadillac Jack* (1982).

The list is long and growing longer. True, the pitch and tone of laughter has changed over the years, but in the West its volume has remained constant. It may well be the grace that keeps the literature of the West from decline and decay. It is a special gift from the God of the Big Sky.